FALL TO THE TEXAS EARTH...

Distantly, as if through a grime-streaked window, he saw Bob with a smoking gun in his hand and heard his wild, triumphant laugh. Somehow he knew without looking that the boy had killed his first man, and the thought saddened him. Movement caught his eye and he turned his head to observe Jim Kelly in pursuit of the third rustler. The black wrangler had his pistol out and was closing quickly for a killing shot.

Then blinding streamers of light flashed before Print's eyes, and for the first time he became aware of something wet and sticky oozing down over his saddle. He clutched for the pommel, but his hand seemed frozen and he saw the Colt fall from his stiffened fingers. When he struck the ground there was no pain . . .

The Savage Land

MATT BRAUN

St. Martin's Paperbacks

This is a work of fiction. All of the characters, organizations, and events portrayed in this novel are either products of the author's imagination or are used fictitiously.

THE SAVAGE LAND

Copyright © 1973 by Matthew Braun.

For information address St. Martin's Press, 175 Fifth Avenue, New York, NY 10010.

ISBN: 978-0-312-96004-9

Our books may be purchased in bulk for promotional, educational, or business use. Please contact your local bookseller or the Macmillan Corporate and Premium Sales Department at 1-800-221-7945, ext. 5442, or by e-mail at MacmillanSpecialMarkets@macmillan.com.

Printed in the United States of America

Signet edition / December 1988
St. Martin's Paperbacks edition / February 1997

St. Martin's Paperbacks are published by St. Martin's Press, 175 Fifth Avenue, New York, NY 10010.

10 9 8 7 6 5 4

TO

GEORGE HUDMAN

A FRIEND FOR ALL SEASONS

AND

THE OMA CORPS OF TROOPERS

BOOK 1

RECONSTRUCTION
1865–1870

CHAPTER ONE

1

The rider topped a hill overlooking the San Gabriel River and reined his mount to a halt. Both man and horse were covered with grimy layers of trail dust and sweat. Motionless, spent beyond the limits of endurance, they stared wearily upon the valley below. Behind them a darkening crept over the land as the sun slowly dipped westward, and cool, deepening shadows settled mercifully over the rider's gaunt face.

The dark eyes of the man slouched in the saddle watched dully as fading streamers of light rippled over the water before him. Then a sharp pain stabbed through his leg, and as if his wits had been jarred he dimly tried to figure the date. But the thought slogged along to nowhere, mired in deadened exhaustion that seemed to numb the very marrow of his bones. Near as he could calculate he had been on the trail something over a month, which would make it the middle of May. After a moment his mouth split in a smile that was closely akin to a grimace. May or June, this year or next, it really didn't seem to matter. Four years had

passed since he last saw this valley and a month one way
or the other just didn't seem real important anymore.

It should. But it didn't.

Abruptly he grunted, cursing the throbbing pain in his
leg and in the same breath damning the fickle bitch men
called fate. The San Gabriel washed away before him and
in his mind's eye came images of shrieking men clutching their shredded guts and bunker walls splattered with
the pinkish gore of raw brains. That was the reality. The
slime, and blood, and torn bodies of those left behind. Fate
was merely an illusion fostered by some cruel god who
took sport in pitting men against their brothers. In the end
the living were no less dead than those buried beneath the
clammy soil of Shiloh, or Vicksburg, or a hundred other
battlefields. They ate, slept, somehow survived from one
day to the next. But the stench of death was always with
them and their insides shriveled up into a hard knot of helpless rage.

They were no longer men, or even animals. Just nothing. Less than nothing.

Still, above ground was better than below. Being rolled
in a blanket and dumped in a mass grave was a hell of
a lot worse than taking a Minie ball and ending up with a
game leg. Maybe there hadn't been anything worth living
for at times, yet there damn sure wasn't much worth dying
for either. Perhaps there had been, when the Confederacy
was young and proud, and everybody went marching off to
teach the Yankees a lesson. But that had lasted only a year,
two at the most. Afterwards it was the generals who still
thought about winning the war—the men in the front
lines started worrying about how to stay alive. On the killing ground that will to survive, the compulsion to somehow see home again, had often been the only thing that
held Old Scratch at bay. Everywhere a man looked he
found death's leering head, and those who weakened made
easy prey.

Four years. Somehow it seemed much longer. He had
marched off a green kid of twenty-one and returned a man

of twenty-five. Going on a hundred. The thought brought a wry chuckle. That's how old he felt right about now. At least a hundred. Sapped of his juices until he couldn't even work up a good spit. Yet he had endured, gone on, pulled through somehow. And he was still kicking. Sort of, anyway.

His hand unconsciously touched the tattered gray rags that hung loosely from his frame, and he idly wondered if he would ever again be rid of lice. Then his shoulders straightened. Christ Almighty, lots of men had cooties. Even generals! But most of them hadn't made it home. Hell, most hadn't even made it past Shiloh. He had, though. Game leg, lice, and all. Which at the moment seemed like a damned sweet victory in itself. Maybe the only victory a man had any right to expect out of war.

The sound of hoofbeats wrenched his mind back to the present and he looked up to see a horse and rider bearing down on him from the Georgetown road. His hand instinctively moved to the Colt .44 Army holstered at his hip. He had taken it off a dead Yankee officer at Bloody Pond, and without it he would never have made it back to Texas. Twice in the last month he had encountered renegades along the road and the threat of the big pistol was all that had saved him. With the war over the South was crawling with bands of highwaymen and robbers—small gangs who ran together like wolf packs savaging the countryside. The only law was what a man made for himself, and to make it stick he had best have no qualms about using a gun.

But as the rider drew closer he saw that it was Willis Crowder, a rancher from over near Little River. He waved, suddenly very aware of his grimy, unshaven appearance. This was the first neighbor he had run into since striking the San Gabriel road, and as grungy as he looked it was sure to make a lasting impression.

"Howdy, Mr. Crowder." When he called out, the older man reined in, looking at him quizzically. "How's everybody over at Georgetown?"

The rancher peered at him uncertainly, noting the ragged uniform and slat-ribbed horse in one, swift glance. " 'Fraid you've got the advantage of me. Face looks familiar but I can't quite place it."

The young man smiled, rubbing his scruffy beard. "Yeah, I guess I have changed some at that. I'm Print Oliver. Jim Oliver's boy. You remember, the ranch over on Yegua Creek."

Willis Crowder just nodded, his uncertainty now replaced with a frown. "Sure, I recollect. You're the one that takes after your ma."

Some people along the San Gabriel had never gotten over Jim Oliver marrying a half-Cherokee. The eldest son had inherited her tawny skin, high cheek-bones and raven hair. Yet the dark, piercing eyes were what reminded people most of his mother, and right now they flashed at the meaning behind Crowder's words. Then the anger faded as quickly as it had come. Hell, it was his first day home and he didn't want trouble with anybody. Not even an old jughead like Crowder.

"How's my folks, Mr. Crowder? You must've seen them around, or at least heard how they're doing."

"Nope. Can't say as I have." The rancher hawked and spit, watching the wad of phlegm raise a puff of dust in the road. "The Olivers ain't too popular in this neck of the woods. Might be you disremember, but Williamson County has got no use for Rebs or their kinfolk."

"I reckon I had forgotten," Print observed stiffly. "What with the war being over I sort of thought things like that would've been laid to rest."

"Not by a damn' sight, they ain't," Crowder snorted. "Some things people just natcherally don't forget. If I was you I'd keep right on ridin', boy. There ain't no room in this county for you or your family. Seems like your pappy's set on learnin' that the hard way."

Print Oliver's eyes went smoky and a dark scowl settled over his face. "Crowder, if you weren't such a busted down old fart, I'd clean your plow myself. But anytime you get to thinkin' you've got my daddy's number, you just ride on over and give it a try."

Print kicked his horse in the ribs and loped off down the road. Willis Crowder watched scornfully for a moment and spat again. Then he reined about and struck out along the dusty ribbon stretching eastward.

Once out of sight Print slowed his horse to a walk. The poor devil didn't have more than one good run left in him, and Print was damned if he'd come home afoot. Some things an Oliver just didn't do, and killing a horse was high on the list.

As he rode, he sifted back over his brief exchange with Crowder. Though he had gotten the last word, he damn' sure hadn't won any arguments. From what Crowder had said, the Oliver clan hadn't been winning many the last few years either. Evidently things hadn't changed an iota, but then that wasn't too surprising. Things rarely changed in Texas. Just got more so.

The thought triggered a long-buried memory, one that hadn't seemed all that important at Shiloh and the other killing grounds he had toured the last four years. Slowly his mind drifted back, sorting scattered pieces of the year the war had started. An ominous political cloud had hung over Texas that year. The issue of secession was all anyone had talked about, especially the wealthy cotton planters along the Gulf Coast and the rich farm lands in central Texas. Then one southern state after another had pulled out of the Union in a matter of days and the flames of secession leaped ever higher. Few people knew what the fight was about, or what they were supposed to be fighting for. But in some vague way they understood that the Yankees were trying to push something down their throats. Exactly what, they again weren't quite sure. Still, Texans weren't disposed to being force-fed and they didn't wait around to find out.

The state legislature forced the issue to referendum, shouting blood and thunder all the while. Early that year it had come to vote and secession carried the state by a landslide. *Except in Williamson County.* There it was soundly defeated, and other than the Olivers and their neighbors along Yegua Creek the entire county had turned thumbs down. The legislature convened immediately and voted to leave the Union on the twenty-fifth anniversary of Texas' independence from Mexico. Sam Houston, who had argued loudly against secession, promptly resigned as Governor and Texas marched off to war.

Except for Williamson County.

There the only ones who had joined up were the eldest sons of ranchers along Yegua Creek, which included Prentice Oliver and many of his closest friends. Like schoolboys headed for a snowball fight they had ridden out full of piss and vinegar, certain beyond a doubt that they would have the Yankees routed well before Christmas. Which was exactly how it had happened at first. But then the worm turned, and after the 2nd Texas Regiment was destroyed at Shiloh, Print had finished out the war with Nathan Forrest's cavalry.

Now the Confederacy and a goodly part of Texas had been devastated, reduced to ashes. The bold leaders and their armies of gray simply ceased to exist, washed away in a carnage of bloodletting that haunted a man's dreams no matter how much distance he put behind him. The South was a defeated nation, and for the first time in three decades Texas had been brought to heel by a foreign power. Military occupation was what they were calling it in Washington. But to Texans it was the end to all they had fought and died for—perhaps the end of Texas itself.

Having come full circle, Print's thoughts again turned to Willis Crowder's words. *There ain't no room in this county for you or your family.* With the Union victory folks in Williamson County would be living high off the hog. After all, they had backed the winning side. And if Old Man Crowder had called it right, then hard times were about to pitch camp on the doorsteps of those who had supported the Confederacy. Especially the Olivers.

Print nudged his mount into a faltering trot. Yegua Creek suddenly seemed far away, and it no longer bothered him that the horse might drop dead beneath his feet.

2

Outside Georgetown Print turned off the San Gabriel road and struck north along a rutted trail. He was nearing home and everything around him now seemed familiar, like an old friend that he had left only yesterday. The wandering trail looked exactly the same, deeply scarred, pitted, a mute testament to nearly three decades of wagon travel. Great stands of live oaks and scrub cedar covered the rolling hills that swept across the countryside. Small meadows and vast, wavering fields were alive with a sparkle of black-eyed Susans, Indian paintbrushes, scarlet buckeyes and dogwood. Spring had come to the hill country, and for a moment it was almost as if he were a boy again. There ahead was where his father had once run a wagon in a ditch, and a little farther along was where he had killed his first deer. But it was those long-ago Saturdays that remained most vivid in his memory. When everyone in the northern settlement rode into Georgetown to shop, and gossip, and get drunk. Those were the days. Grand times, full of laughter and mischief and discovery.

Jim and Julia Oliver had come west shortly after New Year's, 1840. They had journeyed along the Colorado to Austin, then turned north toward San Gabriel country. The rolling hills and sheltered fields were an exciting change from the flatlands of their native Mississippi. Land was free for the taking and upon reaching Yegua Creek they had stopped, awed by the raw beauty all about them. Here they would build their home, raise a family, carve out a future for themselves from this vast wilderness. They would go no farther, for here they had found their Eden and here they would take root.

Print had been born that spring in a log cabin with a dirt floor, the first structure ever erected on Yegua Creek. But Jim Oliver was an ambitious man and that crude, ramshackle cabin was only the beginning. There was black prairie soil for crops, timber for building, and dense, brushy thickets for fattening livestock. Everything a man needed to create a legacy of warmth and plenty for his son.

Yet there was another natural resource to this backwoods wilderness, one which ran wild and like the land was free for the taking. And because of it, Jim Oliver ceased to be a farmer.

Longhorn cattle roamed the dense thickets like deer, living free and unclaimed among the wild things. They were descendants of Spanish cattle brought to Mission San Gabriel a hundred years before, and like the grass and the timber, they were simply part of this new land. From them a smart man could provide meat for his family, rawhide to serve a thousand purposes, and tallow for candles. But more significantly to a backwoods settler, the longhorns could be captured and driven to markets on the Gulf Coast. And sold for hard money—gold—the only currency of worth in a country too new for banks.

Jim Oliver became a rancher, trading cattle for money and money for land, until he controlled thousands of acres north of Yegua Creek. Over the years he sired three more sons, built a rambling log house, and watched his herds multiply with each new spring. While building a legacy for his own sons he had also taken the lead in attracting other settlers to the hill country, eventually creating a tightly-knit community along the isolated backwaters bounded by Yegua Creek on the south and Brushy Creek on the north. Strong willed, determined, fiercely loyal to his neighbors, Jim Oliver became the most influential rancher in Williamson County by sheer force of character. After twenty years of chasing longhorns he had turned the operation over to Print, his eldest, and sat back to watch his four sons crown the great enterprise he had founded.

Then Texas had seceded from the Union and Print marched off to war. Perhaps to end the dream of Jim Oliver on some bloody battlefield where money and power counted for nothing.

Reflecting back as he rode along the trail, Print recalled

that it had been an uncommonly bleak day when he departed in the spring of '61. The family had crowded around him as he mounted, proud of what he was undertaking, yet fearful that he might never return. Jay and Ira, strapping teenagers, were afire with envy, while Bob, still a mere child, had clung tearfully to his stirrup. Then it was time to leave and his mother had taken his hand, speaking with the quiet strength that was so much a part of her dark beauty.

"Never lose hope, son, for without it you are lost. But if it is written that you must die, then die like the great oaks, from the top down. Always keep your roots planted in God."

Jim Oliver had stepped forward then, glancing sideways at his wife. "Print, don't try to do God's work for Him. I've taught you how to handle the tough ones and that ought to see you through. Just do your duty and come on home. We'll be waitin'."

With that Print had galloped out of the yard, waving back as the trail dipped into the woods. Thinking about it now, it seemed hard to believe that four years had passed. It was more like he had ridden into Georgetown only this morning and was returning home in time for supper. The boys would crowd around as he rode up, yelling and squalling for his attention. His mother would appear in the doorway, hand on hip, demanding that everyone wash for supper this very instant. Then, as he dismounted, his father would give him a sly wink, somehow easing the burden of forever being the eldest. That's how it had always been, and while four years had been snatched from his life, that's how it would still be. Even now.

Suddenly he broke clear of the woods and pounded into the clearing. Nothing had changed! It was all there, exactly as he had left it. The log house, a scattering of outbuildings, the breaking corral. Bathed in the dusky glow of sundown, smoke coming from the chimney, just as he had remembered it every night for a thousand bloody nights on the killing ground. The sight brought a moist lump to his throat and all of a sudden he found it difficult to swallow.

They had endured, survived, just as he had. Nothing had touched them, or changed them. It was all as it had been, awaiting only his return. The night would wipe away the four godless years, and with dawn it would be as if he had never left. Just the same, always there—solid, substantial, never changing.

Print slowed the horse to a walk, then came to a dead stop. Like some pale, ghostly thing from the nether world he sat and watched, gripped by a reluctance to test the memory of what once had been.

Then the door opened and a man stepped onto the porch with a cocked rifle in his hands.

"Don't step down, mister," he called. "Not unless you've got business here."

"Jay?" Print choked out the word, unable to believe his eyes. That was Jay standing on the porch. Yet it couldn't be. Jay was still a boy.

Jay started, gaping incredulously at the tattered scarecrow before him. "Print? God Almighty, is that you, Print?"

Leaping from the porch, Jay ran toward him, yelling back over his shoulder. "Ma, it's Print. He's come home!"

The door suddenly filled and people seemed to explode into the yard. Ira and Bob screamed rebel yells and pulled him from the saddle, swarming over him like bear cubs. His mother hugged him fiercely, her eyes brimming over with tears, yet laughing that strong, throaty laugh he remembered so well. In their wake lumbered Jim Oliver, unable to speak, stretching out his hand, then clasping his eldest in a shameless embrace.

Print staggered from one to the other, still not sure that it was real, that they were all there just as he had left them. The boys' excited questions rattled one on top of the other like hailstones. *Were you captured? Did you get wounded? How many Yankees did you kill?* They all jabbered at once, leaving him no room to answer as they bore him along toward the house. But he couldn't have spoken, anyway. Not just yet. For as the shock of greeting wore off he began to see them more clearly, as they really were.

And it was a sobering experience.

Jim Oliver's hair had turned white as fresh snow, and he hobbled along beneath stooped shoulders like some shrunken gnome. The husky, bull-necked pioneer who had hewed a home from the wilderness and sired four sons had been replaced by a stranger. He sounded like Jim Oliver and there was still a hint of fire in his eyes, but this man was only a wispy shadow of the father who had sent him off to war four years past.

Still, it was the boys who shocked him most. Christ, there was no sense calling them boys any longer. They were men, full grown. Jay and Ira had filled out with the broad Oliver shoulders and they both topped six feet now. Another year and they would make him feel like a runt. But it was Bob who made him feel ancient clean down to his bones. That little squirt who used to tag after him endlessly had shot up like a sapling. Unless he missed his guess, the baby of the family was going to put them all in the shade. *Baby!* Print was suddenly staggered by the realization that Bob was now fifteen. He was a baby no longer, and if he was like the rest of the Olivers he wouldn't stand to be treated as one.

Only Julia Oliver hadn't changed. Maybe a few added wrinkles around the eyes and vagrant streaks of grey through the black obsidian of her hair. But otherwise she seemed the same. Tall, straight, still as sleek as a young filly, and somehow stronger than Print ever remembered her. Which struck him as very strange. For his foremost recollection of his mother, even from the days of his childhood, had been the quiet, inner strength she lent to those about her. Maybe Jim Oliver was only a shell of his former self, but Julia hadn't lost an inch in the struggle against time. If anything, she had grown leaner, tougher, and with it, stronger. Perhaps strong enough for both of them.

They had no more than entered the house when Print got

his first lesson in just how strong Julia Oliver had become in his absence. Neither Jim Oliver nor his sons had ever been what anybody could rightly call God-fearing, and the greatest shock of Print's homecoming were the first words out of his mother's mouth.

"Jim. Boys. We'll kneel and say a prayer of thanksgiving for Prentice's safe return. There'll be plenty of time for questions later on."

Without a word the Oliver men assembled around the oaken dining table and knelt. Still somewhat baffled, Print sheepishly followed suit.

Standing over them, Julia Oliver clasped her hands and turned her face to the heavens. "Almighty God, we humble ourselves before you this night and offer up a prayer of gratitude that you have spared the life of our eldest son. Lead him now in the ways of righteousness as you have led him from the valley of death."

Print didn't hear any more though the prayer seemed to go on with no end in sight. His leg began to throb and he looked up to find his father watching him. Jim Oliver grinned and winked, then ducked his head again. Print shook his head, chuckling softly to himself.

Things hadn't changed so damn' much after all.

3

After breakfast Print strolled down to the creek. Curiously, he felt the need to be alone and this shaded glen below the house had always been his favorite spot. Stately pecan trees encircled a spring-fed pond which was lined with ferns and moss. While the pond emptied into Yegua Creek only yards away, it was isolated by a thick cover of foliage; a hideaway he had retreated to since the earliest days of his childhood. Here it was cool and peaceful, a safe harbor from the relentless hammering of the sun. And the prying ways of people. Beside this pond he could wonder and ruminate, puzzling over all manner of things that less inquisitive men rarely bothered to question. Even as a boy he had been a thinker, deep somehow in a way that was different from those around him. More like his mother, folks said, for Julia in her own way was given to profound thoughts and long silences. It was hardly surprising, then, that as a man Print Oliver preferred the solace of his own company at times.

Though others more often than not spoke of him as aloof, coldly distant, it was merely something that surpassed their understanding. He was his own man, dependent on neither God nor neighbor, and he found much to ponder in a world that seemed forever clothed in enigma and riddle.

But on his first morning home he was troubled by something more than the need to be alone. Everything about him seemed to have come apart at the seams, and for reasons that he failed to comprehend he was goaded by a sense of utter futility. Clearly the situation called for decisive action of some sort. Where to start, though, was a thorny puzzler that continued to elude him. The boys' incessant questions at the breakfast table had finally palled on him, and he had escaped to this old hideaway in the hope that alone he might somehow resolve his nettlesome thoughts.

Reflecting back over what he had seen in the past month, he knew that war, or more properly defeat in war, was the root of all their troubles. Coming home he had seen mourning in every household, desolation written in broad characters across the face of the land; cities in ashes and fields laid waste, a nation's commerce annihilated beneath the Union juggernaut. Ruin, poverty, and distress were everywhere; even pestilence had been added to the very cap sheaf of the south's miseries. Yankee forces now occupied a conquered land, and if the last month was any gauge then what was to come would be even worse. *Vengeance is mine, saith the Lord.* Perhaps, but then God had never seen the Yankees in action.

Still, there was an even more pressing problem, one which struck closer to home. The Olivers and their Yegua Creek neighbors were surrounded by Union sympathizers, isolated among the Williamson County loyalists like gold-fish in a sea of sharks. Retribution would be swift in coming, that much was for certain. The only question that remained was what price would be demanded when the rebels were brought to reckoning.

Then there was his father. Perhaps the cruelest blow of all. The most unnerving truth he had yet to face was the fact that the Jim Oliver of his youth no longer existed. Dreams die hard in old warriors, particularly those who have never known defeat. The devastation of war had brought the Oliver patriarch to his knees, turned his hair white, drained him of his manhood. The family was lead-erless, except for his mother's misguided faith in the be-nevolence of God. And in times such as these the absence of a strong leader was a flaw that might prove fatal indeed.

Occupied with thoughts of war, and reprisals, and walk-ing dead men, the hair on the back of his neck suddenly bristled as a step sounded behind him. Instinctively he rolled, jerking the Colt, and came around with it cocked to fire. Behind him, smiling calmly, stood Julia Oliver.

"Ma, you shouldn't come sneakin' up on a man like that." Holstering the pistol somewhat sheepishly, he turned back to the pond. "Sorry. I didn't mean to snap at you that way. I guess my nerves are sort of on edge."

Walking forward, Julia sat beside him, her dark eyes filled with concern. "Son, you've been through a hell none of us know much about. Good food will put the meat back on your bones and plenty of sleep will cure whatever else ails you. And until it does, we've got all the time in the world. So don't you worry about us getting our feelings hurt."

Print just looked at her for a moment, then smiled faintly. "All the time in the world. Seems funny to hear somebody say that again."

"Was it as bad as they say, Prentice? The war, I mean."

"Yes'm, I reckon it was. There wasn't time for anything except dyin'. And nothing much the livin' could do to stop it."

She waited for him to continue, but he just sat there, staring across the pond. "Is that why you avoided your brothers' questions this morning? Because you didn't want to be reminded of it."

Print glanced at her out of the corner of his eye. He had forgotten how shrewd the Cherokee half of her could be when it came to what a man left unsaid. "Something like that. It's not rightly the kind of thing a fella likes to dream about."

"But you have been, haven't you? Dreaming about it, I mean." When he didn't answer, her eyes searched his face tenderly. "Last night I heard you crying in your sleep and when I went into your room you were soaking wet. Your forehead was cool but it was damp, like people get when they have a nightmare."

He made a game effort at grinning, but it came off badly. "Yeah, I suppose 'nightmare' describes it about as well as anything else."

"Prentice, I want you to tell me about it." She saw him stiffen and hurried on before he could object. "Now I won't take no for an answer. You're like a man full of rattlesnake poison, and you'll never be yourself until you get it out. I'll just listen and you tell me how it was."

His eyes remained focused on something across the pond, cloudy as smoked agates, as though he were looking beyond moment and place to a time without dimension. Then he told her. Haltingly at first, but after a few words it came in a rush, like vomit spewing out from a man's sickened bowels.

They had come north under Albert Sidney Johnston to a place called Shiloh on the Tennessee River. This was their first battle and Johnston had cunningly engaged the Yankees before they were ready to fight. They attacked with first light and drove the Bluecoats north from dawn till dusk. Back past Shiloh Church, past the peach orchard, past Lick Creek, and finally into some woods beyond a shallow pond gone red with blood.

But General Johnston had bled to death from a leg wound that afternoon, and the Union artillery had secretly taken position on the high ground to the north. As night approached the Confederates pulled back across the creek to await morning, and the victory that was theirs. Yet even as they rested, the issue was being decided by a cigar-chomping Yankee general.

Ulysses S. Grant ordered gunboats up the river that night, and under cover of darkness moved four fresh divisions into the lines. With dawn the Yankees struck, lobbing shells in from the bluffs to the north while raking their flanks with the gunboats' eight-pounders. When Grant's infantry charged at dawn the Confederate lines collapsed. They fled back past the peach orchard, and Shiloh Church, and by noon what started as a withdrawal had become a full-fledged rout.

Sometime during the fighting that second morning, Print had taken a Minie ball through the thigh. But he bound it up and went on, gritting his teeth with each step. Behind lay death and blood-soaked tables where they hacked off men's legs like butchers in a charnel house. To stop meant to die, and he hadn't come that far only to fall in his first battle.

That night the Confederates began retreating toward Corinth, twenty-five miles away, and the Union artillery shelled them every step of the way. Along toward dark Print came upon a soldier whose head wound had blinded him. He was sitting beside the road, helpless and alone. But he had two good legs. And Print had eyes enough for the both of them. They teamed up, the lame and the blind, and somehow managed to hold pace with the retreating army. Toward morning they reached the outskirts of Corinth and fell exhausted in a grove of trees. When Print awoke some hours later his blind companion had hemorrhaged and died.

Later he would learn that of the thirteen hundred men in his regiment who had marched up to Shiloh only two hundred fifty had returned.

The remainder of the war was merely an extension of the horror and confusion that began at Shiloh. First Corinth, then Jackson, finally Vicksburg. There, on the banks of the

Mississippi, Print saw the Confederacy die. The fighting had gone on, to be sure, but it was only a matter of time. Like a man with a mortal wound, the southern forces faltered then fell before the Union onslaught. Will alone wasn't enough.

Shattered beyond repair, the Confederate army headed southwest out of Vicksburg. Victorious, the Yankees marched east under Sherman. Toward Atlanta and the sea.

When Grant and Lee met at Appomattox Courthouse nearly two years later the carnage was ended at last. Only then, with the dream finally laid to rest, did Print Oliver turn his eyes toward Texas, and home.

Julia Oliver had listened quietly while he talked, revealing nothing of the cold horror that tore at her heart. It was worse than the newspapers had said, more terrible even than the rumors that had drifted back to Texas. But what could she say to him now? What could anyone say who hadn't killed, or gone hungry, or slept beside the bloated, rotting corpse of a boyhood friend? Only time would change that. Time and love.

Some minutes passed before she could trust herself to speak. "Son, I'm glad you told me. Maybe sharing it with somebody will lighten the burden. God works in mysterious ways, and what's happened might be His way of preparing us for the days ahead."

Print looked around, the corners of his mouth twisted sardonically. "Well let's hope God has done His job, Ma. What's ahead isn't gonna be a hell of a lot better than what we just come through."

"Don't blaspheme, Prentice." Julia's gaze bored straight through him. "We have much to be thankful for, and with what you've seen in the war I shouldn't have to tell you that. You've come home to us unharmed and sound of mind. The fighting passed us by, we've got no rebuilding to do, and our cattle have multiplied beyond anything that's natural. God has been good to us, son, and He deserves more from you than a sharp tongue."

Print just grunted, slowly shaking his head. "Ma, do you have any idea of what's about to happen in Texas? Or for that matter, right here in Williamson County. The Yankees are gonna be out to collect their pound of flesh, and our turn-coat neighbors will be right in there swillin' at the same trough. The war's not over, Ma. It just started."

"Don't you think I know that, Prentice? Why do you think I came down here to talk to you?"

"Ma'am?" She had taken him unaware and his startled response showed it.

"Surely you can see that your father isn't the man he used to be. I mean, he's aged beyond his time. It just happens to some people."

"Yes'm, I saw that last night. But I still don't get what you're drivin' at."

"Well, someone has to take over as head of the family," she informed him. "Lord knows, I've tried, but it hasn't been easy. You're the eldest and it looks to me like you'll just have to pick up where your father left off."

Print regarded her for a moment without expression. Then he nodded, just once. "That's about the way I had it figured, too."

She came to her feet, effortlessly and in one movement, the way Indians do. "You're a good man, Prentice Oliver. And a good son. I've always loved you and been proud of you, but never more than right now."

She turned and walked off toward the house before he could speak. But it really didn't matter one way or the other. He was all talked out for one day.

Words wouldn't mean a good goddamn anyway—not if he was any judge of what the Olivers were likely to meet down the road.

4

That afteroon Jay and Print rode out to have a look at the cattle. Over dinner the boys had joshed around and cut their eyes at one another, stating matter of factly that he had a real surprise coming. From their good-natured banter Print knew something was up, but he was wholly unprepared for what Jay showed him.

Everywhere they rode they found small clusters of longhorns. Not just a few scattered here and there, but bunch after bunch after bunch. Until it seemed that every foot of Oliver land was being contested by at least two cows and a couple of calves. Turning upstream along Yegua Creek they rode west for over an hour, flushing mossyhorns like coveys of quail. Before them fled cattle of every color, yellows, brindles, some as black as midnight, many with horns spanning six feet or more.

With the sun high overhead they headed north into the rolling hills. These low granite knobs had boiled out of the earth's bowels in eons past; polished by centuries of wind, and rain, and snow. Between them lay the cedar breaks haunted by cattle for warmth in the winter and shade in the summer. Along with cows they began scaring up deer, wild turkey, and bear, till it seemed to Print that they had somehow stumbled onto a kingdom inhabited solely by wild things.

When they reached Brushy Creek some miles to the north, Print reined in and began loading his pipe. Jay hadn't said much during their ride, and he knew that his younger brother was relishing his baffled expression. After touching a sulphur to his pipe, he nodded back toward the hills. "When I rode out in '61 I thought we had more cows than anybody rightly deserved. But that beats any goddamn' thing I've ever seen."

Jay flashed a quick smile, immensely pleased that his elder brother was duly impressed. Like all the Olivers, Jay was big and rangy with his daddy's burnt-amber hair and blue eyes. Only Print took after their mother, showing signs of their distant Cherokee blood-kin. But unlike his brother, Jay Oliver had somehow been whelped with a natural-born aversion to words, and what he generally left unsaid could have kept a flock of blackbirds busy till first frost. Right now he was still a little awed by Print's sojourn among the Yankees and he was even more laconic than usual.

"You've only seen 'em comin'. There's just as many going back."

"Well they're thicker'n fleas already, so I don't reckon it'll come as any shock. How many you figure there are all together?"

Jay mulled it over for a moment before answering. "Near as we can tally there's somewheres close to five thousand. You recollect we had less'n half that when you left. But they been breedin' like flies ever since."

"Damnation." Print was genuinely dumbfounded. "With numbers like that I take it you sold off little or nothin' while I was gone."

"Nope. Just enough to keep bread on the table." Jay jerked his head around at the brushy landscape. "We're sorta off the beaten track and nobody come buyin', so we didn't go sellin'. Besides, what with cows runnin' wild for the takin', people was payin' piss poor prices anyway."

"Wait a minute. Are you tryin' to tell me you haven't made a gather in four years?"

Jay gave him a mockish smile. "Who the hell with? Me and Ira? Shit, Print, we're talkin about *five thousand* cows. You couldn't hire hands during the war if you had a goose pumpin' out gold eggs."

"No damn' wonder I didn't see much branded stock when we rode through." Print puffed on his pipe and thought about it for a minute. "That means you didn't cut none of the bulls."

"Cut 'em?" Jay hooted. "Christ, we can't even catch 'em. There's more critters with balls out there than you could count. Too damn many, matter of fact. Got so they fight like tigers when the cows come in season. Just wait'll you try ropin' one of them monsters. In case you ain't noticed, big brother, the Oliver spread is over-run with some of the wildest boggers this side of a goddamn jungle."

That had been some speech for Jay, damn' near the longest he had ever made. Print treated it with due respect, falling silent as he chewed over what the younger man had said. Jay was right about one thing. Those were the meanest looking cattle he had ever laid eyes on. Hardly a one

of them weighed less than a thousand pounds and many of
the bulls would top fifteen hundred easy. More unsettling
still, they had been running wild for four years and rounding them up was going to be a little like herding bears
with a willow switch. The Olivers had their work cut out for
them. That is if a man could rightly call it work tangling
with a half ton of horn and muscle.

Some folks might call it suicide.

As the sun dipped westward they turned south and
headed home. Along the way they crossed a flatter stretch
which was rimmed with scattered clumps of yucca, Spanish
bayonet and prickly pear. Such things began petering out in
the hill country but there was still enough to go around.
Even bull nettle flourished here and there, but a man did
well to steer clear of it. While pretty enough to the eye, it
ran a close second with scorpions for being poisonous to the
touch. Somehow it put Print in mind of the drought back in
'59. Creek beds had run dry that summer and if it hadn't
been for the springs their herd would have pulled up in
tough shape. Then the graze just withered away to nothing
and things really got fierce for a while. Finally Jim Oliver
had put the boys to burning the spines off prickly pear and
afterwards fed them to the stock.

Thinking about it, Print had to chuckle. There was something downright ridiculous about watching cows munch
prickly pear like it was popcorn. Then he snorted to himself. Before they got through gathering these wild bastards
again they might be wishing they had some little goody to
lure them out of the brush.

After the supper dishes were out of the way that evening,
Julia called the family back around the table. The boys exchanged sour glances and Jay muttered something about it
being a little early to call a prayer meeting. But Print had
caught a certain look in the old lady's eye, and it came to him
that the female side of the family had spent the afternoon
hatching a new dodge to her latest scheme. Then he looked
over at his father and any lingering doubt was fast erased.

Jim Oliver had been primed like a three dollar pump.

Whatever he had on his mind chances were better than even it had been put there by the lady of the household.

When they were all seated Julia nodded to her husband and smiled reassuringly, then sat back like her divining rod had just brought in a dry hole. The boys caught this little byplay and turned in unison for a fast look at the old man. But if they expected to find some miracle at work they were sorely disappointed. Jim Oliver appeared no different than he had that morning, or a hundred mornings before. The thick, ropy muscles in his shoulders had gone soft loafing around the house and the straight, hard jawline of days past had fattened into pink, whiskered jowls. When the Confederacy died some part of him had died also, and he appeared to be exactly what he was. A man who had given up on life before it gave up on him.

Still, there was a slight twinkle in his eye that hadn't been apparent earlier in the day, and it seemed plain enough that something had pleased him vastly. The boys joined their mother and sat back to wait him out.

Looking around the table, his gaze settled on Print. "What d'ya think of what Jay showed you?"

"Pa, just offhand I'd say the Olivers'd be rich if we could figure out some way to catch all them cows."

Jim Oliver laughed soundlessly, something like a steam whistle fresh out of juice. "Well, what're you gonna do about it?"

"What do you mean?" Print knew well enough, but for the old man's sake this little charade had to be played out to the end.

"I mean that's what this meetin' has been called for. There comes a time when ever' man should step aside. I kept this outfit together while you was gone, but by damn', I've earned me a rest. It's your turn to wear the spurs and I don't begrudge you the job even the least bit." Then he paused, studying the boys for a moment. "These three ain't the hellions you were, but you're still gonna have your hands full bein' head of this family."

The old man darted a glance toward the opposite end of the table, and it came to Print that in his own sly way Jim Oliver was warning him about meddlesome women. "Pa, I'll try not to let you down. Even if it means bendin' the rules here and there."

Oliver's bleary eyes crackled with mirth and he slapped his leg. "By gravy, that'll get it! But if anybody gets to sassin' you, just send 'em to me. I'll straighten 'em out on who's callin' the shots around here from now on."

The boys exchanged quick looks and broke out in wide grins, like three bears in a honey barrel. They didn't understand it all just yet, but they purely liked what they had heard so far. With Print running the outfit there would be some excitement for a change. And maybe fewer prayer meetings.

Then Julia Oliver spoke up, and things got very quiet around the table. "Prentice, you're the eldest, and your daddy has done the right thing in making you head of the family. Now we're all waiting to hear what it is you've got planned."

"Ma, I'm sorta short on plans, but I know the first thing we're gonna do." Print smiled at Jay and Ira who sat across from him, then gave young Bob a dig in the ribs with his elbow. "Just as soon as I can hire some hands we're gonna gather the Oliver herd. After that we'll make damn' sure nobody takes 'em away from us."

"A-a-amen," intoned Ira, who sometimes stuttered when he got excited.

Julia Oliver shot him a withering look, then headed for the kitchen to make fresh coffee. Back at the table she heard snickering from the boys and Print's deeper voice shushing them. Those boys needed a strong hand what with their daddy retreating farther and farther into his own little world. It was good that Prentice had come home in time to set them on the right path. But she would have to caution him about cursing at the table. Even the eldest had to mind his manners in a Christian home.

5

Early next morning Print rode north again. This time he went alone, for his errand had nothing to do with cows or Oliver interests. What he had to do was strictly personal, and while he hadn't yet unscrambled it, he somehow dreaded the next few hours.

Almost four years ago to the day he had made this same trip. Then, bursting with the excitement of a young man marching off to war, his purpose had been to say goodbye to Louisa Reno. Now, humbled in defeat, he was confused, his emotions snarled and tangled in deep-rooted conflict. When he rode out in '61 Louisa had promised to wait for him. But whether she had or not just didn't seem worth the bother anymore. And this numbed indifference was what had him baffled.

Perhaps watching other men die did that. Turned a man cold, hardened him to the softer passions. Maybe not the first, or the second, or even the tenth. But when they fell by the hundreds and finally by the thousands, it did something to a man's insides. Like slaughtering hogs in the fall. After awhile a man no longer heard the squeals, or saw the blood, or smelled the stench when death loosed their bowels. He was just a spectator. Numbed.

Still, there was more to it than that. There had to be. As he rode Print puzzled over it, reflecting back to those frantic days four summers past. Texas had seceded from the Union, with the exception of most of Williamson County. Which included Louisa Reno and her family. The Renos ran a small spread north of Brushy Creek, and like most of the people in the county, they were separated by a wide political chasm from the Olivers and their neighbors.

Sam Houston was still something akin to God in those days, and the people of Williamson County had loyally stuck with him throughout the long fight over secession. When they lost, watching Houston become a pariah in the very land he had wrested from the Mexicans, their bitterness knew no bounds. Texas, and the man who had given it independence, had been betrayed by the wealthy slave owners, the landed gentry. This was a rich man's madness, war for the sake of a privileged few, and the Union loyalists turned their rancor on the rebels of Yegua Creek.

Though they owned no slaves, and were far from rich, the Olivers and their neighbors suddenly found themselves outcasts among people they had known and worked beside for more than twenty years. When Print and his young friends joined up with the Confederate army that summer the issue was sealed. The settlers along Yegua Creek simply ceased to exist insofar as the rest of Williamson County was concerned. Like lepers stoned from the colony, they became something that other men no longer acknowledged.

They were there, but no one saw them. They were dead.

Curiously, the political discord of their elders had had no outward effect on Louisa and Print. While they held opposing views they had been too much in love to allow such worldly matters to come between them. They had been sweethearts from childhood, lovers since Louisa's sixteenth birthday, and the petty bickerings of those around them had seemed too trivial to matter. For a time.

Only when Print made it known that he was joining the army did Louisa change. For more than a week she had cried, pouted, and cajoled, pleading with him to reconsider. Not for the sake of politics, or even because it was the loathsome Confederates he intended to join. She tried to sway him solely because wars killed men and she wanted him alive, with her, just as they had always planned. When her entreaties had failed to move him, she finally gave it up, seemingly reconciled to the fact that some men held duty above all else. Even love.

But she never forgave him. Though they were to have been married that spring she convinced him that it was best to postpone the wedding. When he returned, if he returned, then would they take the vows.

Louisa was a very practical woman. Grass widows were used merchandise, far less sought after than demure young maids. Only in later months, after hearing the same tale from countless men, did it dawn on Print what she had done. And it had left an acrid taste in his mouth for four long years.

Perhaps that was what lay behind his reluctance to see her again. Yet that didn't hold water either. He couldn't honestly fault her for being practical. If the shoe had been on the other foot he might have done the same thing. Maybe it was the war after all. Some men weren't killed but they had lost more than their lives at places like Shiloh and Vicksburg. Whatever it was that kindled love—the nameless thing that fired compassion in a man's soul—had been seared out of them. They weren't animals, yet they had become something less than men.

They saw, they breathed, their senses functioned. They just didn't feel.

Maybe it had happened to him. Outwardly he was alive, unchanged, but his innards felt like cold ashes in a dead fire. Still, everything had its price, and perhaps learning to kill without thought or remorse exacted the highest price of all.

Print's thoughts abruptly returned to the moment as his horse passed through the gate of the Reno place. Ahead he could see the house, just as he remembered it. The porch swing was still there, although the cushions looked faded now; the smell of honeysuckle was as overpowering as ever and off in the distance he noted the wooded hill where they used to make love on warm evenings. It was all as he had left it four years ago, yet somehow different. Nothing a man could put his finger on really, just something he felt in his gut. But it left him uneasy, more perplexed than ever.

The door opened as he dismounted at the hitching post and Louisa stepped onto the porch. For a moment he just stood there, frozen by memories of things past. Long ago, faraway things. Dreams mostly. The dreams of children born of childlike love.

Yet there was nothing childlike about the woman standing before him. Louisa Reno had matured in four years, and where she had once been pretty, she was now downright stunning. The taffy-colored hair and hazel eyes were the same; she was still tall and graceful, still had that pert, button nose and oval features. But the similarity ended there. She had filled out in the right places, enough to give any man the dry sweats, and her face had assumed form, symmetry. Perhaps even beauty in a fresh, wholesome sort of way. The girl of summers past had blossomed somehow, like a butterfly gathering vibrant colors on the warm winds. In her place had emerged a woman.

"Print, it's good to see you again." Louisa smiled, trying not to show the strain. When he didn't speak she moved off the porch and came a few steps closer. "We heard you were home. I wanted to see you, but you hadn't written or anything, so I just. . . ."

She faltered, waiting for him to say something, but he still couldn't find the right words. Then she came a step closer. "I'm awfully glad you weren't hurt. Every single night you were gone I prayed you'd come back safe."

"Lou, I. . . ." Print's words drifted off like wisps of smoke on a still day.

Louisa blinked away tears and just for a moment she was the young girl he had left behind. "Print, I waited. There's been no one else. There never was."

"And I came back," he rasped huskily.

Suddenly she flew across the yard and threw herself into his arms. He pulled her to him, feeling the soft flesh yield beneath his hand, and their lips came together in wet, hungry union. After a moment they parted, breathing heavily, and she nuzzled against his neck.

"Oh, Print, I love you so. When I think of the way I sent you off it just makes me sick. Makes me hate myself for being so foolish."

"Hush, Lou. I'm back and nothin' has changed. It never did."

Louisa brushed his hat off and ran her hands through his black, wavy hair. Then her arms encircled his neck and pulled his mouth to her again.

CHAPTER TWO

---∞ΙΙΙΙΙ Ω ΙΙΙΙ∞---

1

The riders waited in a stand of live oaks on a low hogback. Below them, shimmering in the soft glow of a full moon, stretched a wide, unbroken prairie. Rolling hills surrounded the open expanse to their front, and as the men waited a gentle breeze drifted back over them.

While most of them were dismounted, they neither smoked nor talked. Motionless, eyes fixed on the open ground, they silently waited. Like hunters they had uncommon patience, heedless of the long hours and cramped muscles. Sometime soon their prey would appear below and the excitement of the chase was made all the sweeter by this time of quiet suspense that came before. Even their horses understood how the game was played, and though they had been there the better part of three hours, the animals remained as still and watchful as the men.

Print Oliver stood off by himself, his gaze concentrated on a brushy thicket between two hills some distance to the front. The black man, Jim Kelly, had scouted this setup for a week running, and if he was right the longhorns would

emerge from that thicket sometime before midnight.
They had held off gathering this bunch until full moon,
for the tracks indicated a large band and they would need
plenty of light once the action started. Jay and another crew
of riders were hidden in a grove of trees across the way, quietly awaiting Print's signal to open the ball. When it came
they were to circle in from the north, blocking the cows'
retreat.

After that it was every man for himself.

Less than three weeks had passed since Print announced
his decision to gather the Oliver herd. Time had lost all
meaning in a rush of getting things organized, but not a
moment had been wasted. Print was in the saddle from
dawn till late at night, working seven days a week, yet he
had never felt more alive, charged with energy. Running a
cow outfit was something he understood, what Jim Oliver
had trained him for since childhood, and he was once again
in his element. Wallowing in it, as a matter of fact, like a
buffalo bull that had stumbled into a great, juicy mudhole
in the midst of summer.

The first step had been to hire a crew of brushpoppers
who savvied cows. Surprisingly, this proved to be no
problem whatever. Austin, which was less than a day's ride
south, was crawling with former Rebs, and many of them
had cut their eyeteeth on a rawhide *reata*. Work was scarce,
money even more so, and a man offering both could be
mighty choosy about picking only top hands. After standing drinks in a half-dozen saloons, Print had been swamped
with likely candidates. Within two days he had his crew and
was headed home.

Like most cow outfits, the men who signed on under the
Oliver brand were a mixed assortment. Ace Whitehead had
chased mossyhorns from the Pecos to the Rio Grande, and
read more books along the way than most schoolmarms
had ever seen. Which made him a rarity among cattlemen,
particularly when he started spouting Shakespeare. Doughbelly Ketchum had been a range cook ever since a bronc
stunted his growth, and had won some little renown for his

shotgun coffee. He was fond of noting that it was too thick
to drink and too thin to slice, but just right for floating
buckshot. Jim Kelly, on the other hand, was a black horse
wrangler who laid claim to being a natural-born liar. He
had spent the war years in western Texas hunting mustangs
and he had few peers with either horses or an intricately
fabricated whopper. Harry Strain, Lee Wells, and Bumpus
Moore rounded out the crew. Each in his own way was independent as a hog on ice, yet Print had a sneaking hunch
that they could be molded into a top-notch team. Maybe it
would take a couple of busted heads and some knuckle
dusting to get it done, but that was all part of ramroding a
bunch of bad-assed individualists. With Jay and Ira he had
seven working hands, which was fewer than he wanted but
near about as many as the Oliver treasury could support at
the moment. Figuring roughly, he calculated that they only
had to catch seven hundred cows apiece. But that was merely
time-consuming, the hard part came afterwards.

Letting go of a longhorn was generally a damn' sight
trickier than latching on.

After scouting the hills and thickets and cedar breaks for
close to a week, Print had organized the gather along the
lines of a military operation. Like any well-executed raid,
catching longhorns depended largely on the element of
surprise and forcing the cantankerous beasts to fight on
ground not of their own choosing. With four years of absolute freedom behind them, the cattle had reverted to the
wild, roaming unchecked through the countryside as the
will moved them. Not unlike deer, the longhorns had become nocturnal in habit, laying up in the thickets during
the day and venturing out to feed only after darkness settled over the hills. They were spooky, ill-tempered as turpentined bears, and a formidable threat to man or horse
with their curved, saber-like horns.

They were the enemy, dangerous, unpredictable, born
killers. Matching wits with them wasn't for the fainthearted, and the man who got careless more often than not
ended up taking the long sleep.

Tactics, everyone agreed, was what gave the edge. The longhorns had to be out-generaled before they could be out-fought. Accordingly, Print set the crew to building stout log corrals in strategic locations near their favorite watering holes. Long wings were then constructed in a V-shape fanning out from the corral gate for as much as two hundred yards. The next step was to catch and tame a small herd of fifty cows. This was accomplished by the simple expedient of chasing them from the brush, dragging them roped fore and aft to a corral, then starving them until they had become wholly dependent on their captors. Not that any longhorn could ever be civilized, or trusted for that matter, but at least they became tractable. Docile in a peculiarly lethal sort of way.

Afterwards the tame herd had been used as decoys. They were moved to a meadow and held there while the wild ones were flushed from the thickets. Once the tigers had mixed with the tabby cats they were surrounded by shouting riders and driven to the nearest corral. There the starving and taming process began all over again.

Some of the *ladinos,* the real outlaws, became escape artists of the highest order. Many scaled the corral fences like panthers, while others merely waited until the latest starvation session was ended then darted back into the brush. But there were ways to educate even these stubborn misfits. When the *ladino* was captured again he found himself yoked to an ox who outweighed him in every department, including sheer stubbornness. After a week or so of being dragged around by an ox the longhorn generally decided there was much to be said for life among the herd.

Then there were the spooks, the wary, ever vigilant breed that defied every lure or enticement the hands could devise. Like ghostly shadows they clung to the impenetrable thickets, never showing themselves till late at night when the two-legged predators were fast asleep. These skittish ones were the wildest of the lot, cunning beyond belief and slippery as greased pigs. They had to be run to earth one by one, hauled bellowing and pawing to the corrals, there to

be starved into submission or treated to a short course in
manners by the implacable oxen.

The little sortie Print had planned for tonight was to capture just such a bunch of flighty holdouts.

When the longhorns finally appeared the men had to
blink to make sure they were real. One minute the meadow
had been empty of life and the next there were close to
thirty cows standing there grazing. *Goddamn' critters were
like ghosts, popping up in thin air when a man least expected them.* Print motioned for the men to mount, never
taking his eyes off the cattle. When everyone was ready
his arm swept forward and he spurred his horse down off
the hill.

The riders fanned out and came storming over the open
ground screaming rebel yells, uncoiling their *reatas* as they
rode. These lariats were handmade, braided rawhide that
had been stretched and tallowed, generally forty feet long,
and strong enough to hold a boar grizzly at his prime. Each
of the men rode rim-fire saddles, double cinched to take
the shock of roping a full grown longhorn, and the off end
of the *reata* was snugged tight around the saddle horn.
Their legs were covered with bullhide *chaparejos* to protect them from thorns and brush, and heavy gauntlets
stretched halfway up their forearms. They had fast ponies,
plenty of savvy, and good equipment. All that remained
was to outwit the spooky longhorns.

The cattle veered off as they saw the riders bearing down
on them and tried to dodge back into the thickets. But Jay
and his crew had cut off their retreat and within moments
the battle was joined. Each rider selected a cow and took
off in pursuit. Urging his pony forward, the man would
quickly close the gap, dab a loop over the outstretched
horns, then spur his horse dead away. When the cow hit the
end of the lariat the horse sat back on his haunches and a
thousand pounds of longhorn swapped ends in the dust.
Leaping from his saddle, the rider then raced forward with
a piggin' string, started grabbing legs in bunches, and with
any luck had the brute hogtied in a matter of seconds. If his

luck played out he started dodging horns and hooves instead, muttering prayerfully that his pony wouldn't let any slack creep into the *reata*.

The next few minutes were filled with enraged bellowings, clipped curses, and a couple of quarts of blood. But when the dust settled and the men paused to catch their breath, eighteen she-cows and one bull were trussed up like suckling pigs. Better still, fourteen spring calves were nosing their mammies and blatting to beat thunder because dinner was running late. With the exception of one broken nose and a slight case of gored rump, the men had suffered only minor damages. All in all it had been a pretty good night.

Tomorrow this bunch would be earmarked, branded with the Oliver Sunburst, and any young bulls castrated. The ★ brand, with a point representing Jim Oliver and each of his four sons, had been burned on the flanks of close to five hundred head in the past fortnight. But there were still ten times that many hugging the thickets, and it was disturbingly clear to Print that this operation needed goosing if the full herd was to be gathered before winter.

Print was ruminating on this very subject when Jay pulled up beside him and began building a smoke. "Well, big brother, looks like the white-eyes won another round."

"Yeh, but this ruckus isn't movin' fast enough." Print's gaze roved around the clearing making a fast recount. "Something's got to change or we're gonna be trackin' cows through snow clear up till Christmas."

"Wouldn't surprise me none if you was right. But there's only so many hands and so many hours."

"That's what it boils down to all right, and I've been doing a heap of thinkin' the last couple of days. Maybe we can't buy hours but we can damn' sure buy ourselves some more hands."

Jay's head swiveled around. "Yeah? What with? In case you ain't looked in the cookie jar lately there's nothin' left but crumbs."

"Cows, little brother. Cows." Print's teeth flashed in the

pale moonlight. "With what we've gathered I figure we can cut out two, maybe three hundred head of beeves. We're gonna drive'em down to Galveston and trade 'em for some cash money."

"Shit fire, Print! You oughta know better'n that. Money's scarce as snake tits nowadays. Nobody's damn' fool enough to start trailin' cows yet."

"That's what I'm bankin' on, bubba. Could be every sonovabitch and his dog is just sittin' on their cows thinkin' the same thing."

Print chuckled and nudged his horse in the ribs. "One thing's for sure, though. We're gonna go have a looksee and find out for ourselves."

2

Julia Oliver straightened up from her washtub in time to see Print emerge from the woods on the Georgetown trail. The moment she spotted him she knew he had returned with good news. Print often reminded her of her mother's people, the Cherokee. Sometimes he could be as solemn and close-mouthed as a stuffed owl, yet there were other times when his dark eyes softened and his whole face seemed to brighten with laughter. Much like a small boy who had just taught his pet squirrel a new trick. Watching him as he rode forward, she knew that this was one of those times.

Close behind him came Ira, Jim Kelly, Harry Strain, and the cook, Doughbelly Ketchum. They had been gone almost six weeks to the day, which meant they couldn't have spent more than a night or two in Galveston. Julia was thankful for that, and grateful to Print that he hadn't tarried overlong in that heathen port. Not that she was worried about him. After all, he was a traveled man and knew how to resist the Devil's temptations. But Ira was just a boy and she had heard much about the wickedness and sinful ways along the Gulf Coast. Just the thought of it made her shudder.

What mothers never know about their sons, or simply re-
fuse to admit is often a blessing. And right at that moment
Julia Oliver was perhaps the most blessed of all. Young Ira
had stuttered his way through the fanciest whorehouse in
Galveston, and if it had tainted his mortal soul it certainly
didn't show on his face.

Toward the middle of June, Print and his men had put
something over three hundred head on the trail for Galveston. Behind he left a skeleton crew, with Jay in charge, to
tend the ranch. The drive had taken close to a month, and
along the way Print Oliver had learned considerably about
trailing longhorns. The first day out had been sheer hell
as the foul-tempered beasts tried again and again to turn
back toward their home range. Worse still, they had stampeded twice in the ensuing weeks, scattering across the
countryside the first time and plowing under a cotton field
the second. Thinking about it later, Print pretty well figured
what had set them off on that first run. Longhorns shared the
uneasiness of all wilderness animals around watering holes,
and when a flock of ducks exploded right in their faces the
whole herd had spooked.

But that second jamboree still had him shaking his head.
The unpredictable bastards had run for no apparent reason,
leastways none that he could understand. Maybe they didn't
like the looks of that cotton field, or maybe they just felt like
a little exercise. One guess was as good as another. But he
had filed the knowledge away for future reference, and on
the next drive he would be a damn' sight more watchful.

Still, even with stampedes and three cows lost in quicksand crossing the Brazos, they had reached Galveston with
three hundred eleven head. Finding a buyer had taken less
than an hour. Just as Print suspected, these were the first
beef cattle seen on the Gulf Coast since the close of the
war, and he had dickered until he got prime money. In gold.
Scrip might be all right for city folks, but country boys
knew that gold spends anywhere, no questions asked.

That night Print treated the crew to a ballbuster first class.
After quenching their thirst and touring a few gambling

dives, the boys had voted to get down to serious business.
Galveston was famous for its shady ladies and according to
Doughbelly Ketchum, every man among them had been
sleeping with a stiff pecker for the last month. Ira didn't
say anything, but Print knew from the grin plastered across
his face that wild horses couldn't have dragged him away.
Reflecting on it later, Print concluded that it had been the
boy's first time with a woman. But then there were worse
places for a fellow to lose his cherry than in a spiffy whore-
house.

Ira had acquitted himself well. The madam knew a
shorthorn when she saw one and had paired him with a
nubile young thing who bore the promising sobriquet of
Sugartit. When they emerged from the brothel an hour later
Ira appeared a little dazed. After awhile he had looked up
with a sheepish smile. "Print, it's like a big sweet t-t-
toothache that all of a s-s-sudden don't hurt no more."

The boys went into fits of laughter at that and all the way
home had razzed Ira unmercifully. To hear them tell it, he
had gotten his log sapped, greased his pole, and played stink
finger and hide the wieny, all in one night. Which was a
pretty tall order for a boy just shy of twenty. But Ira had
accepted the joshing good-naturedly. A wet-nosed kid
had gone down the trail and a full-grown man had returned. Since he now knew the difference the crew's coarse
ribbing seemed a small price to pay.

When Print and his men pulled up in the yard Julia
Oliver dried her hands on her apron and walked forward.
"Prentice, you look like a cat that just swallowed the ca-
nary. Evidently you had success."

"Yes'm," Print agreed, white teeth flashing against his
dark skin. "And it's the kind that jingles."

"God helps those who help themselves," Julia observed.
"Why don't you come on in the house and tell your daddy
all about it."

She started off then turned back, giving Doughbelly Ketchum the fish eye. "Mr. Ketchum, I'm almighty glad to see

you home safe. Your friends in the bunkhouse eat like starved wolves."

Doughbelly doffed his hat and started sputtering but she was already headed for the house. Just then Jay rode up with the rest of the crew for dinner and there was considerable back-thumping and horseplay for the next few minutes. When the men trooped off toward the bunkhouse to start swapping lies, Print and the boys followed their mother inside.

Jim Oliver was huddled near the fireplace, swathed in blankets. The boys crowded around expressing concern, but he assured them it was just a touch of the ague, then inquired about the drive. For an answer the eldest son pulled a leather sack from inside his brush jacket and poured a stream of gold coins all over the dining table.

"Pa, that's within spittin' distance of twenty-five hundred dollars. We got eight a head and no argument on price."

"Wowie!" Bob shouted, darting forward to run his hands through the pile of coins. We're rich, Ma. Filthy rich!"

While they were by no means rich, the Oliver family stared at the gleaming coins with something approaching awe. In a war-torn land where most families managed nicely on a couple of hundred dollars a year this unexpected windfall seemed like a godsend indeed. Though none of them had said anything, they had each had misgivings about Print's scheme. It was almost as if the money were too good to be true.

"Robert, act like you had good sense." Julia's tone hushed the boy and after a moment she looked around at Print. "Son, we're proud of you. That's more cash money than we've seen in five years. But I get the feeling you don't mean to bury it for a rainy day."

"No ma'am, I don't." Print paused, glancing first at the boys, then at his father, finally back to the old woman. "Bobbie was right. We are filthy rich. But it's all on the hoof out there in those hills. The way I see it this money's to be used for hirin' hands, buyin' more horses, gettin' this outfit ready to trail cows to wherever there's a market. We oughta be able to sell upwards of two thousand head a year, and this money is what will get us started."

His mother nodded, eyeing the gold thoughtfully. "What you're saying is that we gamble this against the chance that people will be wanting beef just as bad next year."

Before he could answer a young girl came through the hallway and stopped just inside the door. She was vaguely familiar somehow, but for a moment Print couldn't put a name to the face. Then it dawned on him. She was Elmira Gardner, the daughter of a neighbor farther down Yegua Creek. She had been a homely child when he went to war, but four years had done much for her figure, if not her looks.

"Print, you remember Elmira." Julia's voice had an odd catch to it, and he could see pinpricks of fire in her eyes. "She and Jay decided to get married while you were gone. Preacher Titus said the words just last week."

Print was thunderstruck. So far as he knew Jay had never had a beau in his life. But then the Oliver's second eldest was a quiet one, rarely ever taking anyone into his confidence. From the way the old lady was gritting her teeth, Jay hadn't even told her.

Recovering his wits. Print gave Jay a hearty handshake, then crossed the room to kiss the bride. Closer up, she was even harder to take, and he was glad she didn't belong to him. But as he hugged her he somehow sensed the taut swelling beneath her ribcage, and it suddenly came clear. *The homely little devil was about four months gone!* Now he understood why the old woman was in such a snit. Jesus, that must have rocked her to the very foundation. Her own son getting a neighbor's girl in a family way. Silent Jay Oliver and his knocked-up bride! By god, you had to watch those quiet ones. They'd fool you every time.

Julia Oliver saw the crafty glint in his eye, and before he could remark one way or the other she grabbed the lead. "Prentice, let's get back to this matter of money. Now it's all right to dream, but there is such a thing as biting off more than you can chew. My feeling, and I'm sure your daddy agrees with me, is that we should tuck some of that money away for lean times."

Print smiled and shook his head. "Ma, you've been outvoted."

"Outvoted?" The old woman's gaze slewed around the room, but no one would look at her. "Who by?"

"Me. The reins was passed along when Pa made me head of the family, so don't go tryin' to kick the traces. We'll do it my way and I don't reckon there's much to be gained by arguin' about it."

There was a moment of profound silence. Julia's black eyes crackled with hurt and outrage, but Print met her look squarely. Everyone in the room sensed that a fiery battle of wills was being played out right before them, and it was somehow frightening to watch mother and son grapple for power. They were so much alike, these two, dark, moody, easy to provoke and quick to strike. It had been only a matter of time until they clashed, even Bob had seen that, and whoever got their ears pinned back would play hob ruling the roost afterwards. There was room for only one head wolf in any pack, and it was plain to see that Print meant to settle the matter here and now. Once and for all.

Presently Julia Oliver lowered her eyes and whirled back to the stove. She threw open the door and began stoking the fire, still not having said a word. Gradually the tension eased and everyone started breathing again. Print had won. For now, anyway.

Jay cleared his throat, trying not to look at Elmira's swollen belly. "I'll tell you something, big brother. You'd better hire lots of men with that money. Our catch pens over near North Springs was raided last night. Got away with twenty cows and near about as many calves."

"Rustlers?" Print couldn't believe it for a moment. With cattle so plentiful it didn't make sense to steal them. But then it was always easier to rustle tame cows than it was to catch wild ones. "Were they branded?"

"Nope. We'd just finished starvin' them and we was gonna brand 'em this mornin'. When we got over there they was gone."

"Well it had to come sometime. With so many drifters around and work scarce, there's bound to be some that'll steal. Tell you the truth, I'm surprised it hasn't happened before now."

Bob tugged at Print's sleeve. "It's not just us, Print. They hit old man Kuykendall three nights back. Are we gonna kill'em." The boy drew himself erect, trying for a manly look.

"Not you, sport." Print ruffled his hair, smiling gently. "But if we catch 'em we might tie a knot in their tails."

"Go easy on that talk of killin'," Jim Oliver growled, looking up from his chair by the fireplace. "I been through it in the old days, and it works both ways. Remember that. Both ways."

The comment took everyone by surprise, for the old man rarely said anything these days. Even Julia paused, and everyone stared at him for a moment, digesting the truth of what he said. Still, the only thing lower than a rustler was a horse thief, and a man had a right to kill one wherever he found him. Otherwise nobody or nothing they owned would be safe back in these hills.

After a moment Print broke the silence. "Bobbie, run out to my horse and bring me that new rifle."

The boy darted across the room and out the door, returning moments later carrying a rather short, strange looking weapon. Print took the rifle and flipped the trigger guard down, throwing a shell out on the kitchen floor. When he snapped it shut a new cartridge seated itself in the chamber.

"This is a repeating rifle. Fires seven shots just as fast as you can flip that lever. Yanks used 'em during the war. Called it the Spencer Carbine."

Jay stepped forward, eyeing the rifle curiously. "Where'd you get a piece like that, Print?"

"Not one, bubba. Ten. Plus a dozen Colt pistols and a

barrelful of shells for the carbines." Heads snapped around all over the room and he chuckled softly. "While the boys was havin' a drink one night I scouted up a gun runner that's shippin' weapons down to Maximilian in Mexico. I had the gold and he had the guns, so we made ourselves a deal."

Jay regarded him suspiciously for a couple of seconds. "You knew all the time we was gonna get hit by rustlers. That's why you brought back all them guns."

"Close enough," Print agreed. "I didn't exactly know who it'd be, but it figured that someone would hit us sooner or later. Yankees, rustlers, you name it. Whenever a fella finds a way to make money you can bet your socks somebody's gonna try to skim off the cream." Hefting the carbine, he grinned. "With these we'll be ready. Fires a .52 caliber slug and makes a hole big enough to put your fist through. Takes some kinda man to come back for a second dose."

Julia Oliver slammed a pot down on the stove and strode across the room, disappearing out the door. The boys were fascinated with the Spencer and paid no attention to her stormy exit. Print handed Jay the carbine and followed after her. When he got outside his mother was standing at the back of the house, looking off into the green hills.

"Ma, I didn't mean to upset you in there, but it's time we got it out in the open. If I'm runnin' this outfit, then it's me that has to make the decisions."

Her answer startled him. "You're fixing to start the killing, aren't you, Print? Just like they taught you in the army."

"Yes'm. If I have to." He kicked at a clod of dirt, knowing word for word what she would say next. "But I never killed a man that wasn't tryin' to kill me."

"That was war, son." Her dark eyes bristled with fervor. "Thou shalt not kill. So saith the Lord God Jehovah."

"Ma, there's different kinds of war. Sometimes a man has to fight just so he can survive. Sometimes he has to kill to make it safe for his loved ones."

He hesitated, gathering his thoughts. This wasn't how he would have preferred it, but it was as good a place as any.

"We're on our way to makin' a potful of money, and I figure it's time I settled down. Louisa and me are gonna be
married just as soon as I can arrange it. That's the reason
for the guns, Ma. I mean to make these hills safe for you
and your grandchildren."

The old woman shot him a withering look and he read
her mind like it had been chalked up on a slate-board.

"No ma'am. Louisa's not in a family way. The only one
you've got to worry about on that score is back inside."

Julia Oliver spun on her heel and marched back into the
house. Staring out over the fields of bluebonnets and the for-
ested hills beyond, Print had the feeling that first frost had
come early this year.

3

The Oliver ranch had suddenly become a large-scale operation. Within days of his return from Galveston Print had
hired eight new hands and started rebuilding the bunkhouse.
Before the week was out the sleeping quarters had been doubled, with an attached mess hall and an enlarged kitchen
tacked on the far end. Dough-belly Ketchum now had a
pearl diver to assist with general chores and couldn't have
been prouder if he were head chef at the Cattlemen's House
in Austin.

Along with hiring men Print had also bought some
horses, but good mounts were scarce and the remuda was
far understocked for the job ahead. Each hand needed at
least six horses in his string, including brush mounts, cutting ponies, and a reserve or two. When it became apparent
that decent horseflesh wasn't to be had around Austin,
Print sacked up some gold and sent Jim Kelly riding west.
The wrangler was instructed to buy unbroken, mustang
stock, and return with all speed. Bumpus Moore had gone
along to help out, but Print made it clear that Kelly was in
charge. Over the weeks on the trail to Galveston he had
come to admire the black man's cool confidence and his

uncanny instinct for the right move in a tight situation. Without Kelly those two stampedes could have gotten hairy indeed, and so far as Print was concerned the wrangler looked a little whiter with each passing day. Moreover, he was a damn' fine companion, witty, sharp as a tack, and probably the most entertaining liar Print had ever run across. All things considered, he was a hell of a find, and Print felt damn' lucky to have him riding for the Sunburst outfit.

Somewhat like a general deploying his forces, Print next split the crew into two working units. Jay headed one and was assigned to work the northern range, while Ace Whitehead ramrodded the other on a sweep of the hills bordering Yegua Creek. Each crew established a network of catch pens throughout their territory and as the herds grew the job of flushing longhorns from the brush became considerably easier.

Though he hadn't mentioned it to anyone, Print also had another reason for separating the outfit's hands. Men just naturally had the urge to compete, and in a large crew it generally worked down to every man trying to outdo the other. But split up as they were, the pack instinct took over, sort of like kids choosing up sides for a rock fight. They stopped worrying about the man next to them and started working as a team, pulling together in their determination not to be outdone by the other side. The spirit of the thing had even carried over into the bunkhouse where the hands had divvied up the space so each crew could have its own quarters.

Print was playing with fire, for if it ever got out of hand he might find himself refereeing a small war. But that was a risk he was willing to take. Right now the strategy was working, and the score was all in his favor. Within the past two weeks something over a thousand longhorns had been branded with the Oliver Sunburst, and he had never seen cowhands so eager to hit the saddle. Ace Whitehead's crew was leading by a nose, but Jay's bunch was gaining fast, and it promised to be a damn' interesting race.

Print generally divided his days between the two

crews and on this particular morning he was headed over to work with Whitehead's outfit. Young Bob had started riding along with him on his daily circle and he was pleased to see the boy's curiosity about the business taking shape. Until now Julia had kept him close to home learning the three Rs and helping out with chores. But shortly after the Galveston drive Bob had attached himself to Print like a wood tick and hadn't let go since. Clearly the turning point for the youngster had been Print's little set-to with his mother over who called the shots.

Once the dust had settled, Bob evidently decided that his older brother was the closest thing to a curly wolf the Olivers had. Afterwards he was never very far from Print's coattails and showed no inclination to return to the schoolbooks. Julia had sulked around at first, but after a few days nothing more was said. Either she felt the boy was ready for a man's guidance, or else she just wasn't overly anxious for a rematch with her eldest son.

Print really didn't care one way or the other, and Bob was so taken with his brother that the whole thing passed over his head. The youngster had suddenly awakened to a homegrown hero larger than life itself, bigger even than those slick-talking knights and kings in his reading books. He wanted nothing more than to grow up like his big brother. Soft spoken but tough as a rawhide whang, and a dead shot with either hand. That was real, something a fellow could get his teeth into, and it beat the whey out of those sissified knights with their swords and battleaxes.

During their daily excursions through the hills Print and the boy generally discussed little besides longhorns and their ornery dispositions. But this morning Bob seemed quieter than usual, like something was bothering him, and Print had the distinct feeling he was talkng to himself. They had been following a cattle trail west along Yegua Creek when it occurred to Print that the youngster hadn't said ten words in the last half-hour.

"What's the matter, sprout? You seem sorta off your feed."

The boy cut his eyes away, then mumbled, "Nothin'."

"C'mon now, don't sull up on me." Print grinned and poked him in the ribs. "Maybe you've been beatin' your pud too much."

"Have not!" Bob said, but it came a little too fast and his face turned red as ox blood.

"Well don't get your dander up, I wasn't accusin' you. Besides, it's nothin' to be ashamed of, anyway." They rode a little farther in silence and Print decided to try another tack. "Listen, sport, it's not like you to be tongue-tied. Why don't you level with me and tell me what's got your goat?"

The boy looked everywhere but at Print, and for a moment it seemed that he wasn't going to speak. Then his gaze swung around, setting hotly on his brother. "I heard Ma talkin' to Pa last night. She said you're gonna marry that Louisa Reno."

Print couldn't have been more astonished if the boy had spit on him. Louisa had set the date only yesterday evening and it had been well past bedtime when he got home and informed his mother. She must have awakened the old man straightaway and in the process roused Bob, whose bedroom was next to theirs. But the really baffling part was the boy's reaction. He seemed angry, or hurt.

"Well now, I'll tell you, Bob. I sorta meant to spread the good news myself, but I reckon you heard right. Louisa and me are gettin' hitched Sunday week." He paused, watching the boy out of the corner of his eye. "I had in mind you'd be happy for me, but all I see is a long face."

The youngster ducked his head, kneading the saddle horn with his fist. "What d'ya wanna do a thing like that for?"

Print chuckled, keeping his tone light. "You're old enough you shouldn't have to ask. What's the matter, you don't like girls?"

"No, they're all a bunch of lamebrains and showoffs," Bob replied peevishly. "Especially that Louisa Reno."

The moment the words were out something clicked in Print's brain. *The young squirt was jealous of Louisa!* Big

Brother had thrown him over for a female and the kid was rankled clear down to his hocks.

"Whoa back, hoss." Print didn't laugh this time. It was plainly dead serious business in the boy's mind. "You better haul off and come again. Appears to me you've got the idea Louisa's gonna split us up somehow."

"Well what d'ya think she'll do?" Bob choked out. "Women are all alike. She'll have you fetchin' and carryin', and we'll never get to do nothin' together. Just wait, you'll see."

Print didn't say anything for awhile, then he sighed heavily, trying his damnedest to look hurt. "Bob, I'll have to admit that sorta bites deep. You must not think much of me if you believe I'm the kinda man that'd let a woman put a ring in his nose. Even if she was my wife."

The boy's eyes got wide as saucers and a look of revelation came over his face. "You mean you wouldn't let her do that? We'd still be able to pal around and go off huntin' cows?"

"Why sure we would." Print grinned and punched him lightly on the shoulder. "You didn't really think I was gonna let some punkin'-nose female tell me where to head in, did you? Not by a damn' sight!"

"Woowie!" he howled. "I just knew you wouldn't, Print. I knew it."

Spurring his horse, Bob took off up the trail, loosing a boyish imitation of a rebel yell. Print shook hs head, thoroughly mystified that the boy would have latched onto him that close. Then he gigged his own horse into a lope. That damn fool kid would scare every cow in Kingdom Come straight for the thickets.

Less than a hundred yards farther on Print rounded a bend and had to swerve aside to keep from colliding with Bob's horse. The boy had stopped at the edge of a treeline bordering a funnel-shaped break between the hills. Motionless, seemingly unable to speak, he was staring intently toward the north. When Print got his horse straightened out he looked in the direction of Bob's gaze and saw two men milling close to fifty head of cattle. They were jabbering excitedly at one another while trying to keep the small herd from drifting. Clearly the men had been pushing the cows south when they spotted Bob. Most likely they intended to ford the creek and take one of the backwoods trails on the other side.

That left only one question unanswered. Whose brand were those cows wearing?

Print ordered Bob to stay put and rode forward, pulling the Spencer from the saddle scabbard as he closed in on the men. There was a holding pen a mile or so north of here and he had a pretty good idea where the cattle had come from. But Ace Whitehead and his crew were working farther west today, so that meant he would have to handle this deal by himself. Still, there were only two men and he had faced worse odds. Lots of times.

When he was about thirty yards out he pulled up. Every cow he could see had the Oliver Sunburst burned on its flank, which settled the question of ownership, if nothing else. The two men were watching him closely, apparently uncertain as to their next move.

Print didn't waste any time on niceties. "Gents, I'd like to know how you came by those cows."

"What's it to you, mister?" The question came from a stout, red-faced man who seemed to be the leader of the two.

"My name's Oliver and those cows are wearin' my brand. Now where'd you get 'em?"

The two men glanced at one another, then the stout one waved his hand off toward the hills. "We bought 'em from a feller back north a ways."

Print grinned, but it was more like a wolf showing his teeth. "Glad to hear it. We're in the business of sellin' cows. I don't suppose you'd mind showin' me your bill of sale."

There was a moment of dead silence while the men stared at him. Then the talkative one clawed at his side and came up with a pistol. Print's saddle horn disintegrated an instant before he heard the report, but he didn't have time to worry about it. Throwing the Spencer to his shoulder, he triggered a shot and grunted with satisfaction as the big slug blew the stout rustler clean out of his saddle. Before he could lever another shell into the carbine his horse bunched and went crow-hopping across the clearing. Though he cursed, he really couldn't blame the dumb brute. That Spencer made a hell of a racket.

When he finally got his horse straightened out Print saw the second rustler headed due north at a full gallop. While he probably could have brought the man down he really didn't want to be treated to another bucking spree. Besides, somebody had to carry word back that rustling Oliver cows was a risky proposition. From the way that fellow was flogging his horse, he wouldn't lose any time getting the message home.

Just then Bob rode up and stopped his horse a few feet away from the dead man. He stared down on the body for a couple of seconds, then turned away with a queer look on his face. For a moment Print thought he was going to puke, but the boy took a deep breath and smiled weakly.

"I never seen anything like that in my life." Then he glanced back at the dead rustler. "You was right about that gun. He's got a hole in him you could put a gourd through."

Print gave the body a detached look, noting the size of the hole and the gout of blood soaking into the earth. Dead men all looked the same so far as he could tell, and when a man spent four years on the killing ground death sort of lost its novelty. Suddenly it occurred to him that this was doubtless the first dead man Bob had ever seen. More to the point, the kid just barely missed flushing those two birds himself. If he had been alone that might be an Oliver lying in the dust. He was young, but not so young somebody wouldn't kill him if he stumbled onto the wrong game.

Print turned his horse back toward Yegua Creek, mulling the thought further. Things being what they were, it wouldn't do any harm at all for young Bob to have a few lessons in what separates the quick from the dead.

4

Georgetown was a pleasant little village situated on the banks of the San Gabriel. The square was dominated by the courthouse, which overlooked various business establishments lining the town's four thoroughfares. While there were a few small farms scattered about Williamson County, its economy was dependent for the most part on cattlemen who had settled the hill country before the war. Sorghum, maize, and broom corn were grown in some quantities along the river bottoms, but everyone in Georgetown was quick to admit that their livelihood rested squarely on the longhorn herds roaming the backwoods thickets. Banks and mercantile stores, as well as the local saloons and gaming dives, existed solely to serve the cattlemen; without them Georgetown would have been nothing more than a wide spot in the road. Even the town's single cathouse catered to men smelling of horses and cow dung— only the churches suffered for lack of patronage.

Georgetown knew which side its bread was buttered on, and anybody with a lick of sense went out of his way to cultivate the backcountry ranchers.

But with the cessation of hostilities, and the military occupation of Texas, a new force had entered the scheme of things in Williamson County. While it had been the only country to vote against secession in 1861 it was still a part of the Lone Star state, a small yet hardly insignificant part of a defeated nation. Loyalty to the Union was expected to yield handsome dividends once the fighting ceased, but Georgetown was quick to discover that the spoils of war sometimes blind the conqueror. Where plunder was involved friend and foe all too often looked exactly the same—past loyalty became a distinction that counted for little among men who had been given a license to steal. And in Williamson County, the man who held all the cards was Cal Nutt.

Formerly an Iowa dirt farmer, and not a very good one at that, Cal Nutt had attached himself to the Union army's coattails as it advanced across the South. Before the war was over he had garnered friends in high places, serving mainly as a panderer to their lust and general handyman in dirty work whenever the need arose. When the shooting stopped and the pillage began, he had gotten in line with the rest of the carrion eaters; like vultures eyeing a bloated corpse they gathered to cut up the South and parcel out the sweetmeats. For services rendered, Nutt had been awarded Williamson County. Though his status was strictly unofficial, without title or office, there was little doubt that the balance of power had shifted in Georgetown's hierarchy. He was the spokesman for the Yankee bigwigs in Austin, and so long as his schemes contributed a steady flow of gold they would back his play to the hilt.

Cal Nutt had Williamson County by the short hairs, and anybody with sense enough to spit between his teeth knew it.

Just at the moment, though, Georgetown's resident carpetbagger was getting a hard way to go from a most unlikely source, Sheriff Ed Strayborn. The two men faced one another across Strayborn's desk in the courthouse and Nutt was fast losing patience with the lawman.

"I don't give a good goddamn whether you like it or not. I want Oliver arrested and I want it done today. Him and his whole family are nothing but Secesh trash, and I mean to nail their hides to the wall. Am I making myself clear, Sheriff?"

"Yessir. You couldn't be no clearer if you was U.S. Grant hisself." Ed Strayborn had a soup strainer on his upper lip, watery eyes, and a remarkable instinct for self-preservation. Right now he felt like a man walking a tightrope in a high wind. "But what good's it gonna do to arrest the Oliver boy if the grand jury won't return no indictment?"

"Jesus H. Christ," Nutt groaned. "Talking with you is like holding a conversation with a brick."

Not unlike many farm-bred people, Cal Nutt was a stocky, muscular man who gave the appearance of being smaller than he actually was. There was hardly any way of telling where his neck ended and his shoulders began, and while he seemed built on the order of a beer keg he was only a couple of inches shy of six feet. Despite expensive tailoring and daily sessions with the barber, his clothes forever looked rumpled and his wide, dour face was in constant need of a shave. Looking at him, folks just naturally sized him up as a man who was partial to dirty underwear. Yet beneath his soiled clothing he was a man of brute physical strength, and he possessed a hyena-like cunning that made him a deadly adversary.

Glaring at the Sheriff now, his muddy brown eyes seemed void of warmth, as if something human had been left out. "Strayborn, just what the hell makes you think the grand jury wouldn't indict him? This is a case of murder, pure and simple. Why he just shot that man down in cold blood. The story's all over town."

"Mr. Nutt, you haven't been around here long and you're gonna find out that killin' a rustler in cow country ain't considered murder. Maybe Print Oliver is Secesh, but folks hereabouts frown on rustlin' a damn' sight more'n they do a man bein' a Reb. They're not gonna indict him 'cause like as not they'd find themselves in the same fix somewheres down the road."

Strayborn paused, toying with his mustache, not just sure how far he should push it. " 'Course, the way I get the story is that the other feller shot first. There's even talk—just gossip, mind you—that he was on your payroll."

Nutt's gaze hardened and his beady eyes narrowed into slits. "That's dangerous talk, Sheriff. Especially coming from a public official. Are you making some kind of accusation?"

"No sir, not at all. Just repeatin' what's bein' said."

"Are you aware of who my supporters are in Austin? The men who sent me here."

"Yessir, I reckon I am. Leastways I was given to understand you had the military governor and the attorney general behind you."

"That's right. And are you also aware that if I rode down to Austin this afternoon I could have your ass out on the street minus that tin star by nightfall? Maybe even sooner."

"Yessir, I reckon I know that, too." Ed Strayborn swallowed hard on a knot hung in his craw, and tried not to wilt completely under the other man's harsh stare.

Strayborn, like every other Texan, whether Loyalist or Reb, was caught in the grandest squeeze play ever devised in the agile minds of Northern politicians. When the war ended Lincoln had granted amnesty to those who had served the Confederacy, and his successor, Andrew Johnson, had allowed the amnesty to stand. But not without certain hooks designed to snare the hide-bound Secessionists.

Tens of thousands of Confederates, both civilian and military, were denied amnesty under the broad restrictions laid down by the government. They were noncitizens, disenfranchised, ineligible either to vote or hold public office. The lure of ultimate pardon was dangled before them like a carrot before a mule, but exactly how this miracle was to come about was left shrouded in mystery. Those who had been granted amnesty were required to take an oath of allegiance, purging themselves of any aftereffects of their rebellious conspiracy. Yes, here again, the government held a loaded gun in reserve.

Military commanders of the occupation forces were authorized to disqualify anyone they believed to be swearing false loyalty. Proof and rules of evidence went by the boards; men were denied amnesty on suspicion alone. Moreover, military authorities were empowered to remove from public office any civil official suspected of disloyalty, even though he might already have sworn the oath of allegiance. This god-like power was not long left wanting for men of devious and unscrupulous motives.

Across the South, carpetbaggers surfaced overnight, waiting like jackals to share in the kill. Loyal Unionists, northern born, they came to occupy thousands of civil posts vacated by the despotic whim of military commanders. For the right price a New Yorker could be appointed circuit judge in Georgia, or an Ohioan could become post-master in Louisiana, and they swarmed over the South like maggots on putrid meat. Next came the Scalawags, Southern born and bred, swearing mealymouthed allegiance to the Union in return for a license to rob their neighbors and kin. Many became governor, state senator, attorney general, and in league with the carpetbaggers and corrupt military commanders set about performing civil and economic rape of a defeated land.

With law in the hands of the conquerors and their shabby henchmen Ed Strayborn had every right to be frightened of Cal Nutt. The carpetbagger's threat had been no mere idle boast. Should it suit his whim he could have Strayborn dismissed as sheriff, disenfranchised as a citizen, and perhaps even indicted for public malfeasance simply by paying a call on his cohorts in the State House. The threat was very real, and Nutt had made it in dead earnest.

"Sheriff, you strike me as a man who knows how to keep his head above water." Nutt pulled a fat cigar from his pocket and lighted it with great care, letting Strayborn hang on his words. "Now suppose I told you to go on out there and arrest Oliver. What do you think you'd do?"

Strayborn let out a long, wheezing breath, like a man with a gimpy lung. "Mr. Nutt, if that's what you got you're mind set on, why I reckon I'd do it. But I'd be bound to tell you, it's liable to start a war nobody wants. One that nobody'll win, if I'm any judge."

"How so?" Nutt very deliberately blew a cloud of smoke in the Sheriff's face, enjoying himself immensely now that he held the whiphand.

"Them Olivers are mean people. Print in particular. Leave 'em alone and they'll mind their own business, but you get 'em riled up and you got yourself a handful. Before the war I seen Print and his daddy clean out a whole saloon one night when somebody called 'em traitors. If I go out there to arrest Print, they'll fight. And once it starts they'll have ever' hardrock Secesh on Yegua Creek fightin' right alongside 'em. You think on it and you'll see I'm right."

The carpetbagger did just that. Puffing on the cigar, he leaned back in his chair and ruminated for what seemed a full minute. Finally he came erect and very casually stubbed out his cigar on Strayborn's desk top. "You sold me, Sheriff. We'll get Oliver and his Rebs, but I just decided to make them squirm a little while we're doing it."

As he turned to leave, Strayborn rose. "Mr. Nutt, I'm not bein' a wiseacre, you understand, but I wonder if you'd mind me askin' you a question?"

"No, just so long as you keep it short. What's on your mind?"

"Well, it's been botherin' me ever since I heard that rumor we was talkin' about." The Sheriff pulled at his mustache, not quite sure how to put it. "What I'm tryin' to say is, how in tarnation did you get a gang of rustlers operatin' when you've been in town less'n a month?"

Cal Nutt grinned and his muddy eyes brightened with sardonic amusement. "Sheriff, I'm not saying I did organize the rustlers, but it wouldn't have been much of a chore for a smart man. Williamson County is crawling with two kinds of people. Them that hates Rebs, and them that haven't got enough to eat. When you find a man pulling double harness on both counts, you've got yourself a cow thief."

Then he turned and walked from the room, leaving Ed Strayborn wiser but not particularly enlightened.

5

"Now pay attention. You're tryin' to do everything at once. If you rush it, you're gonna miss every time."

Print's arm swept upwards in slow motion, exaggerating each movement. His hand closed around the butt of the Colt, snapping it forward and clear of the holster with a rolling motion of the wrist. As the Colt cleared leather he rotated it out and upward, bringing the gun barrel level in the same moment he extended it forward about chest high. His elbow was slightly crooked, but locked tight as steel cable, and his wrist formed a perfect line parallel with the six-gun's barrel. There was an instant of hesitation, his arm frozen in position, then the Colt roared and a fruit jar ten yards away disappeared in an explosion of glass.

This was Bob's third lesson in the ways of the pistol. After the incident with the rustlers, Print had decided it was none too soon to teach the boy how to defend himself. Like most ranch kids Bob had cut his teeth on a rifle, hunting squirrels and rabbits from childhood, later graduating to deer and wild turkey. Print had seen him shoot, and with a long gun he was as good as most men, maybe even better. But he had never fired a pistol in his life, and it was this gap in his education that Print meant to correct.

They were standing along the edge of a dry wash fifty yards back of the house, shooting at jars lined up on the opposite bank. So far Bob had emptied his pistol twice and had scored only four hits. Print had fired six shots, missing once. The boy had improved markedly over their last session, but it was apparent that he had a long way to go.

As they began reloading Print gave him an encouraging smile. "You're doing just fine. Another week or so and you'll be hittin' regular."

The boy frowned and seated another ball in the cylinder. "The way I'm shootin' I wouldn't do nothin' but scare 'em to death."

"You can't do it all in one day. Takes time to learn how to make a pistol behave." Print paused, watching him measure powder and tamp the balls home. "Always remember what I told you. Every morning you draw your loads and start fresh. Then a couple of times during the day you check your loads and caps to make sure nothin's out of kilter. Misfires have killed more than bad shootin'."

Bob nodded, still somewhat disgusted with himself. "There's nothin' wrong with my loadin'. I just can't get the hang of puttin' the slug where I'm aimin'."

"Maybe that's the trouble. You're still tryin' to aim it like you would a rifle. Pistols don't work that way. Generally you're shootin' at a man less'n ten yards away and there's no time to aim. But don't ever try any of that foolishness of shootin' from the hip, even if somebody's firin' at you. Not unless you're bent on suicide. Get the gun in front of you so you can see it out of the corner of your eye, then aim like you were pointin' your finger. Pretty soon you'll get to where you can freeze that barrel right where your eye is lookin'."

Print holstered his gun and rose. "Let's try it again. Now think about it this time. Shootin' a gun is mostly in your mind. Pullin' it fast is important, but it don't mean a damn if you can't hit what you're aimin' at."

Bob stepped forward, nodding soberly, and let his arms go limp. The holster he wore was exactly like Print's, army issue with the flap and top leather carefully trimmed away so that the hammer and trigger guard were exposed. Suddenly the boy's arm streaked upward, jerking and cocking the Colt all in one motion. The moment it came level he fired, so quickly that the report of the gun and the blurred movement of his hand were one and the same. A geyser of dust erupted about six inches to the side of the fruit jar and the boy instantly triggered another shot, kicking up dirt almost a foot in the opposite direction.

Print didn't say anything for a moment. The kid was fast. Maybe faster than anybody he had ever seen. But without control speed counted for nothing. If the boy ever managed to put them together he could be deadly. Somehow he had to get it through the kid's head that there was a difference between fast and too fast.

"Sport, you're only problem is that you've got speed on the brain. If that had been a man you would've hit him, but he'd still gotten off a shot. Now maybe you don't understand when I talk about being deliberate, taking your time. So lemme say it another way. When that gun barrel comes level you've got to freeze it right there and make sure it's on target. I'm not sayin' you count to ten, or anything like that. But you delay a fraction of a second, sort of like the blink of an eyelash, just to make dead sure you've got that gun pointed straight. You draw, get it out there, and wait. Don't rush. You'll know when it comes dead center. When it does, *shoot!*"

Print spun, dropping into a crouch, and the Colt appeared in his hand. Then a mere fragment of time elapsed, indiscernible to anyone not looking for it, and the gun jumped with a dull boom. Across the wash a jar blew to smithereens.

Turning back, he regarded the boy solemnly. "Bob, that's what separates dead speed demons from live sure-shots. You'd best get it through your head while you're still shootin' at bottles."

Bob just looked at him for a moment. Then he whirled, pulled, and locked his arm chest high. Only this time there was a split second of hesitation and when the pistol bucked a jar splintered in a shower of glass. Even before the reverberations died away, he shifted, froze in an instant of stillness, and busted another jar six feet from the first.

Looking back, he had a big grin plastered from ear to ear. "How's that, teacher?"

Print returned the grin, visibly impressed. "Button, you just went to the head of the class. Trot on up to the chicken yard and catch a couple of hens. Then bring'em back here with some twine. I think it's time for your next lesson."

Bob gave him a puzzled look but took off toward the house. Minutes later he returned with a squawking hen under each arm and a roll of twine stuffed in his pocket. They crossed the wash and Print knotted a piece of cord around one chicken's leg. Then he tied it to a tree, leaving about six feet of play so it could move around. Repeating the process, he tied the second hen to a tree a few yards off to the left.

Moving back to the other side of the wash, he stopped and watched the hens for a moment. Then he looked around at the boy. "The only reason a man pulls a handgun is to kill another man. Now's as good a time as any for you to get used to seein' something die every time you squeeze that trigger. Kill 'em."

Print jerked his head toward the chickens and the boy stared at him pop-eyed for a couple of seconds. Then he turned, drew, and calmly dropped the first chicken in a flurry of feathers and blood. When the gun roared the second hen began squawking louder than ever, running in tight circles at the end of her string. Bob tracked her with the Colt, waiting until she stopped to change directions. His first shot clipped her tail feathers, but before she could move he fired again and the hen was blown apart where she stood.

As Bob holstered the gun Print squeezed his shoulder, smiling tightly. "Good work. Just remember, whenever you pull that gun you're gettin' ready to watch something cash in. I want you to bring a couple of chickens down here every week and kill 'em so's you won't forget."

The youngster glanced at him sideways. "Ma won't like me shootin' her chickens. 'Specially since there ain't enough of 'em left to eat."

"You let me worry about Ma. I'll buy 'er a crate load of hens next time we go to town. You just keep practicin' like I taught you, and make every shot count. The time's comin' when an Oliver won't be able to afford a miss."

Gathering powder flasks and loading gear, they walked on back to the house. Julia and Louisa were sitting in rockers on the front porch, frowning like a couple of scalded owls. Bob ducked his head and shot through the door, with Juila hard on his heels. Print saw which way the wind was blowing and braced himself for a little family rhubarb. They had been married less than two weeks, but sometimes it seemed that the only thing Louisa had on her mind was getting him to set aside his guns. The fact that his mother kept harping on the same subject hadn't improved his disposition any—quite the contrary, it had only made him more stubborn. Some days he felt like a proddy old bull surrounded by blathering females.

Louisa gave him a smoky look, then went back to work on a pan of snap beans in her lap. "Print, it's bad enough that you've killed a man. But you're going to wake up someday and regret what you're doing to that boy."

He sighed grumpily and leaned back against the porch banister. "Lou, you seem to forget that I killed lots of men in the war. One more isn't gonna doom my mortal soul. Besides, he was tryin' to kill me. Should I have just sat there and let him take another potshot?"

"You always say that, like you didn't have a choice in the matter." She attacked the beans with a vengeance, not looking at him. "If you hadn't been wearing a gun nothing would have happened."

"If I hadn't been wearing a gun," Print retorted sharply, "he would have killed me and then stolen the cattle. Did it ever occur to you, Lou, that those rustlers were makin' off with about five hundred dollars on the hoof?"

"That's neither here nor there. And it certainly has nothing to do with you taking Bobbie down there and letting him shoot poor, defenseless chickens."

"Ah, that's what this is all about. The chickens." Print should have known that Julia Oliver wouldn't miss seeing her chickenyard raided. "Well, I'll tell you. If I have to sacrifice a few scrawny hens to teach Bob how to defend himself it's a small price to pay."

Louisa glanced at him hotly. "Print, it's not the hens. You're teaching that boy to kill. Don't you understand what a terrible, sinful thing that is?"

"I'm up to my ears with sin. Damned if I'm not!" He took a deep breath, clamping down hard on his anger. Some moments passed before he trusted himself to speak again. "Lou, I don't know if you'll understand this but I'm gonna try to explain something to you. I spent four years watchin' men die fightin' for the right to live their own way. I made up my mind that if I got through that I'd never again let a man push me around or take what's mine. Soldierin' with men that aren't afraid to get killed for what they believe in changes a man. Maybe some folks can live with themselves by turnin' the other cheek. I can't. The war burned that out of me, and nothin' you say is gonna change it."

Louisa's hands fell still on the beans, and for a long moment she just stared at her lap. Then big tears formed in her eyes and her lip quivered. "Print, it's you that doesn't understand. You could kill every man in Williamson County and I'd still be right here waiting when you got home. It's just that my insides are tied up in knots worrying that they'll kill you instead."

Shoving off the banister, he strode forward and knelt at her side. Lifting her chin, he wiped away the tears and smiled gently. "Honey, there's not a man been born that can take my number. I'm not ready to die. I've got too much to do. Besides, if I let some jasper put me under where would a homely old thing like you find somebody else to nag at?"

Louisa sniffled and smiled through her tears. Then she threw her arms around his neck and hugged him fiercely. But even as she did so, she promised herself that the matter wouldn't end here.

Only the tactics would change.

Print Oliver might be bullheaded and set in his ways, but there were certain things no man could resist. Or do without.

CHAPTER THREE

———◆———

1

They had been on the trail two months and three days. Though the longhorns had actually put on a little weight, the men were lean and ripe. Their last bath had been a cloud-burst almost a month past, and many nights in between they had fallen into exhausted sleep with nothing cover-ing their backbones but an empty stomach. They were dirty, tired, and thoroughly disenchanted with the ways of longhorn cows. But the Kansas-Missouri border was only fifteen miles away, and from there it was less than two weeks' drive to the railhead at Sedalia. After close to a month crossing the Indian Nations, trailing through the Missouri farm country would be a cakewalk.

Print brought them to a halt along the south bank of the Neosho, ten men and a mixed herd of a thousand longhorns. There was graze, fresh water, and lots of open space just in case their Indian friends got playful. They would camp here for the night and ford the stream at first light. Then it was only a day's drive to Baxter Springs where they would turn northeast toward the railhead.

Once the cows were watered and bunched on the open grasslands, the hands wearily collected around the chuck wagon. Doughbelly Ketchum already had a fire going and was slinging together a stew in a charred Dutch oven. They had been on the trail long enough that everything they did had now become routine, and there was no need for Print to issue orders. The cattle were put out to graze, Jim Kelly hobbled the remuda nearby, and throughout the night the crew rode herd in two-man shifts. After wolfing down a hot supper they generally swapped tales round the fire for a while. But not for long. Shortly after dark the talk came to an end and as if by unspoken agreement, the men crawled gratefully into their soogans. The camp would be up, fed, and ready to move a full hour before sunrise, and that left a man precious little time for sleep.

Watching them now, as he lingered over a last cup of coffee, Print felt damn' lucky to have such a crew. They had been through a lot in the past couple of months and there wasn't a quitter among them. Not that the drive had been as bad as he expected. On the contrary, they had had only one stampede and a couple of brushes with Indians that had proved more irritating than dangerous. But the work alone had been enough to test what kind of grit a man had in his craw.

Shortly after Christmas Print had decided on Sedalia for the next trail drive. Though it was more than six hundred miles as the crow flies, it was the nearest railhead, which meant there would be cattle buyers from the northern packing houses. He reasoned that with the war ended there would be great demand for beef in the north; not since the hostilities began in '61 had a herd been trailed out of Texas. That meant higher prices for the man who was willing to risk his cows, not to mention his own life, and Yankee gold was much on Print's mind these days.

If Sunburst was ever to be more than a ragtail outfit it needed a steady influx of hard cash—the fact that it was tainted Yankee gold didn't bother him a whit. Texas was cow rich and money poor, which made things slightly lopsided the wrong way. Ranchers who were to survive the military occupation must swallow their pride and start thinking like sharp Yankee traders.

Which was exactly what Print Oliver did.

Their neighbors along Yegua Creek thought the Olivers were being led straight into the jaws of ruin and hard times by the eldest son. But after spring gather Print had a thousand head of old stuff cut out and in early May headed them north. With Ira at his side, he led them across the Red River, struck the Shawnee Trail, and pushed on past Ft. Gibson toward the Missouri border. The trail plowed straight through the Nations, hilly country, with dense woods and steep-banked streams that made each day a small test of a man's endurance. Yet if the terrain was unpleasant, the Indians were downright belligerent. While they were called the Five Civilized Tribes, the Great White Father had clearly neglected to explain just what that meant. Both the Cherokee and the Choctaw had stopped the herd and demanded a toll of fifty cents a head to cross their lands. After lengthy bargaining sessions he had gotten them to accept cows in place of money, the only alternative being that they would stampede the herd. Thinking about it later, he concluded that the Indians were perhaps more civilized than he had at first suspected. Leastways they traded near about as shrewd as any Yankee he had ever run across. Still, the boys had gotten the herd through in good shape and they were on the last leg of a damn' fine drive. All things considered, they had been fortunate beyond his wildest expectations.

Print was about ready to call it a night when he caught the sound of horses splashing through the stream. Along the trail he had drilled the crew for moments just such as this and they reacted instantly, without a word being spoken. Each man scrambled from his bedroll, grabbed the Spencer carbine he had been issued, and ducked into the shadows out of the firelight. Print moved to the side of the chuck wagon, levered a shell into his carbine, and waited.

The horses came to a halt some distance off and a voice called out. "Hallo, the camp."

Print eased a step away from the wagon. "Ride in, if you're a mind. But keep your hands high. Otherwise you'd best move on."

There was a moment's hesitation before the voice answered. "We're comin' in. Don't get itchy."

The horses came forward at a slow walk and four riders appeared out of the darkness. They had their hands in plain sight and only when they were well within the circle of light from the fire did they rein to a halt. From their dress and their rigs, they were Texans, but Print wasn't taking any chances.

"State your business, gents. It's sorta late to come callin'."

"Friend, you couldn't be righter." This came from a young man about Print's own age. "Name's Jim Daugherty and these are what's left of my hands. We got bushwhacked by the Jayhawkers this afternoon."

Print didn't have the least idea what Daugherty was talking about, but he now knew for sure that the man was a Texan. One far off his home range. "Step down, Mr. Daugherty. We'd be mighty interested to hear what happened. Doughbelly, rustle up some grub for these men. The rest of you boys come on into camp."

Daugherty smiled and shook his head when the Oliver men emerged from the shadows. Then he dismounted and shook hands with Print. "Mister, I sure 'nough wish we'd had you fellas with us today. With a few more guns backin' our play I'd be about five hundred cows richer."

"Name's Oliver. Print to my friends. Now what's this business about gettin' bushwhacked?"

Daugherty squatted by the fire and waited while Doughbelly poured him a cup of coffee. "You trailin' to Sedalia?"

"Unless somebody's built a railroad closer," Print replied.

"Thought so." Daugherty took a big swallow of coffee and wiped his mustache. "That's where we was headed, too. Leastways till we ran into them Jayhawkers."

"What the hell's a Jayhawker, anyway?" Print didn't

mean to sound short, but it was like pulling teeth to get straight facts from the young Texan.

Daugherty looked around in surprise. "Christ, I guess you ain't heard. Maybe nobody has 'cept me and my boys. The Missouri legislature has passed a law bannin' longhorns from crossin' the border. Seems like their livestock is catchin' Spanish fever from our cows. Anyway, that's the way they tell it. Somebody drove a herd up here last year and damn' near wiped 'em out."

Print scratched his head, thoroughly baffled by the whole affair. "Well what'd they think we're gonna do with all them cows? Trail 'em back to Texas?"

"Damned if I know," Daugherty observed hollowly. "They just don't want 'em crossin' their line."

"In a pig's ass!" Ira declared hotly. "We didn't bring a herd s-s-six hundred miles just to turn around and take 'em back."

"Friend, I wouldn't go off half-cocked, if I was you." Daugherty glanced at Ira, then back to Print. "I felt the same way till we run up on them Jayhawkers. They wanted three dollars a head to let us cross the line. When I bowed my neck they killed one of my men and stampeded my herd. Somebody got rich, but it sure as hell wasn't me."

A hush settled over the camp as the Oliver hands mulled that one around. This deal was getting dicier by the moment, and Print still wasn't sure he had the straight of it. "You started to tell me what a Jayhawker is."

"Friend, a Jayhawker is nothin' but a goddamn' robber, pure and simple. Whole gang of 'em just across the line. They're supposed to be patrollin' the border to turn back longhorns, but if you pay 'em off they'll let you through. If you don't they start shootin' and just take your herd."

Later, after Daugherty and his men had been fed and bedded down, Print lay awake thinking about this new development. Ira was right. They hadn't come this far only to turn back. Somehow they were going to sell the herd—too much depended on that gold for them to return home empty handed. Jayhawkers be damned! Anybody that tried to stop them just might not walk away.

But as it turned out, young Jim Daugherty clearly wasn't a man to stretch the truth. When the Oliver herd neared the Missouri border late the following afternoon, twenty armed men rode forward on line to block their path. Print had briefed his hands that morning on what must be done, and within a matter of seconds they had taken positions in front of the herd. Each of the men dismounted, moved to the offside of his horse, and laid a Spencer repeater across the saddle. The Jayhawkers watched them curiously for a moment, then their leader rode closer.

"Hey, you Texans!" His voice rang out across the open ground separating them. "The law says you gotta pay three dollars a head to cross them beeves. Get it up or we'll scatter them cows clear back to the Nations."

Print had taken a calculated gamble that they could slip by without encountering the Jayhawkers. With that option gone he had only one choice left. "Mister, you'd better take your men and ride out. The first one that heads this way is gonna get you killed."

The Jayhawker leader sat still as stone for a moment, then turned his horse and headed back the way he had come. Suddenly he whirled his mount in a tight circle, bellowed something at the top of his lungs, and led the gang forward in a headlong charge. The Jayhawkers had drawn pistols as they put their horses into a gallop and began firing even before they were within decent range. But the noise alone was enough to spook the longhorns. Their heads came up and for a moment they stood dead still. Then one old mossyhorn roared like a bull elephant and in the next instant the entire herd stampeded southward in a rumbling cloud of dust.

Print didn't even look around. Aligning his sights on the Jayhawker leader's chest, he squeezed off a shot and saw the man tumble backwards out of the saddle. Guns began to bark on either side of him as the Oliver hands worked the Spencer levers with dizzying speed. The Missouri gang ran fulltilt into a hornet's nest of lead as the Texans laid down a barrage of close to seventy shots in less than thirty seconds. Horses screamed and pitched head first to earth, catapulting their riders from the saddle. But even as they jumped to their feet and took off running the Jayhawkers were cut down by the withering fire. Others were simply swept from their saddles by the deadly .52 caliber slugs and sent rolling in the dust. Within the space of a few heartbeats the charge was broken and the remaining Jayhawkers took off at a full lope in blind retreat.

When Print ordered ceasefire, the open ground to their front was littered with the bodies of nine Jayhawkers and five horses. The Texans had only two men wounded and one horse crippled by a wayward slug. For some moments the Oliver hands held their positions, staring mutely at the carnage their repeaters had wrought. Many of them had been in the war, but for sheer killing power they had never seen anything to match the deadly little Spencers.

Shoving his carbine in the saddle boot, Print mounted and looked around at his men. "The fight's over, boys; Bumpus, that horse of yours is done for. Shoot him and climb up behind Ira. The rest of you get mounted and let's go catch some cows."

Without another word he spurred off after the stampeded longhorns. They had three hours before dark and he fully intended to have that herd gathered come nightfall. Tomorrow they would head them north again.

Toward Sedalia and the Yankee gold.

2

Cal Nutt kept an office over Jackson's Feed & Grain. While there were more pretentious buildings in Georgetown, he had chosen this particular office with certain advantages in mind. Foremost was the fact that it had a private entrance by a back staircase, which meant his visitors could come and go without being observed. Another consideration was that the office afforded a good view of the town square while being high enough to prevent passersby from gawking in his windows. Though his office took up only half the second story, the remainder was storage space crammed to the ceiling with grain sacks. The partition separating the two rooms was uncomfortably thin, yet there was small likelihood that anyone would overhear what was said in the carpetbagger's quarters.

Which was exactly as Cal Nutt had planned it. The discussions held in his office would seldom bear repeating. Not if a man wanted to keep from getting gunned down some dark night by an irate citizen.

The room comprising the office was somewhat like the man himself, unkept, furnished with a second-hand desk and chairs, almost spartan in appearance. Nutt maintained a room at the local hotel, which he considered luxury enough for the moment. Later, when Williamson County had been sucked dry, he would return east and build himself a mansion, perhaps even become a gentleman farmer. But right now it was best to keep his activities cloaked behind a plain and simple front. Even the door to his office lacked a sign. It was just a door. One opened by few people, and only then on matters of the utmost urgency.

Nutt was seated at his desk, staring aimlessly out the window, when a knock sounded at the door. Without moving, he called over his shoulder, "C'mon in. It's open."

Grip Crow stepped into the office and closed the door behind him. For a moment he stood there, waiting for Nutt to say something, but the Northerner didn't even look around. Finally he walked forward and took a seat before the desk. "Mr. Nutt, you oughta be more careful about leavin' your back to folks. There's some around here that might take that as an invitation."

Nutt slowly turned from the window and his thick lips spread in a smile. "Don't let it bother you, Grip. Only two kinds of people come up here, and they're both crooks. What's on your mind?"

Crow nodded, not quite sure he liked being pegged a

crook, even if he was. Like many men in the South he had
returned from the war thankful to be alive, yet determined
that he wouldn't go back to grubbing in the soil or hazing
cows for a livelihood. There had to be better ways to earn
a dollar, honest or otherwise, and he had been at loose ends
when Nutt found him in an Austin saloon. They had gotten
along famously from the start, for at heart Crow was
crooked as a dog's hind leg, and Cal Nutt knew it before
they had exchanged ten words.

Some people even thought Crow looked like a desperado. He was generally unshaven, wore a battered old slouch
hat, and had two Remington six-guns hitched around his
waist. Though shy of six feet, he was whipcord lean and
gave the appearance of being taller. While he wasn't a
powerful man, he moved with the lithe smoothness of a
tawny cat. He was what folks called a sudden man, especially after they had seen him handle a gun. Yet it was his
eyes that convinced most people they were looking upon
one of Lucifer's own. Not that his eyes were mean, or piti-
less, or even threatening. They were just blank. Double
ought. Cloudy emotionless agates that somehow put a man
in mind of thin ice over a pail of clabbered milk.

The eyes of a man who would be good at slaughtering
pigs. Or people.

Cal Nutt had hired him for these very reasons, and within
a week Crow had recruited a band of Renegades who shared
his longing for easy money. So long as the work wasn't
strenuous and the paydays were lush, they were game for
anything. Cattle rustling sounded tailor-made to their
way of thinking, and when Crow explained the set-up in
Williamson County, they had signed on for the duration.
After scouting the country southwest of Yegua Creek, they
found a hidden meadow tucked away deep in the hills. The
layout was perfect for holding cows while their brands
were doctored, and once the gang erected a rough log cabin
they were in business. Over the ensuing months they had
done a fair amount of rustling—and considerably more
loafing and whoring around. Crow had been as good as his

word; to a man they agreed that the outlaw life was the greatest thing since churned butter.

The only fly in the ointment so far had been Print Oliver. Still, Clarence Tubb's getting caught red-handed with a bunch of Sunburst cows had been a freak, something a man couldn't rightly foresee. When Oliver killed him it hadn't made them any less bold, only more watchful. Since they didn't have to bother themselves about the sheriff, they had free run of the backcountry, what amounted to a license to swing the long loop wherever they pleased. Most ranchers showed a decided aversion to fighting over longhorns, anyway, which just sweetened the pot all the more. The few hard cases like Oliver would eventually have to be weeded out, but there was no hurry. Right now the gang had all the cows it could handle, and then some.

Crow returned Nutt's smile, watching him through hooded eyes. He wasn't afraid of the Yankee, for he feared no man. Not so long as he had a gun close at hand. But he did respect Nutt's political connections in Austin; without them rustling might easily become a hazardous occupation. He decided to pass on the remark about crooks. "Just thought I'd bring the boys in for a little celebration and let you know what's cookin'. Tomorrow we're gonna start a thousand head for the coast."

Nutt lit a cigar and peered at him through a cloud of blue smoke. "You're driving a thousand head all at once?"

"Boss, you know me better than that." Crow chuckled, trying to hide his vexation at being questioned like a schoolboy. "They'll be split up in five herds and go down by different trails. Some'll go to the hide and tallow plants and some to the beef shippers. Not as much money that way but it keeps people from gettin' nosey."

Nutt studied him for a moment, then abruptly switched subjects. It was a device he purposely used to throw others off balance. "There's talk that ranchers over in the eastern part of the country are being raided. I thought I told you to stick to that Secesh bunch for the time being."

Crow grimaced and shot his carpetbagger boss a dark

look. "Damnation, we only hit a few of 'em. Just enough to give us a breather over around Yegua Creek. If we keep raidin' the same places all the time they're gonna start layin' for us."

"Grip, let's get something straight." Nutt's brow furrowed and he jabbed the air with his cigar. "When I give you an order that's exactly how I want it. Without any sass, either. Understand?"

"Sure, boss, whatever you say." The gang leader swallowed his anger, hesitant somehow to push the Yankee too far. "I just thought it'd be best to keep 'em guessin', that's all."

"Well don't think so much. Just follow orders. So long as we stick to those Rebs nobody in Williamson County will say a word. But if we start raiding Loyalist ranchers that could change. Besides, I want to see Oliver and his neighbors nailed to the cross. Just as fast as they gather a herd, you rustle it."

Since it was none of Crow's business he didn't add that he had designs on more than rustled longhorns. If the Olivers and their neighbors could be pushed to the wall financially their lands could then be acquired through tax auctions. Where the landowners were former Confederates it was purely a matter of form and being done every day across the South. What worked elsewhere would work in Williamson County. Perhaps even better.

"You just concentrate on that Secesh trash. If they ever run out of cows then's when we'll start thinking about the other ranchers. Not before."

"You're the boss. But you oughta know that things are liable to get a mite touchy. Them Johnny Reb's'll fight if we push 'em too hard. Don't think they won't."

"Let me tell you something, Grip, my boy. I didn't hire you for your gentle nature. I brought you into this deal so I wouldn't have to worry about little problems like teaching the Olivers to pull in their horns. Do you follows me? What I'm saying is—you take care of it and don't bother me with details."

Crow understood perfectly. The Yankee bastard had hired someone to do his dirty work for him, and if it came down to a shooting war that was part of the deal. But he had to admit that it really didn't trouble him too much. Hell, somebody was always getting themselves shot, and so far he had managed to make sure it was the other fellow.

After a few minutes of idle conversation Crow excused himself and headed for the door. Just as he shut it, he glanced back and saw that Cal Nutt had returned to staring out the window. Whatever the tricky scutter was chewing on it must be powerful medicine.

Then Grip Crow chuckled softly to himself. Sonovabitch was probably figuring out some way to rob the church poor box.

3

Print returned from Missouri with more money than the Olivers had ever seen in one lump sum. After paying off the crew and deducting trail expenses he had cleared $11,000. The gold was stacked in shiny pillars on the kitchen table and there was much rejoicing along Yegua Creek that night. Even Julia Oliver admitted that Print had been right, not so much with words as in the way she looked at him and quietly served his favorite dishes for supper. Afterwards the gold was secreted beneath a loose slab in the fireplace hearth, and the family gathered around to listen as Ira and Print related their experiences among the Indians and Yankee Jayhawkers.

But when the stories were over and the excitement had waned, Jay had something of his own to tell about. While Print was off jousting with border rabble, Jay and the remaining hands had been fighting a few skirmishes themselves. Rustling activity had picked up noticeably, and it was no longer a matter of isolated raids involving a few cows. Every rancher north of Yegua Creek had been hit. Not once but repeatedly. The raids were staggered so that no one knew who would be next, yet the rustlers struck like clock-work no less than twice a week. They were clearly well organized and led by someone who knew his business.

When Print questioned him further on this point, Jay observed somewhat heatedly that the raids had been re-stricted to ranchers with known Confederate loyalties. Though it was strictly a rumor, word was circulating around Georgetown that the rustlers were in cahoots with the county's resident carpetbagger, Cal Nutt. This tallied out about right, Jay noted, when a man considered that none of the pro-Union ranchers had suffered more than token losses.

Still, the most chilling aspect of this deal was the rus-tlers' new willingness to stand and fight. Before it had beeen a hit and run proposition; the raiders had many times left the cows and taken flight rather than trade lead. For the past month, though, they had been getting bolder. More apt to start shooting instead of turning tail. Old Man Kuyken-dall and Bud Abbott had already exchanged shots with them, and while no one had been hurt it was getting to be damn' serious business.

Then Jay brought Print up on the edge of his chair. "It's gettin' pretty close to home, too. Last week me and Bob was ridin' over to the pens west of Stinkin' Springs and some-body opened up on us without warnin'. They was hid in the brush so we couldn't rightly see 'em, but there must've been four or five of 'em. I near had to whip Bob to get him to skedaddle out of there. The little nitwit wanted to stay and fight. Against five guns, mind you!"

Bob leaped up from where he had been seated by the fire and shook his fist in Jay's face. "Watch who you're callin' names! You're not so big I can't take you down a peg or two."

"Kid, you haven't got sense enough to shell peas." Jay smiled, trying to soften his remark. "Now simmer down. All I'm sayin' is that you gotta learn how to mix guts with a little smart."

"Yeah, well you better get to learnin' it the other way round." Bob strutted back to the fireplace, then turned and sneered at his brother. "We could've whipped 'em if you hadn't been so all-fired set on runnin'. Betcha we lost fifty head just 'cause you got cold feet."

Jay flushed and started out of his chair, but Print's gruff command brought him up short. "Hold it! Both of you. We've got enough trouble on our hands without fightin' among ourselves. Now you two roosters just back off and save your spurs for somebody besides family. I've got an idea there'll be enough fightin' to go around before we're finished."

The two boys exchanged raw looks and backed off. But the spirit of Print's homecoming had been dulled by their anger. Shortly everyone began yawning and talking about bed. One by one they made their goodnights and drifted out of the room. Bob hung around for a while, looking sort of sheepish, then finally followed suit. Before long Print found himself alone with Louisa and his mother. The house had grown still and for some moments they stared into the dancing flames, each absorbed in thoughts of the trouble that had come to Sunburst.

Julia Oliver sighed at last and looked around at Print. "Son, I let you have your way with Robert because he was getting too old to stay tied to my apron strings. He needed a man's hand, and as head of the family it fell on you. But he's turned into a young hellion and none of us can handle him anymore. Something has to be done and it seems to me that it comes to rest on your doorstep."

"Ma, he's just a kid." Print smiled, but his troubled eyes belied the light tone. "All boys get feisty when they start out to be a man. Why when I was his age you pretty near tore your hair out by the roots."

Julia wasn't diverted by his joshing manner. "Prentice, you were my first born and I haven't forgotten a moment of your life from that time to this. You were a naughty, unruly boy, even wicked sometimes. But not in the way I'm talking about with Robert. He was always hot-headed, and now that you've taught him to use a gun he's gotten cocky. Too much so for his own good. That temper of his will one day bring grief to us all unless you take a strong hand."

Print regarded her in silence for a moment, then turned back to the fire. The stillness deepened, broken only by the spitting fire and the creak of timbers as the house settled for the night. When it became obvious that Print wasn't going to speak, Louisa couldn't hold her peace any longer.

Leaning forward, she placed her hand on his arm. "Honey, your mama isn't blaming you. She's only trying to make you see that Bob is turning wild." She glanced around at Julia for help, but the old woman didn't flick an eyelash, Grasping for some way to make him understand, she then chose the thing that frightened her most. "Surely you can't doubt it after what Jay told you tonight. Bob would have stayed there and fought those rustlers even if he got himself killed. Every day since you left he's been out practicing with that gun, and it's just like your mama says. He's gotten so cocky he thinks there's not anything or anybody that shouldn't step out of his way. He's just a boy, Print. He doesn't know there's a difference between killing chickens and killing men."

Print shifted uneasily, his mouth twisted in a frown. "Lou, he's not a boy. He's going on seventeen, and in this country you're either a man by then or you might never make it. These are hard times, and man or boy, he has to know how to take care of himself."

When neither of the women said anything he knew he was licked. Females had a way of working on a man with silence when everything else failed. Silence and tears, always one or the other. "All right, I'll talk to him. But I'm not gonna put him on a short rope. Sooner or later he'll have to stand on his own, and I want him ready when the time comes."

Julia Oliver's smoky gaze met his straight on. "Just don't let him get killed in the meantime. You're the eldest and these boys follow where you lead. Whatever happens, I hold you to account for their well being. Perhaps that's not fair, Prentice, but it's part of what a man shoulders when he becomes head of the family."

Mother and son stared at one another for a long moment, and Louisa had the feeling of someone caught between two scarred old warriors as they circled to give battle. Watching them, it seemed the living incarnation of the irresistable force and the immovable object. Only so far one or the other had always been willing to back off before it went beyond the point of reason. She shuddered to think what would happen should these two proud and fiercely determined people ever join in final struggle. There, in a single moment, the Oliver family might be no more, consumed within itself like a barn full of hay suddenly bursting into flame.

Just when the tension seemed unbearable a moment longer, Print rose and stalked off through the house. Turning down the long hallway where the bedrooms were located, he halted before Bob's door and knocked. There was a muffled response and he entered, wondering not just why he was there, but more disquieting still, what the hell he was going to say.

Bob was propped up in bed cleaning his pistol with an oily rag. When Print closed the door he looked up with a brash smile. "Well, don't tell me. They sent you down here to pound some sense in my head and make me mind my manners."

"Maybe I should," Print growled. "The way you've been lippin' off since I got home you're overdue."

"Aw, hell, Print. It's them and their stuffed-shirt ways." The boy rubbed on the Colt furiously, groping for the right words. "Just because I'm the youngest don't mean they have to treat me like a baby."

Print understood only too well what Bob was going through, and it went against the grain to put the kid on the spot. "No, I reckon you're not a baby anymore. But there's more to being a man than packin' a gun. There's such a thing as responsibility, and when a fella figures he's through being wet-nursed then he's got to tote his share."

"Responsibility? Hellsfire, I been doing a man's work

around here all summer, and it wasn't me that hauled ass when them rustlers started potshootin' us."

"Sport, that's just what I'm gettin' at. There's a time to fight and there's a time to run. A man knows the difference, and he's not 'shamed whichever way he heads."

Bob studied him for a moment, then a sly look came over his face. "I didn't see you turn tail that day we flushed them two birds north of the creek."

Print swallowed a grin. The kid had spunk and he was sharp as a tack. "That's a fact. But I had the drop on 'em, and that made it even money. If there had been five of 'em you'da been eatin' my dust all the way home."

The boy shot him a skeptical look. "Aw, quit your funnin'. You would've stayed right there no matter how many there was."

"You could lose your saddle makin' foolish bets like that. What I'm tryin' to get across to you is that a man thinks, where a boy just wades in with his eyes closed. You think fast, but you act slow. You never rush in unless you've got the upper hand. The same thing goes whether it's a gunfight or a knuckle-dustin' contest with your brother."

"Meanin' I oughta wait a couple of years before I lock horns with Jay."

Now Print grinned. "Something like that."

When the youngster laughed Print shushed him, then eased out the door. There were all kinds of ways to make a point, and the women didn't have to know that he had done it without calling down thunder and lightning. Besides, the kid was right.

Jay was a stuffed shirt. Not to mention being a natural-born pain in the ass.

4

Print rode into Georgetown early next morning. While he had at first thought to go alone, on the spur of the moment he decided to take along one man to cover his back. What he had in mind probably wouldn't involve gunplay, but with the way things were shaping up a man couldn't afford to take chances. Whoever had it in for the Olivers had already proved they weren't above backshooting, and having another gun along might sandbag the odds just enough. Every gambler worth his salt knew when to hedge his bet, and today seemed like a damn' good time to start.

Curiously, Print chose Jim Kelly to back his play. Thinking about it afterwards he felt a twinge of guilt at having picked the black horse wrangler over the other hands. But if he had learned anything during the war it was that the color of a man's skin counted for nothing when the shooting started. The only thing that mattered was how straight a man could shoot when the chips were down, and of all the hands on Sunburst, Jim Kelly had no equal with a pistol. Print found that a little odd, too, but he didn't waste any time puzzling over it. The black man had clearly learned to use a gun with deadly skill—where or how didn't mean a hill of beans. Print just felt damn' lucky to have such a man on the payroll, black, white, or candy-striped.

Before they left for town Print had briefed Kelly on what he intended doing. He made it clear that if the black man didn't like the game he could pass and no hard feelings. Kelly had simply flashed a toothy smile and gone to saddle his horse. Men who thrived on danger seldom made any big show about it, and Print had a sneaking hunch that the black wrangler had buried his share. Kelly plainly didn't care who they were after or why. So long as it was his outfit doing the fighting, that was enough.

When they reached Georgetown Print went directly to the courthouse. Julia and Jim Oliver had reared their sons to respect the law, and if a man had real trouble he was duty bound to make sure he stood right with the authorities. Little things, like a couple of rustlers, he handled himself. That was accepted practice in cow country and nobody saw any need to bother the law with chores that were rightly personal business anyhow.

Print left Jim Kelly on the courthouse steps and made

his way to the Sheriff's office. When he entered Ed Strayborn was hunched over his desk, thumbing through a sheaf
of papers. The lawman looked up and a peculiar expression
came over his face. Observing the sudden change in manner, Print had a gut feeling that the Sheriff knew why he
was there. Instantly he was on guard. Something about this
deal didn't rhyme the way it should.

"Mornin', Sheriff. How's things going?"

"Just fine, Print. Just fine." Strayborn had himself in hand
again and he smiled woodenly. "How's your folks gettin'
along? Haven't seen'em in quite a spell."

"Couldn't be better," Print replied easily. "The old man's
gettin' fat as a pig and Ma's just as stickery as ever."

The Sheriff's laugh was forced, like a man with a fresh
toothache. "And Louisa? Say that's some sweet gal you've
got there, Print."

"Thanks. She's just fine, too." Print took the chair indicated by Strayborn, replacing his smile with a solemn look.
"Sheriff, the reason I'm here is to ask for some help. Rustlers
have been hittin' us pretty hard, and it looks to me like it's
gonna take the law to stop it. Maybe you've already heard
about what's happenin' out there."

"Matter of fact, I have." Strayborn put on his professional
lawman's look; concerned, interested, just the least bit for-
mal. "Jeb Kuykendall was in last week. Said he'd lost more'n
a hundred head in the past month."

"Sunburst has lost double that, maybe more." Print studied him for a moment, unable to shake a growing suspicion. "Any idea who's behind it?"

The Sheriff's eyes wavered for an instant, just enough
to show that the question had rattled him. Then he got busy
shuffling the papers on his desk. "Damned if I can figure it
out, Print. But I will, don't you worry about that. Just as
soon as I get things straightened out around here. What
with all the paper work and reports the military governor
demands these days, I haven't hardly had time to squat."

Print never had thought much of Strayborn as a peace
officer, but he was an even worse liar. Keeping his voice

casual, he decided to go whole hog. "Sheriff, the word's around that a fella named Cal Nutt might have a hand in this rustlin'. You heard anything about that?"

Strayborn jumped like he had been goosed with a hot poker. "No, not a word. Don't hardly seem likely, though. Cal Nutt's a businessman. Land speculator, so I hear."

"Carpetbagger'd be more like it, wouldn't it?" Print really didn't expect an answer. He had already found out what he wanted to know. Shoving his chair back, the cattleman nodded and headed for the door. "Nice seein' you, Sheriff. We'll let you know if things get so bad we can't handle it."

Ed Strayborn quickly gathered his wits and came around the desk. "Now, Print, don't you go takin' the law into your own hands. I understand you've already killed one man out there."

Print looked back from the door and smiled grimly. "Ed, there's gonna be a whole passel of dead men out there if they don't stay clear of Sunburst land. You might pass the word along." Then he turned and walked out.

Outside the courthouse he inquired directions to Cal Nutt's office, then collected Jim Kelly and took off across the square. When they reached the alley behind Jackson's Feed & Grain, Print instructed Kelly that no one was to be allowed up the stairs until he came out. The black man's pearly smile assured him that he had nothing to worry about on that score.

Print mounted the stairs and pushed through the door without bothering to knock. Cal Nutt sat motionless in his chair, watchful, perhaps a bit curious, but not at all alarmed. Somehow he reminded Print of a bright pig. Wide, flaring nostrils; jaw a little underslung; narrow, beady eyes.

Bright and more than likely dangerous.

The two men stared at one another for a moment, each taking stock and filing away what he saw. Then Print strode forward, halting before the desk. "If your name is Cal Nutt, I've got a message for you."

The carpetbagger appeared mildly puzzled, but not in

the least intimidated by the big man's brusque manner. "I'm Nutt. Who are you?"

"Name's Oliver, from Yegua Creek. Ring any bells?"

Cal Nutt masked his surprise with a blank look. "Can't say that it does. Why, should it?"

"Maybe. Maybe not." Print didn't like anything about the man, and some hidden instinct told him that he was on the right track. "Depends on how you feel about cows wearin' the Sunburst brand."

"You lost me, Tex. What have your cows got to do with me?"

Print smiled tightly, finding it hard not to admire the man's calm bearing. "Unless it's your men rustlin' them, why I reckon they don't have nothin' to do with you."

Nutt's gaze hardened a little around the edges. "Rustling is a serious charge. If you're accusing me of something perhaps we should step over to the Sheriff's office."

"No need. What I've got to say is just between us. You see, I don't like my family being shot at, Mr. Nutt. Rustlin' cows is one thing, but shootin' at people named Oliver won't get it. I just rode in to tell you that if anything happens to my family, I'm gonna come back here and turn you into a lead mine. Savvy?"

"That's dangerous talk from a paroled Reb. Maybe I should have you locked up before you harm someone."

"Maybe I oughta just shoot your left eye out. How's that sound?" Print grinned when the carpetbagger's face went ashen. "Your Yankee friends in Austin can't help you up here. Even if you had me jailed you'd still get a quart of buckshot up your gizzard some night. You just keep thinkin' about that."

Nutt's jaws clenched and his voice shook with rage. "You Secesh trash don't scare me. Now get out of here, and take your threats with you!"

"Yank, you don't seem to understand. You mess with me and I'll kill you." Print leaned across the desk and punched him in the chest with his finger. "And if you hurt my family, I'll cut your balls off and feed 'em to the hogs."

The Texan turned and walked from the room without a backward glance.

Cal Nutt remained dead still, listening to the jangle of Print's spurs as he tromped down the stairs. Then he rose and stepped to the window, looking on as the cattleman and his black wrangler crossed the square to their horses. After a moment he grunted and his beady eyes squinted into thin slits.

Somebody was going to lose his balls, right enough. But it wouldn't be Cal Nutt.

5

They rode in as dusk gave way to night. Silent men, grim-faced, their eyes troubled and cold. Most of them were lean and weathered beyond their time. Men who had challenged a raw, savage wilderness and endured, where others had faltered, even perished. They had survived hardship and hunger, blizzards and Comanches, prevailed in a moment of time when men of less grit simply vanished beneath the onslaught of an untamed land. They rode tall and proud, having seen the worst of both God and man. About them was the quiet strength of those who had been baptized in the crucible of blood and sweat and human gore.

They came to talk of a new threat. One as sinister and deadly as any of old—and not a man among them would shrink from the gruesome job ahead.

They dismounted before the Oliver house and trooped inside. Print met them at the door, greeting them as old friends though in many cases he was but half their age. Jim Oliver and the boys were waiting in the parlor, and as the men found seats around the room Julia brought in a pot of coffee, then retired to the kitchen. What would be discussed here tonight was men's work, and from times past women knew that these affairs were best left to those who had the stomach for such things. Slowly the parlor filled with the men of Yegua Creek, and by full dark they were all there.

Fourteen men, including Jim Oliver's younger sons, a pitifully small number for the task before them.

Print waited until everyone was settled and the small-talk had subsided, then he moved to the fireplace and faced them. "We're all here, so we might as well get started. Everybody knows why I asked you to come, and I reckon none of us needs to hear it laid out with fancy speeches. We've all had cows rustled and it seems pretty clear somebody's set on drivin' us out of Williamson County. That brings it down to a matter of what we're gonna do about it."

Jeb Kuykendall cleared his throat and glanced around the room. He was a prune-faced old cuss, a grizzled human wrinkle with a mustache white as fresh-fallen snow. But he was still a fighter, hard as nails and merciless as honed steel. Not a man present doubted what stand he would take. "Print, your pappy and me was the first to settle these hills. We ain't exactly strangers to this business of cow thieves. There's only one language they understand. A strong rope and a stout limb. Works everytime."

"Jeb, you old fire eater, skinnin' a cat might be harder than killin' him." Fred Smith, whose spread bordered Kuykendall's, chuckled in his easy-going way. "What I'm sayin' is that hangin' a few rustlers won't cut it. Appears to me somebody with some real brains is back of this deal."

"Damn it all, boys," Kuykendall growled, "I ain't talkin' about hangin' a few! Hang 'em all!"

Grady Morrow, who was himself no stranger to killing, came up on the edge of his chair. Though slow to anger, he was a burly, powerful man and rough as a cob underneath. Over the years his neighbors had learned to listen when he spoke. "Now hold it, both of you. Print's the one that called this meetin' and I'd sorta like to hear what he's got to say. The rest of us've been sittin' around like a bunch of mugwumps and he might just have something worth listenin' to."

Every eye in the room shuttled from Morrow back to Print. While they knew he had taken over as head of Sunburst, most still considered him a boy. Granted he had fought in the late war, but among the old campaigners seated here, he remained the dark-eyed youngster who as yet was untested on home ground. They knew he had Jim Oliver's spunk—before the war they had seen him whip grown men half again his size—they just didn't know if he had inherited his daddy's horse sense.

Print could read their thoughts like a well-chalked slate-board. Though their faces were open and friendly, he knew they were reserving judgment until he'd had his say. When it came to taking advice this bunch could be independent as a hog on ice. Even more so if it involved some young whippersnapper telling them how to save their hides.

Print had thought all this out before they arrived, and his words had been picked after considerable deliberation. "Grady, I don't know that I've got all the answers, but some things seem pretty plain to me. You all know that we drove a herd to Sedalia. What you don't know is that we sold a thousand head for close to $13,000."

The men started with shock, staring at one another incredulously as they repeated the figure. The sum was more money than most of them had cleared in the last decade, and the implications were enormous. While none of them ran a spread as large as Sunburst, it didn't take a mental giant to calculate that they each had a fortune on the hoof wandering their ranches at that very moment.

Before they could begin peppering him with questions the young cattleman pushed on. "While we were in Missouri I found out that the railroads are building west toward Kansas. Within a couple of years that means we'll have railheads close enough to ship a herd every spring. People in the north are hungry for beef. The way the buyers in Sedalia snapped up our herd proves that. So what I'm gettin' around to saying is that every man in this room can be sittin' pretty if we stick together."

Bud Abbott popped up out of his chair and began pacing across the room. Short-fused and somewhat excitable, he was noted for a hair-trigger temper and a waspish disposition. "Boy, you sure as hell know how to hit a man where he lives. That's big money. Bigger'n most of us ever even dreamed about. But what's us stickin' together got to do with it?"

"Just this, Bud. Trailin' to Sedalia, we learned the hard way that a small herd with a few men is askin' for trouble." Briefly he related the problems they had encountered with Indians and Jayhawkers, observing that if it hadn't been for the Spencer carbines they would have returned empty handed. The men nodded, grinning appreciatively when he described how they had wiped out the border gang in a matter of seconds. "What we've got to do is form one herd among us and send along enough men that nobody'll be tempted to jump us. Indian or white. That way our cows'll get there and we'll also get a better price. I've already wised up that a man with a big herd can talk a tougher deal than somebody with a bunch of scrubs and a boil on his ass."

Jeb Kuykendall chortled and shook his head, regarding Print with a curious twinkle in his eye. "Son, somewheres between here and Appomattox you done turned into a sure enough meateater. If I'm hearin' you right, you're sayin' we oughta get organized some way or t'other."

Print's ruddy face brightened with excitement. "You hit it dead center, Jeb. We've got to band together, unite somehow. Make it sound big, so folk'll know they're not dealin' with a bunch of shorthorns. Call ourselves something impressive, like maybe the Yegua Creek Cattlemen's Association. Something they won't forget, or be real keen to tangle with."

Fred Smith spoke up then, looking just the least bit skeptical. "Well boys, I'm all for stickin' with my neighbors. But I'm just a mite confused. Print, if it's gonna take a couple of years for them railroads to get built what in tarnation're we gonna do with our cows in the meantime? The way you talk we'd have to fight a small war every spring just to get 'em into Missouri."

"Next year we'll trail 'em to Colorado Territory and the northern plains." The men all started talking at once and Print held up his hand for silence. "Now hear me out.

There's thousands of gold miners up there that haven't tasted cow since before the war, and a whole slew of army posts that need beef, too. We'll trail out of here when the snow melts, get there first, and make'em pay through the nose for some good Texan longhorn. By the spring after that the railroads'll be in Kansas and we'll be primed and waitin'."

The men silently looked around at one another and Print could see that they were convinced. Still, it didn't surprise him all that much. He had been working this out in his head all the way home from Sedalia and he was confident beyond question that the plan was a good one. The only thing that remained was to get it organized and pull it off. Which would probably be a damned sight more ticklish than he had let on a moment ago.

Suddenly the men stopped chattering among themselves as Grady Morrow broke in. "Well, all this talk about formin' an association is jim-dandy. Don't mistake me, I'm all for it. But what the hell's it got to do with cattle rustlers? Christ, the way things are going they could have us wiped out before we ever made the first drive."

Everyone turned back to Print, their faces reflecting Morrow's question with sober unease. Somehow, within the space of their brief meeting, Jim Oliver's eldest son had been designated leader of the Yegua Creek cattlemen. Young or not, he had a head on his shoulders. More to the point, he seemed to have the answers.

Besides, he was the only one among them who had yet killed a rustler, and that was no small thing in itself.

"Gents, where rustlers are concerned I reckon I side with Jeb. They've got to be killed off. Whether we hang 'em or shoot 'em makes no difference. It's purely a matter of get them before they get us."

The men nodded gravely, in complete accord with every word he said. They had come there tonight with the same thought in mind, knowing full well that their only hope lay in exterminating the rustlers with no more mercy than they would show a den of rattlesnakes. The only difference was, Print Oliver had put it in words.

From his chair by the fireplace Jim Oliver cackled softly. "I told you fellers he was a tough'un, didn't I? Just a chip off the old block. By gum, you'll believe me next time."

Before the old man could get carried away, Print again grabbed the lead. "I had a little talk with the Sheriff yesterday and that's one reason I figured we'd better get organized. Looks to me like Strayborn is carrying water for a carpetbagger name of Cal Nutt, and unless I'm wide of the mark, he's the one behind the rustlers. What I'm sayin' is, it looks like we're not gonna get any help from the law."

Then he paused and looked around at the ranchers' somber faces. "If you catch a rustler, hang him on the spot. But before you do make damn' sure he spills everything he knows about a fella named Cal Nutt."

CHAPTER FOUR

━━⊶⊷━━

1

Print Oliver and Jim Kelly reined their horses to a halt on a stunted knoll overlooking the North Fork of the Loup. Behind them trailed two pack horses loaded with jerky, hardtack, assorted camp gear, and four saddlebags stuffed with gold. Before them stretched a shimmering sea of blue-stem grass, lapping in unbroken waves as far as the eye could see. There was no need to ride farther. The northern plains lay dead ahead, six hundred miles of rolling grasslands running straight as a string through Nebraska and the Dakotas.

They had found what they came to see.

Late in April, some four months past, the first herd of the Yegua Creek Cattlemen's Association had headed north. The mixed herd numbered two thousand cows and the crew was comprised wholly of hired hands. Print wanted no disputes with the other owners along the trail and part of the conditions he had laid down was that he alone would ramrod the drive. After road-branding the longhorns he had pointed them due northwest, toward the Colorado gold fields. Over the ensuing weeks he had pushed them along at a leisurely pace, letting the cows graze their way north-ward as the spring grasses ripened beneath their hooves. They had crossed the Red, the Arkansas, and the Republican without incident, and in late July turned west on a dead reckoning for Denver.

But news of the herd had preceded them. When they reached Badger Creek, some fifty miles east of the mining camps, they found an enterprising Denver merchant wait-ing with a sackful of double eagles. Though the business-man dickered like a horse trader, Print had him over a barrel. Fresh beef would command sky high prices in the gold fields, and they both knew it. Before the hour was out they had settled on a price of eighteen dollars a head for three-fourths the herd. Print wrote him out a bill of sale, accepted payment, then sent Bumpus Moore and ten hands along to see the cows safely to Denver. Once the long-horns were delivered they were to return directly to Texas. After they had pulled out, Print and the remainder of the crew pointed some five hundred cows north along Badger Creek and headed them toward the South Platte.

Over the next few weeks they had gradually worked their way north and east along the Platte, selling longhorns at even stiffer prices to isolated army posts dotting the plains. Late August found them at Ft. Kearny without a cow to their names and $37,000 in gold crammed in their sad-dlebags. Print paid off the hands and started them down the trail for home. Afterwards he and Jim Kelly rigged the gold aboard one pack horse, loaded another with camp gear, and struck out for the sweeping grasslands north of the Platte. With the black man along Print had no fear for the gold, and now that the cows were off his hands, he was free to tackle the second part of his objective in making the drive. Namely, to scout the water and graze on the northern plains.

Now, as the two men gazed out over the vast grasslands, Jim Kelly clucked his tongue in marvel. "Mistah Print, it's the Jordan range, sure 'nough."

Print nodded agreement, slowly scanning the distant sweep of the rolling land. "Beats anything I ever saw, Jim. That's for damn' sure. I've got an idea the folks back home are gonna brand us a couple of liars when we tell'em about this."

The black man grinned widely. "Can't say's I'd blame'em too much. Jest 'tween us, if I hadn't seen it for myself, I wouldn't rightly believe it neither."

"Yeah, it does take a little gettin' used to, at that." Print blinked and looked again, half expecting it to evaporate in a puff of smoke. "Sorta makes home look like a parched cabbage patch."

For men who had been born and reared in the southwest, where good graze was a sometimes thing, the northern plains were indeed an eye-opener. Back at Ft. Kearny Print had heard the commanding officer jest that Nebraska had one month of spring, thirty days of summer, and ten feet of snow the rest of the year. While it was easy to see that the windswept prairies could be damn' uncomfortable in a blizzard, Print wasn't concerned with winter. Right now he was thinking only of summer, and all that grass.

The land around them swayed gently in a hot breeze, a carpet of deep green that seemed to grow by inches right before their eyes. Over the grayish snarl of buffalo grass the hardier bluestem and wheat grasses grew thick and lush, tall enough to hide a suckling calf. Wildflowers of every description flourished alongside the grasses, and it was as if a man had suddenly stumbled onto a landscape dobbed and splotched by an artist gone mad with color. It was a sight to warm the heart of any cattleman, and in his mind's eye Print could see thousands of longhorns cutting a swath through the belly-high graze. This land had fattened millions of buffalo for untold centuries, and it could just as easily add precious tallow to the ribs of young Texas steers. Easier, in fact, since the brush-reared longhorns weren't used to such abundance.

"How you reckon them Texas cows would do up here,

Mistah Print? They so lean and hungry, they might jump right in there and founder themselves."

The black man's question snapped Print out of his reverie. "Founder? Naw, I doubt it, Jim. I've got an idea the young stuff would put on about a pound a day, and those slat-ribbed old *ladinos* would probably do even better. Leastways till they got filled out. Inside a month they'd be fat as butterballs. Give'em a summer and we'd probably have to cart'em out of here in wagons."

"Now wouldn't that be somethin'? Cows fat as pigs!" Kelly chuckled to himself, trying to conjure up a picture of broad-beamed cows waddling across the prairie. "Purely puts a man to thinkin', don't it, boss?"

"It purely does, Jim," the young cattleman allowed thoughtfully. "It purely does."

When they were alone Print often caught himself slipping into the black man's slurred, rhythmical way of speaking. Yet it wasn't done to be patronizing, or even as a harmless joke as some whites were fond of doing. Jim Kelly wasn't a man to be patronized, as Print had well learned over the past year. Nor was he a man to shuffle his feet and grin shyly while someone made a jackass out of him. Though good-natured and loyal to those who befriended him, he was near about as dangerous as a spooked rattler to anyone who stepped out of line. Print had seen him clean house on three cow hands one day, but he hadn't tried to interfere. The white men had gone too far with "nigger this" and "nigger that", and when Kelly had had enough he just waded in and demolished them. Afterwards everyone around the place had walked light with their nigger talk. Kelly's reputation as a dead shot was already common knowledge, and anyone that lethal with his fists was just naturally a man to step around.

Print suspected that Jim Kelly had been busting heads and deflating white arrogance long before Abe Lincoln got into the act. More than likely that was why he had spent all those years chasing mustangs in West Texas. Out there tough was all that counted, and anytime a couple of fellows got crosswise of one another they generally played it for keeps. Since Kelly had returned no worse for wear, it seemed pretty clear that he had learned how to hold his own in a white man's world.

Strangely, Print didn't resent the black man's touchy manner. Instead he was sort of proud of Kelly, like someone who had made friends with a grizzly bear. Though the wrangler never buttered him up with the "yassuh" and "nosuh" patter that most Negroes used, Print had long since ceased to notice, or care. Kelly addressed him simply as mister or boss, and at times the cattleman had even considered having him drop that. But the black man seemed to prefer it that way—it was as if he wanted to maintain some hairline of separation between them. While they could laugh with one another, even josh around in a polite sort of way, Kelly made it clear that their alliance was still somewhat tenuous. There were times Print got the idea he was being tested—like maybe they could be real friends someday if his marks came up to Kelly's satisfaction. But by whatever standards the black man was measuring him, Print found him to be an easy companion on the trail and damned handy to have around in case of trouble. Which was exactly why he had picked the wrangler to accompany him on this little jaunt up north.

They had been watching the grassy plains for some moments in silence when Kelly darted a curious glance in his direction. "Boss, I'm gettin' a hunch you got somethin' tricky up your sleeve. You got some idea of seein' if that grass'll really put porkchops on cows?"

"Well, maybe yes and maybe no," Print replied vaguely. "Depends on a lot of things. Mostly what to do with them after we get'em fattened up."

The black man thought that over for a minute, watching Print out of the corner of his eye. "Seems like I recollect hearin' the Sioux was sorta picky 'bout lettin' folks move in on their stompin' grounds. Might be lean cows is better'n fat ones if a man has to trade his hair in the deal."

"No might be to it," the cattleman observed. "We've got lots of cows, but a man's only got one head of hair. Course, settlers are movin' west all the time, and that colonel back at the fort told me that railroad's building this way fast. Something like that could make a big difference in a year or so. Hard tellin'. We'll just have to wait and see."

The wrangler flashed a big grin and rolled his eyes toward the cloudless sky. "Lord o' mercy! Mistah Print, I sure hope I can get some dimdot to cover my bet."

Print gave him a quizzical look. "What bet is that?"

"Why, that we is headed back this way come next spring, boss man. Jest you don't tell them boys down home what we seen here and I'll clean 'em out. Leave 'em ridin' bare-backed and poor-mouthed!"

"Jim, I might take a piece of that myself." Print laughed deeply and reined his gelding about. "Let's go home, hoss wrangler. I've got an itch that won't get cured this side of Yegua Creek."

Jim Kelly threw back his head and howled like a wolf. "You don't have to ask this nigga twice on that score. Maybe all this grass makes cows fat, but my innards is sure 'nough groanin' for some of Doughbelly's cornbread and beans."

The two men roweled their horses into a fast trot and struck out south across the plains. Neither of them turned to look back. But both had seen something in that shimmering sea of grass that would be a long time fading from their minds.

2

Cal Nutt stood by a window, staring out over the Capitol grounds while Attorney General Horace Davidson finished signing some papers. The burly carpetbagger saw little of what he was looking at through the window, however, for his thoughts were back in Williamson County. Things weren't proceeding according to schedule and he had come to Austin seeking assistance.

Advice he could do without.

Though he reported directly to Davidson, and funneled a slice of every deal through the Attorney General's office, he was given the latitude to act as he saw fit in his own bailiwick. That made his visit this morning all the more distasteful. Somehow he saw it as an admission of his own shortcomings; anyone who had his own house in order didn't have to come running to the big augurs for help.

Still, Nutt had been here before and today's session likely wouldn't be the last time. Davidson had sponsored him, and served as his go-between with the military authorities, which meant that he had small choice in the matter. When help was needed, this was the place to come. As Nutt knew only two well, every Carpetbagger and Scalawag in the Fifth Military District had trudged through the Attorney General's anteroom at one time or another. For in the State of Texas, Horace Davidson was the influence peddler who could open all doors. But the knowledge did little to ease Nutt's sour disposition. It still grated on the bone for him to admit that he hadn't yet broken the backs of the Yegua Creek crowd.

Davidson's belated acknowledgement brought him out of his funk. "Sorry to keep you waiting, Cal. But you know the military and their paperwork. Now, what can I do for you?"

Turning from the window, Nutt moved across the room with something akin to reluctance. He didn't relish this talk at all, and it was obvious from the dour look on his face. "Mr. Davidson, I'm not happy with the way things are going in Williamson County. That Secesh bunch is still holding on, and I want them off that land. I was wondering if we couldn't talk some more about declaring the Oliver family disloyal. They're the ones putting starch in the rest of those Rebs."

The Attorney General sighed heavily and his smile faded. "Cal, we talked all that out before. I thought you had plans to run those people off their ranches."

Horace Davidson was an imposing figure of a man. Tall, silver-haired, with the soft, melodic speech of a Southerner.

Patterning himself after Sam Houston, he had not supported the Confederacy. When the war ended, and the army of occupation marched into Texas, he had promptly made his loyalties known to the military authorities. Since he was a conniving rascal at heart, as well as a lawyer by trade, the military governor had eventually appointed him to the post of Attorney General. With unlimited power, and Yankee bayonets to back his dictates, Davidson had quickly become the most infamous Scalawag in the Lone Star State.

Squirming under the politician's stare right now, Cal Nutt had good reason to choose his next words carefully. "Yessir, I still plan to run them out. But it's taking much longer than I intended because of the Olivers. Mainly, Prentice Oliver. If we could just get that family judged disloyal and confiscate their property the rest would all fall into place."

Davidson's eyebrow lifted with a small frown. "You're making me repeat myself, Cal; I had that family checked out thoroughly, and the property is owned solely by the old man. Since he was never personally involved in the Rebellion there's no way we can touch him. Moreover, the Reconstruction Act explicitly states that even the property of a disloyalist must be *abandoned* before we can confiscate it. Even under military law the father can't be held accountable for the actions of the son."

"Well goddamn, Mr. Davidson," Nutt growled testily. He was speaking out of turn, and he knew it. But this business had him rankled, and just for a moment he didn't care. "I've seen that law bent to accommodate other situations. Hell, all that cotton that got gobbled up over on the coast wasn't abandoned. Way I heard it the owners weren't even dyed-in-the-wool Secesh."

"That's right, they weren't." The Attorney General pursed his lips, seeming to deliberate for a moment. "Yesterday the Military Tribunal sentenced a man to two years in Dry Tortugas for insulting the flag. Does my point become clear?"

Nutt's forehead wrinkled with puzzlement. "No sir,

I'm afraid I don't see the connection. Seems like apples and oranges to me."

"Hardly. We are living in a time of extremes and absurdities, Cal. You can shoot just about any Texan you choose—so long as he's not black—and go free. But defame the Union and you're shipped off to a dungeon. Conversely, the Reconstruction Act can be manipulated to ruin the large land holder, break up the plantation system. That's acceptable. However, it is expressly forbidden that it be used against the little man, no matter what his politics. Now do you grasp what I'm driving at?"

"I understand, well enough," the Carpetbagger replied, "but I don't agree where the Olivers are concerned. There is nothing little about them, Mr. Davidson. They own more land than anybody in Williamson County. Their ranch is the plum. The one I've had my eye on from the start."

Horace Davidson looked like a man whose patience had been tried to the limit. "I don't know whether you're stubborn or just dense. You say you understand, then you come right back with another feeble argument. The point I'm trying to make is that we won't skirt the letter of the law unless the deal is big enough. Unless there is sufficient money involved. The Oliver land is nothing but brush and hills. Valueless to anyone except another hand-to-mouth rancher. Frankly, Cal, I can't be bothered with tacky schemes like that."

Cal Nutt was as tenacious as a bulldog, but he knew when to keep his mouth shut. The Attorney General was running a business, something on the order of a candy store. He sold political appointments, pardons for unreconstructed Rebs, slightly used plantations, and freshly confiscated cotton. Anything of value in a market place where guile and power ruled absolute. But he had no interest in a ranch whose only notable assets ran wild in the brush. That had been made brutally clear, even to the hardheaded carpetbagger. While it stuck in his craw, Nutt decided there wasn't a damn' thing he could do about it. Sometimes a man who pushed too hard ended up having his ass handed to him as he was ushered out the door. Besides, he still had a few trumps left to play against the Olivers anyway.

When Nutt held his peace, Davidson smoothly switched topics. "Tell me, Cal, how are you doing with the Freedman's Bureau? Most of the boys have been meeting some pretty stiff resistance back in the sticks."

"Well, we're about the same, I guess. Maybe not so bad." Nutt had regained control of his temper and once more exhibited the studied calm of a faro dealer. "We've got the Negroes organized, but I don't think we'll ever control the vote with them alone. You know, that's ranching country and there just aren't that many blacks around. Strange enough, we are getting some trouble from the whites though."

Davidson smiled, his humor restored now that they were no longer at loggerheads. "You sound surprised. What's so strange about that?"

The Carpetbagger seemed mildly baffled by the question. "Let's just say it wasn't what I expected. After all, Williamson County did stay Loyalist through the war. You'd think they would jump on the bandwagon. But evidently they don't like blacks any better than the Rebs. Makes you wonder why they stuck with the Union."

"I keep forgetting that your county didn't support the rebellion." Davidson rubbed his jaw thoughtfully. "Damn' nuisance. Especially when it's the only one in the state. But don't let that hobble you, Cal. As I've said before, whatever's not nailed down you figure out some way to put it in our pockets. So long as we have the military backing us we still hold the whip hand. With or without the vote."

Then he paused, glancing shrewdly at his henchman. "Remember, though, we are only interested in property that can be converted into cash. Or in selling our influence to the highest bidder. Forget about those back-country ranchers and concentrate on the real cream."

Cal Nutt covered what he was really thinking with a tight smile and nodded obediently. Davidson was thinking of the here and now, what could be skimmed off fast and loose. But to an observant man it became increasingly clear that the future of Texas lay in cattle. Not farms, or run-down plantations, or even town property. Cows were about to become big business. Still, Davidson would be satisfied with a few tidbits here and there, and he could take care of the Olivers in his own good time. What the Attorney General didn't know wouldn't hurt him.

Particularly when one Calvin Nutt emerged with the deed to half of Yegua Creek in his pocket.

Widening his smile, Nutt rose and stuck out his hand. "Whatever you say, Mr. Davidson. We'll keep those hayseeds jumping through the hoop one way or the other."

"That's what I like to hear, Cal." Davidson gave his hand a hearty squeeze. "Now don't be such a stranger. Next time you come down maybe I won't be so busy and we can really make a night of it."

The Attorney General walked him to the door and pumped his hand again. Moments later Nutt stepped from the Capitol building and headed for the livery stable where he had left his horse. Striding along Austin's busy street in the warm noonday sun, he let his mind drift back over the conversation. Damned if he wasn't almost glad that Davidson had turned him down. Somehow it reduced the debt. Politicians were masters at getting a man indebted and then holding it over his head like a club.

Favors owed—to be called on demand by the bearer.

But today's little session had erased some of that red ink. More than anyone suspected. Perhaps one day soon he wouldn't need Horace Davidson, or his protection. The name Cal Nutt alone would be reckoning enough.

The chunky Carpetbagger smiled to himself and ambled on through Austin.

3

The door of Louisa's bedroom slowly opened and Print stuck his head through. Her eyes sparkled at the sight of him and a tiny gasp of delight escaped her lips. Flinging

the door wide, he rushed forward and knelt at the side of
the bed, scooping her up in his arms. She smothered his face
with kisses, ignoring the rough stubble of his beard and the
trail grime that covered his clothes. Then she pulled his
mouth to hers and for a long moment they embraced like
young lovers still courting. When they finally came up for
air Print held her face cupped between his calloused paws
and his dark eyes softened.

"How's my girl?"

Louisa's face glowed with happiness. "Better than butter."

Print chuckled, then his look sobered slightly. "Sorry I
couldn't make it home in time."

She smiled and playfully squashed his nose with her finger. "You always were the tardy one. But don't take it to
heart. There'll be a next time."

Her meaning took a moment to register, then his deep,
rumbling laugh filled the room. "Damnation! Kissin' and
makin' babies. Ain't nothin' like it, woman. Nothin' at all."

Print reached for her again, but a tiny bundle on the far
side of the bed suddenly erupted in a squall of protest.
They came apart and Louisa gently lifted the bundle in
the crook of her arm. The lusty screams ceased at the sound
of her soft cooing and she lovingly peeled back the layers
of delicately quilted blankets. Slowly a round, pink face
emerged, and a pair of button eyes blue as a summer sky
flickered open. The baby gurgled, working his mouth with
small sucking noises, and wet little bubbles formed on
his lips.

"This is your son, Print." Louisa's eyes glistened as she
searched his face. Then she glanced back at the baby, jiggling him proudly. "Just like his daddy. Loud and hungry."

Louisa lowered the bodice of her gown, exposing a
swollen breast, and shifted the baby closer. Without the
slightest coaxing his tiny fists clutched at the soft flesh and
his mouth settled over the nipple with a smacking sound.
Butting roughly with his head, he suckled in greedy silence
and a few drops of warm milk trickled down over his fat
cheeks.

Print watched every movement with open-jawed fascination, completely at a loss for words. *His son!* The words rang through his head like a clapper striking thunderous blows on a church bell. His skin felt prickly and an electric charge surged throughout every fiber of his body. There was a distant sense of unreality to the whole thing, yet what his eyes saw somehow possessed a godly vitality that could not be denied. This was his son. As if gorging himself on the words he silently mouthed them again. His son. It was at once frightening and grandly exhilarating beyond anything he had ever known. There, rooting and grunting for his dinner, was a living breathing part of him. A bawling, blue-eyed offshoot of his own flesh. It surpassed belief.

Glancing proudly from father to son, Louisa saw the look of wonder written across Print's face. "See, what did I tell you? Just like his daddy."

Still he didn't say anything. Couldn't. Not just yet. Never in his life had he been touched by the profound sense of love and tenderness coursing through his veins right at that moment. Louisa cuddled the baby closer and nuzzled him lovingly with her cheek. Watching her, it came over him that he had never seen her so radiant, so alive and vibrant. She was no longer the pretty, vivacious girl he had married. She was breathtakingly beautiful. The mother of his son.

Suddenly a kind of warm glow of discovery flooded over him. Women possessed a strength that came all too seldom to men—an inner power that could stand before any brute force and ultimately win hands down. Whatever name a man put to it, he was left with the realization that it was simply, and finally, the power of love. That selfless, unguarded giving of oneself. Without strings, or holding back, or even a hint of fear. Just pure, unadorned giving.

Then, in a voice that hardly seemed his own, he spoke. "Lou, could I touch him?"

Louisa laughed with spontaneous joy. "Why, of course, silly. He won't break. He's an Oliver."

The baby had finished feeding and was gurgling contentedly to himself. When Print stuck out his hand the little one closed a chubby fist around one finger. Gently the young cattleman pulled his hand back, but the baby held on tightly, determined not to let go now that he had captured this rough, thorny thing. Whatever it was, he wanted to explore it further, and he jerked on the finger with lusty strength.

Print smiled, watching raptly as the soft little hand tested his finger. "Honey, you do good work. He's cuter'n a bear cub."

"Why, thank you, sir." Louisa ducked her chin and coyly batted her lashes. The pose gave her an appearance of shrinking modesty that was very engaging. "Just place an order anytime."

Her invitation sparked an amused grunt, but Print never took his eyes off the baby. Then in a solemn voice, he said, "James Johnston Oliver."

They had decided on the name months ago in the event it was a boy. Something which would honor both the patriarch of the Oliver clan and that late Confederate hero, Albert Sidney Johnston. But as she heard it now, Louisa's lips puckered in a small frown. "I do hope the next one is a girl. This house is getting overrun with men."

Print snorted, flashing a wide grin. "You'd better not set your sights too high. The Oliver family runs to men. Always has."

"Well a girl can hope, can't she?" Louisa crinkled her mouth in a sly pout. "Besides, it takes a man around the house to make babies anyway."

"Ouch! You got me dead center that time." He laughed and climbed to his feet. "Tell you what. I promise I won't get out of sight before next spring. You behave yourself between now and then, and we'll work on gettin' you a little girl."

"Oh! Just listen to the rooster crow, would you. Promises, promises. That's all I ever get around here."

Print leaned over and kissed her, stealthily squeezing her ripened breast. "You'll get more than that when you're able."

"Mr. Oliver, please!" Louisa's brow lifted with mock indignation. "Not in front of James Johnston."

Chuckling deeply, he headed for the door. "You'd best start restin' up right now. I'll be back sooner'n you think."

"Print," she cried sulkily, "you just got home. Now you're off again."

"Honey, I'm just gonna talk to the folks for a while. I'd no more'n come through the door when they told me about the baby and I came tearin' back here. You take a little nap and I'll be back quicker'n you can say scat."

"Isn't that just like a man? Can't wait to start bragging about where he's been and what he's done. You're all alike."

"Woman, when are you gonna stop pokin' around in my mind?" Still grinning, he looked back from the door. "Sometimes a feller's got reason to brag. You be a good girl and I'll tell you all about it later."

The door closed, then opened a crack, and he stuck his head back in the room. "Ma'am, I just wanna tell you. You sure got some powerful recipe for babies."

Laughing at the expression on her face, he struck off down the hall. Maybe there were better days in a man's life, but he doubted it seriously. The day a fellow's first son was born would be hard to touch. Mighty hard indeed.

Moments later he entered the living room and found the family waiting anxiously. After everyone had again congratulated him on the baby, he briefly related details of the drive north. Then he casually mentioned that Sunburst's twelve-hundred head had brought nearly $23,000. For a moment everyone stared at him in stunned silence, hardly able to believe their ears. Abruptly they all started carrying on at once, laughing, shouting, the boys dancing wildly around the room. The Olivers were rich, just as Print had said they would be. Everything he had told them had come true. In spades! Even his mother got misty-eyed, telling the old man again and again that it had come to pass exactly as Print promised.

Some minutes went by before everyone calmed down, and when the heady atmosphere cleared a bit Print began to tell them of the northern plains. Slowly at first, then with mounting excitement, he described the vast, rolling grasslands. Nothing was left out. Everything he and Jim Kelly had seen was recounted to the smallest detail, embroidered upon, until they each began to grasp the immensity of a land unlike any they had ever known. A sea of grass. Belly-high to a longhorn. It was something to ponder. On that they all agreed.

But it was Julia Oliver who brought them back to reality. "Prentice, you've never done a thing in your life without a reason. Now tell me plain. Have you got some notion of moving this ranch to that wild country?"

"No'm. Not exactly." He paused, feeling the weight of their curious stares. "But that mightn't be a bad idea. Some day, I mean."

Julia eyed him shrewdly. "Then why did you ride all that distance out of your way? Why are you telling us about it?"

"Ma, I can't rightly say." Print shook his head, thinking for a moment. "Maybe if the railroad gets up there it would be a good place to fatten cows for fall shipment. That grass'd sure do it. More'n that, I haven't really thought it out."

His mother clearly didn't believe a word of it. "Fools walk in where angels fear to tread. You just keep that in mind, Prentice. That's Indian country up there, and besides, how would cows graze with all those buffalo wandering about?"

"Yes'm, I know all that. I'm not sayin' we're gonna pull up stakes next week——"

"Well I should hope not!"

"——it's just something to keep in mind. Something to think about for the future."

Jay butted in before his mother could reply, sounding just as caustic as ever. "Well, you'd better start worryin' about what you've *got* before you run off conquering new empires."

"What's that mean, Bubba? The rustlers been givin' you trouble while I was gone?"

"You bet your sweet patootie, they have. Killed Fred

Littins three weeks back and drove off ever' cow on his place. Been hittin' us regular, too, but we haven't seen hide nor hair of 'em. Seems like they always manage to amscray before we get close enough to start shootin'."

Print's mouth twisted in a grim smile. "Well, I guess Mr. Nutt knows good advice when he hears it."

Jay gave him an owlish look. "What're you gettin' at?"

"Nothin', Bubba. Just thinkin' of a little talk I had with Cal Nutt once."

Jim Oliver brought his rocker to a sudden halt and his weathered brow scrunched up in a furious scowl. "Them Pettyfoggin' Yankees oughta be run out of the country! And if you boys got the sense God gave a turnip, you'll get to hangin' them rustlers. You better hear what I'm tellin' you before it's too late."

"The words of the wise are as goads," Julia observed in her prayer-reading voice. Stalking forward, she gave the old man a sharp glance that had *shut up* written all over it.

"Same song, second verse," Jay remarked acidly.

Julia Oliver turned on him like a grizzly sow with a sore snout. "Now just what does that mean, young man?"

"Nothin', Ma. I wasn't sayin' anything about you quotin' scripture. Honest! I was talkin' about what Pa said. Him and everybody else is always yellin' about hangin' rustlers, but I haven't heard anybody tellin' us how to catch 'em."

"Amen," Ira noted soberly.

"And hallelujah," Bob slipped in with a crafty smirk.

"That'll do for one sittin'," Print ordered. "You boys are talkin' when you oughta be listenin'. Pa's right. The way things are it's gonna get worse before it gets better. Maybe a lot worse. But the only way it'll get straightened out is to hang a few ornaments up and down Yegua Creek."

"Big brother, we're all ears and a yard wide," Jay cracked. "Suppose you just tell us how you plan on collectin' them ornaments."

"Just offhand, I can't rightly say. Might take some high powered figurin'. But I'll let you know when I get it puzzled out. Till then everybody keep your eyes open and your mouths shut. You'll learn more that way."

Then his eyes brightened and he returned their stares with a faint grin. "Now if you folks will excuse me, I think I'll just take another peek at my son. Jay, get them gold sacks stashed away and tell Doughbelly to roust the crew out an hour early. We're going huntin' come first light."

Before anyone could speak he turned and walked from the room. The Olivers, both old and young, were left in a quandary, thoroughly baffled by his last cryptic observation.

4

The crew slouched around the large central room of the bunkhouse. Like most such places there was nothing noteworthy about the living quarters of Sunburst's hands. The furnishings included several rickety chairs, a patched settee, one commode with a dull, warped mirror, and a roughhewn table littered with faded magazines and newspapers. There was a chill nip to the night air and most of the men were gathered around a huge potbellied stove, talking quietly among themselves about what to expect in the next few hours.

Though opinion was divided on that topic, there was one thing they agreed on down to the last man. The pace of things sure picked up whenever the boss came home. Real quick.

Across the room Print had a large map of Sunburst range spread out over one end of a long mess table. Grouped around him were Jay, Ace Whitehead, and Bumpus Moore. Bob stood off to one side, hanging on every word like a young wolf sniffing fresh meat.

Print was just then circumscribing an arc with his finger around the northern boundaries of Oliver land. "Ace, I want you to take your men and start over here at the west end.

Jay, you come straight down the middle. That leaves the east side for you and your bunch, Bumpus. Everybody starts on Brushy Creek at exactly ten o'clock. Get your men fanned out and comb every inch of open ground as you drive south."

He paused, chewing on his lip as he deliberated for a moment. "Now, one of three things is gonna happen. First, we might not find a goddamn' thing. On the other hand, you might come across fresh tracks. If you do, follow 'em up at a run. Lastly, you might get lucky and actually flush somebody rustlin' cows. But there's one thing I don't want no mistake about. Whatever happens, you're not to lock horns with anybody up there. Stay right on their tail, but drive 'em straight south toward Yegua Creek. When you're a couple of miles from the creek, get a man up on some high ground and have him empty his carbine. That way we'll know which way the birds are being flushed and everybody can converge at that point. The way I figure it, you'll hit Yegua Creek about two o'clock if nothin' happens. Sooner, if it does."

"That's just peachy keen," Jay said skeptically. "But what makes you think today's the day they're gonna hit Sunburst?"

Print gave him a slow, piercing look. "Bubba, from what you've told me about their raidin' habits, it appears likely we're overdue. That's for openers. Next, I've got a hunch the head wolf of that outfit figures to let me know he's not losin' any sleep over the fact that I'm back home. Thirdly, I've got a twinge in my big toe that tells me it's today. That satisfy you?"

Jay's ears turned beet red, but he didn't back off. "Well, where are you and your big toe gonna be while this wild goose chase is takin' place?"

"Glad you asked that." Print's hand shot out and stabbed at a spot on the map. "I'm gonna take Ira, Bob, and Jim Kelly, and wait smack dab in the center of Yegua Creek. Assumin' you boys do flush something our way, we'll hear your warnin' shots and pin 'em down till you come in from behind. But remember, I'd rather hang 'em than shoot 'em.

I'd like to hear somebody do a little talkin' about the boss of that outfit before we put 'em out of their misery. Understood?"

The three men just nodded, staring silently at the map. Print hesitated a second, going over it again in his mind to make sure all the holes had been plugged. Then he looked around and smiled. "All right, let's move out. Time's a-wastin'."

When the hands trooped out of the bunkhouse the sky had gone slate-colored with the first dusky glow of false dawn. Stars were still visible, though fast disappearing, and there was a crisp bite to the fall air. Within minutes the crew had separated into three indistinct knots of horses and men. The jingle of spurs and the creak of cold saddle leather could be heard across the compound as the hands mounted and waited for the order to ride out. There was no talk now, for each of them had heard what was said back in the bunkhouse. Today they would hunt for two-legged game—the kind that could shoot back—and it was entirely possible that some of them would return draped across their saddles.

Print walked up to the corral fence where his gelding was tied just as Ace Whitehead and Jay mounted. Moving between the horses he began adjusting his cinch, then looked around with a sudden thought. "Ace, hold up a second. Couldn't rightly ask you back inside there, but I was wonderin' how all this sets with the men."

Before Whitehead could answer, Jay gigged his horse viciously and took off. Both men stared after him with troubled frowns, aware that his surly attitude was in part their own doing. Whitehead had proved himself a top-notch cattleman, more so than anyone on the spread, and Print had officially made him ramrod before departing for the northern plains. Jay had taken it hard, sulking for days afterwards, and it was obvious he thought Print hadn't given him a fair shake. Since returning Print could see that close to five months hadn't improved the boy's disposition much, if any. Jay had always been jealous of his older brother in a sneaky sort of way, but now he had turned into a backbiting little scorpion. The knowledge hurt Print, but there wasn't a hell of a lot he could do about it. He had a spread to run, and brother or no brother, he couldn't afford to play favorites.

Whitehead worked his jaws and squirted a fence post with a shot of tobacco juice. What he thought about Jay he kept to himself. Print had asked him a question and it had nothing to do with wet-nursing kid brothers. "Boss, I reckon the crew's a little skittish, but they're game. You've treated 'em square, and they ain't likely to forget."

Still thinking about Jay's snotty attitude, Print jerked the latigo taut as a bow string. The gelding grunted with surprise, then rolled his eyes and farted in outrage. Print suddenly felt disgusted with himself for taking it out on the horse and he didn't look around. "Much obliged, Ace. I'll see you on Yegua Creek."

Whitehead rode off and moments later the three scouting parties loped out of the compound, headed north. Print mounted and turned the gelding west along the creek, trailed closely by Bob and then Ira. Jim Kelly brought up the rear, whistling softly to himself as he calculated the odds on burning a little powder. The more he thought about it, the better the chances seemed, and his pearly teeth glinted wickedly in the hazy dawn. *The boss man had finally got his craw full, and high time, too!*

While the black wrangler's thoughts had only to do with rustlers, he wasn't far wide of the mark on a whole slew of things. Print was discovering that being head of the family wasn't any snap. The responsibility was constant, unrelenting, and lately the load had begun to appear formidable indeed. The physical operation of the ranch, organizing trail drives, even matching wits with rustlers—these things weren't so bad. Jim Oliver had raised him from boyhood to assume such responsibilities, and it was as much a part of him as his smoky temper. Moreover, he enjoyed working with cows, secretly admired the wild streak peculiar to the longhorn breed. He was what he had always wanted to be—a cattleman—and he wouldn't have traded places with anyone on earth.

But being head of the family didn't stop there, and that was what had lodged in his craw like a tiny fishbone. The constant bickering with his mother. Jay's petty jealousy. Catching hell because he had put Bob on the road to being a man. On and on it went, with no end in sight. Now Ira had married one of the simpleminded Morrow girls, which just meant more people and more responsibility. The thought reminded him that Jay was also the father of a son, born only a month after the last drive had started.

Suddenly it came over him that the ranch compound would soon become a swarming anthill of squalling babies and sour-tempered women—all named Oliver. With every last damn' soul looking to him to feed them, clothe them, and rule with the wisdom of Solomon in arbitrating their dizzy squabbles. He could see it coming, just as sure as snow fell and shit stank. Small wonder that the old man had crawled in his shell and passed the deal.

The way things were shaping up he might turn out to be the smartest coon on the whole goddamn' place.

Ira and Bob had learned the hard way that Print was best left alone when he was in one of his sulky moods. Once they reached a point midway along Yegua Creek, the boys and Jim Kelly very wisely kept to themselves. Print wandered off a ways and sat with his back against a tree, looking sort of like he had lost his last friend in the world. There he remained for the rest of the morning and on into early afternoon, absorbed in thoughts that had little to do with cows. Rustled or otherwise.

Shortly after the sun had passed directly overhead, Bob decided enough was enough and started over to have a try at joshing Print out of his foul temper. But just as he was about to open his mouth a string of gunshots drifted in from the northwest. Instantly all four men were on their feet, counting. When the last echo died away they ran for their horses. Seven shots meant that somebody had ridden to the top of a hogback and very deliberately emptied a Spencer carbine. That in turn could mean only one thing. Ace Whitehead was close on the heels of someone who was driving cattle toward the creek.

Ten minutes later Print skidded the gelding to a halt along the treeline bordering the stream. Kelly and the boys reined in beside him and saw immediately why he had stopped. Three riders were coming hell for leather across a wide meadow and they kept peering back over their shoulders like Old Scratch himself was on their tails. Print ordered the others to fan out along the treeline and follow his lead. But there was to be no shooting unless he started it. He wanted these birds alive and kicking.

When everyone was in position Print nudged the gelding out of the trees and rode forward at a walk. Out of the corner of his eye he could see that Kelly and the boys were on line with him and holding their horses on a tight rein. Directly ahead the three riders spotted them and slammed to a halt. For a moment they just sat there, staring bug-eyed as they tried to decide what to do. Then they started forward again. They didn't know for sure what was behind them, but it figured to be a lot more men than they saw dead ahead. This late in the game a man couldn't do any more than play the odds, which was exactly what they did.

When they were within thirty yards Print reined in and held up his hand. "That's far enough, gents. The trail stops here."

One of the riders smiled nervously and rode a bit closer. "Mr. Oliver, you know me. Dave Fream. We don't know who you're after, but it ain't us. We was just ridin' through from up Little River way. Ain't no harm in that, now is there?"

Print's eyes flicked over the other two, then settled back on Fream. "Dave, I'm sorry you've taken to keepin' bad company. Maybe it's just as well your daddy didn't live to see it. Now you boys just be real careful with your hands and start shuckin' them gunbelts."

"Whoa back, Mr. Oliver," Fream said hotly. "We ain't done nothin' wrong. Why should we hand over our guns?"

" 'Cause if you don't, Dave, I'm gonna shoot you right out of that saddle. Now do like I told you and be quick about it."

"Mr. Oliver, that don't hardly seem fair." Fream darted a glance back at his partners and they began edging their horses off to either side. "You're talkin' like we rustled your cattle, or somethin'. Hell, all you got to do is look and you can see we ain't drivin' no cows. Yours or anybody elses."

Print shrugged, noting that Kelly and the boys had the other men blocked off. "Dave, I'll tell you once more to drop that gun. Then I'm gonna kill you."

"What if I do drop it? What then?"

"Why, I reckon we'll set down and have ourselves a little talk."

"What you mean is, we'll talk some and then you'll hang us."

"You said it, Dave. I didn't." Print jerked his head back across the meadow. "Depends on whether my boys find any cows in those woods."

"Well damnation, Mr. Oliver. You've known me all your life. You know I wouldn't do——" Fream's hand suddenly snaked to his side and came up with a pistol.

Print cursed himself for a fool and clawed at his Colt. But even as he cleared leather, Fream's gun spouted flame and a sledgehammer blow took him full in the chest. He grabbed the saddle horn and fell forward, bringing the Colt to bear even as he was hit. The six-gun cracked and a red dot appeared on Fream's shirt front. Reeling in his saddle, the young cattleman thumbed off a second shot and saw the rustler's throat blown away in a frothy scarlet spray.

Distantly, as if through a grime streaked window, he saw Bob with a smoking gun in his hand and heard his wild, triumphant laugh. Somehow he knew without looking that the boy had killed his first man, and in some vague way which he couldn't quite grasp, the thought saddened him. Movement caught his eye before he could sort it all out and he turned his head to observe Jim Kelly in pursuit of the third rustler. The black wrangler had his pistol out and was closing quickly for a killing shot.

Then blinding streamers of light flashed before Print's eyes, and for the first time he became aware of something wet and sticky oozing down over his saddle. He clutched for the pommel but his hand seemed frozen in a clawlike vise and as though dreaming he saw the Colt fall from his stiffened fingers. Slowly he toppled from the saddle, somehow floating gently in a suspended fragment of motion and space. When he struck the ground there was no pain, no feeling at all, just a heady sensation of lightness and freedom. But it seemed desperately important that he remember something he had just seen——something that was trying to elude him in the swirling lights.

Suddenly he saw it again in an instant of vivid clarity. It was Ira. Poor Ira. Looking on in horror at the killing, unable even to draw his gun.

Then a cold darkness settled over him, and there was nothing.

5

The fire cast golden tongues of light across the living room, tracing shadowy, formless images along the walls. A single lamp sputtered dimly, and its cider-glow lent a soft warmth to an otherwise tomblike quiet. Louisa was seated before the fireplace near the old man, rocking gently back and forth with the baby cradled in her arms. The boys and their wives were scattered about the room, watching, waiting, saying nothing. For the last hour no one had spoken, and the only sound was the faint jangle of Bob's spurs as he restlessly prowled the house.

Watching his youngest son, Jim Oliver was reminded of a caged bear mindlessly pacing itself into exhaustion. The boy had taken it hard, perhaps harder than anyone except Louisa. Somehow he had drummed up the notion that he was to blame—that he could have prevented it had he kept his eyes on Dave Fream instead of going for the other rustler. His rage had been stoked even higher by Ira's witless performance. When the youngster discovered that Ira had never drawn his gun, much less fired a shot, it had taken both Ace Whitehead and Jim Kelly to restrain him. Even now he couldn't look at Ira, who was huddled in a corner shivering with shame and self-loathing.

But if Ira's behavior left the family revolted and bitter, Louisa had shown mettle enough for a dozen men. Instead of screaming and going off into crazed hysterics as most women would have done, she had crawled from her bed and come straightaway to the living room. There, rocking the baby to keep him quiet, she had endured the ungodly waiting without a sound. Though tears streaked her face, she had kept a tight grip on herself, never once uttering even the smallest cry. Staring into the fire with glazed eyes, she willed God to watch over her man, and for the past hour her only thought had been an endless repetition of the Lord's Prayer.

While Jim Oliver wasn't much for praying he could see her lips moving silently, and it somehow brought a soggy lump to his throat. Beneath the sorrow that clutched at his own heart he found himself overcome with love for this tall, spirited girl. His eldest son had done them all proud by bringing her to live among the Olivers.

The kitchen door opened and the creaking of Louisa's rocker suddenly stopped. Everyone in the room froze, watching breathlessly as Julia Oliver and Dr. Clement Doak emerged from the kitchen. The physician gently closed the door and turned to face them. His shirt front was splattered with blood and as he followed Julia into the living room they could see that his face was grim as death warmed over. Halting beside Jim Oliver's chair, he spoke to the family as a whole, but his eyes never for a moment left Louisa's pale, drawn features.

"We got the bullet, but he's lost a lot of blood. If he can make it through the night, he has a chance." Then he paused, trying to think of something to add. He had faced many families under similar circumstances and they were rarely satisfied with a bare recitation of clinical facts. "Fortunately he was shot with a .36 caliber gun. I've taken those little slugs out of many men still living today. Don't give up hope. He is strong and he's fighting hard."

There was a moment of chilled silence, then Louisa rose and faced him directly. "Doctor, you don't have to hold anything back on my account. I'll ask you straight out. Will——is Print going to die?"

Clement Doak had been a physician for twenty years. He was a short, dumpy man with a pencil-thin mustache and an unstinting belief in his own skills. But he had long since lost all faith in the power of miracles. Men lived or died for a variety of reasons, none of which had anything to do with God. Not even remotely. The man lying on the kitchen table at this moment had a fair chance to pull through. Just that, nothing more. Had he not been carried so far on horseback, or had this house been closer to his office in Georgetown, Print's chances would have improved greatly. Still, that was neither here nor there. The fact was that come morning he would either be dead or on his way to recovery. What he said to this girl now meant absolutely nothing, and for that reason he decided to be less than truthful.

"Young lady, if I know Print Oliver he won't give up the ghost that easily. He is a man with a strong will to live, and I just suspect he'll pull it off." He saw the strain wash out of her face and he smiled reassuringly. "In any event, I'll spend the night. He's resting easy, but we can't move him before morning. I've dosed him with laudanum and I doubt he'll awaken much before then anyway."

Louisa just stared at him for a moment, then she crossed the room and handed the baby to Elmira, Jay's wife. Turning, she came back and stopped in front of Julia. "Mother Oliver, I want to see Print."

Without a word Julia spun on her heel and led the way

toward the kitchen. When they came through the door Louisa halted and a small gasp escaped her lips, but she held onto herself with iron will. Print was stretched out on the long oaken table, covered from toe to chin with a downy comforter. His face was chalky, drained of its tawny color, and his labored breathing reminded Louisa of a lung-shot buck she had once stumbled across in the woods. Somehow the pallor of his skin frightened her more than anything else. But as she moved closer she saw that he was resting comfortably. The expression on his face was composed, almost peaceful and it was clear that the doctor had given him enough opiate to fell a horse. Yet Louisa had the eerie, crawly feeling that she was standing in a mortuary——that she had come one last time to view the remains of all she held dear in life.

She touched his face and found it cool, but she couldn't remember whether that was good or bad. She had never seen a man die before, yet she vaguely recalled hearing that a fever was the dread sign. Looking up, her courage faltered and for the first time her voice went shaky. "Is he dying, Mother Oliver?"

"Hush, girl. You heard what Doc said. Prentice will outlive us all. Now you just set your fears aside and trust in God."

Julia Oliver's eyes were hollow, darkened pits, and the desolation written across her face belied the conviction of her words. The ordeal of the last few hours had taken its toll, and Louisa sensed that this flinty, resolute woman was struggling against the anguish of watching her first-born fight for life itself.

"Do you think God really hears our prayers?" she said, gazing again upon her husband's pallid, waxlike features. "There must be thousands and thousands of people dying right at this moment, and every one of them begging for mercy. Why would He stop to listen to us?"

Julia wiped her brow and tried to remember why. There was a slight tremor in her hand as she searched for the reason why He always heard. Something she had read in the

Good Book, long ago. Then, as if in answer to a lifetime of unquestioning faith, it came to her. "Are not five sparrows sold for two farthings, and not one of them is forgotten before God?"

Louisa's head snapped around and huge tears welled up in her eyes. "Oh, Mother Oliver, I wish I could believe that. Truly believe. Ever since they carried him in I've been sitting in front of that fire praying that God be merciful. But in my heart I couldn't believe—not truly—that the Lord would trouble Himself with someone who purposely rides out to kill other men. That's a terrible thing to say, I know. But I can't help thinking it, even if I do love him better than life itself."

The old woman looked down upon her son and a curious warmth came over her face. "We all love him, Louisa. But we can't change him. There's too much of my flesh in Prentice for him to be anything other than what he is. He's not a godly man, but in his own way he listens to the Lord." Then she glanced up and the rocky stoicism again covered her features. "Perhaps we wouldn't like the man he became even if we could change him."

The girl stared at her for a long while, as if seeing her for the first time. At last, a fleeting smile played over the corners of her mouth. "Underneath all that starch, you're an old softie. But don't worry, I won't give away your secret. Now why don't you go get some rest. You must be worn to a frazzle after helping Doc operate." Louisa shook her head in wonder. "I don't know how you did it. I'd have been scared to death."

"You won't be. Not when the time comes." Julia Oliver put an arm around her shoulders and guided her toward the door. "You run along and take care of my grandson. We've got to make sure he grows up big and strong like his daddy. Doc will spell me till you get the baby down for the night. Then you come on back and we'll talk some more."

Louisa smiled knowingly and bobbed her head. Then, with one last glance at Print, she opened the door and went out. When it closed behind her the old woman walked back to the table and stood over her son. She gently stroked his dark hair, tucking each wayward strand in place as she had done so often when he was a boy. After a moment she blinked and a lone tear rolled down over her cheek.

"A wise son maketh a glad father: but a foolish son is the heaviness of his mother." Then her lip quivered and she bent forward, kissing him on the brow. "My reckless little man. Where will it end?"

CHAPTER FIVE

1

Print put the bay into a gallop for the last mile. Though late February, the ground was still frozen and the gelding's hooves made a sharp clicking sound on the crusted trail. Leaning into the crisp bite of the wind, he feathered the horse's flanks with his spurs, urging him to stretch out. Beneath his legs he felt the gelding respond with a surge of power, slamming his rump back against the cantle. While he had been forking horses for more than twenty years the young cattleman never ceased to wonder at the raw, animal vitality of this spirited bay. There were times over the past year when he felt like a man saddled to a roaring twister, and anyone who had seen the gelding in action hardly needed to ask why Print had named him Cyclone.

Jim Kelly had bought the gelding for ten dollars at an auction in Austin. The auctioneer had freely admitted that the horse was a killer, with a reputation for pulverizing riders, saddles, and anything else that got within range. But the black wrangler had an instinct for horseflesh that rarely failed him. Some inner hunch told him that no one had ever explained things to this fire-eater in just the right way, and his miserly bid had gone unchallenged.

Besides, his boss man was just then beginning to hobble around the place again, and Kelly had had a feeling that this four-footed whirlwind was just the tonic he needed.

On looks alone, the gelding was enough to set a man's pulse to hammering. Bigger than regular cow ponies, he was a magnificent barrel-chested animal standing fifteen hands high, and topping a thousand pounds by a goodly margin. But it was his color that set him apart from other horses. Blood bay, with a black mane and tail, his hide glistened in the sun like dark blood on polished redwood. He had a strong, wide brow, fiery eyes that glowed like coals, and a temper just short of a boar grizzly on loco weed. Not that he was unfriendly, or particularly enjoyed stomping on things. He just didn't like people. Especially those who tried to climb on his back.

Kelly had an idea the bay had been running a sandy on folks ever since he was big enough to saddle. Probably never in his life been topped off by someone with real horse sense. Though the wrangler disdained the use of a spade-bit, he did fit the gelding with a hackamore, then spent the next week riding him into a puddle of sweat. Day after day the horse sunfished, rolled backwards, banged full tilt into corral fences, acted in general like he was willing to commit suicide so he could commit murder. He was big, stout, and ornery, with a neck so thick and stiff it could hardly be bent with a block and tackle. But he had never crossed trails with anyone quite like Jim Kelly. The black wrangler took root in the saddle and refused to budge, almost as though horse and man had been transformed into a dusky onyx centaur. Morning and afternoon for a week running, Kelly took everything the bay had to offer and rode him straight into the ground.

When it was over the gelding still didn't care much for people, but he had gained a whole new outlook on life. The black man had convinced him that acting the part of an outlaw had its drawbacks, and being smart as well as ornery, he decided to call a truce. When Kelly had turned him over to Print, the bay behaved like a little gentleman, confining his tantrums thereafter to a few civilized crowhops on cold mornings.

Now, returning from a business trip to Austin, Print found himself again amazed at the gelding's remarkable stamina. The brute was seemingly inexhaustible. They had covered close to sixty miles today and still he was ready to gallop clean into the next county. Cyclone thundered out of the woods and halfway across the compound before Print skidded him to a halt. Tossing the reins to a hand, with orders to cool the gelding before feeding him, the young cattleman strode off toward the main house at a fast clip.

Dusk had settled over the hill country only moments before, and as he barged through the door the family was just preparing to sit down to supper. Marching straight to the table, he pulled a leaflet from his coat pocket and waved it in their faces.

"Hey, quit stuffin' your mouths and take a look at this." Grinning broadly, he walked around the table with the leaflet held high. "It says come spring we're trailin' a herd to Kansas."

Everyone suddenly stopped eating and started talking. Print listened to the clamor for a moment, still smiling like a possum, then held up his hand. "All right! Let me get a word in edgewise." When they fell silent he tapped the leaflet with his finger. "This here was put out by a man named McCoy. He's built a town in Kansas called Abilene and the railroad's already there. Ready and waitin'. This McCoy has got agents all over Texas tellin' cattlemen to bring their herds to his town. Every cattle buyer in the north will be there, payin' cash on the spot. All we've got to do is deliver the cows. They even gave up a map through the Nations. Accordin' to this McCoy, some fella named Chisholm laid out a trail that starts just north of the Red. By damn, I told you the railroad was comin' west! Remember?"

The expressions around the table were a grab-bag of conflicting emotions. Jim Oliver nodded thoughtfully and went back to work on his beefsteak. Julia and Louisa exchanged worried frowns, saying nothing. Bob didn't say anything, but his mind was furiously mulling arguments that would get him included in the drive. Jay smiled in a sour sort of way, like he had just finished a bowl of green persimmons. Then, when nobody else spoke up, he couldn't resist a chance to show-off.

"Appears to me you're tradin' a bird in the hand for two in the bush. We've done all right trailin' up to Colorado and the forts. Why quit a sure thing?"

Print had asked himself that same question on the ride home from Austin. They had done well on the high plains, there was no disputing that. Last spring's drive had been more profitable than the one the year before, even without him along. The chest wound he received in the fall of '67 had been slow in healing, and to complicate matters further, he had contracted pneumonia that winter. When spring rolled around he had been as weak as a kitten and it was on into summer before he fully regained his strength. But Ace White-head had trailed the herd north just like he had been doing it all his life, and came back with a barrelful of double eagles. Jay had gone along as *segundo*, and Whitehead later reported that he had been a great deal of help on the drive. That trip had made Jay a self-appointed authority on cattle drives, which was why he had no hesitation in questioning this latest plan. Still, Print had to admit he had a point. Kansas could be a complete washout, a disastrous one if everything in McCoy's handbill weren't true.

On the other hand—if he had things figured right—a third drive to the high plains could prove even riskier.

"Bubba, you could be right as rain," Print conceded. "But the way things shape up it's sorta the lesser of two evils. I suspect there's gonna be lots of outfits trailin' to the high plains this spring. Likely they heard it's good money and they'll try to cash in. Which means prices'll drop fast."

Jay had mellowed some with time, but he still resented Print having the final say. "Maybe. But you're just guessin'. Prices might be even worse in Kansas."

"Might be. Course, with a town full of cattle buyers I've got an idea a fella could play 'em off against one another and come out smellin' good. Up north it's gonna be a matter of whoever gets there first. The second man is liable to end up givin' his cows away."

"Yeah, but you're bankin' everything on a handbill put out by some jasper we never heard of. For all we know, he's just another Yankee sharper waitin' to cheat you blind."

Print curbed his impatience, hoping to resolve the matter without any fireworks. "Whichever trail we take, it's a gamble, Bubba. Has been, right from the start. I'm just trying to calculate the one with the best odds. Besides, the Injuns up north have been gettin' more hostile every year, and I've got a hunch it's gonna get real fierce this summer."

"Jumpin' Jehosophat!" Jay snorted. "You talk like there weren't no Injuns between here and Kansas. Have you forgot why they call it the Nations?"

"No, little brother, and I don't need you to tell me." Print tossed his hat in a corner and sat down beside Louisa. Damned if Jay didn't have a way of getting under his skin without even half trying. "But I'll tell you something there's no argument on. Kansas is near two hundred miles closer to home. Which means going and coming, we'll spend about a month less lookin' over our shoulders. Savvy?"

While Jay was trying to think of a snappy comeback their mother broke in. "Prentice, have you made up your mind that Kansas is the best place?"

"Yes'm, I have." He started filling his plate as Louisa passed him the serving dishes. "Thought it all out ridin' home and I figure this fella McCoy and his new town is our best bet."

"Then it's settled." Julia looked down her nose at Jay, just in case he hadn't gotten the message. "Let's have no more argument at the supper table."

Everyone got very quiet for a while and concentrated on

the food. Since the old man had been shoveling it away with both hands while they followed the conversation, it quickly became apparent that someone was going to leave the table hungry. During the lull, Louisa gave Print a sly squeeze on the thigh and shot him an amused side glance. Though she never entered into these family donnybrooks, she found them a constant source of humor—a fact which her husband had never fully been able to appreciate.

Bob hadn't missed a stroke with his fork the whole time, but his eyes were riveted on Print. Finally he couldn't hold back any longer. "You know, Print, I been thinkin'. This season it oughta be my turn to go up the trail. Jay and Ira've already gone and that sorta makes me next in line."

Print stifled a smile and kept right on eating. "Got it all tallied up, have you, sport?"

"Dang it all, I'm ready, Print." The boy glowered back at him like a stuffed chickenhawk. "I'm doing a man's work around here, and I don't hear you or Ace complainin' none. I figure it's time I had a little of the fun."

"Fun!" Print almost choked on a wad of mashed potatoes. "Boy, you've got a lot to learn. Trailin' a herd of cows six hundred miles ain't exactly my idea of a good time."

Bob opened his mouth to reply, but Julia cut him off. "We'll hear no more of such talk. Robert, you are still too young for trail work. Just put those thoughts out of your head and eat your supper."

"Aw, Ma, you haven't got no call——"

"Robert!" Julia gave him a stony look.

"Yes'm." The boy ducked his head, mortified at being treated like a runny-nosed kid.

Print took a last sip of coffee and cleared his throat, fixing the old woman with a level gaze. "Ma, I don't like to go against you, but the truth is, I'd been plannin' all winter to take Bob along."

Julia carefully laid her fork in her plate and met his eyes. "I don't want him to go yet. He is too young for such blasphemies. Don't look so surprised, Prentice. I know what goes on in those towns."

Louisa shot him a puzzled little glance and he knew he had a tall job of explaining ahead of him later to night. "That's neither here nor there, Ma. Bob's going on nineteen, and like he said, he does a man's work. It's time he saw the elephant. You know, he's not a baby anymore. The way he saved my bacon in that shootout oughta prove——"

"Prentice, I won't have that affair discussed at my table." Julia fully realized that the boy had been forced to shoot that day, but she had never quite forgiven Print for teaching him to kill while still so young. "If you must take him, then do so. But be very careful you don't let those heathens in the bunkhouse corrupt him. Do you understand me?"

Print certainly did, and from the way Louisa's eyes narrowed it was pretty damn' certain she got the drift, too. Which left him toe to toe with how a man went about explaining cowtowns to his wife. Then he glanced over at Bob and that was forgotten for the moment. The boy's eyes were shiny bright, and clearly it was all he could do to keep from howling with sheer delight.

Damn' right, Print repeated to himself, it's high time he saw the elephant. A kid's only young once, and not for very long at that.

2

They pulled up before the Red in early May. After close to a month on the trail the hands were just getting their second wind, and as Print sat watching the turbulent waters he decided they were going to need it. The river was running fast, so foamy and full of silt that it looked like a man could walk on it. But twenty-five hundred longhorns sure as hell couldn't, and the next few hours promised to be a dicey proposition at best. For a moment he considered holding the herd south of the Red until morning, then just as quickly chucked the thought. Spring rains might keep the river cresting for another week, and he didn't have any time to spare.

They would cross now.

Reining about, he jerked his hat and signaled the point riders to come ahead. Within moments they had the lead steers strung out and walking briskly, moving the herd toward the river in a pie shaped wedge. The swing and flank riders moved in from the sides, hazing the longhorns into a narrow file as they approached closer to the south bank. Print drove his bay gelding into the swift current only moments ahead of the lead steers, letting the horse have his head as he struck out for the opposite shore. The point riders began yelling and popping their lariats, driving the longhorns into the water before they had time to mill and form a bottleneck. The hands riding swing and flank kept the herd moving steadily forward, crowding those in front into the river with constant pressure from the bawling, wild-eyed steers just behind. The drag riders held their positions at the rear of the herd, gradually easing more cattle into the funnel, so that the steady stream of longhorns never ceased.

Toward sundown the last of the herd scrambled ashore on the north bank, with Jim Kelly and his *remuda* hot on their tails. All things considered, it hadn't been a bad crossing. They had lost twelve steers, one horse, and no riders. Casting one last look out over the roiling waters, Print was struck by the thought that they had come off damn' cheap. The Red was a fickle old bitch, and it could have treated them a hell of a lot worse. Waving to Bob, who was riding drag, he roweled the bay lightly and headed forward. While they still had a month or more ahead of them—not to mention Indians and another half-dozen river crossings—their luck was running strong so far. Still, Print was just as superstitious as the next gambler—he didn't believe in counting his chips before the last card was dealt.

With Doughbelly Ketchum piloting the chuck wagon and twelve hands hazing the longhorns, Print had turned north from Yegua Creek in late April. He had learned much about the ways of cows since that first drive to Galveston four years past, and he ordered the herd be pushed along at a brisk pace. Before nightfall they had covered twenty-eight miles, and the longhorns were so worn out they could barely stay awake to graze, much less harbor thoughts of returning to their home range. Thereafter they had held the drive to an outside of fifteen miles a day, with Print blazing trail and the two most experienced hands, Bumpus Moore and Harry Strain, riding point. Much to his disgust, Bob had been assigned to eat dust riding drag. But his older brother played no favorites, at home or on a drive. Shorthorns always got the dirty jobs their first time up the trail. Just because the youngster's name was Oliver made him no different in Print's eyes.

Only more so.

In the days that followed Bob had come to understand why anyone but a slick-eared kid would never consider trail driving a sporting diversion. Work began early and ended late with Print ramrodding the show. The hands saddled by starlight each morning when the air was still crimpy and their ponies were full of snorts and meanness. Once they got the herd strung out and moving, the steers were allowed to graze along for three or four miles in a northerly direction. Then they were hazed steadily until noon, or until Print found a good grazing spot for a midday break. Doughbelly and his chuck wagon were generally close by so that the men could wolf down a cold bait of beef and biscuits.

Sometimes they went from dark to dark with nothing in their bellies but loud rumblings.

Whether fed or left to go hungry, the noonday halt seldom gave a man time for any rest. When the steers started lying down to chew their cuds Print knew they had grazed long enough, and gave the signal to resume the drive. Riding on ahead, he then scouted out a likely place with graze and water to halt for the night. Toward sundown the hands drove the herd onto the bed-ground, and if everything went without a hitch, they were usually unsaddled and scrubbed for supper by dark. Yet their work day was far from over.

Every hand, old or young, rode night guard in four-hour

shifts. As the old timers were fond of noting, longhorns were temperamental beasts, easily offended. Without someone to keep them company during the long, lonely night they might take a vote and decide to stampede clean out of the country. Just for the hell of it.

But when a man had already spent fourteen hours in the saddle since morning, he could get real droopy riding night guard. Some of the hands had a home remedy called rouser—a dab of tobacco juice under the eyelid. Which was a sure-fire cure for drowsiness, among other ailments. Bob Oliver only had to try rouser once—the memory alone was adequate to keep him awake for the rest of the drive.

Still in all, the hands did get their sleep, sometimes as much as three or four hours a night. Then, as it seemed that a man had just closed his eyes, Doughbelly would rout them out of their soogans and start serving pork 'n beans and six-shooter coffee. This latter appellation derived from the fact that Doughbelly's coffee was thick enough to float anything from a loaded six-gun to a small cannonball. With their ribs firmly glued in place, the hands barely had time to stow their bed-rolls in the chuck wagon before Jim Kelly drove the *remuda* in for saddling. The work day had begun again.

Though the work of horse wrangler was generally considered beneath a dyed-in-the-wool cowhand, few men made light of the job done by Jim Kelly. Each man in the outfit had four horses in his string, which meant that the black wrangler and his nighthawk had the full time chore of shepherding close to sixty snake-eyed ponies. While the *remuda* consisted solely of geldings, Kelly had brought along a bell-mare. Should the horses get scattered in a stampede, or otherwise wander off, the Sunburst crew would have been out of business. But so long as they could hear the mare's bell, there was little fear of the ponies straying. Gelded they might be, but dead they weren't, and even an old crowbait mare could still arouse their crippled instincts.

Now, with the crossing of the Red behind them and the herd bedded down for the night, the hands returned their horses to Jim Kelly's watchful eye and began gathering in Doughbelly's savory little domain. According to some, the area immediately surrounding the chuck wagon was nothing less than a kingdom, ruled over by a crotchety, turd-faced old tyrant.

But they were very careful never to say it within hearing distance of Doughbelly Ketchum.

Like most cow outfit cooks, the head pot-walloper of Sunburst considered himself one of the anointed few, answerable only to God and the ramrod. Even the latter walked on eggshells around the chuck wagon. Cooks were a capricious breed, and more than one drive had been brought to a standstill because some crusty old curmudgeon had gone on strike with a case of hurt feelings.

Doughbelly had certain rules for those who frequented his picnic grounds, and woe be to the hands' stomachs if anybody stepped out of line. First, he had to be supplied with grub, wood and water. Without those essentials the cooking just didn't get done. Next, there was to be no wash water dumped around the chuck wagon or tobacco juice expectorated into the cook fire. These were absolutes, never to be profaned, and the offender would likely as not find himself slowly starving on meager rations. Lastly, and this was the cardinal rule, there was to be no jabberwocky about the quality of the cooking. Them that didn't like it didn't have to eat it, but they were forewarned to keep their traps shut. Otherwise Doughbelly's Revenge—in the form of running trots—would be visited on the entire crew. For men who spent their lives in the saddle, this represented the ultimate threat. Doughbelly was king around the chuck wagon, and for the common good of all, his dictates were followed to the letter.

Yet, hard as it was to keep from bending the rules, there were certain advantages to the arrangement. Namely, the scrumptious meals Doughbelly could whip up if the mood struck him. Perhaps because his beloved chuck wagon had made it safely across the Red, he was in fine fettle this particular night. When the hands lined up with their tin plates they found themselves presented with a princely feast.

Son-of-a-bitch stew, which consisted of loins, sweetbreads, liver and heart simmered in a spicy gravy. Spotted Pup, a racy combination of rice, raisins, and brown sugar. Stewed canned tomatoes with generous chunks of salt pork added. Sourdough biscuits and molasses. Dried apple pie sprinkled with cinnamon. And that old standby, without which no feast was ever truly complete, six-shooter coffee.

Doughbelly had outdone himself, and the hands dug in with an assortment of grunts, slurps, and appreciative belches. After some minutes had passed without a word being spoken, Bumpus Moore loosened his belt and leaned back against his saddle. Fumbling around in his war bag, he pulled out a stick of Pigtail and some corn shuck papers and started building himself a smoke. Once he had the cigarette going to his satisfaction, he looked up with a wide smile. "Doughbelly, I have to hand it to you. You're nothin' but a natural born wizard. Never thought I'd see the day a man could put out that kind o' meal with a couple of pots and a Dutch oven."

Print and the rest of the crew got very alert all of a sudden. Bumpus Moore and his sidekick, Harry Strain, had a running battle of wits going with Doughbelly. The trick was to needle him without insulting him. Particularly on his sore point, the cardinal rule about never harassing the cook. In a sense the two men were toying with the gastronomic fate of the entire crew, but it was such a fascinating game that no one had the heart to call them off. Sort of like watching a couple of fellows play tag with a real live tarantula.

Doughbelly just grunted, ignoring Moore's comment, and went back to banging his pots.

Harry Strain waited a minute, then held a sourdough biscuit to the firelight and studied it carefully. "Yessir, Bumpus, you couldn't be righter. Now you take them biscuits. They're burnt on the bottom, raw in the middle, and salty as hell."

Doughbelly's pot clanging suddenly stopped and he straightened up, nailing the cowhand with the withering scowl.

Strain popped the biscuit in his mouth and began munching like a gopher. "But they're shore fine, just the way I like 'em."

Doughbelly glared at him a moment longer, then returned to his pots with a derisive snort. Jim Kelly rode in just then and dismounted. Wranglers always ate first or last, depending on the time of day, and right now the crew actually appeared relieved to see the black man. They were still snickering to themselves about Strain's little joke, but they had been amused enough for one night. Nobody wanted to see Doughbelly on the prod, and another zinger like that would just about do the trick.

Print lighted a cigar and waited for the wrangler to get himself seated across the fire. "Jim, looks like we might be gettin' some weather tonight. Take care your horses don't get spooked off."

Kelly chuckled around a mouthful of Spotted Pup. "Boss, don't you worry none 'bout them hosses. They ain't like cows. They's like people."

"People?" Moore raised up and gave him a quizzical look. "Jim, just how the hell you figure hosses are like people?"

"Why, that's easy, Bumpus," the black man replied. "Hosses ain't afraid of big things, like thunder and lightnin'. Maybe it riles 'em up, but they ain't afraid. What spooks 'em is what they ain't expectin'. Could be some little somethin', like a twig fallin', or a field mouse comin' at 'em through the grass. Ghosty kinda things. Quiet and scary. Same things that scares people."

Jim Kelly's favorite sport was telling big windies, and it was often difficult to separate the whoppers from the real article. The men crowded around the fire watched him closely for any telltale sign that he was joshing. After a moment, Lee Wells, one of the older hands and a noted liar in his own right, spoke up.

"Jim, these boys mightn't read your sign, but I hear you talkin'. Puts me in mind of brandin' time once up in Young County. I was chasin' one of them wild she-critters plumb back to breakfast when all of a sudden a big grizzle bear jumps out from behind the bush. Well sir, I'd no sooner'n whipped out my hogleg when this hammerhead I'm ridin' goes off in four directions at once. When I picked myself up I'd lost my hat, shot off my boot heel, and dropped my pistol. Now don't you know I took off runnin' like greased lightnin'. But boys, when I looked back there was that god-damn' wooly bogger up in the saddle, building himself a loop with my rope. And I wanna tell you, he flat knew how to make a cow pony behave."

Wells stopped and stared innocently around the fire, waiting for someone to bite. Finally Bob Oliver couldn't stand it any longer. "Well what happened, Lee? Did he get you?"

"Why shore he got me, son. That grizzle bear dabbed a loop on me pretty as you please, then jumped down and ear-marked me with a double underbit." Wells turned his head and tapped one ear, which had been mangled in a saloon brawl some years earlier. "Been wearin' the Rockin' W's mark ever since."

The crew roared and slapped their legs with great amusement. Even Doughbelly managed a sour sort of grin. But Bob turned red as beet juice, and the best he could pull off was a sheepish little smile.

When the laughter died down, Jim Kelly leaned over and punched Bob on the arm. "Don't let 'em get your goat. There's lots o' things these jaybirds ain't never seen."

The hands quieted now, certain they were about to hear a real whopper, and the black man glided into the story without a pause. "You see this happened before I come west, when I was jest a boy back in Arkansas. Now my pappy was a man for growin' corn. Corn and hogs. Loved one near 'bout as much as he did t'other. But this year I'm talkin' 'bout, he got to noticin' somethin' was natural cleanin' his corn field down to the last ear. And Lordy Mercy, next time he looks round his hogs is disappearin'. But the whole thing's got him bumfuzzled, you understan'? There ain't no sign of anything killin' his hogs and there ain't so much as a shuck down in the corn field. Well now, my pappy starts huntin' sign and he finally spots tracks leadin' off to a patch of woods. He snakes his way back in there and directly he comes on a little clearin'. Sure enough, there was his hogs. Somebody had closed 'em up in a nice rail pen and them hogs was fatter'n butterballs."

Kelly casually started to build a smoke and glanced around the fire. "Now here's the part I wanted you fellers to hear. My pappy'd been sittin' there jest a while when the bushes starts cracklin' and along comes two bears with their arms loaded down with corn. Seems like they'd been watchin' him and learned all there was to know 'bout this business of raisin' hogs. Jest goes to show you, hosses ain't the only critters that acts like people."

The crew grinned and nudged one another with their elbows, but they didn't laugh like before. It struck too close to home, and they got the feeling the black man had made some point they didn't understand. Print exchanged a sly look with Kelly, then climbed to his feet.

"Boys, I reckon we'd better pack it in. The day's long and nights are gettin' shorter all the time."

When the men drifted off toward their soogans, Print stepped around to the front of the chuck wagon. Gazing up at the brilliant sky, he spotted the pointers of the Big Dipper, then lined up the North Star. Bending, he grabbed the wagon tongue and hauled it around until it was pointed due north.

Straightening, he peered again into the starry heavens and smiled. Another day, another dollar, and another mile closer to Abilene.

3

When Cal Nutt walked through the door he sensed that something had changed. Nothing he could put his finger on right away, but it was there nonetheless.

Horace Davidson came around his desk and strode

forward with a wide smile and an outstretched hand. The Attorney General was an affable man, to be sure, yet Nutt had never known him to greet an underling with such warmth and cordiality. The carpetbagger was immediately on guard. Somebody was out to do a job on someone else, and he had the distinct feeling that Mother Nutt's oldest son had been selected as the pigeon.

Davidson ushered him to a chair then took a seat close by instead of returning behind his desk. Nutt's hackles really came up, as he had the eerie feeling he should look over his shoulder. That desk was Davidson's symbol of authority. Seated behind it he could leer, scowl, smile benignly, always keeping the vassals under scrutiny while he manipulated their lives with lordly hauteur. For the scalawag to abandon his throne, seating himself like a common man, was reason enough to be wary. Coming back to back with his oily good humor made it an ominous sign indeed.

"Very good of you to come, Cal." Davidson offered him a cigar, then occupied himself for a moment snipping and lighting his own. "Hope I didn't drag you away from anything pressing."

Nutt took a slow pull on the cigar and mentally braced himself to play the game. "No, nothing that won't keep. Out in the sticks there is always tomorrow, or the day after."

The Attorney General laughed with just a bit too much levity. "Cal, you're a born philosopher. Did you ever read a fellow by the name of Shadwell?" Nutt exhaled a small gray cloud and shook his head. "No? Well you should. He once wrote that the haste of a fool is the slowest thing in the world. Make a man wonder when he sees all the hustle and bustle here in Austin. Greed does strange things to men, Cal. Strange things."

When the carpetbagger remained silent, Davidson smiled and gestured dismissively with his hand. "Well, that's enough deep thinking for one day. Now tell me about yourself. Haven't seen you in months. What's the latest up in Williamson County?"

"Nothing much to tell really," Nutt informed him.

"We've still got a lock on most of the county offices and we control voter registration, so there are no problems to speak of. Other than that, things are pretty much the same."

Nutt saw no need to enlighten him further. The fact that he had consolidated his political base in Williamson County was common knowledge. To what extent, he had no intention of revealing to anyone, including the Attorney General. Davidson was clearly a man who preferred to keep a tight grip on the reins of power; there was nothing to be gained by telling him that a fellow named Cal Nutt now held the whip hand in Georgetown. He would continue to take advantage of the Attorney General's influence in the State House. But in terms of running Williamson County, he could manage that nicely by himself.

Davidson still received his share of all shady deals emanating from Georgetown, and so far as the carpet-bagger was concerned, that was enough. Any schemes Nutt had for feathering his own nest were plainly, and simply, none of the Texan's business.

Not anymore.

Horace Davidson appeared curiously relieved that Nutt's operation remained free of problems. "That's fine, Cal. Real fine. Wish I could say the same for the rest of the state. Unfortunately, not everyone has grown under my tutelage the way you have. Of course, now that I dwell on it, I remember a time just a couple of years back when you gave me a bad moment or two."

Nutt almost laughed. It was the oldest trick in the book. Pat a man on the head, then remind him what a dunce he is. Very blandly, with just the right touch of surprise, he said, "Oh, when was that?"

The politician waved his cigar in a deprecating manner. "Nothing to concern yourself with, Cal. Shouldn't even have brought it up. Matter of fact, I can't even recall the particulars. Something to do with a ranch you had your eye on. My recollection is that I felt our operation up there would be endangered if you persisted in antagonizing this penny-ante rancher."

"Yeah, now that you mention it, I do remember that." The carpetbagger smiled and shook his head, staring off into space. "Seemed real important at the time, but it sort of got lost in the shuffle along the way."

What he neglected to say was that the scheme had never for a moment left his mind. If anything, he was more determined than ever to destroy the Yegua Creek ranchers. The memory of Print Oliver's contemptuous visit to his office was still vivid in his mind, not to mention the fact that the Olivers had killed four of his men. But as he had grown in political power so the Oliver family had grown in wealth, and from his vantage point, one seemed to offset the other. Still, the day of reckoning would come. Sooner than anyone suspected. He had grown smarter as well as more powerful, and he had learned that patience is an ally openly cultivated by the wise. Print Oliver would make *the* big mistake someday, his kind always did. When it happened he would find himself being crunched in a legal nutcracker operated by none other than Mr. Cal Nutt. Then those Seceshers on Yegua Creek would discover that there are all kinds of ways to steal, some of them even perfectly legal.

Nutt's reverie was broken as the Attorney General cleared his throat and shifted uneasily in his chair. The silver-haired Texan had grown more distinguished-looking with time, and right now he was clearly working himself up to something that required all the diplomacy he could muster. Cal Nutt was gripped with the sudden awareness that the old reprobate was suffering from a very skillfully disguised case of the shakes.

Davidson regarded him with a tight smile for a moment, then resumed in an oblique manner. "Cal, there's the smell of change in the air. Whether for good or bad, things seldom remain constant. Over the years it has been my observation that the only certainty in life is the certainty of change. I have a feeling that Texas is approaching just such a period at this very moment."

The square-jawed carpetbagger just nodded and watched

him silently. Whatever the politician was leading up to, it was plainly something with far-reaching effects on their corrupt activities. Otherwise why would Davidson bother with this petty charade of bonhomie and good will? Or go to such lengths to mask his rattled state of mind?

When Nutt held his silence, the old scalawag chose his next words carefully. "Just to be frank about it, I've been holding conferences this week with county organizers from across the state. Men like yourself, who got their start through the auspices of my connections in the State House." He paused for a heartbeat to let the import of his statement sink in. "In the days ahead, Cal, you would do well to bear that thought in mind. Should one falter, we might all be toppled in the storm to follow."

Nutt's curiosity was now aroused, but as he framed a question Davidson held up his hand. "No, let me finish. The reason I called you here was to tell you that Texas will be readmitted to the Union early next year. When that happens the tides could change drastically. Depending on who occupies the State House, we could go on just as we have for the past four years, or we could find ourselves the object of a very messy investigation. Some of the boys plan to pack their bags and quietly disappear with their ill-gotten gains. I thought it only fair to afford you the same opportunity. Personally, I intend to stick it out and see what happens."

Horace Davidson had every reason to view the future with a measure of uncertainty. With military authorities backing their corrupt schemes, carpetbaggers and scalawags had ruled unopposed in Texas since the close of the war. But as the Attorney General had so aptly perceived, change was in the wind. Only last Christmas President Andrew Johnson had proclaimed universal amnesty, thereby liberating hundreds of thousands of former Confederates from the limbo of banishment and disgrace. Yet Davidson's latest piece of intelligence, which was not yet common knowledge, was of far greater significance.

The Texas State Legislature had girded itself to comply

with every demand laid down by Congress in the Recon-struction Act. Once that was accomplished the Lone Star State would again take its place as a full-fledged member of the Union. Military rule would cease to exist—the day of the carpetbagger and scalawag would end forever—and for men like Davidson and Nutt it might well prove a time fraught with great personal danger.

Thinking about it now, Horace Davidson took small con-solation from the fact that Texas was the last state of the Confederacy to bow before the dictates of Washington. The determination of its citizens not to submit had extended military rule in Texas, to be sure. But the demise of an era was fast approaching. Just as every state in the South had done over the past two years, Texas was preparing itself to genuflect meekly before its conqueror. When it did, poli-tics in Austin would become a whole new game. One with a fresh deck of cards, and quite likely, a reformed dealer.

Watching him now, Cal Nutt had to admire the old scoundrel. Win, lose, or draw, he meant to hang around to see how it turned out. After a while Nutt pulled the cigar out of the corner of his mouth and grinned. "Guess I might as well stick, too. Whichever way it falls, I suppose it's just rightly something a man has to see for himself."

Observing the smile that came over Davidson's taut features, he had to restrain himself from laughing out-right. Whatever happened, Cal Nutt had made himself a sanctuary in Williamson County that would see him through any storm. The interesting part in sticking it out would be to watch the expression on Horace Davidson's face when somebody finally got around to stretching his scrawny neck.

4

Print wasn't particularly surprised when the Indians ap-peared. Ever since crossing the herd into Indian territory a fortnight past he had been about half expecting them to show up. Now, as the crew hazed the last of the longhorns across the Salt Fork of the Arkansas, the mounted warriors suddenly materialized as if they had sprung from the earth.

The Indians had their ponies fanned out in line blocking the trail, and for the moment, at least, seemed peaceable enough. By rough count Print made out eighteen warriors, which didn't mean a damn' thing one way or the other. They could have double that number waiting behind the blackjack-studded hills that bordered either side of the trail. Abruptly one of the red men kneed his pony forward a couple of yards and raised his hand overhead, palm outward. The peace sign. Print followed suit and shoved his hand up in the air. But even as he did so it occurred to him that somebody ought to rename it the truce sign.

Where Indians were concerned peace was a sometimes thing.

Still, this was the land of the Five Civilized Tribes and they were supposedly friendly to white men. Or so the desk-bound bureaucrats back in Washington kept telling everybody anyway. Farther west the Kiowa and Comanche made no bones about their hatred of white-eyes, and a fellow at least knew where he stood with them. But this pack of gut-eaters blocking the trail could be anything. Civilized or savage. Maybe even a little of both. One thing was for certain. The rifles they carried looked damn' hostile, even if the head man did have his paw stuck up in the breeze.

Print ordered the crew to hold the herd and yelled for Jim Kelly to come forward. The black man had spent some years on the Llano Estacado chasing mustangs and had a passable knowledge of Indian ways. When Kelly pulled up beside him, Print didn't have to say anything. The situation spoke for itself.

They rode forward, halting their horses some twenty yards in front of the Indians. The black man again signed peace, then stuck his right hand out with the fingers slightly curled and twisted his wrist back and forth.

The head Indian eyed him stonily for a moment, then pointed back at the cattle. Raising both hands in front of his face, with the fingers and thumbs joined, he rotated his hands to the left in a circular motion. Then he extended his left arm and chopped across it with his right hand.

Kelly puzzled over it for a few seconds before turning to Print. "Near as I can make out, this feller's sayin' they wants fifty cents a cow 'fore they'll let us cross their land."

Print didn't have to mull that over at all. Give or take a little, fifty cents a cow came to a neat twelve hundred dollars. "What kinda Injuns are they, Jim?"

"Beats me, boss." The wrangler looked back with a wide grin, slowly studying their dress and equipment as he spoke. "Never saw nothin' like 'em on the Staked Plains. Might be Choctaw or Chickasaw. Even Cherokee. No tellin'. Don't know as it means nothin', but they ain't wearin' war paint."

"You think they've got any friends hid out behind them hills?"

Kelly shook his head, still smiling broadly for the Indians' benefit. "Naw, if they was gonna bushwhack us they'd only sent a couple o' their boys down here. They're tryin' to run a sandy on us by trottin' out the whole bunch."

Print turned in his saddle and saw the hands lined up in front of the herd, each man cradling a Spencer carbine over his arm. Without a trace of emotion, he said, "Jim, tell 'em we won't pay. Tell 'em our men have guns that speak many times, and if they don't haul ass out of here the birds'll be pickin' their bones before sundown. Make it strong."

Kelly's pearly teeth flashed even wider and he turned to the Indians. Some moments passed as his hands darted and chopped, circled and slashed, translating the message with obvious relish.

When he finished there was a heated muttering among the Indians, and some of the warriors brandished their rifles angrily. Then their leader barked a guttural command and they fell silent. Looking back at the black man, he signed again toward the herd, turned both hands palm up, with fingers and thumbs extended, and thrust his hands forward.

Kelly nodded understanding and glanced at Print. "Says he'll take ten cows 'stead of the money."

Print's response was short and sweet. "Tell him no. It's haul ass or fight. His choice."

The wrangler's ebony hands again whirled in the sunlight. When he finished the Indian gazed at him for a moment without expression. Abruptly his face twisted in a sullen scowl. Raising his hands, he spread his fingers wide apart and rapidly jabbed them together in unison. Then he pointed directly at Print, placed his palms together and twisted with a rubbing motion.

Kelly was still smiling, but his eyes looked a bit troubled. "Well, it comes out somethin' like this. He claims this here's their land and we've got a war on our hands if we don't pay up. Says to be sure and tell you that you'll be the first to get rubbed out."

Print's face went grim, but before he could say anything the black man tossed in a final thought. "Mistah Print, 'fore we starts shootin' you best figure some. Even if we kills this bunch there's more of 'em around somewheres, and they'll likely stampede them cows to hell and gone 'fore mornin'. But if you wants to fight, let's do it quick while they ain't primed."

The Texan's dark gaze never left the Indians as he weighed Kelly's words. At last, he gave a great sigh of disgust. "It goes against the grain, but tell him we'll give 'em five cows. No more."

Kelly hands went to work again and Print had the feeling he was talking more than called for. Probably telling them what a bad hombre his boss man was—that they had better take what they could get while the getting was good. Whatever he said, it worked. The leathery-faced head man signaled agreement, and Print called back for the boys to cut out five of the puniest steers. When the longhorns were hazed forward the warriors circled around and drove them off with shrill gobbling whoops.

The Indian leader favored Print and Kelly with an amused look, did a few more tricks with his hands, then spun his pony around and took off after the other braves.

The wrangler chuckled and started building himself a

smoke. "He said to tell you he figures you're too dark to be a white man. That last thing he done, the cut throat sign. That's the sign for Sioux. He said the way you trade you must be a Sioux."

Print had some Cherokee blood in him, true enough, but he didn't like road agents, red or white. While he might have donated his last cow to a hungry Indian, it stuck in his craw to be robbed with such backhanded arrogance. Especially when there wasn't a damn' thing he could do about it.

Still, five cows more or less didn't mean a hill of beans, and they had a good three hours left before dark. Turning, he signaled the hands to get the herd strung out, then kicked the bay into a lope up the trail. Graze and water were what he had to worry about now, but he couldn't resist hoping those red bastards choked on that good Texas beef.

Toward sundown Print found a stretch of prairie along a little creek, and well before darkness closed in the herd had been driven onto the bed ground. When he rode in for supper he noted that the air had turned still and sultry, a bad sign. There hadn't been any clouds to speak of that afternoon, so maybe it was just another spring shower. On the other hand it could just as easily be a storm brewing, and that would mean real trouble. The season for it was fast approaching, and the smell of the warm, fetid air gave him an uneasy feeling down in the pit of his stomach. Plains storms had put the fear of God into more than one cattleman, and he wasn't ashamed to admit that it was the thing he dreaded most on a trail drive.

Jim Kelly rode in about then and squatted down with his plate on the opposite side of the fire. Matter of factly, he mentioned that he had heard an owl hoot earlier in the afternoon. None of the men said anything and Print didn't comment one way or the other. But they all knew what the black man was driving at. There was a widely accepted superstition among cattlemen that the hoot of an owl during daylight meant a bad storm was on the way. Print didn't particularly believe or disbelieve in such things. But he had seen it work out often enough to know that it was more than mere coincidence.

Yet there wasn't a hell of a lot they could do about it even if a storm was headed their way. Print ordered the men to picket their night horses close to camp and told Doughbelly to keep the coffee pot full. Other than that, there was nothing to do but wait and keep an eye peeled on the starless sky.

Along about ten that night, with the herd scattered over the wide prairie, a sudden gust of wind swept through camp. The rush of air came like a slap in the face, and every man in the crew came erect, wide awake in an instant.

No more than a few seconds elapsed before the wind died and a faint breeze drifted over them. The longhorns came to their feet a moment later and turned their heads to the northwest, scenting the gentle current. Suddenly great breaths of hot air stuck like the pounding of a giant fist, buffeting the men back on their heels.

Then a dead calm settled over the prairie and the heat seemed to bear down with crushing force.

Print yelled for the men to get mounted, but even as they climbed aboard their horses the herd started drifting south at a fast walk. Abruptly there came a gust of cool air with the smell of rain and ozone. Then the atmosphere became charged with electricity. It crackled in the men's hair, brought silvery flashes from the rowels on their spurs, and sent sparks of static leaping from their horses' ears.

Suddenly the darkened sky came alive with a blinding flash of light that seemed to turn the whole world blue-white. Then a great dart of lightning flashed from the clouds and struck the ground, gathering itself into a ball of fire as large as a house. It rolled across the prairie like a tumbling sunburst for perhaps a hundred yards, only to disappear in a numbing explosion that shook the very earth.

Even before the clap of thunder sounded, the herd stampeded. The clattering of their horns as they surged together, mixed with the steady drum of hooves and their terrified bellows, sent a quaking tremor across the bed ground. Sparkling balls of fire played across the tips of their horns and as they ran a wave of scorching heat clung in their wake. Bolts of lightning flashed in every direction and the thunderous concussions that followed each streak seemed to freeze the motion of all living things in a brilliant white glow.

The roar of the wind swelled to a deafening pitch, and with it came the rain, tearing and slashing with brutal force as great torrents of water deluged the earth. Men and animals were tossed like corks in an angry sea as the shriek of the wind and the searing sting of the rain buried them in a thunderous, fiery cataract. Along the outskirts of the seething mass of cattle the trailhands quirted their horses savagely, riding in a blind, mindless fury. Barring an act of God Almighty nothing known to man could stop the longhorns from running, and while the storm lasted their only hope lay in somehow keeping the herd in sight.

Six miles and a couple of lifetimes later, the raging torrent that had once been the Salt Fork of the Arkansas brought the steers to a halt. The crew quickly circled them back from the water and forced them to a milling standstill. Behind lay a string of trampled steers, dead and dying, ground into a soggy grave under the hooves of those who had lived.

Cursing God and longhorns alike, Print Oliver reined in overlooking the swirling, muddy waters. They were right back where they had started earlier that afternoon. Where they had been waylaid and robbed. Only in some curious way he no longer begrudged those Indian bucks their five steers.

The return trip had been a hell of a lot more costly, and not nearly so entertaining.

5

Print topped a slight rise and brought his gelding to a halt on the limestone bluffs overlooking the Smoky Hill. Abilene lay on the north side of the river, built on a vast prairie that sloped gradually downward to the military road and the timbered mile-wide Smoky Hill. Print could see a small

creek alongside the town, which emptied into the river, and
off in the distance he spotted three herds being held on
the rolling grasslands. But the thing that caught his eye
was the loading pens adjacent to a railroad siding. He estimated that the pens could hold upwards of three thousand
head, and even then longhorns were being loaded into cattle
cars. The bright June sun beat down mercilessly and from
across the river he could hear the cows bawling in protest
as they were prodded up the chutes.

But it was music to his ears. The music he had ridden
six hundred miles to hear.

Joseph McCoy's handbills hadn't lied. Abilene was
everything he promised. Perhaps even more. It was a cowtown, the first of its kind, built with no other purpose in
mind than to serve as a way station for rangy Texas beef.
Print couldn't have been prouder if he had built the whole
shebang himself.

Backtrailing, he had the crew hold the herd on a grassy
swale just south of the river. The hands could see Abilene
for themselves now, and they started whooping with excitement. They had been on the trail sixty-three days. They
were caked with dust, smelled of cow dung and sweaty
horses, and right at that moment wanted nothing quite so
much as a hot bath. Unless, perhaps, the town had such a
thing as cold beer. Or wicked women.

Print knew just how they felt, but right now it was first
things first. They had come north to sell a herd, and before
any celebration got started, they had best find out the going
rate on Texas steers. Leaving Bumpus Moore in charge, he
forded the Smoky Hill and rode toward Abilene.

The military road brought him directly to a cluster of
buildings along the railroad tracks. The main part of town
was situated just north of the tracks, but he had a feeling
that cattle buyers would be found somewhere near the loading pens. Facing him was the stockyard office, a bank,
and a sprawling, three-story building called the Drover's
Cottage. The latter was painted a dusty tan with bright green

shutters and was quite obviously Abilene's single hotel. He decided to try the Drover's Cottage first.

Once inside, Print found that in addition to rooms for hire there was a bar, a cafe, and a cozy billiard parlor. All the comforts of home. Throw in a few dancing girls and the place could have been fashioned straight out of a cowhand's wildest dreams. Jim Gore, the hostelry's amiable manager, came forward to introduce himself, and within a matter of minutes had Print shaking hands with a half-dozen cattle buyers in the bar.

Thirty minutes later Print emerged from the hotel feeling slightly giddy. Tucked safely in his pocket was a contract for one herd of longhorn steers at $24 a head. On the hoof, sight unseen. Clearly, there was a great demand for beef in the north. If it had horns and was able to stumble up a cattle chute, the buyers eagerly outbid one another like a swarm of squabbling fish merchants. Counting losses and trail expenses, Print calculated he would return to Texas with close to $55,000.

Mounting the bay in a bounding leap, he loosed a shrill Rebel yell, and thundered back down the military road. Now the celebration could begin in earnest. Tonight the Sunburst crew would be riding high, wide, and handsome. On Yankee gold. Somehow, the fact that it was northern buyers who had paid through the nose made the moment all the more savory.

Shortly after dark had fallen that evening, Print and half the crew strolled from a public bath house, fresh scrubbed, clean shaven, and smelling of lilac powder. They had new duds from the skin out, and besides a very tall thirst, nothing they wore had come up the Chisholm Trail except their boots and hats. And their pistols, of course.

Abilene fairly bristled with armed men. With the summer only just begun, something over thirty thousand head of cattle had already been shipped north. Estimates for the season ranged upwards of one hundred thousand head before winter closed the trail. Each day saw more herds arriving, and with them came grungy, trail-weary cow-hands who had little on their minds besides the Three H's. Whoring, hell-raising, and hurrahing the town. On any given night the town's main thoroughfare was a jostling, seething mass of drunken Texans, red-eyed teamsters and howling buffalo hunters. It was an explosive mixture. Half a thousand men stirred well with Kansas Popskull and a small battalion of shady ladies. One which could erupt with volcanic fireworks at the drop of a hat.

While the dimly lighted street was lined with twenty frame buildings, Abilene's commercial endeavors dealt solely with man's gamier pursuits. There were eleven saloons, three dance halls, one mercantile store, and a livery stable. That left only the four whorehouses, which were by far the most popular establishments in town. Not that a fellow couldn't get his pole greased in the back room cribs at the dance halls, but there was something mighty comfy about a cheery little parlor house just crawling with naked women. Somehow those chattery Soiled Doves had a way of making a trailhand with a case of the lonesomes feel right at home. Naturally, they could never take the place of that sweet little thing waiting faithfully back in Texas. But it sure beat the living hell out of Mother Thumb and her four daughters.

Over the past year the daily train from the east had disgorged a formidable array of gamblers, bunco artists, whores, and common drifters. The flotsam of the underworld from Kansas City, St. Louis, and other outposts bordering the frontier had caught the scent of fast money on the freshening winds. This grimy, godforsaken huddle of shacks on the western plains had little appeal to the eye of an eastern dude. Quite the contrary, it was a squalid, stench-ridden eyesore, flung together with whipsawed lumber and erected slap-dab on a reeking sea of horseshit.

But the horses who regularly unloaded on Abilene's streets were from Texas, and the men who rode them into town had just been paid off in coin of the realm. They dismounted with a hellacious thirst, a reckless disposition, and a hard, throbbing lump beneath the crotch of their trousers. They each had upwards of a hundred dollars to blow on a dizzying round of gambling, boozing and fornicating. Though untutored in many things, the sporting crowd were excellent mathematicians. Abilene was the first western boomtown to arise in close to a decade, and during the five month trailing season somebody stood to tap the rambunctious Texans for many hundreds of thousands of dollars. The lure was strong, and sharpers flocked to the Smoky Hill like gaunted wolves trailing a gut wagon.

Print and his crew made one sashay up and down the main drag before choosing a watering hole. They had come to see the elephant and they meant to do it up in real Texas style. Tonight was their night to howl. They had money in their pockets and a powerful itch to see what it would buy in this spangley circus called Abilene. Tomorrow they would likely be broke, with heads big as watermelons, but that wouldn't matter. When they returned to camp, where the rest of the crew was standing night guard, they would have been the first from Yegua Creek to sample the wild and woolly wickedness of Gomorrha on the Plains.

Naturally enough, they selected the Alamo Saloon to begin the festivities. Trooping through the bat-wing stained glass doors, they stood gaping at a swirling anthill of painted women and rowdy Texans. The smoke-filled room reeked of whiskey, stale sweat, and cheap perfume. Gaming tables of every description were flanked by a brass mounted bar, and from the walls hung a scattering of French plate mirrors and fake Renaissance nudes. Toward the rear, past a cluster of tables, there was a small dance floor. A three-piece band struggled along discordantly, while spurred cowhands tromped and stomped and howled, clutching frowsy saloon girls cheek to cheek in sweaty embrace.

Print's boys had decided that the first order of business was to get a little firewater under their belts. Then maybe they would take a crack at the gaming tables and sample a little of that fancy dancing. Afterwards, when everybody was in the proper frame of mind, they would waltz on down to the cathouse and play dip the wick. Once everyone was so wrung out they couldn't pull their peckers out of a pail of lard, they might just return to camp. That remained to be seen. Right now it was like the boss always said. First things first. With the night's agenda nicely planned, they bellied up to the bar and ordered drinks around.

Sipping their whiskey neat, the boys started making up for lost time. A man couldn't rightly appreciate all of this fun and hilarity till he had a glow on, and they meant to get there quick. Bob was pop-eyed with the wonder of it all, gawking around the room like a speckled pup with his first bowl of cream. The hands had told him what it would be like, but they hadn't done it justice. Not by half. Still, the best part was being shoulder to shoulder with Print, drinking, ogling the painted women, getting himself primed for what would come later.

His first shot at a live, naked lady.

Just thinking about it set his heart to pounding, and he started lapping up the forty-rod as fast as the barkeep filled his glass.

When the boys had worked their way through the better part of a pint apiece, they started getting restless. But just as they decided to have a fling at a bit of faro a fight erupted between a trailhand and a moth-eaten buffalo hunter. Before anyone quite realized what had happened, a burly ox of a man materialized out of nowhere and laid his pistol upside the Texan's head. The cowhand went down colder than a wedge and the fight came to an abrupt halt.

Print instinctively started forward, but as the big man turned he caught the gleam of a star. Then he knew who it was. Bear River Tom Smith. The man everybody along the trail had been talking about. Imported by Joseph McCoy to tame Abilene and teach the Texans to leave their uncouth ways south of the Smoky Hill. The Marshal wore two nickel-plated Colts and was reputed to have killed enough men to fill a small graveyard. But as Print looked him over now, he had the unsettling feeling that Bear River

Tom Smith really didn't need those guns. He was built along the lines of a granite statue and the cold glare from his steely eyes made a fellow think twice.

Taking hold of the lawman might be a hell of a lot easier than letting go.

Suddenly Bob wobbled away from the bar and braced himself like he was getting ready to draw down on a fruit jar back at the ranch. "You goddamn shitkicker," he yelled drunkenly. "Why'nt you mind yer own bishness? Why'd you clobber a Texan 'stead of that hunk of wolf bait?"

Print was so stunned that for a moment he couldn't move. But Bear River Tom Smith labored under no such handicap. Eyeing the boy's belligerent stance, he smiled sardonically. "Sonny, you'd better button up your lip before you get hurt."

Bob tensed and his hand clawed at the Colt on his hip. "You dirty——"

There was a mushy splatt as Print's fist connected with the youngster's jaw. Bob hurtled backwards into a faro table and sunk to the floor like a limp dishrag. Rubbing his knuckles, Print looked around to find the lawman appraising him coolly.

"Mister, that was a smart move." Bear River Tom Smith cocked an eyebrow toward the unconscious boy. "You'd best keep that young coon home till he gets full-growed."

Nodding, the Marshal holstered his gun and sauntered toward the door. When the stained glass bat-wings closed behind him the saloon suddenly came back to life. The band blared out with a raucous tune, dancers began tromping the boards once again, and the bar was swamped with shouting, laughing men. The excitement was over, no one was killed, and it was time to get back to really serious business.

Striding across the room, Print hefted Bob over his shoulder and steered a course for the door. Master Robert Oliver had a lot to learn about what separates the men from the boys. The young squirt would have to wait for another night to get his cherry busted. Tonight he was going to get his ears boxed, and listen to a few well chosen words on how not to get yourself killed.

But as he pushed through the doors it occurred to Print that the kid draped over his shoulder wasn't all that much to blame. Like Ma would have said: he had been shown the way. Still, the cattleman's anger flared again just the same.

Maybe he had brought the boy along too fast. But he damn sure hadn't taught him to draw down on the likes of Bear River Tom Smith.

Drunk or otherwise.

BOOK 2

CATTLE KING
1871–1875

CHAPTER SIX

1

The lobby was deserted when Print came down the stairs. From the bar he could hear the steady drone of men's voices, mixed with laughter and the clink of whiskey glasses. The cattle buyers were doubtless holding court, spreading good cheer and bad liquor in the hopes they could give some Texan the fast shuffle on a herd of cows. Before the night was over they probably would, too. Fools came in all shapes and sizes, and more than a fair share seemed to spend their lives trailing cows north only to be bamboozled by Yankee sharpers.

Print debated having a drink, then decided against it. The buyers had been after his herd for two weeks now, and he was bored sick with their slippery ways. Crossing the lobby, he stepped out onto the hotel porch and took a seat in a rocker. Maybe after supper he would play some cards. Then again, maybe he wouldn't. Holding nearly four thousand cows outside town was getting to be a damn' expensive proposition, just in wages alone. Not to mention the amount of grub those waddies were wolfing down at cowtown prices. Maybe instead of loafing around the gambling dives he would be better off making the best deal he could and getting the hell on back home.

Lighting a cigar, he propped his boots up on the porch railing and let his gaze drift out over Ellsworth's dusty main street. The day had been a real scorcher and as the sun settled into the west he could still feel rivulets of sweat running down his backbone. Exhaling, he watched the smoke hang in the still air and grunted with disgust. The hill country along Yegua Creek wasn't the coolest place on earth, but it couldn't hold a candle to these baked, godforsaken Kansas plains.

Sunburst had sent two herds north that summer. Print had ramrodded the first and Bumpus Moore followed him by two days with the second. Over the past couple of years they had learned the hard way that it was best to keep the herds small, somewhere around two thousand head. What with Indians, prairie storms, and the temperamental nature of longhorns, it was just a hell of a lot smarter to hold the herds to a more manageable size. This summer they had been uncommonly lucky. The gut-eaters had been bought off cheap enough, and a freak thunderstorm had cost them less than fifty head. Otherwise both herds had made it through without incident and been put to graze on the rolling prairies north of town.

But unlike the past two summers, they had not trailed to Abilene. The Union Pacific was rapidly building west along the Smoky Hill, and by the spring of 1872 it became clear that Ellsworth was to be the next great cattle center. Abilene had turned into a sodbuster town anyway. Joseph McCoy had been booted out as mayor and the Grangers Committee had taken advertisements in Texas newspapers warning cattlemen they were no longer welcome. Wild Bill Hickok's gunfight last season with Phil Coe and a bunch of cowhands had been the last straw. The reformers had promptly fired Hickok as marshal and declared Abilene out of bounds to anyone riding a ramfire saddle.

The Texas cattlemen looked on the whole affair as a big

joke. Since Ellsworth was some sixty miles southwest of Abilene it made the drive slightly shorter, and so long as somebody paid top price for their cows the name of the town mattered little. Joseph McCoy had brought the best part of Abilene to Ellsworth at any rate. With the help of a small army of carpenters, he had dismantled the Drover's Cottage, loaded it on a train, and resurrected it with great ceremony in the new cow capital. The sporting crowd had been close on McCoy's coattails, and what with the same old faces in their regular haunts it was sort of difficult to tell the difference between the two towns anyway. Ellsworth had the usual swarm of whorehouses, gambling dives and saloons, and most were operated by the very characters who had once made Abilene a paradise for heathens of every persuasion.

So far as Print was concerned personally, the change meant absolutely nothing. Double zero. The only reason he left Texas was to trade cows for Yankee gold, and where it was done seemed vastly unimportant. Abilene, Ellsworth, even smack dab in the middle of the Smoky Hill was all right with him. So long as the flow of double eagles didn't slacken. Looking back over the last two years, he had to admit that God and the Yankee cattle buyers had been mighty good to the Olivers. Just about in that order, too. He now had two husky sons, James Johnston and Nathan Forrest, who were spitting images of their daddy. Louisa was expecting again, and with any luck he would be home in time to welcome the latest arrival. The Oliver clan was fast becoming one of the wealthiest families in Texas, and unless he was wide of the mark, the old man and his mother now felt a measure of security unlike any they had known since settling on Yegua Creek.

All in all, life had been damn' good to everyone on Sunburst.

Reflecting on it now, as he rocked back and forth on the hotel porch, Print was still a bit awed by the way time and circumstance could alter a man's life. Only seven years ago he had ridden home from the war broken in spirit, limping from a leg wound, and so shamed by the South's defeat that he was hardly able to look another man in the eye. The leg still bothered him sometimes, especially when it rained, but on every other count he had no complaints whatsoever. The military occupation, along with Reconstruction politics, had ended two years past, and Texas was again being ruled by Texans. Not that they weren't as corrupt and conniving in their own way as the Yankees had ever been. Curiously, many of the scalawags still remained in office, neatly switching sides with an agility that again hornswoggled the voters completely. The Governor had even organized a State Police force, which operated as his personal army and at times made the Bluebellies look like milk-fed gentlemen by comparison. Still, they were Texans. With the exception of a few like Cal Nutt, who had somehow managed to hold his own in Williamson County. Perhaps the men who now ruled Texas were no less crooked then their Yankee predecessors, but at least they were the homegrown variety of thief. A man could live with that, for as Jim Oliver was fond of saying—the human race had been getting shortchanged by politicians ever since Adam begat enough sons to hold an election.

The thought just naturally led Print to think of Cain and Abel, and as he watched the sunset from the porch of the Drover's Cottage, it occurred to him that the only thing bothering him these days were his own brothers. One of them anyway. Jay and Ira weren't all that much trouble, no more so than any other sharp pain in the ass. They spoiled their wives unmercifully, kept fathering another brat every year, and did only enough work to justify their share of the loot from the spring cattle drive. They hadn't pulled their own weight in the last two years and showed no signs of doing so any time in the future.

But like conniving politicians, that was something a man could learn to live with. Bob was another kettle of fish entirely. While Print still thought of him as a kid, the youngest Oliver was going on twenty-two and in some ways he was a full-grown man. There wasn't a hand on Sunburst who worked harder, spent longer hours in the saddle, or gave more unstintingly of himself to the outfit. The boy earned his keep, and then some. Yet there was a wildness in him that overshadowed all else—made people forget the dawn to dusk buckets of sweat he devoted to the ranch. Whenever he went into Georgetown it invariably ended in a saloon brawl, and many times he would have pushed it to the limit if anyone had been foolish enough to draw on him. After each escapade Print lectured him sternly, and for a while he would walk the straight and narrow. Then, just as regular as clockwork, he would explode like a Roman Candle and pull some reckless stunt.

Print had spent many sleepless nights worrying about the kid, but short of locking him up there wasn't a hell of a lot he could do about it. The only step remaining had been to keep Bob at home as much as possible, especially during cattle drives. After the boy had tried to square off against Bear River Tom Smith it became apparent he just couldn't be trusted in a cowtown. The Kansas railheads somehow brought out the worst in a man—whether he had a violent streak or not—and there were plenty of cold-eyed Yankee marshals who wouldn't think twice about letting daylight through a smart-aleck young Texan. Bob didn't kick up too much fuss about being left behind on the trail drives but it hadn't really solved anything. With Print gone he just treed Georgetown a little more often, sort of like a wild cat that had missed the rabbit and grudgingly settled for a squirrel instead.

Mulling it over like a worrisome riddle, Print suddenly became aware that someone had taken the rocker next to him. Looking around, he found Abe Campbell, one of the eastern cattle buyers, watching him with a sly grin.

"Abe, how's tricks?" He flipped the cigar stub into the street. "Figured you'd be in the bar greasin' some cowman for the quick slide."

Campbell laughed, showing a mouthful of yellow teeth. "Why, Print, you know me better than that. I'm just an old country boy out trying to make a living."

"Sure, Abe." Print had to smile, remembering the man's homespun way of throwing a sucker off guard. "You're just a regular Good Samaritan, aren't you?"

"Land's sakes, I just never knew Texans were such cynics." The cattle buyer stared back at Print with round, guileless eyes. "Here I came out to make you an offer on your herd and all you do is rake me over the coals."

"Now, Abe, you know I'm not gonna sell those cows till I get my price. I must've told you that fifty times in the last two weeks."

"Oh, I recall that, right enough," Campbell replied. "But if you hold off much longer you'll wind up wintering that herd in Kansas."

The cattleman chuckled softly. "Well, I'll tell you. The way you fudge on the price I'd probably come out ahead doing just that."

"Now there you go again, letting personal feelings stand in the way of business. I really mean it. I'll make you a good offer."

"You know my price, Abe. Same for you as anybody else. $30 a head."

"Twenty-four and I'll take the whole shootin' match off your hands."

The price was still low, but it surprised Print. Yesterday it had been two dollars lower. "Mr. Campbell, I get the feelin' you know something I don't. Like maybe the market price in Chicago has jumped. $29 a head is the least I'd take."

"Print, you're a hard man to do business with. I'll go $25, and that's my last offer."

"Twenty-seven and you got yourself a deal."

The easterner did a quick calculation and grinned. "Call it $105,000 even."

Print was no slow poke with figures himself. "Abe, you just bought yourself a herd of cows."

The two men shook hands and stepped back inside to seal the bargain with a drink. Abe Campbell had saved himself forty cents a cow. Print Oliver had made an extra

$3,900. His rock-bottom had been twenty-six from the start.

2

Print, Jim Kelly and Bumpus Moore walked through the door of Nick's Place and headed straight for the bar. The herd had been driven into the loading pens that morning and after the tally was double-checked Abe Campbell had presented the young cattleman with a draft on the local bank. Tomorrow the draft would be exchanged for double eagles, and with the gold stored in a false bottom specially built into the chuck wagon, the Sunburst outfit would head for home. But between now and then, Ellsworth was going to be hurrahed in proper style.

The crew had been paid off and quickly fanned out to their favorite watering holes and cathouses. From past trail drives, Print felt fairly confident he would spend a good part of the night bailing rowdy cowhands out of the local hoosegow. Their heads would be sore as boils and most wouldn't recover till they were south of the Red, but they would have some great stories to swap throughout the long winter. Trail driving was a backbreaking, thankless job, and the thing the men looked forward to all year was this one wild, rip-snorting spree of perfumed women and cheap whiskey. They had earned it, whatever the effect on their heads and their wallets. Without it, trailing cows north would have been the sorriest business known to man.

When the barkeep came over, Print told him to leave the bottle. After filling their glasses right to the lip, he raised his drink to Kelly and Moore. "Boys, here's to the best goddamn' crew any outfit ever seen or heard tell of."

The three men tossed off their drinks and shuddered when the fiery liquor hit bottom. Jim Kelly took a deep breath, half expecting to see flames shoot out of his mouth. "Lordy mercy, that t'rantula juice'd near 'bout draw blisters on a rawhide boot."

"Jim, what'cha talkin' about? That's first class drinkin' whiskey." Moore filled the glasses again and gave the black man a crafty smile. "Listen, one time in Abilene I got hold of some booze that if a man drunk it straight he could get shot in the head and it wouldn't kill him till he sobered up."

"You know, I seem to remember that trip, now that you mention it." Print looked past Moore and winked at the wrangler. "Near as I recollect Bumpus came crawlin' into camp with such a foul taste in his mouth he took his store teeth out and buried 'em."

Moore swelled up indignantly. "Now, Print, you know that ain't so. Ever' tooth in my head is the ones I was borned with."

Kelly hooted derisively. "No, boss, you got it right. I was right there, seen it for myself. That was the time he went crazy as a parrot eatin' sticky candy, and we had to rope him to the chuck wagon to keep him from hurtin' hisself."

"Well, Mr. Hoss Wrangler, I've seen you bent out of shape a few times myself." Moore's rubbery mouth twisted in a mocking grin. "Now just fer example. You take last year in Abilene. Why, you was stumblin' around like a blind dog in a meat house. Ever' man in the crew tried to get you to. . . ."

Print didn't hear the rest of the story. Glancing around the saloon he caught sight of four men playing poker at a back table. One of them jogged his memory and he suddenly recognized the man as Tom Kennedy, old Martin Kennedy's youngest son. The Kennedys owned a spread down near Corpus Christi and the old man had bought him many a drink in the years they trailed to Abilene. Then he recalled hearing that Tom had cut loose from the family a couple of years back. Which wasn't too surprising since Martin Kennedy made no bones about holding on to the pursestrings till the day he gave up the ghost. Print downed his drink and headed toward the poker table. Kelly and Moore would spend the rest of the night getting soused and jawboning about past drunks, and they damn' sure didn't need a referee.

Halting beside the table, he waited till the young Texan looked up. "Howdy, Tom, remember me? Print Oliver."

Kennedy's face went blank for a moment, then brightened with recognition. Rising, he grabbed Print's hand and started pumping like he was filling a water trough. "Damnation! Print Oliver. Boy, it must've been a month of Sundays since we crossed trails. Where you been keepin' yourself, old buddy?"

"Mainly between here and there," Print said, returning the youngster's smile. "Just pushin' cows and tryin' to make a dollar. Where's your daddy? Haven't seen him this year."

Kennedy snorted. "Just wait around long enough and he'll show up. That old goat wouldn't miss a trail drive if he had one foot in the grave."

Print caught a sour note in the boy's words, but he didn't let on. "Well how are things down to home? Mart gettin' along all right, is he?"

"Fair to middlin', last time I seen him." Kennedy plainly didn't want to talk about it; he darted a glance at the other players. "Looka here, I've gotta get back to the game. Maybe we can have a drink later."

"Yeah, that's right," one of the players growled. "He's into me for a wad and I'd like a chance to get even. You boys have your reunion later."

Print looked around, noting that two of the men were Texans, clearly old timers who had just sold their herds and had a yen to buck the tiger. The third appeared to be a gambler by the cut of his clothes and the soft, well kept look of his hands. Print felt a twinge of surprise that the boy could hold his own in such company. Kennedy was a big, rawboned fellow, sort of lean and shad-bellied, but he wasn't what a man would call overly bright. Print seemed to recall that he was one of those lamebrains who had his own theory about filling inside straights. Still, everybody hit a lucky streak now and then, even the dumb ones.

He nodded to Kennedy and started to turn when the gambler spoke up. "Mister, five makes a better game and there's a chair open. You're welcome to sit in if you've a mind."

Print saw the boy frown and glance sideways at him. Probably didn't want to be bothered with more talk about his family. But with Kelly and Moore rehashing past escapades, he was at loose ends. Besides, he was sort of partial to the game. "Thanks. Don't mind if I do. Just till suppertime anyway."

One of the Texans started shuffling as he sat down. "Oliver, is that yer name? Well, son, she's wide open and cut throat. Table stakes. Check and raise. Stud or draw."

Print emptied a rawhide bag of double eagles on the table as the man began dealing stud. Kennedy was seated to his left, flanked by the two cattlemen, and the gambler was to his right. The dealer caught an ace on his first up card, whooped with delight, and bet a hundred. Plainly he was a man who believed in buying pots, even when it amounted to nothing more than the ante. Print peeked at his hole card and folded. Kennedy had a queen showing, but he surprised Print by also turning over. Somebody, quite clearly, had been teaching the youngster the game of poker.

The deal passed around the table with talk limited to betting and an occasional curse when luck took a wrong turn. As the game progressed Print quickly got a handle on the two ranchers. They were inveterate bluffers, trying to sledgehammer everyone around the table with loud talk and wild bets. He also had the feeling they were betting on each other's hands whenever one of them caught good cards. But young Kennedy and the tinhorn still had him buffaloed. The gambler played good poker, very cool and conservative, which was to be expected. Yet there were times when Print could have sworn he was overbetting his hand. While it built extremely large pots, these were the very hands the gambler invariably lost. It was sure enough puzzlement, one he couldn't quite figure.

Tom Kennedy, on the other hand, was downright astonishing. He folded early when his cards looked bad and rarely stuck around if he was beat showing. When he made a hand he bet cautiously, suckering the cattlemen into raises, then lowered the boom on the final go round. Curiously, he even managed to snooker the tinhorn, especially on the larger pots. He was playing cards like he had just stepped off a riverboat, and he was winning. Not that he didn't lose, but he was winning the big ones, and the pile of double eagles in front of him was growing steadily.

After something over an hour of play Print figured he was down perhaps fifty dollars. Considering the size of the bets he could have been hurt a lot worse if he hadn't caught a couple of good hands. The two old reprobates across from him were losing their shirts, ass over teakettle. The gambler was ahead, but no more than a few hundred dollars at the outside. Butter and bread money for a seasoned campaigner, and from the looks of him this character had been weaned on a deck of pasteboards. The winner was Martin Kennedy's strapping young son. Print judged the boy to be out front by close to a thousand dollars just since he had joined the game. From what was said before, he had probably been winning ever since the play started.

The tinhorn was dealing when Print suddenly came to his senses. Unless his eyes deceived him, the bastard had just dealt seconds to Tom Kennedy. *Not to himself, but to the young Texan!*

Then it came clear. Thinking back, Print recalled that the gambler never built a pot unless he was dealing. No wonder! The son-of-a-bitch knew who was going to win. He was in cahoots with Kennedy and they were out to trim the two well-heeled cattlemen. The tinhorn boosted the raises knowing the boy would pull down the pot, and no one the wiser. After all, who would suspect a Yankee cardsharp of slipping winners to a green Texas cowhand? For that matter, who would believe that the son of Martin Kennedy would rig a game against his own kind?

Now it all made sense. The boy knew the game was crooked and that was the reason for his frown when the gambler had invited Print to take a chair. The card-slick didn't give a damn for friendship. He had sized Print up as a herd owner and figured the more the merrier. Once they had him hooked he might have sat there all night trying to get even. And gone busted piecemeal. Just like the two codgers across from him.

But Print hadn't played poker from Shiloh to Appomattox without learning his way around a card table. The Confederate Army had had its share of marked decks, hold-out artists, and card mechanics; those who hadn't taken the trouble to learn such dodges more often than not spent the war on short rations. Unless this tinhorn was something special, it shouldn't prove too hard to get the goods on him and his young accomplice.

One of the cattlemen was high with a king and he gleefully bet a hundred. From the look in his eyes he had a pair wired back to back. Print glanced around the table and saw that Kennedy had a ten showing. More than likely he had it matched in the hole, with a third slated to appear toward the end of the hand. Print peeked at his hole card, casually inspecting the top for any unusual designs that would signify a marked deck. Nothing seemed out of order. Next he tested the card for shaved edges. That, too, was a washout. Since it was a queen he knew damned well it had been tampered with in some manner. Still, he couldn't be too obvious about handling it. He called the bet and waited for the third card to be dealt.

The highroller across from him caught a deuce and Kennedy a nine. Print found himself holding a pair of queens, which meant that the tinhorn intended to sucker him along also. Again he took a peek in the hole, letting his finger glide gently across the face of the card. Eureka! It was marked with tiny pin pricks, indiscernible to anyone who didn't know what to look for. Print called the cattleman's bet for two hundred and let his eyes slide naturally to the tinhorn's hands as he began dealing.

That cinched it.

The bastard was wearing a ring on his left hand. Right now the safest bet in the house was that a small needle marker would be found on the underside of the ring band.

Kennedy's fourth card was no help, but the cattleman paired his deuce. That gave him kings and deuces, and he crowed like an old rooster as he chucked five hundred into the pot. His partner folded, the tinhorn raised another five hundred, and Print got out. Kennedy just called. Both the herd owner and the gambler raised again, then it was time for the last card.

Print smiled to himself when a ten floated across the table and landed in front of Kennedy. The cattleman still had two pair and the cardsharp came out with what looked like a busted flush. With a pair of tens showing Kennedy was now high, but he checked after darting a nervous glance at the old Texan's hand. Print had to admire the boy's act. Somebody had drilled him letter-perfect in how to bait a trap. The cattleman studied Kennedy for a moment, then grinned like a horse eating briars. Confident now that the kid had two small pair, he bet a thousand. The tinhorn stuck to the script and folded. Kennedy gave a good impression of a man sweating blood, then swallowed heavily and raised back. The old cowman snorted happily and goosed it another thousand. Kennedy called and waited for the Texan to flip his hole card.

Every head at the table snapped around as Print gave it to the cattleman without any frills. "Mister, you've been greased and they're about to drop you through the chute. You're holdin' kings and deuces, but this fella's got you beat."

Looking over at Kennedy, his mouth set in a grim line. "Tom, you've got a third ten in the hole, and I reckon you just bought yourself a barrelful of trouble."

"What the hell you talkin' about, Print?" Kennedy blanched and shot a nervous side glance at his partner. "There's no law against a man holdin' three of a kind."

The boy's hot words had carried across the room, and the saloon suddenly got very quiet. Print looked from the young Texan to the gambler and back again.

"Not unless they're marked and somebody is dealin' you seconds. Your tinhorn friend here has got 'em all marked up nice and pretty with that ring of his, and he's been sand-baggin' these gents by raising on your cards. Wasn't no gamble really since he knew what you were holdin'."

The gambler's hand streaked toward a Derringer secreted in his vest, but the whirr of a Colt hammer being thumbed back froze him dead still. Jim Kelly moved forward, covering him with a cocked pistol, then lifted the hide-out gun from his vest and stepped back.

Print's voice was gritty as ground glass. "Kennedy, you and your friend better make tracks out of Ellsworth. Just leave the money on the table. We'll see that it gets divvied up."

Kennedy's eyes watered with rage. "You rotten sonovabitch. I never yet seen anybody with a big mouth that didn't have a long nose. Well, by Judas, I got a remedy for that!"

The young Texan launched himself out of his chair and swung a haymaker that would have torn Print's head off. Except that it never landed. Print ducked beneath the blow and belted him in the jaw with a short, chopping right. The boy's head exploded in pinwheels of light and before he could recover, Print busted him in the gut. When he doubled over Print caught him square in the face with his knee and Kennedy's teeth clicked together with a loud pop. The youngster straightened upright like his head had been fired out of a cannon, then slowly crumpled to the floor.

Print stood over him, ready to dish it out again if he wanted more. But the boy was out cold. Blood gushed out of a deep cut over one eye and his nose looked like a rotten apple. He might rise to fight again, but it wouldn't be soon.

The anger slowly drained out of Print as he stared down on the youngster's mangled features. Then to no one in particular, he said, "That boy just don't know how lucky he is. If his daddy had caught him cheatin' Texans he'd probably have killed him."

Turning, he fixed the white-faced gambler with a murderous glare. "Tinhorn, I oughta cut your nuts off, but I reckon the kid's gonna need some help. Get him out of here, and when you hit the street, just keep makin' dust."

Print scooped up what he figured he had in the game and stuffed the coins in his pockets. Wheeling away from the table, he stalked off toward the door. Kelly and Moore were hard on his heels, but the black man's eyes never left the gambler till they emerged on the boardwalk outside.

3

When the knock sounded, Print opened the door of his room and found Sheriff Chauncey Whitney standing in the hall. It passed through his mind that the Sheriff didn't let any grass grow under his feet. Less than an hour had elapsed since the fracas with Tom Kennedy and he was just now getting around to changing his blood-splattered clothes.

"Afternoon, Mr. Oliver," the lawman greeted him pleasantly. "Mind if I have a word with you?"

Print pulled the door back wider. "Don't mind a bit, Sheriff. What can I do for you?"

Whitney was built sort of low to the ground, what someone of a charitable frame of mind might have called portly. Age had rounded the craggy edges of his youth, leaving a spongy, rather florid face that looked a bit like a child's image of St. Nick. The soup strainer on his upper lip was a mottled gray, which made him appear all the more benign. But Print wasn't deceived by the man's rotund, somewhat harmless appearance. Chauncey Whitney had been an army scout and lawman for close to two decades, and his faded blue eyes didn't miss a trick. He was a cool old bird, and among cowtown lawmen he was noted as being one of the deadliest when the chips were down.

The Sheriff stepped into the room a few paces, then turned as Print shut the door. "No sense beatin' around the bush, Mr. Oliver. What I come about is that ruckus this mornin' with young Kennedy."

Print gave him a slow nod, his eyes flat and guarded. "Seems to me you're talkin' to the wrong man."

"Maybe. But I ain't been able to have a word with the boy just yet. He looks sorta like a stampede of hogs run over him." Whitney shook his head in mild wonderment. "You did a job on him."

"He had it comin'," Print observed dryly.

"Don't doubt it for a minute. Had a hunch him and that tinhorn was holdin' hands. They drifted into town a couple of months back actin' like they didn't know each other. Already been a couple of squabbles over the way they deal, but it never was anything we could prove."

"You've got the proof now. Why don't you just run 'em out of town?"

"Well, it ain't all that cut and dried, Mr. Oliver." Whitney's look was about half apologetic. "The Kennedy boy has a lot of friends here, and it ain't all just the sportin' crowd neither. You know there's a goodly number of trailhands that sorta likes to see a big cattleman get hisself skinned in a card game. Crooked or otherwise."

Print eyed him a little closer, not at all sure he liked the drift of this conversation. "From where I sit, Sheriff, I don't reckon they've got too much choice. I told 'em to make tracks and not look back."

"Now that's what I come to talk to you about." The lawman looked up from studying his boot tops and met Print's gaze squarely. "'Pears to me it sorta works down to whose ox gets gored."

The Texan gave him a quizzical glance. "Meanin'?"

"Meanin' if you tried to send Kennedy down the road his friends'd more'n likely take a hand. Course, your boys'd just naturally back your play, and 'fore you knowed it we'd have ourselves a regular war. That's something I don't look to have happen in my town. If you savvy what I mean."

"Suppose you just put your cards on the table, Sheriff. Are you giving me some official kind of warnin'?"

"Nooo. Wouldn't rightly call it that." Whitney tried to soften it with a smile. "Just figured you wouldn't mind stayin' clear of the boy while you're in town. Sorta in the interest of civic betterment, you might say."

Print's face darkened in a tight scowl. "Mister, I planned on leavin' town tomorrow mornin' myself. But if you think I'm gonna walk around that young pup while I'm here, you've come to a goat house lookin' for wool."

"Seems to me I've heard that chestnut before. Most of the tough talkers has gone up the flume though."

"Come straight at me with it, Sheriff. I'm not much for riddles."

"Why, I'm just sayin' that if you start tradin' lead with Kennedy and his bunch there's gonna be a lot of dead men on the street. You might be one of 'em. No sense to it. None atall."

Print saw the logic to that, but it still curried him the wrong way. "Tell you what. While I'm here I'll stay out of Nick's Place. You keep Kennedy out of my hair and I won't go lookin' for him. That's about the best I can do."

"Fair enough," Whitney allowed. "I'll have a talk with the boy and make him see the light. Course, the way he looks I suspect he ain't real anxious for another waltz with you anyhow."

The Sheriff was still chuckling at his own profundity when Print showed him out the door. The whole thing didn't sit well with the cattleman, but it was really no skin off his nose. Ellsworth was Whitney's town, and he had a right to run it any way he saw fit. If that included kowtowing to cardsharks, then there was nothing to be gained by forcing the issue. Still, it rankled him no end.

Print changed into a fresh shirt and clean pants, then buckled on his gunbelt and headed for the lobby. Kelly and Moore were waiting for him on the porch and he briefly outlined the gist of the Sheriff's visit. After a moment's discussion, they crossed the street and walked toward the Ellsworth Billiard Saloon. Though he had agreed to stay out of Nick's Place, Print was still of a mind to play poker, and there was sure to be a game in the billiard parlor.

When they reached the saloon door, Kelly turned aside,

glancing up and down the street. "Boss, I reckon I'll jest catch me a little nap out here in the sun. You need me, you jest call."

Print smiled, hardly fooled by the black man's casual manner. Kelly intended to stand guard, just in case young Kennedy got any bright ideas about settling the score. The entire front of the saloon was made up of large windows which were left open in warm weather. A row of chairs had been placed on the boardwalk next to the building and the wrangler chose one directly before the window. From here he had an unobstructed view of the street, and by turning slightly in his chair he could see the inside of the saloon as well.

Bumpus Moore wasn't much of a poker player, so he decided to have a crack at the billiard tables instead. Print left him chalking a cue in the front of the saloon and ambled on back toward the rear. There was only one game in progress and after watching for a few minutes he took a chair. The men were all Texans, with the exception of a lone drummer, and it proved to be a congenial group. Not that they weren't playing for blood—the object of the game was to win, and if a man sat in he had to figure charity began at home. But compared to the cut-throat game that morning in Nick's Place it was a regular Sunday school class.

The next two hours passed quickly and Print was enjoying himself immensely. The cards seemed to be falling right and he calculated he was well over a hundred dollars ahead. Just in the past half hour he had filled on a one card draw, caught a small full house, and bluffed his way through once with nothing but an ace showing. His luck seemed to be running strong, and if it held, he might just have a crackerjack story to tell the old man when he got home.

Print had taken a chair facing the door when he joined the game, allowing himself a good view of the front of the saloon. Just in case. But he remained unaware that there was a storage room in the back, with a door that opened onto the alley. Just as he dragged down his second pot in a row, the store room door opened a crack and Tom Kennedy cautiously peeked around the corner. What he saw was Print's back and Bumpus Moore stretched across the billiard table for an awkward shot. Friends had scouted the saloon only minutes before and he already knew that the nigger was posted out front.

Striding quickly across the floor he came up on Print's left from the rear. His six-gun was out and cocked, and none of the players even looked up until he spoke. "You sonovabitch, I'm gonna cash you in right now."

Print moved even as he heard the voice, throwing himself backward out of his chair. The pistol roared, still aimed at where his head had been, and a ball tore through his left hand. The cattleman clawed frantically at his holstered Colt as he toppled to the floor, but he never had a chance. Kennedy swiveled around and triggered two blinding shots. The young Texan had rushed his shots, though, for he knew he had only moments to finish the job and disappear before Bumpus Moore joined the fight. The first slug caught Print in the thigh and the second plowed through his groin, exiting in a gory mass just beneath his left buttock. Grinning evilly, the boy raised his pistol very deliberately and drew a bead on Print's head. This time he wouldn't miss.

Suddenly there was an explosion from the front of the saloon and Kennedy spun around as a slug ripped through his hip. Just for a moment he caught sight of Jim Kelly standing in the open window with a smoking gun in his hand. Then a dark curtain settled over him as the black man's second shot struck him full in the chest. Hurled backwards, Tom Kennedy's eyes went glassy and he dropped dead on a gritty carpet of sawdust.

The card players came up off the floor where they had dived for cover and crowded around Print. Though he was unconscious, he was still breathing, and a call quickly went up for the doctor. Moore and Kelly forced their way through the jumble of men and knelt beside the fallen man. There were tears in Kelly's eyes and he silently cursed himself for not thinking of the back door. Then, because it seemed the thing to do, they gently lifted the cattleman and carried him toward the front of the saloon. After stretching him out on a billiard table, Kelly shredded his shirt and went to work trying to staunch the flow of blood. Print was spurting bright crimson rivulets like a stuck hog, and it was apparent to everyone in the room that he would bleed to death if something weren't done damn' fast.

Moments later the doctor elbowed his way through the crowd and ordered everyone out of the room except Kelly, who was applying pressure on the wounds with his blood-soaked shirt. Opening his bag, the doctor spread a white cloth on the billiard table, then began laying out neat rows of swabs, sutures, and shiny instruments. After examining the wounds, he rolled up his sleeves and went to work with a probe.

Something over an hour passed before the little physician straightened and stood back to view his handiwork. Satisfied that he had done everything possible, he turned to the black man. "Your friend is a very lucky man. Blessed, in a manner of speaking. There were no vital organs damaged and all three bullets passed clean through. Of course, part of his watch chain is embedded in that groin wound, but we'll worry about that later. Right now, I want him carried very carefully to a clean bed. Then I'll give him an opiate so he'll sleep through the night."

As Kelly signaled to Moore through the open window, the doctor let his gaze settle over Print's pallid features again. "Yessir, he's a mighty lucky man indeed. If that wound had been two inches higher they'd be fitting him for a box just about now."

The wrangler glowered around, not understanding, and the doctor smiled diffidently. "No cause for alarm. It's just that when they're gut-shot the first thing I do is call for the undertaker. That or a preacher." Then he shrugged and began repacking his bag. "A man does what he can. Sometimes it's just not enough."

4

Jim Kelly came through the door just as a bunch of cattlemen were leaving. Print's room at the Drover's Cottage had become something of a gathering place for Texan herd owners and cowhands alike over the past month. Along with the black wrangler, he found himself a hero of sorts after the shootout in the billiard parlor. The man who had exposed the cardsharps and put them to rout. While he hadn't fired a shot in the gunfight, he was nonetheless lionized for bringing the affair to a head. To his fellow Texans' way of thinking, it was as though he had struck a blow against all Northern scoundrels by unmasking the Yankee tinhorn and his turncoat accomplice.

The wrangler had been patronized on an even larger scale for his role in the shootout. After all, it was his flawless skill with a gun which had saved Print Oliver from certain death. Not to mention the fact that he had downed the assassin in the bargain. Still, he was a black man, and there was a certain reserve attached to the back-slapping and good will extended by the Texans. Though they gladly bought him drinks, and never tired of listening to his version of the gunfight, they couldn't quite forget that he was a nigger. Fast, deadly, a better man than most, to be sure. But still a nigger.

Print and Kelly laughed about it in the privacy of the room they now shared. Kelly, with his great gift for storytelling, would mimic the highfalutin' airs of his white admirers, adding spice to the tale with his own pungent commentary. Bed-ridden as he was, Print looked forward to the black man's daily histrionics with immense relish, rocking the room with great belly-laughs that sometimes threatened to rupture his wounds.

These carefree moments, along with sharing living quarters, had brought the men closer together than ever before. Whatever hesitancy Jim Kelly had once felt about binding himself to a white man had been washed away in the single act of pulling a trigger. When he saw Print Oliver gunned down, and reacted instinctively out of sheer rage, the last restraint between them had been broken.

They were no longer white rancher and black wrangler. They were friends.

Closing the door behind the departing Texans, Kelly came to stand beside the bed. "Gettin' on to suppertime. Or is you so wore out from talkin' you done lost your appetite?"

"Goddamn, Jim, you're gettin' to sound more like a wife every day." Print's sly smile brought a snort from the black man. "Those boys didn't wear me out, but they sure as hell got me excited. They just got back from summering their herds in the Platte country. Some of 'em are even thinking of moving their outfits up there lock, stock, and barrel."

Kelly rolled his eyes heavenward in mock despair. "Lawd, look down here and save us from white men eatin' loco weed." Glancing back at Print, he shook his head ruefully. "Boss, somebody ain't been tellin' you the full particulars. That land up there is crawlin' with Sioux and Cheyenne and ever' other kinda Injun you can name. 'Bout the only time they ain't on the warpath is when the snow's deep enough to frost your whiskers."

"Could be," Print conceded. "But those boys that just left here didn't have a speck of trouble. They trailed up there last spring, grazed their cows all summer, and shipped 'em out two weeks ago. Got better prices than we did, too."

There was much to be said for the Platte country and it was a common item of interest whenever cattlemen gathered. While the mild Texas winters were better for calving, the bluestem range north of the Platte, with its endless supply of water and cooler summers, could produce heavier beef in a far shorter period of time. Print's latest visitors estimated that their steers had gained at least an extra hundred pounds apiece by summering on the lush northern grasses. That meant another $2 to $3 a head when a man started talking to cattle buyers, upwards of an added $10,000 cash money every season. The only drawback in the past had been the lack of a railhead in the north country. But the Union Pacific had now laid track across the plains, thus establishing a ready means for shipment to the eastern markets.

While Print hardly discounted the Indian threat, this was offset to his way of thinking by a rather remarkable aspect of the Platte country. There were no rustlers on the sparsely populated northern plains, and perhaps wouldn't be for another decade. Thinking about it now, he felt that if forced to a choice he would almost prefer to fight Indians. With the redskins, a man at least knew *who* his enemies were.

"Well, it don't make me no never mind, I guess." The rolling cadence of Kelly's words brought the cattleman back to the present. "I done scalped ever' kind o' Injun there is down our way, so I reckon I could do the same up there. Besides, once you gets your mind made up, there ain't no sense talkin' 'bout it anyway."

Print gave him an amused look. "Now, Jim, you're putting words into my mouth. I never said a thing about us trailin' north. I just said them other fellas seemed to be havin' plenty of luck at it."

"Whooeee! Listen to that man talk, would you." The wrangler cocked his eyebrow like an old horned owl. "You think I don't 'member the look on your face that time we rode up there? Boss, you ain't foolin' this nigga. You been thinkin' 'bout trailin' up there ever since. And I bet you been layin' in that bed kickin' yourself in the rump 'cause you let them other fellers beat you to it." Kelly flashed a pearly grin and turned toward the door. "Now if you is through spinnin' windies, I'll go on down to the cafe and get you some supper. 'Pears to me you needs somethin' in your gizzard 'sides hot air."

Print was still chuckling when Kelly went out the door. But beneath his laughter the black man had touched a raw nerve. He was irked that someone had beaten him to the northern plains. No sense in denying it. The idea had been his from the start and he should have acted on it, instead of taking the easy route and trailing to Kansas every year. Just pure damn' laziness. That's all it amounted to. Still, it wasn't too late. Not if a man planned far enough ahead.

Like maybe next spring.

Then he started chuckling again. Kelly had him pegged all right. That black devil could see through him like he was made of glass. Curiously, since he had always been a man to keep his own counsel, it didn't bother him that someone else could figure him so easily. Not Jim Kelly, anyway. The last month had been a real eye-opener on that score.

Kelly and Moore had carried him back to the Drover's Cottage that day after the doctor finished patching him up on the billiard table. Evidently the sawbones had given him enough laudanum to fell an ox, for he had awakened sometime the next afternoon to find Kelly dozing in a chair beside the bed. While Print was still woozy, he was able to follow the wrangler's account of the shootout, and it hadn't required much thought to see that he was damn' lucky to be alive.

Only luck didn't have anything to do with it. Jim Kelly was the reason he had pulled through. Just that. Nothing more.

Some days later, when the doctor pronounced him out of danger, Print called in Bumpus Moore and instructed him to take the crew home. Though reluctant to leave, Moore agreed that it would serve no purpose to hang around. Print would be laid up for a month, perhaps even longer, and the men had plenty of work awaiting them back at Sunburst. Fall roundup wasn't all that far off, and Ace Whitehead would need all the help he could get. Moore didn't much like the idea of taking all that gold with him, but Print insisted. He still didn't trust bankers, especially Kansas Yankees, and Sunburst needed that money to keep operating. On the other hand, Print observed, he did trust an old waddie named Bumpus Moore. With close to twenty cowhands guarding the chuck wagon, he had every confidence the gold would reach Yegua Creek safely. Moore had got a big lump in his throat when Print said that, and was so proud he damn' near twisted his hat into shreds.

Somehow, there was never any question about who would remain behind to look after Print. Reflecting on it later, he decided that Jim Kelly must have given the boys the message in a way that left small room for argument. The black man stayed, everybody else went home, and Print went about learning the meaning of true pain.

The doctor took him off opiates after the crisis had passed, and the young cattleman was abruptly introduced to a throbbing hell that never seemed to sleep. While the wounds in his hand and leg were bothersome, it was the groin wound that left him soaked in sweat and at times clenching his teeth. Jim Kelly had a cot moved into the room and stayed with him constantly that first week. The wrangler told a seemingly endless round of stories, badgered him into rambling discussions on the cattle industry, and sometimes talked to him around the clock to divert his mind from the pain.

Though his wounds were healing nicely, Print was unable to move from bed, and this grated on him almost as much as the pain. For the first time in his life, he found himself as helpless as a child. But as the plump little sawbones commented after seeing Jim Kelly in action, the patient was in good hands. Like some black angel of mercy the wrangler ministered to his needs—feeding him, changing his linen, even emptying his bedpan. As the pain began to fade, and the days lengthened into weeks, Print Oliver slowly awakened to the fact that between himself and Jim Kelly the time for testing had passed. Whatever it was that bound them together had endured mightily, and neither man felt the need to speak of it. They knew, and that was enough.

While he had never been much for reading, over the weeks Print took to studying the Bible as a means of passing time. The hide-bound views of his mother had never appealed to him, but surprisingly enough, he found that the

Old Testament made damn' good reading. Even entertaining, in a stiff sort of way. Curiously, since the black man could neither read nor write, he discovered that Kelly was well versed in the scriptures. Thereafter they spent many hours arguing certain cryptic passages of the Good Book, and Print came away convinced that after his own fashion, the wrangler was a deeply religious man. The effect on Print wasn't exactly profound, but it did give him pause for thought. Perhaps there was more to the Bible than he had ever taken the trouble to unearth.

When Kelly returned with his supper tray, the young cattleman was deeply engrossed in Jacob's sojourn into Egypt. He had read this section of Genesis time and again, speculating that there was a certain similarity between Jacob's life and his own. Jacob had been at odds with his brother, and in some strange way attached to his mother. Moreover, he had traveled widely in search of his destiny, almost as if the grass always looked greener over the next hill. Then there was his large family, numbering more than seventy toward the end. That damn' sure struck a chord. Given a few more years, the home place at Sunburst would put Jacob in the shade by a goodly margin.

After fluffing Print's pillows and getting him settled with the tray, Kelly glanced over at the open Bible. "Still chasin' old Jacob, huh? Lordy, that man has got you under a spell, sure 'nough."

Print's appetite had returned with a vengeance and for a moment he was too busy stuffing his mouth to answer. Finally he came up for a breather and stabbed the air with his fork for emphasis. "Listen, sport, don't go underratin' Mr. Jacob Israel. He was a wise old bird. Knew exactly what he was doing all the time."

"Sure, I ain't arguin' with you." The wrangler stopped and peered up at the ceiling, like he was studying some riddle that had suddenly appeared on the cross beams. "Course, he did let folks flimflam him around with their smooth talk. I mean it ain't like he was 'nother Abraham, now is it?"

Grunting indignantly, Print paused with a piece of beef-steak in mid air. "Now that's a hell of a thing to say! Lemme tell you something, Jim. Anybody that can live to a hundred forty-seven ain't exactly the village idjit. Whatever the old boy's secret was, it must've been powerful medicine."

The black man shot him a crafty side glance, then got busy rolling a smoke. "The secret—is not turnin' your back on unlocked doors."

Print started to say something, then thought better of it. Sometimes his ebony-skinned friend had a way of striking right to the marrow. Which left a fellow damn' little room for a snappy comeback.

But he was sure as hell right about one thing. From now on it was back to the wall and one eye cocked.

Even in a friendly game.

5

The train chugged to a halt at McDade Station, belching smoke and cinders like some iron dragon after a heavy meal. The grimy little station house served the town of Thrall, which was some twenty miles east of Georgetown, and the Oliver clan had come to welcome home their wandering kinsman. Watching the car windows expectantly, Louisa felt a mounting sense of excitement as the train ground to a screeching stop. Bob was just plain fidgety, nervously pacing up and down the platform trying to catch a glimpse of Print. Jay and Ira stood off to one side by themselves, glum-faced as a couple of deacons at a tent meeting. The four of them made up the welcoming party. Julia Oliver and the old man had remained behind to make sure all was in readiness for the return of their eldest son.

Though it was early September the day was unusually warm, and Louisa had already started worrying about Print's comfort on the long wagon ride back to Sunburst. While she had never ridden on a train, she also had a feeling that being cooped up in those stuffy coaches for four days wouldn't have done much for her husband's disposition. Print and Jim Kelly had gone by rail from Ellsworth to Kansas City, taken another train from there to Ft. Worth, then switched again for the final leg of their journey. Coming such a distance in a rattling chair car could try the patience of any man accustomed to the freedom of horseback, particularly one who probably wasn't feeling up to snuff anyway.

But Louisa was in for an even greater shock than she imagined. From the tone of Print's cheery letters she expected him to alight from the train with nothing more than a bad limp. Instead, he came down the steps cradled in the arms of the black wrangler. He was sallow and puny looking, and as Louisa ran forward she could tell he had lost considerable weight. More than that, he was clearly too weak to stand on his own or he would never have submitted to being carried like a child. Print Oliver was too proud a man for such indignities. Unless he had no choice.

Still, he managed a wide smile and his eyes brightened noticeably as she reached him. Kelly's massive arms held him securely, and he was able to reach out and embrace Louisa in a tight squeeze. Yet the strength she knew so well was gone from his touch and through his coat she sensed that he had been reduced to skin and bones.

Tears welled up in her eyes, but she fought them back and gave him a big kiss smack on the mouth. Then she cocked her head saucily and gave him a good once over. "Well, Mr. Oliver, it's about time you decided to come home. Land sakes, a body would think you weren't even interested in seeing your new son."

Louisa had given birth to their third son, Jeb Stuart Oliver, two weeks after Print had been shot. Looking at her now, it occurred to him that he had yet to be home when one of his children was born. Chuckling softly at her brave little act, he touched her cheek. "Lady, what would I do without you?"

She sniffed and cut her eyes around mockingly. "Why, swell up and burst. What else?"

Print snorted and looked up to find the boys watching him closely. From the expressions on their faces it was obvious they were shocked by his condition. Unlike Louisa, they weren't able to cover their feelings with light words. Nodding to each in turn, he spoke their names, and his gaze came to rest on Bob. He was somewhat taken aback to see that the boy had grown a big, bushy mustache over the summer.

"Sport, you're lookin' chipper as a bluejay. Where'd you get that cookie-duster?"

Bob's hand went mechanically to his brushy upper lip and he smiled sheepishly. "Well, Print, you know. I just sorta figured—"

"—that an old married man oughta look the part."

The boy blushed right up to his hairline. "Yeah, something like that, I guess."

Louisa had written him that Bob and Jenny Franklin had been married in early August. The news had left him speechless at first. But then, as he thought it over, it came to him that the baby of the family was a kid no longer. Perhaps Bob would always remain a kid in his mind, simply because he was the youngest. But to anyone else he was clearly a full-grown man. He was by far the tallest in the family, packing more muscle than any of the Oliver men, and the mustache made him look years older. Watching him now, Print could only hope that he had matured in other ways as well. Marriage had a way of settling most men, and it would be a godsend to everyone on Yegua Creek if Jenny Franklin somehow managed to clip Bob's wings.

Before the other boys could get a word in, Louisa took charge. "Now, Jim, you just bring him on over to the wagon. We've got a nice pallet all laid out in the back and he can ride home in style."

"Yes'm," Kelly grunted, jiggling Print in his arms like an overgrown doll. "He ain't the heaviest thing I ever toted, but he ain't exactly a feather neither."

The small crowd around the station looked on curiously as the black man marched to the wagon and gently deposited

Print in the back. The three brothers trailed along behind and Bob helped Louisa over the sideboards into the wagon. While she was tugging at blankets trying to make him comfortable, Print caught Jay's eye. "How's the folks?"

"Sassy as ever," Jay informed him. "Course, they been some worried about you, but the way you wrote we sorta thought you was on the mend. They'll likely get a little bent out of shape seein' you carried in the house."

Print shrugged it off. "Well, they've seen me down before, so it won't be nothin' new."

"Yeah, I guess you're right." Jay paused, inspecting him with a critical eye. "What'd them doctors up there say about you gettin' well?"

"Why, Bubba, they said I'd live to be a hundred. Maybe even a hundred and forty-seven." Out of the corner of his eye he saw Jim Kelly crack a smile. "Just takes a little time to get your wind back when a fella puts three leaks in you. Know what I mean?"

Ira popped up in a faltering voice, licking his lips nervously. "Are you gonna be able to r-r-ride again? I mean, are you gonna have to k-k-keep to the house, or what?"

Print saw a look pass between the two brothers and it suddenly dawned on him what they were hinting at. "Don't you boys get in a sweat. I'll be fit as a fiddle come spring roundup. Just relax and keep makin' babies. Uncle Print'll make sure everybody gets their turn at the gravy bowl."

Bob guffawed and slapped the side of the wagon with a loud whack. Jay and Ira ducked their heads sheepishly, which only confirmed what Print had thought. The lazy clods were scared shitless they might have to take over running the spread. If being an invalid weren't so almighty boring he might just lay up on his backside and let them have a try at pulling the load. Damn' if it wouldn't serve them right!

After glowering at them for a moment, he smiled tightly. "Keep your dauber up, boys. All's well. We've got big plans come next spring. Real big." Turning his head, he winked slyly at the black man. "Ain't that right, Jim?"

"Yassuh, Mistah Print." Kelly went into his faithful old darkey routine. "Come spring it's gonna be big doin's, sho 'nough."

The three brothers looked at the wrangler like he had lost his marbles, then their gaze swung back to Print. Before anyone could pose the question he cut them off short. "Don't fret, you'll hear about it in due time. Now suppose we get this outfit headed west. I'd sorta like to see my new boy."

Jay and Ira headed for their horses without a word, glad to have the conversation done with. Bob hung back, waiting till they were out of earshot. "Print, it's not true what the hands said, is it? About that feller downin' you without you gettin' off a shot."

Print smiled, then reached up and punched him lightly on the jaw. "Sport, I learned something real important up there in Ellsworth. You might say it has to do with a man gettin' too big for his britches. Soon as we have some time I'll tell you all about it."

He heard Kelly's deep chuckle from the wagon seat and a moment later the black man put the team into a slow walk. Bob ran for his horse and Louisa scooted around so that Print could rest his head in her lap. She began smoothing his hair back and he closed his eyes, luxuriating under her touch. After a moment he took her hand and gave it a gentle squeeze.

"Woman, it's good to be home. Damned if it's not."

CHAPTER SEVEN

———————

1

New Year's had come and gone, and for Cal Nutt, 1873 promised to be a banner year indeed. Fortune had conspired in such a manner as to alter the political power structure in Austin, and for the first time since coming to Texas the dour-faced carpetbagger was free from obligation to the State House. More to the point, so far as his immediate plans were concerned, the power struggle taking place in the capital had presented him with a hefty new clout in the political arena.

For the last three years, marked by the end of Reconstruction in early 1870, Nutt had schemed and plotted to free himself from the dictates of Horace Davidson. Yet despite his best efforts, the backroom skulduggery had been notably unproductive. By clinging assiduously to the Governor's coattails, Davidson had weathered the housecleaning that occurred when Texas was readmitted to the Union. Though few scalawags survived the transition unscathed, the foxy old Texan had somehow come out of it with his power undiminished in the new regime. When the dust settled he was still Attorney General and had been appointed commander of the dreaded State Police. Far from being ridden out of Austin on a rail, he had emerged the second most powerful man in Texas.

Cal Nutt once again found himself bound to Davidson in a virtual state of serfdom. Short of cashing in his chips and catching the next train east, there was no way to break loose from the silver-haired old scoundrel. Not that he didn't try—there was just no sane means of ditching the Attorney General and still maintaining the power base he had so carefully engineered in Williamson County. With the State House and the Governor's private army backing his play, Horace Davidson held the winning hand. In spades.

But power, like fame, had proved a fleeting thing.

The Attorney General and his uniformed mercenaries had ruled unchecked for more than two years, riding roughshod over anyone who dared to oppose his will. Then, early last fall, the state legislature had staged a palace revolt. The citizens of Texas had their bellies full of scandal and corruption, and the lawmakers had been the first to sense the changing tide. Their own political survival was at stake, and when the clamor for reform swelled across the state, they had jumped aboard the bandwagon with the fervor of true zealots. Their wrath centered wholly on the Governor at first, for if he were toppled his organization would go under with him. But like partisans the world over, they quickly perceived that the way to depose a tyrant was to destroy his palace guard.

The legislators had turned their hungry gaze on Horace Davidson.

The Attorney General was a pragmatist, if nothing else, and he knew a loser when he saw one. His administration was so riddled with graft and corruption that a ten-year-old could have uncovered the facts; in a very real sense, exposing him would prove child's play for the nimble-witted legislators. All it took was a concerted will on the part of the lawmakers and his house of cards would come tumbling down around his ears. Horace Davidson organized his retreat with all the aplomb of a Chinese bandit. After secretly selling off all his holdings he embezzled an additional tidbit in the amount of $37,434 and fled to Belgium. Courtly Texans were all the rage in Europe those days, and prince that he was, the old scalawag planned to live out his years in a royal manner.

The Attorney General's nifty escape caused a furor in Austin. But if the legislature had failed to tack Davidson's hide to the wall, they could at least use the scandal to bludgeon the Governor. The lawmakers quickly passed a bill abolishing the State Police, neatly jerking the Governor's fangs in one fell swoop. The roar from the State House could be heard west of the Pecos, and the Governor promptly vetoed the bill. Both houses of the legislature just as promptly overrode the veto, and on April 22, 1873, the Governor's hired Janizaries passed into oblivion.

The writing was on the wall, clear for all to read. The State House, as well as the power structure of Texas, was up for grabs. Politicians of every persuasion began jockeying furiously for the inside track.

From his inner sanctum north of Austin, Cal Nutt had watched the decline and fall of Horace Davidson with undisguised glee. When the legislature axed the State Police as well, Nutt sensed that his years of waiting were about to pay off handsomely. Patience, after all, brought its own rewards; as he scented the shifting winds, it came to him that the situation was tailor-made for a man who knew how to play his cards with audacity and skill. Since he controlled the political apparatus of Williamson County, he had something the power brokers desperately needed as the struggle in Austin intensified. Votes in the Senate and the House of Representatives were being courted openly by both factions, and it hardly came as any surprise that Cal Nutt owned Williamson County's legislators body and soul.

Negotiating with shrewdness, and utter confidence in the strength of his own position, the carpetbagger committed his votes to the Governor's enemies in return for a certain legal myopia on the part of the new Attorney General. Williamson County became his private hunting preserve, inviolable now even to state law. Whatever went on in Cal Nutt's sacrosanct little domain was nobody's business but his own, and short of outright sedition his schemes would be overlooked by the new guard in Austin.

Ever since a hot summer day in 1866 Nutt had bided his time, waiting for this moment. That was the day Print Oliver had stormed into his office and threatened his life, berating him as if he were some dirty-necked fieldhand in a cotton patch. For seven years the memory of that day had smoldered in his mind, feeding upon itself like some cankerous growth. Never had a man spoken to him in that manner and lived to tell the tale.

With the lone exception of Print Oliver.

Money, power, even a certain eminence in the community had come his way with time, but there remained the bitter taste of ashes about that day so long past. Slowly, as the memory ate at his pride like a nest of worms and year faded into year, he became a man obsessed with a dream of retribution. Somewhere, somehow, he would bring Print Oliver crashing to earth. But it must be done in a way which would humiliate the Texan, break him as a man, leave him destitute in both mind and worldly possessions.

While he had never admitted it to himself, Oliver's threat had held him back at first. Simple fear for his life had caused him to limit the raids on Sunburst range. To be sure, the Cattlemen's Association had hung or shot nine of his rustlers over the years, and the message wasn't lost on him. Later, of course, Horace Davidson had tied his hands even more, and the Olivers' growing wealth had presented a formidable obstacle in itself. Curiously, there always seemed to be some reasonable argument for delaying his revenge farther, and at times it appeared the gods themselves were watching over the Seceshers of Yegua Creek.

But now the last stumbling block had been removed. Neither God nor man nor the State of Texas watched over the

Olivers any longer. They had been abandoned to the uncertain mercies of Cal Nutt—and he meant to exact a fearful price for the arrogance of their eldest son.

These pleasurable thoughts were foremost in the chunky carpetbagger's mind when Grip Crow knocked and stepped through the door of his office. While he hardly needed the money these days, Nutt had never been able to let go of the rustling operation. There was something about the sheer lawlessness of it that appealed to him greatly, and he found the organization and logistics of stealing other men's cows a very diverting pastime. Then too, he had grown quite attached to Grip Crow. Much in the same way a naturalist studies bugs or the mating habits of snakes, he was fascinated by the very perversity of the man's soul. The gang leader was cunning, endowed with neither conscience nor moral awareness, and was easily the coldest son-of-a-bitch Nutt had ever met.

It was a rare combination, one which gave the politician many pleasant hours of idle speculation.

Motioning the rustler to a chair, the corners of his mouth lifted in a dry smile. "Grip, I'm about to unchain you from the shackles that have too long held you in check."

Crow's pale eyes were as blank as sugar cubes. " 'Fraid you lost me on the turn, Mr. Nutt."

"No matter," Nutt replied, feeling very magnanimous tonight. "The reason I called you in is very simply stated. You are now free to begin raiding the Oliver ranch in earnest. With no strings attached."

The gang leader didn't flicker an eyelash, but he was clearly impressed by the news. "They're overdue, for a fact. Been wonderin' when you'd cut the wolves loose."

"Consider it done. For a variety of reasons that don't concern you, there is nothing to stop us from digging Print Oliver's grave."

"You mean I can shoot the bastard? By God, I waited a long time to hear that."

"No. I very decidedly don't mean that." Nutt leaned forward on his desk, speaking in low, bristling tones. "I want

Oliver kept alive. Whatever happens to the rest of his family doesn't matter, but he is not to be killed. Is that understood?"

"Sure, boss," Crow nodded. "However you want it. Just seems like a waste, though. Not to kill him, I mean."

"Hardly a waste, my friend. More like a well deserved mockery." The politician's eyes narrowed, and behind the slitted lids a smoky hatred kindled. "I want you to terrorize that entire family. Men, women, and children. Steal their cattle, drive them out of the country, make them less than paupers. But do it slowly, do you understand? Make them feel it every inch along the way, and when you're done, don't leave them with the means to wipe their ass."

Crow smiled like a hyena, and a deadly glint appeared in his eyes. "I get'ya. Force 'em up against the wall and shit all over 'em. Rub their noses in it."

"That's it exactly," Nutt growled. "Crudely stated, but just what I had in mind. From now on I want you to spend your days thinking up ways to make the Olivers sick to their stomachs with fear."

"Don't give it another thought, Mr. Nutt," the rustler chortled. "We'll have 'em pukin' like buzzards inside a week."

"Good. But remember, Print Oliver's not to be harmed. I want him to see it happen step by step, right down to the last." Nutt tilted back in his chair and gazed out the window. After a moment he looked back with a sudden thought. "One other thing. I want you to break a rancher named Smith. Steal every cow on his place."

"Fred Smith?" Crow's brow lifted in puzzlement.

"That's right. I want you to clean him out. Cows, livestock, everything he's got."

"Hell, boss. Smith's outfit ain't worth two bits. Why waste time on him?"

"Grip, sometimes you ask too many questions. Just do it and let it go at that. Now suppose you get on back to camp and start thinking up some tricks to pull on the Olivers."

Crow nodded and unfolded from his chair. "Don't you

fret none, boss. I guaran-damn-tee you we'll make 'em sit up and blink. Gonna be a real pleasure, too."

When the door closed behind the gang leader, Cal Nutt sat for a moment hearing his last words again. *A real pleasure.* That cold-eyed illiterate had hit it right on the head. Making Print Oliver crawl on his belly was going to be that, and more.

Much more.

2

The Lone Star Saloon was the Texans' favorite watering hole in Ogallala. Like most business establishments in the high plains cowtown, it was a clapboard cracker-box with a false front and not much for looks. But the whiskey wasn't watered down all that bad, and the barkeep had been a trailhand till he got busted up in a stampede, so the cattlemen had made it their unofficial headquarters.

When Print walked through the door, Bob and Jim Kelly knew immediately that something was wrong. He was scowling like a grizzly with his paw in a rusty bear trap and looked mad enough to eat nails. Without so much as a glance in their direction, he stalked up to the bar, demanded a glass, and downed two fast shots. The wrangler had learned from experience not to ask questions when Print was in one of his moods, and Bob was smart enough to follow suit. They just stood there quiet as a couple of church mice and let him boil. Sooner or later he would give them the lowdown. But only after he had gotten so damn' mad he couldn't hold his peace any longer. Until then a man was well advised to just keep his mouth shut. Which is exactly what they did.

Some minutes passed while Print sipped his third drink in silence. Finally he turned and looked at them as if they had just popped out of the woodwork. "Well boys, it's a sorry day and gettin' sorrier all the time."

Kelly and the youngster exchanged looks, then the black

man took the lead. "When you come stompin' in like a scalded owl we sorta got the idea it wasn't good news."

Print shot him a sour frown. "Good news? Shit! It's about as good as a swift kick in the ass." He drained his glass and for a moment just stood there, staring at nothing. "Seems like we're a week late and about four dollars short. That's how much the price of cows has dropped since Monday."

"Well, I'll be dipped," Bob said, gawking at him bug-eyed.

"Double dipped is more like it," Print snapped. "In a barrel of chicken shit."

"Great bals o' fire, boss," Kelly mumbled. "This here's only Friday. You mean they whacked off a dollar a head ever' day this week?"

"Damn' near it. Accordin' to the cattle buyers things are gettin' shaky back east and beef prices have gone to hell."

Bob absently twisted the ends of his mustache. "What's that mean? Shaky."

"I'm not real sure," Print admitted. "Hell, even the buyers are just playin' Polly Parrot for something that came over the wire. Near as I can make out there's some kinda money scare back east and banks have tightened the drawstring."

"Four dollars a head." Bob repeated the figure like he still couldn't believe it, then his jaw suddenly went slack. "Jesus Christ, Print! We just lost close to $8,000."

"That's right, sport. Or if you wanna figure it another way, it's the same as losin' three hundred head of cows at the regular price. Whichever way you slice it, though, we just lost the profit on this herd. Now you see why I'm bent out of shape."

"Yeah," Bob murmured. "But what are we gonna do? Hold 'em and see if the price goes up?"

"Hell no!" Print grunted. "I sold the whole kit and caboodle to the first buyer that offered twenty-five. The way things look it's gonna get worse before it gets better, and I don't aim to winter a herd of cows on the South Loup."

"Amen, brother," the wrangler added quietly. "Amen."

Print filled his glass again and stared morosely at the amber liquid. "Well, it's not a complete washout. Ace must've sold his herd in Kansas close to a month ago. So it's pretty damn' certain he got top dollar, anyway."

Nearly five months back Print had decided to split the herds this season, sending one to Nebraska and the other to Kansas. That way they weren't putting all their eggs in one basket, and it would give him a chance for a closer look at the high plains. With Bob and Jim Kelly in his crew, he had trailed the first herd north toward the Platte in late April. Ace Whitehead and Ira had been tapped to take a second herd up the Chisholm Trail just as soon as spring roundup was finished. That meant they had probably left in early May and sold the herd in Kansas sometime around the middle of July. Jay had been assigned to stay behind and look after Sunburst. Which suited him fine, since there wasn't a hell of a lot to do with most of the hands scattered all over Kingdom Come.

Print's outfit had forded the Platte at Ft. Kearney in late July. Only a day's ride north they had stumbled across the valley of the South Loup and decided to summer the herd there. The bluestem was thick and lush, there was plenty of water, and a grove of cottonwoods along the river made a perfect spot to set up camp. The rest of the summer they had hunted buffalo and antelope, lazed around camp in the warm sun, and watched their steers tallow out like they were feeding on shelled corn. The last week in August they began trailing slowly toward the railhead at Ogallala, which was only a week's drive west along the South Platte.

When they brought the herd to the holding grounds east of town earlier in the afternoon, Print had been bright-eyed and bushy-tailed. The steers were sleek and fat, certain to command top dollar, and he had just spent a month reveling in a cowman's paradise. The valley of the South Loup was everything he had ever dreamed of, even better than the stretch of prairie he and Jim Kelly had seen back in '67. The summer graze could put tallow on anything that walked, and despite what he had heard about northern winters, he was now convinced that longhorns could thrive the year round on the high plains. *If a man had his mind set in that direction.* The thought had a curious appeal, and while it was still just the kernel of an idea, it made for very pleasant daydreaming.

One thing was for damn sure. With his own eyes he had seen the velvety undergrowth of buffalo grass curing on the stem that summer. Like a furry brown blanket it covered the plains clear to the foothills of the Rockies, and there wasn't a cow alive that couldn't winter well with such an abundance of natural hay.

But after dropping Bob and Jim at the Lone Star that afternoon, Print's day had gone straight to hell. Evidently there was some kind of financial panic back east, and the repercussions were quickly being felt on the western plains. Cattle prices had fallen sharply and if the buyers could be believed, the bottom was going to drop out within the next fortnight. Print normally wouldn't trust these slick operators any farther than he could spit, but some instinct told him that this time they had hit it dead on the head. He sold, and was damn' glad to have it done with. Though the profit on the herd had been whittled down to practically nothing, he sensed that it was time to take the money and run.

Print sloshed the whiskey around in his glass, watching little flecks of light shimmer on the surface. Then he tossed it down in one gulp and slammed the glass on the bar. Turning, he gave his brother and the wrangler a hang-dog look. "C'mon, I wanna get some fresh cigars. Then we'll hightail it back to the herd. I told the buyer we'd have 'em in the pens before sundown."

As they walked toward the door Bob searched his face. "You plannin' on stayin' in town long before we head home?"

The cattleman snorted, and his gruff tone made it clear that he was still ticked off. "Just long enough for the boys to get their poles greased and tie on a drunk. Matter of fact, I might just give 'em a run for their money on both counts. The way things are going, I could stand a few laughs."

"Poontang and panther juice," Kelly snickered. "Cures what ails you ever' time."

Print limped on out the door without comment. Though he had recovered completely from the wounds suffered last summer in Ellsworth, he still felt more comfortable on a horse than he did on foot. Sometimes he wondered if the fragments of watch chain embedded in his groin had anything to do with his gimpy leg. Yet it didn't hardly make sense. There was never any pain to speak of, and the doctors had decided to leave well enough alone, so it probably amounted to nothing. Still, it was damned irksome to be hobbling around on a half-game leg all the time. Especially on a day when he had been diddled out of a year's profits.

Crossing the street, the three men entered a mercantile store and came to an abrupt halt just inside the door. A glass display case full of pistols had caught their eye and they crowded around for a better look. While most of the guns were the garden variety cap and ball, there was one revolver unlike any they had ever seen.

Walking forward, the storekeeper stopped behind the case. "Afternoon, gents. See you spotted our new Colt. Remarkable weapon. Really remarkable."

Print bent down for a closer look. "Mister, what sorta gun is that, anyway?"

The merchant opened the case and lifted the pistol out. "Well sir, it's not like anything you've ever seen before. Just got 'em in on the noon train. This here is a Colt Peacemaker. Old Sam really come up with a doozie this time." Thumbing the hammer back to half-cock, he flipped open the loading gate and spun the cylinder. "You see this isn't a cap and ball. Uses shells just like the newer rifles. All you do is slip the shells in the cylinder, snap this dojigger shut, and you're in business."

Print took the pistol out of his hand and inspected it carefully. After a moment he turned and swung the gun on line with a barrel of pickles, testing it for weight and balance. A smile formed at the corners of his mouth and he hefted it again, looking back at the storekeeper.

"What kinda shell does it fire?"

The little man beamed. ".45 caliber. Guaranteed to down anything on four legs. Or two, as the case might be."

"Damnation!" Bob muttered. "Print, lemme have a look at that thing."

Print handed him the Colt, then fixed the merchant with a steady gaze. "How many of them guns you got?"

"Well, I've got this one on display and five more. Six altogether."

"I'll take 'em."

"All six!" The storekeeper appeared a bit flustered. "Why, I can't rightly sell you all six. They just came in today and I've got regular customers to think about."

Print leaned across the counter and glared at him. "Mister, I reckon you didn't hear me. I just bought your whole stock. You're open for business and that makes it first come, first served."

The man got a little pale around the gills when he saw the look in Print's eyes and backed up a step. "Well, all right. You don't have to get sore about it. But you haven't even asked the price."

"Don't matter. I'll take 'em. How many shells you got on hand to fit this?" Taking the Colt from Bob, he thumbed the hammer back and sighted on a lady's bonnet at the back of the store.

"Happens I know exactly, since it all came in the same order. Twelve hundred shells, right on the button."

"I'll take them too. Put the guns in one sack and the shells in another."

"Good Lord, man. You must be planning to fight a war." The merchant shook his head with a dumb-founded expression. Suddenly he brightened and gave the Texan a sly smile. Turning, he pulled a rifle from the rack and thrust it at Print. "Since you're so keen on guns, maybe you ought to take a look at the new Winchester. Greatest thing in rifles since the Henry carbine."

Print set the Colt aside and began examining the rifle. He worked the lever, sighted again on the lady's bonnet, then hefted it for weight. He ran his hand over the stock, caressing it as he would a woman. Lowering the hammer, he glanced around at the storekeeper.

"What's it shoot?"

".44 caliber, but more powerful than the old Henry. Holds fifteen shots."

"How many you got in stock?"

"By jingles," the little tradesman crowed, "I'll send you back to the well this time. I've got four left and they're forty dollars each."

Kelly chuckled and the three Texans exchanged amused looks. The storekeeper stared at them for an instant, then his face turned red and his gaze came back to Print. "Don't tell me—I know. You'll take 'em. Mister, you must be the richest man in Texas."

"Not yet," Print grinned. "But I'm workin' on it. Box me up a thousand shells to go with the rifles, too."

"So long as you're not paying in Confederate I'll box up the whole store if you like. Sure you don't want to buy a wagon to cart all this artillery?"

"No thanks. We'll manage." The cattleman opened his shirt and began loosening a money belt. "Now suppose you just tote up what we owe."

Ten minutes later the Texans rode east out of Ogallala, with a fair sized load of pistols, rifles, and sacks of ammunition tied to their saddles. Print had one of the Peacemakers stuck in his belt and every few minutes he would pull it out and start inspecting it all over again. They had just passed the cattle pens when he suddenly jerked the gelding back on its haunches.

"Sonovabitch!"

Bob hauled up short and looked back. "What's the matter, Print?"

"Wouldn't you know it. I clean forgot my goddamn' cigars."

Jim Kelly started laughing and within moments the three

men were whooping like they had just come off a dose of forty-rod. Then they put the rowels to their horses and set a course for the holding grounds.

Somehow, the day didn't look quite so bleak anymore.

3

When Print and his crew returned from the Platte in late September, they found a strange disquiet had settled over Sunburst. Even as they rode into the compound the cattleman sensed that something had changed, and not for the better. With the exception of Print, the boys had built their own homes among the stately pecan trees lining the creek. As head of the family, his place was in the big house; though Louisa would have preferred a home of her own, she had adjusted to sharing a roof with the old man and Julia. But there was an eerie stillness about the place this evening, and for a moment Print couldn't put a name to what bothered him.

Then, as he glanced around, it struck him what was missing. Toward sundown, with supper finished and dark coming on, the compound was normally overrun with a gathering of loud, rambunctious children.

Tonight, there wasn't a child in sight.

As he dismounted in front of the house Lou came through the door and ran toward him. One look at her face and he knew for certain that something was bad wrong. While she was smiling there was an odd cast to her eyes. Fear— perhaps grief—something that didn't belong there.

"Oh, Print. Print." She threw herself into his arms. "God, I've never been so happy to see anyone in my life."

Holding her close, he felt her shiver beneath his touch. "Honey, what the hell's going on around here? Are the kids sick?"

"No, no. They're fine." She hugged him tighter, burying her face against his chest. "Honestly, just fine."

"The old man, then. Or Ma?" Grasping her shoulders,

he stepped back and bent down to look in her eyes. "Dammit, something's wrong. Now what is it?"

"Sweetheart, everybody's all right. I promise." Tears began to well up in her eyes. "It's what they're doing to the animals."

Before he could question her further Jay and Ira came walking up, and he could tell from their expressions that something fearful had taken place while he was away. Then Bob came running across the compound, clearly in a rage about whatever had happened. Evidently Jenny hadn't wasted any time in spilling the story.

The youngster skidded to a halt and looked from the boys to Print. "Have they told you?"

"Nobody's told me anything, yet," he said with a touch of irritation. "But we're gonna solve that real quick. Let's get inside."

With his arm around Lou he led the way into the house. His mother was waiting just inside the door and again he saw the same strange look that seemed to be in everyone's eyes. After hugging her, he strode forward to where Jim Oliver was seated in his rocker and they shook hands. Whatever else was wrong, at least the old man wasn't scared out of his wits. His grip was strong and his gaze seemed firmer than Print could recall in a long time.

"Pop, you're lookin' mighty spry. Ma let you sneak a jug into the house, did she?"

Jim Oliver cackled and threw him a sly wink. "Not yet, she ain't. But I was hopin' you might've brung me one from up north."

Print nodded his head with a movement that was barely perceptible and grinned. Then he glanced around the room and turned back to Lou. "Where are the kids?"

"They're playing in their room." The lines around her mouth remained tight. "Maybe you should wait to see them. After we've talked."

His brow wrinkled in a small frown. "Why? What difference does it make?"

"They'll ask you why—" Her face went pasty and she couldn't go on.

"All right," Print grated. "I guess it's about time somebody gave me the lowdown. Jay, what the devil's got everybody walkin' on eggshells?"

Somehow Jay didn't look his usual smug self. There were dark circles under his eyes, and when he spoke, his tone seemed to be less cutting, not so smart aleck anymore. "After you and Ace went up the trail we started gettin' raided again."

"So? We've been rustled before. How many head did they get?"

"About two hundred, near as I can figure. But that ain't what's wrong."

"Well, spit it out," Print demanded hotly. "You act like somebody was tryin' to pull your teeth."

Jay swallowed and just for a moment he looked a bit unnerved. Then he straightened, meeting Print's gaze levelly. "Whoever it is has been doing bad things to the stock. They cut the throats on a bunch of she-cows up by North Spring, and when we found 'em the calves was so weak we had to shoot 'em. Another time they hung a calf from a tree over the creek path. They was close enough we could hear it cry when they strung it up."

"Didn't you go after 'em?"

"No, it was night and we was short-handed. Like as not they had us outnumbered. Besides, since this started, we been bringin' all the kids in before dark and stayin' close to home."

That explained why there weren't any children in the compound tonight. Print scratched his jaw thoughtfully for a moment. "Jay, it appears to me that this somebody you're talkin' about has got the Indian sign on you. You don't stop 'em by barrin' the doors and crawlin' under the covers."

"That's easy to say if you ain't around. If you'd been here the night they got to the horses, you might be a little nervy yourself."

"What d'ya mean, the night they got to the horses?"

"Well, I was sorta holdin' off on that till you got the picture." Jay glanced around at the others as if seeking support. "They snuck up on the nighthawk 'bout the end of August and knifed him. Didn't kill him, but they come close to it. He came to while they was still doing their dirty work and played possum. Otherwise I reckon they'd have finished him off. Anyway they hamstrung nine horses before the rest broke loose and took to the hills." Then his eyes wavered, and for a moment he stared at his boot tops. "They was mostly mares. We shot 'em the next mornin'."

Print's face knotted in a towering rage and he scowled at his brother. "You mean you just shot the mares and left it at that. You didn't try and track them down? Bubba, I don't know whether you've got jelly in your guts or not, but that's something you just don't let a gang get away with. You hear me? You find 'em and you kill 'em!"

"Don't blow your cork at me!" Jay shouted, his face mottling with shame. "The women and kids was scared silly, and I figured the important thing was to look after them. Whoever it is struck into the compound a couple of weeks later and gutted a dog. Left it right out in the open where we wouldn't miss it. Your big, tough foreman was here then. Why don't you go yell at him?"

Julia Oliver broke in gently. "Prentice, he's right. Screaming at each other won't help anything. You were gone and Jay did what he thought was best."

"Maybe so. But his best damn' sure wasn't good enough." Stalking to the fireplace, he stared into the flames till he had his anger in hand. They waited to see what he would say, and finally he turned back to Jay. "Did you think to contact the Sheriff?"

Jay nodded glumly. "Did that first thing. Told me he didn't have enough deputies to be out beatin' the bushes. Said if we caught anybody to bring 'em in and he'd see they went to jail."

"Jail!" Bob growled savagely. "We don't need him or his

jail. Them scutters oughta be strung up and worked over with their own knives."

"Hold your horses, sport." Print waved Bob back and fixed Jay with a dark look. "You said the night-hawk saw some of those men. Did he know any of 'em?"

"Nothin' definite. Said he might've spotted the Kiley brothers, but he couldn't be sure. It was dark and he wasn't too clear headed most of the time they was workin' on the horses. I told the Sheriff and he said something like that wouldn't mean a hill of beans in court."

"Dock and Lawson Kiley?" Bob asked. "The ones that always hang out around Grady's pool room?"

"I reckon. Don't know 'em myself. But some of the boys said they's seen 'em in town off and on."

"More off than on if they're out carvin' up other people's stock." Bob gave Print an appraising look. "What d'ya aim to do about it?"

"Well, I'll tell you. The first thing I'm gonna do is sleep on it. No sense going off half-cocked."

"You think that Cal Nutt feller is behind all this?"

"Hard to say. Might be even harder to prove. Especially since he's become the big augur in town."

Print's deliberate manner nettled the youngster. Sometimes he felt his oldest brother thought things out too much, instead of taking the bull by the horns. "Well, if it was up to me I'd ram a gun in his belly and see if it might not loosen his tongue."

"Yeah, but it's not up to you, sport," Print observed dryly. "Besides, I tried that once and it don't pay to threaten the same man twice. He'll always be layin' for you that second go-round. No, what we've got to do is figure out some way to get the goods on Nutt, or whoever's behind this."

He paused and mulled it over for a couple of seconds, then glanced around at the family. "Like I said, I'll sleep on it tonight. Tomorrow I'll have something lined out. You boys tell your women to rest easy. There won't be anyone around scarin' young 'uns from now on. Leastways there won't without somebody payin' a stiff price in the bargain."

The three brothers seemed pleased to have the discussion done with, and before long they drifted off to their own homes. After they had gone Julia started toward the kitchen, then turned and faced Print. "Son, I've been waiting to hear you say what all this means. Why would men do such terrible things?"

"Ma, I'm not sure I rightly know. Looks to me like somebody might be tryin' to run us out of the country. The thing that's got me worried is that they might switch to people if killin' our stock don't turn the trick."

"The boy's right," Jim Oliver mused out loud. "Nights're dark and lead's cheap as nails."

Print just stared at him for a minute, then took Louisa's hand and headed for the back of the house. Sometimes the old man made more sense than the whole damn' family put together.

Along toward ten that evening Bob Oliver dismounted in front of Grady's pool hall and tied his horse to the hitch rack. When he went through the door his eyes swept over the room at a glance. Grady was racking balls on a back table and Lawson Kiley was lining up a bank shot on the front table. Dock Kiley was nowhere in sight. He would have preferred to get them both at once, though a fellow asking pot luck couldn't be choosy.

"Kiley, I've got something to say to you."

The youngster's blunt words brought everything in the room to a standstill. Lawson Kiley straightened up from the table with a startled look, but before he could say anything the proprietor came rushing forward.

"Now listen here, Bob Oliver, I don't want any trouble in my place. You just turn around and get out of here, if you know what's good for you."

Bob never once looked away from Kiley, but out of the corner of his eye he could see Grady edging toward a small bar along one side of the room. "Grady, I know you got a shotgun back there. Make a move for it and you're a dead man."

Kiley finally regained his voice. "He's right, Grady. Leave it be." Grinning cockily, he laid his pool cue on the table and stepped clear. "Now, honeybunch, what was it you had on your mind?"

Bob's voice shook with rage, but in a queer sort of way he had never felt cooler in his life. "Kiley, anybody that hamstrings horses is nothin' but a low down, good for nothin' sonovabitch. That includes you and your shit-eatin' brother."

"Sonny, you must be tired of livin'." Kiley's mouth twisted in an evil smirk. "What'll it be? You gonna crawl over here and kiss my foot, or do I hafta dust you on both sides?"

"That's the trouble with being yellow, Kiley. You always try to talk a man to death."

Kiley snatched at the pistol on his hip, but as the barrel cleared leather he froze dead still. A Colt Peacemaker had appeared in Bob Oliver's fist and was pointed straight at his chest.

Sweating now, he tried to brazen it out. "Sudden sort of bastard, ain't you?"

"So long, honeybunch." Bob squeezed the trigger, and as the Colt bucked in his hand Lawson Kiley slammed up against the pool table, then fell face down on the floor.

The youngster's cold gaze went around the room, touching on Grady and the other players. "Anybody here don't agree that was self-defense?"

When nobody said anything his eyes settled on the proprietor. "Grady, when you see Dock, tell him he's next."

Backing to the door, he casually holstered the Colt and stepped into the night.

4

Print couldn't deny that Bob's visit to Grady's pool room had been reflected in the attitude of everyone on Sunburst. There was something deep-down satisfying about hitting back, and every hand on the place was proud as punch that the youngster had struck the first blow. Bob was treated to his first taste of hero worship and he found that it had a heady flavor. The crew's remarks about the gunfight came in a joshing, offhand manner, but it was clear that they were slightly awed by his rash and somewhat deadly response to the gruesome raids.

For his part, Bob didn't start swaggering around like a two-bit pistolero, and no amount of coaxing could get him to brag about the shootout. While he secretly gloried in his new reputation, even encouraged it by growing quieter and more solemn, the youngster didn't let it swell his head. When asked, he stated calmly enough that he had just killed a sidewinder, and let it go at that. The hands took that as a mark of true grit, and among themselves they agreed that he had the makings of a real mankiller.

But Print wasn't all that impressed. Like the crew, he was proud of Bob, for it took real balls to face a known gunman and allow him to make the first move. That was cool, deliberate calculation, rigging it so the law had no choice but to declare it self-defense. That he could admire. Blind recklessness was another matter entirely, though. The boy had taken a desperate chance walking into that pool room alone. Without someone covering his back he could have been gunned down before he ever got started. That was just plain damn' foolishness, and the morning after the shooting he let Bob know it in no uncertain terms.

His first mistake, Print had noted, was in playing a lone hand. If he had to do it, then he should have gotten help. Since he knew the answer he would have got had he come to the big house, he should have looked elsewhere. Perhaps Jim Kelly, or one of the older hands. Someone who knew how to handle himself in a tight situation. For that matter, even Jay or Ira would have done, just so he didn't rush into a shootout with his back exposed. Had Dock Kiley been on the premises, Print observed, they might be burying an Oliver instead of the other way round.

Bob had agreed that he acted rashly, but he was really

more interested in hearing about the second mistake. Print informed him bluntly that it was downright stupid to pick a fight on someone else's turf. If there was no way around killing, he had concluded, then the time and place should be to the other fellow's disadvantage. Catch him off home ground. Sucker him into a spot where he had his back to the wall and the sun in his eyes. Then pick the fight.

Julia Oliver raised the roof when she learned that Print hadn't done anything more than lecture Bob on his mistakes. Those who live by the sword shall die by the sword, she pronounced stiffly, declaring that if any harm befell the youngster his blood would be on Print's hands—just as surely as if he had pulled the trigger himself. Print informed her that fighting was men's business and hotly advised her not to meddle in things she knew nothing about. Then he had stormed out of the house, leaving the old woman to reflect on the fact that Sunburst was no longer a family enterprise. It had become the personal empire of her eldest son, and like it or not, there was little she could do to influence his thinking.

While Julia's musings were based sheerly on a mother's instinct, she had never been closer to the truth in her life. Print Oliver had long since ceased to think of Sunburst as a family proposition. Instead he saw it as an exclusive and very private little club, limited to a membership of one. Himself. The responsibility for thousands of cattle and close to fifty human beings rested squarely on his shoulders. The buck stops at the top—that was how he remembered it from the cavalry—and it wasn't something a man took lightly. Right or wrong, the responsibility for what happened was his. Which wasn't exactly the kind of thing that could be shared or shunted off onto someone else when the going got rough. That made the decisions his alone, also. For if no one was willing to share the responsibility, then he damn' sure wasn't willing to share the authority.

Perhaps a man more introspective than Print would have realized that over the years he had fashioned Sunburst to fit his own needs. Whether intentional or by happenstance, he made it into a one-man show, with everyone in the outfit dependent on him for a guiding hand. Not that he couldn't delegate authority. He could, and did. But only with a strong measure of control. For Print had come to see himself as a man of destiny, one chosen to leave a mark that neither time nor circumstance would erase. His lodestar was the image of himself as a cattle baron, one who would found an empire that could be passed on to his sons, and their sons after them. The kind of man who was remembered for having dared greatly—for what he had done rather than what he had been.

While Print knew full well that life could only be understood backwards, he was distinctly aware that it must be lived with audacity. Those who waited for the last card to show before making their move invariably ended up sucking hind tit. Yet goaded as he was by this need to soar even higher, it was a hunger that he never fully comprehended. It was one of those things a man could fathom only when looking back; rarely, if ever, did he recognize it for what it was as he was living it. Sometimes he suspected that it was nothing more than a gnawing in the gut or a lonesomeness of the flesh, for given a full belly and a warm-natured woman he was as content as the next man. Then that indefinable thing that lived inside his head would flare anew, and he realized all over again that the furies of the soul were like some great carnivorous beast. Always hungry, never satisfied, driven on and on to glut itself not on food or even love, but with the mindless will to stand above the petty commonplaces of lesser men.

Sadly, it was the kind of hunger few could imagine, much less attribute to one of their own. Neither his mother, nor Louisa, nor the boys could understand what drove him, and that bothered him at times. It sealed him off, made his life a solitary thing. For there was no one like-minded enough to share his thoughts. Or his dreams.

Yet it didn't diminish what he saw in himself, or lessen

the savor of what he had accomplished. Instead it spurred him in some curious way to test himself even further.

To reach still higher.

But if a man had designs on the future, he must first protect that already gained. Accordingly, he organized a fast-moving band of four picked men to patrol Sunburst range. Since fall roundup was only about half finished four men were all he could spare, but he had an idea the ones selected would be equal to the task. Their job was to scout the hills and back country at odd hours of the day and night. They were to be especially careful not to establish a pattern or schedule, anything that would make their movements predictable by those planning a raid on the Oliver spread. Their orders were to kill anyone who resisted, but to take as many prisoners as possible. Sooner or later they would capture someone who could be persuaded to talk, and at that time the rules of the game would change drastically.

Jim Kelly was chosen as leader of the patrol. The wrangler was an old night fighter from way back, and his years on the Staked Plains had taught him much about the sport of hunting men. Lee Wells and Pinky Simms were picked because they were both crack shots and regular buzzsaws when it came time to make the fur fly. The fourth man selected was Bob Oliver. He wouldn't have had it any other way, and Print felt it only fair that one of the family be assigned to this risky undertaking. The youngster had proved that he could handle himself and that settled it. Though he had a tendency to be reckless, Jim Kelly was just the fellow to teach him that bold men don't always live to be old men.

Not unless they were damn' smart in the bargain.

With that out of the way, Print turned to problems of a different nature. Namely, how to weather the present financial storm and what course to set for Sunburst come spring. After devouring the Austin newspapers and spending an afternoon with the Oliver's lawyer, he made his decision. That night he called a family conclave in the living room of the big house. Though the three boys were invited, their wives as well as Louisa had been excluded. The only female present was Julia Oliver, and as usual, she stood directly behind the old man's rocker.

When everyone settled down, Print opened the meeting. "First things first. This money panic back east has put the squeeze on a lot of cattlemen. Some of 'em just flat got wiped out. That's because they lived high on the hog and figured they could always get a new loan from the banks come spring roundup. We're in pretty good shape, though. We didn't make much profit this year, but we've got a fair size chunk of gold rat-holed back."

"Well we sure oughta," Ira said, trying to lighten it with a quick grin. "No more'n you pay us, this outfit oughta be knee deep in double eagles."

Print ignored the thinly veiled criticism and kept his voice mild. "Ira, you get paid the same as me or the folks. I hold out what the ranch needs to operate and split the profits five ways. If Emma spends too much on foofaraws that's your problem."

"Goshdurn it, Print, that ain't f-f-fair." Ira's ears got red and he started to fidget. "What's a man w-w-work for if he can't give his woman p-p-pre—nice things?"

"Beats me. But a man's got to draw the line somewhere. You and Jay spoil those girls so bad it's a wonder they don't have you wearin' aprons."

"Now hold on just a blamed minute," Jay croaked. "The real trouble is just what I've always said it is. You hold back too dangblasted much money for the ranch. If we all got what was comin' to us there wouldn't be no problem."

"Jay, the only ones with problems is you two." Print forked his fingers like a frog gig and jabbed at them. "The rest of us seem to be livin' good and eatin' pretty regular. Besides, it looks like I haven't been holdin' back near enough. The way things are shapin' up I'm gonna have to ask everybody for a donation."

"Donation!" Jay and Ira barked in unison like a couple of trained seals.

" 'Fraid so," Print observed calmly. "For them that's got

the money to put herds on the trail, next summer is gonna be their big chance. The end of the rainbow. Folks back east will be yellin' for beef, but there'll be a hell of a lot of outfits that won't trail the first cow north. I figure there's gonna be a shortage of beef at the beginning of the season, and that means prices will skyrocket. Whoever gets there first is gonna make it big."

He paused, looking from face to face. "I mean to put four herds on the trail by the middle of May."

"Four!" Ira and Jay came under the wire so close together they gave each other dirty looks.

Julia Oliver decided to get into the act. "Son, aren't you risking an awful lot on the hope this money scare won't last?"

"Yes'm, I guess you could say I am." Print rubbed the stubble on his chin, taking a moment to get his ducks in a row. "But that's what this business is all about. Always has been. Them that aren't willin' to take chances winds up with the leavin's every time. Next year is gonna separate the men from the boys, and I mean to have Sunburst right at the head of the pack."

"Prentice, you've done a wonderful job," his mother said. "Nobody can fault you up to now. But wouldn't it be wiser only to take two herds up till you see how things look?"

"Might be wiser, Ma. But it wouldn't be near as good a gamble." Julia blinked but he didn't bother to clarify that cryptic observation. "Anyway, we're only gonna sell three of the herds. The fourth one will be breeder cows to stock our new spread north of the Platte."

The room suddenly got very quiet and the Oliver family spent the next couple of moments staring at each other in consternation. Print couldn't help but chuckle at their stunned expressions, and the sound of his laugh brought their heads back around.

"Now before anybody gets their nose out of joint, lemme tell you something. I don't aim to move Sunburst up there, but I mean to see that we get our fair share of the goodies. The next big push in this business is gonna come up north. You've heard me talk about it often enough. That land has got the grass, it's got the water, and it's close to the railheads. What I've got in mind is to establish a whole new operation up there. Still Sunburst beef, but a different outfit altogether. All it takes to get it started is some cows and a little money. The land's free."

Jay snorted scornfully. "Well, by jingles, you ain't gettin' me to move up there in that blizzard factory."

"Me neither," Ira parroted.

"Boys, the thought hadn't even crossed my mind. You two don't know beans from buckshot about the cow business. Never took the trouble to learn."

They both started to yell, but Julia Oliver stilled them with a sharp look. "I hope you're not thinking of Robert."

Bob came up like he had been goosed with a pointed stick. "Ma, you got no call to say that. Print wasn't much older'n me when he took over this spread."

"Take it easy, sport." Print waved him down. "I figure we're gonna need you around here the next couple of years anyway. That'll give me time to teach you there's more to this business than ropin' and brandin' cows. Meantime, I'm gonna let Bumpus Moore run that outfit. He's steady and he'll do a good job."

There was a long moment of silence as everyone digested that, then Julia spoke up again. "You said a little money, son. How much does that mean?"

Print studied their faces an instant before answering. "With what we've got in the cookie jar, I figure it'll take another $10,000."

"Ten thousand!" Jay bellowed incredulously.

In a softer, but equally disbelieving voice, Ira said, "J-J-J-Jesus."

"Watch your tongue, young man," Julia snapped.

Print held up a hand for silence. "Now that's not as big as it sounds. It's only two thousand apiece, and within a year we'll get it back double. In five years we'll have more money than a Philadelphia banker."

"Print, you got rocks in your head," Jay croaked. "Even

if I had the money I wouldn't fork it over. And just in case you're wonderin', I don't have it."

"Me t-t-too," Ira sputtered. "I mean I don't have it neither."

Everything got quiet again while Print thought that over. Finally he pursed his lips and nodded. "It figured, I reckon. No need to cry over spilt milk, though. I've got better'n three thousand saved and I'll toss every cent of it in the kitty."

Bob swallowed and took the plunge. "I got a thousand anyway. Maybe closer to fifteen-hundred."

Print glanced at his mother, who in turn dropped her eyes to the old man's balding pate. Jim Oliver slowly brought his rocker to a halt and leaned forward. He had both jaws loaded with tobacco and was all but speechless. When he let go there was a wild hissing and spewing and for a second Print thought he had put out the fire. Then he reached out and tapped the hearth with his cane.

"There's close to nine thousand in gold under there. Me and your ma been squirrelin' it away for a rainy day." Craning his neck around like an old hoot owl, he gave Jay and Ira a sour once-over. " 'Pears to me it just started to pour."

Twisting back, he set the rocker in motion and winked at Print. "Son, I been thinkin' I wouldn't mind seein' that tall grass myself."

Print's eyes glistened with pride and after a moment he found his voice. "Pop, I've got a notion you'll do just that." Looking around, he grinned. "Boys, it looks like we're going to the Platte."

Nobody said anything for a while, then Jay raked him with a bitter glance. "You know somethin', Print? I think you'd spit in the devil's eye if it'd get more graze for your dang cows."

Print laughed, feeling the tension wash out of him. "Bubba, you've only got it half right. I'd shake hands and make him a partner if it meant gettin' that valley we camped in last summer."

"Don't speak blasphemy, son," Julia Oliver admonished him. "Woe unto them that call evil good, and good evil."

The old man squirted the fire again and a sizzling cloud of sparks leaped up the chimney. "The stroke of the tongue breaketh the bones."

His wife grunted like Lucifer himself had nudged her in the ribs, then spun on her heel and stalked off toward the kitchen. But as she went through the door a tiny smile played at the corners of her mouth and she began humming softly to herself.

5

Late the next afternoon Jim Kelly and his men rode out just as the crew began drifting in for supper. The sun still hovered over the westward hills, but in another hour it would be dark. The wrangler intended to patrol along the creek, then swing north for a couple of miles and make a cold camp somewhere around Stinking Springs. Before dawn they would be in the saddle again and circle generally in a southeast direction, back toward the compound. More than likely they would hit the home place just about the time Doughbelly started clanging the grub bell.

Unless they got lucky—which didn't seem to be anything a man could rightly count on. Not lately, anyhow. Rustlers had gotten scarce as hen's teeth it seemed, and in two nights of patroling they hadn't seen hide nor hair of anyone suspicious. For that matter, they hadn't seen anyone, suspicious or otherwise. Kelly was beginning to think someone had put the quietus on their little venture. Up till now they hadn't done anything but lose a good deal of sleep and scare the bejesus out of a few longhorns.

Still, he was convinced that when the raiders struck next they would do so under cover of darkness. With roundup in full swing there were just too many Sunburst hands combing the hills to make a daylight raid anywhere near safe. Thinking about it just that morning, it came to him that it might be wise to start out a little early tonight. The rustlers knew as well as anyone else that the hands came in for supper around dusk. Assuming they were as smart as the next man, they might just use that last hour before dark to cross undetected onto Sunburst land and get themselves situated for a night's dirty work.

Kelly was banking on the fact that the rustlers hadn't yet tumbled to his scouting party. That being the case, it might just be possible to waylay some night riders who figured everybody was back at the compound feeding their faces. It was sort of like hunting wild horses. You had to stand off and look at it the way the other fellow would. Before long— if you really put yourself in his place—you might begin to get a feel for what he was likely to do.

But whether a fellow was hunting mustangs or men, he first had to get himself in tune with the night. That is, if he meant to move about safely and get the job done. Before their first patrol Kelly had explained it to the other men in much the way he had learned it. The night has a feel all its own, something that has no kinship with daytime. If a man is in touch with the dark he senses things instead of seeing them. He tests the wind more often because his nose works better in the soft night breezes. He listens for the sounds that should be there—the katydids, crickets, and frogs—just as he keeps an ear open for those that shouldn't. When he hears a twig snap he knows that it could be a longhorn, maybe even a deer. But more than likely it is something that walks on two legs. Wild things don't make much noise, especially in the dark when there are other wild things waiting to pounce on them. Naturally, the jingle of saddle gear or a shod hoof striking a rock would be dead giveaways. Yet a fellow couldn't count on being that lucky. He had to figure that the man being hunted was just about as smart as the hunter, maybe even more so. He walked light, kept downwind whenever possible, and stuck to the deepest shadows he could find. Otherwise the first sound he heard might be a knife grating on bone as it slid into his gizzard.

Riding along now, though, Jim Kelly's thoughts had little to do with the night and its stealthy ways. Caution and an instinctive awareness for what shouldn't be had long since become as much a part of him as his ebony skin. Instead, he was thinking of the boy who rode behind him.

Over the span of his years at Sunburst he had seen the youngest Oliver grow from a gangling tad to a broad-shouldered bull of a man. In all that time the boy had never traded on the fact that he was an Oliver; if anything, he had worked longer and harder to prove that he was as good a hand as any in the outfit. Now he had proved something else, though it had small bearing on his work with horses and cows. In one explosive instant he had shown the sand it takes to coldbloodedly face another man and force him to draw. There weren't many of that breed around. Kelly knew, for at one time or another he had seen most of the hard cases and tough nuts that ever came down the pike. Sure, there were lots of men who would fight to save their skins, and some of them were damn' dangerous fellows when aroused. But the kind who would call another man out and coolly goad him into a fight were few and far between.

Kelly had concluded long ago that such men probably pissed ice water and had blood about as warm as a snake's. While he had killed his fair share, it had always been the other fellow who started the ball rolling. Whatever it took to prod another man beyond reason and coldly gun him down was something he didn't have. And didn't especially want. But he had thought about it a lot, wondering just which part of a man's insides got twisted around so that he ticked differently than the next fellow. Most people chalked it off to sheer guts, some freakish kind of courage that came along once in a blue moon. Maybe it was, for there was no denying that a man with a stripe down his back sure as hell didn't fit the ticket. Still, it had always seemed to him that there was a little more to it than that.

Courage was something most men had after a fashion—even a cornered rat would give a good account of himself. The cold-eyed killers had something more, or then again, perhaps they had something less. The more he thought about it, the more Kelly came to believe that something had been left out of such men. They weren't braver than anyone else, they just had less fear. Maybe no fear at all. They weren't afraid of the things that frightened other men, whether it was getting shot, or carved up with a knife, or even dying. Like sourdough biscuits with the starter left out, some quirk of nature had neglected to give them their share of fear. Folks generally allowed that this breed of man had nerves of steel, but to Kelly's way of thinking they didn't have nerves at all. They just did what they had to do, and never gave a thought to the consequences. For themselves or anyone else.

Reflecting on it now as they rode through the trees skirting the creek path, the wrangler had a feeling deep down in his guts that Bob Oliver was that kind of man. Maybe not as ruthless or downright scary as some he had seen, but the youngster was getting there damn' quick. Once they got a taste for killing they were hooked for life. It became a habit, sort of like tobacco. Only it was a hell of a lot harder to break.

Unless he missed his guess, young Bob was about to become a heavy smoker.

The black man suddenly snapped erect and reined his horse back. Three riders across the way had just started to ford the creek onto Sunburst land. Since Kelly's patrol had kept to the trees rather than using the path, the strangers hadn't seen them as yet. Surprise was the best edge a man could ask for, and with any luck they might capture all three of these birds without firing a shot.

Kelly looked around and found his partners watching him intently for instructions. Motioning with his hand, he brought them abreast of his horse and waited till the three riders pushed their mounts up the creek bank onto Oliver range. When the intruders broke through the treeline into a small clearing north of the trail, Kelly nudged his horse and moved forward at a walk. Quartering to the west for a few moments, he then swung the patrol on line and halted them off the left flank of the night riders. This had all been done without alerting the three men, and Bob found himself filled with admiration for the wrangler. When the bastards turned they would be staring straight into an orange ball of fire perched atop the hills.

"Hands up!" Kelly shouted. "First man that moves is dead."

The riders scattered like a covey of quail, never even looking back. Plainly they had heard what happened to rustlers caught on Sunburst and they preferred to take their chances on a fast run for the brush. But they had a good fifty yards to ride before they would again be under cover.

Kelly jerked his rifle, spouting orders out of the side of his mouth even as he aimed. "Get their horses! We want 'em alive."

Bob brought the Winchester to his shoulder, swung the sights as if he was leading a duck, and squeezed off a shot. He never did remember hearing the other rifles go off, but all three horses somersaulted headfirst and sent their riders tumbling to earth. Two of the men scrambled to their feet and began popping away with six-guns. The third lay where he had fallen, presumably dead or knocked cold. Curiously, Bob heard the rifles this time. The sharp cracks were a beat apart, and as the blast rolled across the meadow the two rustlers staggered, then pitched to the ground.

Kelly signalled the patrol forward and they moved across the clearing at a walk. When they approached the fallen men it was obvious that the two who had elected to fight were dead as doornails. But as they drew nearer the third man raised his face from the dust and called out.

"If you boys won't gun me I'll get up."

"Take it slow," Kelly answered. "We gets jumpy when people move too quick."

The man came erect very cautiously, raising his hands overhead. "Yeah, I noticed."

Bob felt his pulse quicken as the rustler turned to face them. It was Dock Kiley. The youngster exchanged quick glances with Kelly, then the black man looked back at their captive.

"Mister, you got a choice between some tall talkin'," he said, "or a mighty slow hangin'. Which'll it be?"

Kiley saw the hard look on their faces and knew that they weren't bluffing. "What's in it for me if I do talk?"

"Depends on what you got to say. Jest for openers, who's your boss?"

The rustler hesitated briefly, weighing the alternatives. Then he decided there weren't any. "Feller named Grip Crow."

"Hell," Kelly growled, "we known 'bout Crow far back as I can remember. Jest happens we ain't been able to catch him. I'm talkin' 'bout the big boss. The head wolf."

"I don't know, and that's the honest to God truth. It's somebody in town, but Crow never told us who. Wouldn't even talk about it."

"You ever hear of a feller name of Cal Nutt?"

"Sure I have. He's some high muckety-muck in George-town. Everybody knows that."

Kelly cocked one eyebrow. "And you're tellin' me he ain't your boss?"

The man shook his head dumbly. "I ain't tellin' you nothin' of the kind. I'm sayin' I don't know."

"Maybe you didn't hear what I said 'bout hangin'." The wrangler's teeth flashed in the deepening twilight. "I know a way that takes a man at least an hour to die."

"Damn' right I heard you." Kiley's forehead broke out in a cold sweat. "You don't think I'd string you along facin' a rope, do you? Boys, this Cal Nutt ain't nothin' to me. If I knew I'd say so. That ain't no bull. Honest to Christ, it ain't."

Kelly studied him for a moment, then looked around at Bob. "Hate to say it, but I think the sorry bastard's tellin' the truth."

Pinky Simms and Lee Wells bobbed their heads in agreement, but the youngster got a funny look in his eye. He glanced at the rustler, then his gaze came back to Kelly. "Jim, lemme have him. It's personal."

The black man returned his stare with a sober frown, then slowly nodded.

Bob dismounted and walked off to one side about ten

paces. Turning, he faced the captured man. "Kiley, you know who I am, don't you?"

"Yeah, I know you. Wouldn't be likely to forget."

"Good. Then you know it was me that got your brother. I'm gonna give you the same chance I gave him. Your gun's still in the holster. Use it."

Kiley jerked his head back at the three mounted men. "What about them?"

"Jim, if he beats me you turn him loose. That's the way I want it." Bob hadn't taken his eyes off the rustler and an icy calm settled over him now. "That suit you?"

"Guess it'll have to."

"Then quit talkin'."

Dock Kiley wasn't any faster than his brother. His gun was still in the holster when Bob's slug caught him dead center in the brisket. He grunted, like he couldn't hardly believe it, then folded limply to the ground.

Jim Kelly also found it a little hard to believe. He had seen fast gunhands before, but this boy made the rest of them look like molasses at forty below. The blur of his hand had been all but indistinguishable from the report of the gun, like a snake striking. You didn't see it—you just knew you'd been bit.

But the black man found comfort in the knowledge that Bob Oliver was on his side.

Suddenly he felt very old and very slow.

CHAPTER EIGHT

———◆———

1

The usual courthouse loafers greeted Cal Nutt as he mounted the steps to the north entrance. Their buttery chorus was the same as that reserved for all local bigwigs—judges, bankers, wealthy property owners—the shakers and movers of the community. Though Nutt held no official position, their welcome was no less cheery, for it was common knowledge in Williamson County that he wielded a big stick politically. Moreover, during the Reconstruction era he had acquired considerable town property as well as a vast stretch of farmland along the San Gabriel. Most folks just naturally felt there was ample reason to give the former carpetbagger his due, and then some.

Nutt nodded dourly, without so much as a glance in their direction, and entered the courthouse. By now the bowing and scraping had become old hat, and he no longer took heed of their waxlike smiles. It was simply the way things were, something he expected not so much as he took for granted. When he thought about it at all, it was generally with a note of cynical humor. People had a curious knack

for convincing themselves that their fear was actually respect, and that made it all right for them to kowtow to a man
like himself. No one lost face that way, and the peckerheads
could still sit around telling each other what tough hombres
they were.

In a quirky sort of way it was damn' amusing. They
fooled not only each other, but themselves as well.

Striding down the long central hall, he turned in at the
office of the County Prosecutor. When he came through
the door, Sheriff Ed Strayborn and George Suggins were
waiting for him. The two men greeted him with a certain
deference, much the same as the loafers on the courthouse
steps. Without acknowledging it one way or the other, he
moved forward and took a seat beside Suggins' desk.

"Gentlemen, the reason I called this meeting is to dis-
cuss the grand jury." After nipping the end off a cigar and
lighting it, he glanced up at the County Prosecutor. "I
understand you mean to empanel a new jury next week
sometime."

"That's right," Suggins agreed. "Probably get started on
Monday."

Nutt extracted a sheet of paper from his coat pocket and
flipped it on the desk. "See to it that these men are selected."

Suggins unfolded the paper and let his eyes scan a list
of names. Then he looked up with a puzzled expression.
"These are mostly farmers and saloon bums."

"I didn't ask for a report on their ancestry," Nutt observed
testily. "I said to get them on the grand jury."

"Well sure, I guess we could manage that—"

"I had an idea you might be able to work it out."

"—but it'll cause a godawful stink around town."

Nutt smiled sardonically, exhaling a cloud of thick blue
smoke across the desk. "You just do what you're told and
let me worry about the busybodies."

George Suggins had every intention of doing exactly
that, just as Nutt had known he would even before calling
the meeting. Like the Sheriff and most of the men holding

county offices, Suggins had been elected Prosecutor due solely to Nutt's patronage. The political machine Nutt had put together over the years could pretty well pick and choose who occupied the seats of power, and this fact wasn't lost on those who had aspirations toward public office. The rumpled, cigar-chomping Yankee controlled a bloc of votes that could swing any election, from dogcatcher right on up to county judge. Essentially the bloc was comprised of three elements. Those who owed him favors, which included Georgetown's sporting crowd. Those who owed him money on mortgages, business loans, and notes he had bought up from their creditors. Finally, the immigrant farmers who had settled in Williamson County after answering his advertisements in *The Austin Statesman*. For the most part these were German émigrés who had been taken under Cal Nutt's protective wing shortly after stepping off the boat in Galveston. Some homesteaded plots of land back in the hill country. Others were allowed to buy parcels of Nutt's bottomland along the river on long term mortgages. But wherever they settled in Williamson County the farmers were surrounded by cattlemen, and they were quick to learn that their only friend was the man who had brought them there. Whether by choice or circumstance, they were obligated to the political boss for their very existence. Once qualified to vote, they also did exactly as they were told.

The ranchers grumbled, the townspeople complained, and the opposing party shouted blood and thunder every time an election year rolled around. But it had no more effect than whistling into the wind. Cal Nutt pulled the strings, and the courthouse was his own personal puppet show.

Watching him now, George Suggins wondered just what the hell the wily bastard was up to this time. "Since it's me that has to get them on the grand jury, don't you think I ought to have some idea why?"

"Suggins, the only reason you need is because I said so. When it comes time I'll let you know what has to be done." Nutt glowered at him for a moment, then looked over at Ed

Strayborn. "Sheriff, I've got some bad news for you. Before long you'll have to get off your duff and start making some arrests."

Strayborn smiled tactfully and fingered his mustache. "Whatever sounds fair, Mr. Nutt. Who's the culprit?"

"You've been reading too many dime novels." The politician puffed on his cigar for a moment before answering directly. "The culprit, as you call him, will become known very shortly. Seems like some men are going to be murdered on Yegua Creek."

"Murdered?" Strayborn got a blank look on his face. "That's sorta queer isn't it? I mean you knowin' about it even before it happens."

"Don't lose any sleep over it," Nutt snapped. "Just be ready when the time comes."

The Sheriff bobbed his head agreeably. "Sure, reckon I could do that. Trouble is, I'm not real certain what it is you want done."

"What I want done is exactly what you haven't been doing. The way I hear it there were three men shot out there a few months back and you didn't do a damn' thing."

"Now that's not quite right, Mr. Nutt. I went out there and looked into it personal."

"But you didn't arrest anyone. Or did I miss part of the story?"

"Couldn't arrest nobody. The dead men was rustlers. Caught red-handed."

"Who said so?"

"Why, the Olivers. The boy and three hands that was with him when it happened."

"And you just took their word for it?"

"Didn't see no reason not to." Strayborn darted a glance at Suggins but found no support there. "Besides, messin' with that family isn't exactly like attendin' a church social. Somebody's been using a knife on their stock, and they're sorta primed for bear."

Nutt scowled at him and started puffing on his cigar. Over the past year he had fleshed out quite a bit, and he had a tendency to purple somewhat when angered. "Sheriff, how long have you been in office?"

Strayborn's eyes widened for an instant and he appeared flustered. "Twelve years, just about."

"Well if you have any notions about serving another term you would do well to stop taking other people's word for things. Do I make myself clear?"

Strayborn and Suggins exchanged looks, and the message was clear as a bell. Election time wasn't far off and Williamson County's political boss had just laid it on the line. Either they did as they were told or when the ballots were counted they would be standing around scratching their asses wondering where the good times went.

The Sheriff got hold of himself and managed not to wither under Nutt's glare. "What you're sayin' is that I'd best start takin' your word for things instead."

"You hit it right on the nose, Ed. Couldn't have said it better myself." Nutt rose and favored them with a tight, mealy-mouthed smile. "Now that we understand each other, let's make sure there are no slip-ups when things start popping. Suggins, let me know just as soon as the grand jury has been picked. Then we'll see if we can't serve up some indictments that will make a hero out of the Sheriff."

With that the Yankee walked out the door and left them staring at one another through a haze of cigar smoke. After a long while the lawman let out a deep sigh and slouched down in his chair.

"George, do you get the feelin' that conniving sonovabitch is gonna send some men out to Yegua Creek just so's the Olivers can kill 'em?"

Suggins stuck his thumbs in his vest pockets and peered down his nose like a near-sighted gopher. "Ed, I'm gonna pretend I didn't even hear you say that. If you want some good advice, you'll do just what I'm gonna do."

"Yeah. What's that?"

"Nothin'. Except what that miserable bastard tells me to do."

Ed Strayborn came to his feet and started for the door. Some days it just didn't pay for a man to get up—on either side of the bed. Right now he had the feeling somebody had jammed an auger up his ass and given it a couple of sharp turns.

Halfway through the door he paused and looked back. "Mr. Prosecutor, it strikes me that we're holdin' cards in a game that's about to get dicey as hell."

Then the door closed and George Suggins got busy breaking out a bottle he kept for occasions just such as this. Nerve medicine, he called it. Whether a man was losing his—or just didn't have any to start with—whiskey had a way of working wonders on the spine.

2

Across a wide stretch of prairie below North Springs a herd of close to five hundred breeders had been gathered. Some of the hands were still combing the surrounding hills for she-cows and spring calves, but the main gather itself was just about finished. Three other crews were working different parts of Sunburst in a similar manner, holding heifers, cows without calves, and a sprinkling of bulls. Once the separate gathers were done, a herd of two thousand head would be assembled and put on the trail for the Platte.

Print Oliver's grand plan for the expansion of Sunburst was rapidly taking shape.

Though it presented some difficulties, roundup had been started early that year and the first herd would be trailed out toward mid-April. Since Bumpus Moore was taking eight men along to the Platte, Print had hired twenty additional hands for the season. With any luck, and a lot of long, sweaty days, three herds of beeves would then be shoved up the trail for Kansas a week apart. Figuring losses to quicksand, storms, and the Indians, Sunburst would market something over four thousand steers by the middle of August. With a whole new operation established in the valley of the Loup along about the same time, the Olivers would damn' near have the world by the short hairs. Still, dreams were often like puff weed in a strong wind, and the end of summer was a long way off. Between now and then they had their work cut out for them, with a damn' small margin for error.

Print and Bumpus Moore sat their horses on a small rise watching the gather below. Calves were being dragged blatting from the herd to a small fire where a crew of five men swarmed over them. Within a matter of seconds they were branded, earmarked, castrated, and swabbed. Afterwards, somewhat altered in appearance but no worse for wear, they scooted off searching for their mamas. When the she-cow came to claim her calf they were driven off into the brush, leaving only the breeders marked for the Platte herd on the prairie below.

Bumpus Moore had his leg hooked around the saddle horn and was building himself a smoke. In between licks he shuttled a look over at Print. "Way things are shapin' up we oughta put 'em on the trail day after tommorah. Friday at the latest."

Print nodded absently, watching a hand flank an unbranded yearling with a tremendous heave. "Looks that way. The rest of the crews are just about even with you. Ace's bunch might be a little ahead."

Ace Whitehead, Harry Strain, and Jay had been selected to take the steer herds up the Chisholm Trail to Kansas. Each had his own crew, and the men they ramrodded during roundup were the same ones they would have on the drives. After Whitehead's bunch reached Wichita he would spend the rest of the summer floating up and down the trail, lending a hand in case Jay or Harry Strain got in over their heads. Print intended to reach Wichita a few days ahead of the first herd and remain there throughout the summer. That way he would be on the spot to watch market fluctuations and could make a deal whenever prices peaked.

Moore got his smoke going and spit on the sulphur-head before tossing it away. "How long you reckon it'll be before you get the rest of 'em headed out?"

"No more'n a month," Print replied. "Damn' sight less if I've got anything to do with it. Once we get you and Ace on the trail I'm gonna let the last two crews work on their own herds. That way they'll be ready to leave just about together."

"When you plannin' on leavin'?" Moore asked.

"About two weeks after Ace pulls out," Print noted. "That way I'll get everybody started on the trail and I still oughta be able to catch up with Ace somewheres around Red River Station."

Moore flicked an ash with his pinky and thought about that for a minute. "You still mean to leave Kelly and his bunch here all summer?"

"Don't see why not." Print continued to watch the action below, but a slow smile crept over his face. "What's the matter, them boys been béllyachin' about being left behind?"

"No more'n a grizzle bear with a sore paw," Moore chuckled. "To hear them tell it, everybody else is gonna come back with soft cocks and fur in their mouths, and they won't never have set foot off the place."

Print had thought it out well in advance, and he was taking no chances this summer. Jim Kelly's little band would remain behind to patrol Sunburst throughout the trailing season. Along with the hands who stayed back to tend the spread it should be enough to dissuade the nightriders from getting too bold. Bob had pitched a fit when Print informed him he wouldn't go up the trail this year, but after a few days he had calmed down. Once he thought it over it wasn't such a bad idea after all. Not only would he get to spend the summer with Jenny, he might just get another crack at the rustlers. Which would be a hell of a lot more exciting than eating trail dust for six hundred miles.

"Well," Print observed after a moment, "guess I'll have to make it up to 'em once everybody gets home. Maybe I'll send 'em down to San Anton for a week and let them señoritas iron the kinks out of their tails."

"Say, I wouldn't mind a little of that myself." Moore got a faraway look in his eye and his voice trailed off. "I surely wouldn't."

Print turned and regarded him with deep scrutiny. "Reckon you'll miss Texas, Bumpus? Or aren't you the kind to get homesick?"

"Miss Texas! Me?" Moore laughed shallowly. "Boss, it's just like that Yankee general said. If I owned Texas and Hell I'd be hard put to choose between 'em." Then the smile faded and his eyes went sober. " 'Course, there's places lots worse, I guess."

"Yeah, I expect you're right, at that," Print agreed. "Still, it likely won't be for more'n a year. Bob oughta be ready to take over by then, and if you're of a mind to, you can come on back. Meantime you can find yourself a filly in Ogallala. Hell, you might even wind up gettin' partial to that northern stuff."

"By damn', I might at that!" Moore's face brightened with the thought. "That gal I had when we was there last year purely knew how to jitterate a feller's juices. Makes my mouth water just to think about it."

"Well, don't think on it too much," Print commented. "You've got a lot to do and damn' little time to do it in. By the time you get a bunkhouse up and grub freighted in, winter'll be comin' on. And I've got an idea you and the boys'll spend lots of days in the saddle pushin' cows from one snowbank to another. Remember what I told you. This herd's make or break. If you can't bring 'em through a winter up there, then the whole damn' scheme's a washout."

"Shit, boss, don't let it fret you none." Moore grinned confidently. "Why, come next spring we'll be ass deep in calves. You just wait and see if I ain't right."

"Bumpus, I sure as Christ hope so. Otherwise we're gonna—"

Print's words fell off abruptly as he noted a rider coming hell for leather across the prairie from the south. Nobody pushed a horse that hard unless it was damn' important. Which generally meant trouble in one form or another.

Then he saw that the rider was Lee Wells and there was no longer any doubt. Jim Kelly and his boys had clearly flushed something down south. But that hardly made sense. Anybody who tried rustling cattle during spring roundup couldn't be playing with all his marbles.

The two men roweled their horses into a lope and rode forward to meet Wells. Moments later they came together near the branding fire and Lee Wells lost no time in spitting out the message.

"Boss, we caught four of 'em! Just pushin' a bunch of cows along pretty as you please east of Little Pond. We shot one and another got away, but we got two of 'em live and kickin'. Kelly says for you to come quick."

"Whoa back," Print ordered as Wells started to rein his horse around. "Let's have it a little slower. What about our boys? Anybody get hurt?"

"Just Pinky Simms," Wells informed him, clearly anxious to be off. "The dead jasper winged him in the arm, but when we threw down on 'em the others called it quits."

"I thought you said one of them got away."

"Well, he did. Couldn't be helped, though. He was ridin' drag when the fireworks started and he took off like he'd been turpentined. I went after him myself, but he circled back west and I lost his trail 'bout a mile downstream."

"Who plugged the dead one?" Print asked.

Wells' mouth lifted in a knowing smile. "Didn't figure you'd have to ask. That little brother of yours is a real pisscutter. Drilled him plumb center with one shot."

Print didn't say anything for a couple of seconds, then he nodded. "All right, catch up a fresh horse out of the cavvy. Soon as you're saddled we'll ride." Turning, he found Moore watching him closely. "Bumpus, keep your boys humpin'. This don't change a thing. I'll see you back at the house tonight."

Print kneed his gelding into a trot and started south. Before he reached the far corner of the open grassland, Lee Wells had caught up with him and they set out at a dead lope.

* * *

Slightly less than an hour later the two men reined to a halt beside a small pond no more than a mile north of Yegua Creek. Jim Kelly and Bob came to their feet and walked forward, but Pinky Simms kept his seat under a tree. Obviously he was hurt worse than Wells had let on. The rustlers were trussed up like a couple of pigs and lay on their bellies a few yards away. The dead man was nowhere in sight.

Print dismounted and nodded to Kelly. "See you caught yourself some fish."

The black man shook his head and snorted. "Jackasses'd be more like it."

Still thoroughly puzzled by the whole deal, Print's gaze drifted over to the bound men. "Wonder how the hell they thought they'd pull it off with roundup in full swing?"

"Beats me," Kelly remarked. "I guess some folks jest ain't got sense 'nough to pour piss out o' a boot."

"Did you get 'em to talk?"

"Sure. But they ain't said nothin' worth listenin' to."

"How's Pinky?" Print asked, glancing over the wrangler's shoulder at the wounded man. "Looks a little green around the gills."

"Aw, he's all right," Kelly assured him. "Didn't lose hardly 'nough blood to bait a trap. Give him a dose of snake medicine and he won't even know the difference."

"Well let's have a talk with these roosters. Maybe they've had time to think it over."

Print moved toward the trees and stopped a few paces from the rustlers. Neither of them looked up or gave any indication that they saw him standing over them.

"You boys sorta got yourselves in a fix," Print observed wryly.

"No shit." The younger of the two men was sandy-haired and evidently had a temper to match. "You figger that out all by yourself?"

Print didn't say anything for a while, then he looked at the older man. "How about it? You look like you've been around long enough to know when it's time to save your own skin."

"Eat shit," the rustler snarled corrosively.

"You know, once when I was a kid my daddy and me hung a wiseass like you for horse stealin'. Fella wouldn't give us the time of day, even when we were fittin' him for a noose. Later we come to find out he didn't do it after all."

Print paused to let that sink in. "Guess the joke was on us."

"Some joke," the sandy-haired youngster grunted.

"Sonny, in case you haven't gotten the drift, the joke's on you today. You've got about ten seconds to start talkin'. Otherwise you get strung up."

The two men craned their necks to exchange looks, then the older one cleared his throat. "What'd you have in mind?"

Print squatted down so they could see him better. "Who sent you out here? And don't tell me it was Grip Crow."

"Well, mister," the rustler cracked, "I reckon we just run out of things to jawbone about. 'Cause that's the feller's name."

"Horseshit! I've never even seen this Crow, but I've got an idea he's too smart to send somebody out rustlin' right in the middle of roundup."

"Yeah? Well if you ever do see him, tell him I said he's the dumbest sonovabitch on two legs. He said you'd have all your boys up north around Brushy Creek today. That's the only reason we come out here."

That struck Print as damn' queer. It just didn't make sense one way or the other. "Where might we find this Crow fella?"

"You don't find him, he finds you. Told us to take the cows to a spot on the North Fork of the San Gabriel. Said he'd meet us there in the next day or two if everything came off."

"Then I reckon you wouldn't know where he gets his orders," Print said casually.

The sandy-haired one snickered nervously. "Mister, we don't even know where he drops his drawers to take a shit."

Print came erect and nodded to Kelly. "Get 'em on their horses." Looking around, he caught Bob's eye and motioned to the tree. "Sport, put a couple of ropes over that limb and cinch 'em down tight to the trunk."

Though he had never seen a man hung, Bob didn't even blink an eye. Moving quickly, he gathered lariats from the rustlers' own saddles, tossed them over a stout limb, and snugged them firmly at the base of the tree.

Kelly meanwhile cut the rawhide thongs binding the men's ankles, then Wells helped him to hoist them aboard their horses. Within the space of a few heartbeats they had the rustlers mounted and positioned beneath the dangling ropes.

The older man raised his eyes and studied the rope a moment, then glanced back to see Print mounting his gelding. "Mister, you're sorrier'n chickenshit. We told you all we know and you're still gonna hang us."

Print eased the gelding alongside the youngster and fitted the noose around his neck. Then he reined over beside the other man. "Old timer, you'd better save your wind. You're gonna need it." Then he dropped the rope over the man's head and pulled it tight.

"Go fuck yourself," the rustler growled venomously.

Print backed the gelding away, removed his hat, and swatted the older man's horse across the rump. The youngster's mount needed no such urging and leaped away skittishly in the same instant. Both rustlers swung clear of their saddles, then snapped back as the ropes brought them up short. The older man was the heavier of the two and his neck was broken as he hit the end of the line. But the sandy-haired boy spun around and around in lazy circles, kicking and dancing with his legs like he was trying to find some foothold in thin air. His eyes seemed to burst out of his head, growing huge and distended with fiery red streaks. Then his face turned a peculiar shade of blackish amber and his swollen tongue flopped out over his chin.

The Sunburst riders stared on as if mesmerized, feeling their own throats tighten as the youngster's struggles grew weaker and weaker. Not until he had slowly strangled to death could they force themselves to look away.

After it was over Print's dark gaze settled on Kelly. "Where's the one Bob shot?"

The wrangler jerked his head toward the hills and thick undergrowth. "We pulled him off in the brush."

"Drag him out and string him up beside those two. We'll let'em hang there till they rot. Might be it'll give certain folks something to think about."

Print gigged the bay and headed west through the hills. He still had three cow camps to check and the sun had already edged over the noon hour. Then his stomach grumbled and it occurred to him that he had missed dinner.

But, what the hell? Those three fellows back at the pond wouldn't be hearing any dinner bells either.

3

The first sign of trouble brewing was when the Sheriff showed up bright and early next morning with a wagon. Something smelled high enough to peel paint and all of a sudden Print felt a shade uneasy about the whole deal. When Strayborn announced he was there to collect the dead men, there was no longer the least particle of doubt. The Olivers had been suckered into some sort of trap, and it didn't take much horse sense to see that the bait was even then swinging from a tree out by Little Pond.

Looking back to yesterday, Print recalled thinking that the rustlers had been a bunch of dimwits to come raiding right in the midst of spring roundup. This morning it was crystal clear.

They hadn't come. They had been sent. Expressly as bait for the trap that was now about to be sprung.

Still, it was like the old man always said. Hindsight wasn't no better than hind tit. All it did was make a fellow feel like he had mush between his ears.

Right now, Print felt like he had about as much brains as a cold horse turd.

Only after cutting the bodies down and loading them did the Sheriff seem inclined to divulge the particulars. Seated in the wagon, he glanced up at the three dangling rope ends, then looked back at the cattleman. "Just between us and the fence post, Print, you shouldn't have hung those boys. Sorta puts you betwixt a rock and a hard place."

"They were rustlers," Print grated out. "Since when is it against the law for a man to defend his own property?"

"Well, maybe they was rustlers and then again, maybe they wasn't." Strayborn took out a plug of tobacco and bit off a mouthful. After he got it juiced up, he spit and wiped his soup-strainer. "We've got a man back in town saw the whole thing. Says you killed 'em with no cause atall."

"What d'ya mean, he saw it?" Print had an icy feeling along the base of his spine that he knew what was coming next.

"Maybe you recollect there was four of 'em?" When Print nodded the lawman went on. "Well this feller, name of Will McDonald, was the one that got away. Way he tells it, he circled around atop one of these hills and watched you string his partners up. Says they was just takin' a shortcut across your land on the way to town when your boys jumped 'em."

"That's a goddamn' bald-faced lie!" Print roared. "Those bastards were drivin' better'n fifty head of cattle. I suppose they were just lettin' them cows show 'em the shortcut."

"This McDonald feller says there weren't no cows." Strayborn pursed his lips and drowned a horsefly with one squirt. "Says your boys opened up on 'em before they had time to say scat."

"Then how come one of my men got nicked in the arm?" Print demanded.

The Sheriff shrugged eloquently. "Way he tells it, your boys started the fight and one of his partners got off a shot before he was downed. Then you came along a couple of hours later and just strung 'em up without a by-your-leave."

Print was fighting a losing battle to control his rage. "Strayborn, I don't know where your stick floats in all this, but I'm gonna tell you something straight out. We hung three rustlers, and if anybody comes out here tryin' to arrest my hands they're gonna get their ass handed to them in a sack. You included."

The old lawdog bowed his head for a moment, then squinted up with a bemused expression. "Print, I'm sorry you feel that way. Wouldn't do no good, though. I could always call in the Rangers and you'd just get a lot of people killed needlessly." He spat over the side of the wagon and looked away. "Besides, the charges was brought against you. Nobody else."

Print seemed to calm down when he heard that. "Then there's no problem. I've got four witnesses that'll swear we didn't hang nothin' but rustlers. Four against one oughta just about wrap it up."

"Wouldn't do that, if I was you," Strayborn allowed. "Not just yet, leastways."

"Why not?"

"Well this McDonald feller is going before the grand jury this afternoon. They held off so's I could come collect the evidence. You bring your boys in there to testify and they're liable to hand up five indictments 'stead of one."

The Sheriff paused and shifted his cud to the off cheek. "I wouldn't own up to tellin' you this, but if it was me, I'd save their testimony for the courtroom. You're gonna need it."

"You're sayin' that by tonight there'll be a warrant out on me for murder."

"That's about the size of it. Some folks don't hold for lynchin', and by a queer sorta coincidence, there's a whole raft of 'em sittin' on that grand jury. Am I beginnin' to get through to you?"

Print studied the peace officer's face for a few seconds,

then grunted. "Somebody stacked the jury to make sure they'd see it the right way."

"Reckon you'll have to draw your own conclusions about that. I've already said enough. Too much, more'n likely."

"Guess it wouldn't do me any good to ask you who's behind it?"

When the lawman's features stiffened, Print smiled tightly. "Thought not. Doesn't rightly matter, though. There's only one asshole I know that'd think up a deal like this. Yankee asshole, to boot."

Strayborn acted like he was stone deaf, then after a while he looked around. "Print, I'll have to come for you. Probably tomorrow mornin'. Any need for me to bring help?"

The cattleman hesitated only briefly. "No, I'll come peaceable. If you want me to, I'll meet you at the courthouse about noon."

"I'd be obliged," the Sheriff said quietly. "It'd look better all the way round."

"No, Ed, it's me that's obliged. I know that bastard's got you by the short hairs. Hell, everybody in the county knows it. You went out on a limb tellin' me what you did, and I won't forget it. I owe you one."

"Don't mention it," Strayborn replied. Then the double meaning of the words struck him and he chuckled softly. "Matter of fact, just forget we had this little talk."

The lawman clucked and his team hit the traces. Print held the gelding back and watched him drive off. Maybe Ed Strayborn wasn't the straightest man that ever pinned on a star, but he damn' sure wasn't the crookedest either. Even when he was on the other side of the fence, you had to give the devil his due.

Print decided to call it a day. He had some tall thinking to do and the roundup could get along well enough without him for one day. Come to think of it, the whole shebang—roundup, cattle drive, and family—might have to get along without him a sight longer than a day if the dice went against him in Georgetown. Reining the gelding about, he rode toward the creek, trying to ponder his way through what had suddenly become a sorry goddamn' mess.

One thing was for sure. Somebody wanted the Olivers nailed to the wall. Perhaps even driven clean out of the country. What had happened here this morning only served to confirm what he had thought all along. There was some kind of conspiracy afoot to bring the Olivers to their knees—force them to eat humble pie and start thinking about faraway places. Otherwise why would anyone go to such lengths to snooker him into a murder charge?

Was somebody out to get him personally? Perhaps to settle an old grudge he couldn't even recall.

Or could it be some of those die-hard old Loyalists still intent on teaching the Rebels a lesson?

On the other hand, it might not be all that complicated. Maybe somebody just plain and simple had his eye on the ranch. It wouldn't be the first time folks had been terrorized off a good piece of land.

For that matter, it might tally out to a combination of all those things. Somebody nursing a grudge against Rebs in general and the Olivers in particular. Somebody who meant to grab off Sunburst by forcing the Olivers to pull up stakes and run for cover.

Like hell they would. The Olivers had never run from anything in their lives—and they weren't about to start now.

Then it came to him that instead of saying *somebody* or *they* he ought to just use the name that had been on the tip of his tongue all morning. Cal Nutt.

The sorry bastard fitted the ticket on all counts. He was a Rebel-hating Yankee who had gobbled up land along the San Gabriel for years after the war. Though it couldn't be proved, it was also common gossip that he had been behind the rustlers from the start. Moreover, he had an old score to settle. Thinking about it now, Print remembered telling Bob that it wasn't smart to threaten the same man twice. Evidently once had been enough for Cal Nutt.

But what the hell could be done about it?

Short of killing the son-of-a-bitch there was no way of forcing him to call off the dogs. He owned the law in Georgetown lock, stock, and barrel. Never mind sheriffs and judges—now it seemed that even juries were obligated to do his bidding. Legally there was no way to touch him, and killing him would bring the new State Police—Rangers they called themselves—quicker than a dose of salts through a constipated goose.

It was a thorny problem. One that defied solution.

Then he recalled something Jim Kelly had once said about breaking broncs. *There never was a horse that couldn't be rode; there never was a man that couldn't be throwed.*

Maybe the same thought applied to Mr. Cal Nutt. Even a ruthless shit-heel of a Yankee had to have a weakness somewhere.

Turning the bay toward home, he decided to get some more heads thinking on it. This evening after supper he would call a family meeting and lay it out for them. They had to be told about the murder charge at any rate, and they might just come up with something he had overlooked. Maybe he was so close to it he couldn't see the forest for the trees.

Then he grunted wryly to himself. That could happen to a man faced with a hanging charge.

Sometime after midnight Will McDonald stumbled out of the Tivoli Saloon & Gaming Parlor accompanied by a deputy assigned to safeguard his welfare. Tonight had been the biggest night in his thus far unremarkable life. He was no longer a drifter, or a saloon bum—or worse yet, a common rustler. He was the State's star witness, a celebrity of sorts. Once he had his day in court they were going to stretch Print Oliver's neck a yard long and thin as cat-gut. Then he could just sit back in the shade and live like the swells. That was what Grip had promised him, and he had every confidence it would come true. With the stories he could tell if he was a mind, he didn't dare back out on the deal.

But even if it didn't happen, tonight had made the whole thing worthwhile. Everybody standing in line to buy him drinks and slapping him on the back. Telling him what a grand fellow he was and making a big to-do about the balls it took to face anybody as mean as the Olivers.

Christ! That was the kind of treatment a man could cotton to real easy.

McDonald's reverie was suddenly jarred by a dull thud followed by a soft groan. Turning clumsily, he saw the deputy fold at the knees and slump forward to the ground. There was a jangle of spurs off to one side but he couldn't see a blessed thing. In some dim recess of his mind it occurred to him that like a damn' fool, he was standing in an alleyway pitch dark as a stack of black cats. Then something hard and cold rammed up against his backbone, and even stumbling drunk he recognized the metallic whirr of a Colt hammer being thumbed back.

"Mister, you make one sound and I'll blow your guts clean into next Sunday."

A powerful arm encircled his neck and jerked him off his feet. Before he could quite gather his wits he had been dragged down the alley and unceremoniously slammed up against the back wall of a building. Then a hand that felt like an ore crusher took a firm grip on his throat and the pistol was rammed into his belly clean down to the gizzard.

"McDonald, you got about five seconds to make a deal if you wanta keep on breathin'." The man's voice was gravelly and rough, just about as rough as his way of handling people.

"What d'ya want?" McDonald croaked, trying desperately to sort it all out in his numbed brain.

"My name's Bob Oliver. That mean anything to you?"

The rustler turned songbird stiffened like an icicle. The name gonged through his head like the peal of thunder and he was suddenly stone-cold sober. Though he couldn't see it very clearly in the dark, that was death staring him in the face. Old Scratch himself. Bob Oliver had already killed five men, and if Mother McDonald's pride and glory wasn't real careful he would wind up number six.

The hand loosened slightly around his neck. "My brother tells me you're the feller that's got him wired for a trip to the gallows."

McDonald's lips moved and his voice came out in a gusty rush of pure fear. "I ain't got no stake in this. Honest to Christ, I ain't. I'll get on the witness stand and tell 'em I'm a liar. Tell 'em I didn't see none of that happen. Nothin', you hear. Nothin'. Just plain double ought nothin'."

The hand tightened down on his Adam's apple and he felt his eyes bulge out of their sockets. "You know, Will, I got an idea you can do better'n that. Lots better. Like gettin' your scrawny ass clean out of Texas. Maybe as far away as California. How about it? Wouldn't you like to see the ocean and dip your pecker in some salt water?"

McDonald bobbed his head as much as he could without strangling himself and when the hand again loosened he sucked in great gasps of air. "I'll do it. Honest to God I will! I'll ride out and never look back. Not ever."

"Yeah, I know you will," the gravelly voice said. "I've got a horse all saddled and waitin'. There's two hundred dollars in the saddle bags and enough food to get you to hell and gone."

Suddenly the Colt left his gut and was jabbed underneath his chin so hard it made his teeth click shut. "Don't make any miscues, shithead. You ever show your face around here again and there ain't nothin' on God's green earth that'll stop me from killin' you."

Ten minutes later, Will McDonald, former star witness and minor celebrity, rode west out of Georgetown, flogging his horse like the hounds of hell were right on his heels. Though thankful just to be alive, he couldn't help but curse his piss-poor luck. For a night that had started out so good it had sure turned shitty all of a sudden.

Still, maybe California wouldn't be so bad at that. At least there weren't any Olivers out there.

The thought came sweet and clear, like the warmth of sunlight in a cold dawn, and he sank his spurs halfway up the shaft in the horse's belly.

4

Bob and Jim Kelly waited in the courthouse hall as Print went through the door of the Sheriff's office. They had insisted on trailing him to town and nothing he could say to the contrary had phased them in the slightest. After last night's meeting, everyone on the place remained firmly convinced that somebody meant to hamstring the Olivers by railroading Print on a murder charge. This morning the shock had worn off and they were just plain fighting mad. When Print started out for Georgetown they had outvoted him seven ways to Sunday, insisting he take along at least two bodyguards.

Whatever happened, they meant to see him through safely. After all, anyone underhanded enough to rig him for a quick trip to the gallows wasn't above shooting him in the back on some lonely stretch of road. Just to make sure.

But when Print entered Ed Strayborn's office he sensed immediately that something about the game had changed. The lawman looked like a cur dog that had just been pelted with rocks, and if he'd had a tail it would have been securely clamped between his legs.

Print closed the door and consulted his pocket watch, then came forward to stand before the desk. "I think we agreed on noon. I'm ten minutes early."

Strayborn gave him a sour frown. "Early or late, it don't matter much. You're free to go. For the time being, anyway."

The cattleman's startled look was genuine enough, but Strayborn found it hard to believe he hadn't had a hand in last night's dirty work. "Now c'mon, Print. Don't put on that schoolgirl act with me. I don't mind being tricked so much, but don't play me for an ass in the bargain."

"What the hell're you talkin' about?" Print snapped back.

The Sheriff appraised him with a skeptical gaze. "Are you standin' there tellin' me you don't know what happened outside the Tivoli last night?"

"Tivoli?" Print echoed. "What the Sam Hill does the Tivoli have to do with anything?"

"Aw, not a hell of a lot," Strayborn replied sarcastically. "Somebody just conked my deputy over the head and made off with Will McDonald. You remember him, don't you? The feller that was gonna testify against you. Nobody's seen hide nor hair of him since."

"Well kiss my ass," Print muttered with amazement.

"Yeah, it is sorta peculiar, ain't it? Especially when he was the only man this side of hell that had the goods on you."

Print's dumbfounded look evaporated on the instant and his eyes went hard. "Sheriff, let's get one thing straight. I didn't have nothin' to do with this and I don't know nothin' about it. I don't work in the dark. Anybody that says I do is a goddamn' liar."

Strayborn's gaze again lingered on him for a moment. "Well, I'll have to admit it's not exactly your style. But it's damn' queer, all the same."

Print couldn't deny that, yet his bafflement was rapidly disappearing. Though he couldn't be sure what had happened to McDonald, he had a pretty good idea who was behind it. Still, that was hardly something to be discussed with the law. "You said something a minute ago about me being free to go. How come?"

"How come?" the Sheriff snorted. "Why Christ Jesus, man, we're fresh out of witnesses. That's how come. The County Prosecutor just got through rakin' my ass over the coals for lettin' McDonald slip through our hands. If that's what really happened. Suggins is of the opinion he's long dead by now."

"Does that mean the charges have been dismissed?"

"Hell no, the charges haven't been dismissed. It just means there's no sense holdin' you for trial unless we've got somebody to put on the witness stand. The indictment stays on the books till this thing is cleared up one way or the other."

"So now your friends'll be holdin' a club over my head with an open murder warrant?"

Strayborn smiled disdainfully. "Print, what kind of odds would you give that Will McDonald ain't never heard from again?"

"Yeah, I see your point." The cattleman fell silent, wondering just what the hell had happened to McDonald. Finally it came to him that there was nothing left to be said on the subject. Not here. "Guess I'll be on my way, then. Unless you've got more business with me."

"Don't let the door hit you in the ass on the way out," the Sheriff said grumpily. "And if you ever hang anybody again, I'd appreciate it if you'd do it over in the next county. I'm gettin' too old for this horseshit."

Print didn't even look back. Bob and Kelly fell in beside him as he came through the door and started peppering him with questions. Just then the door to the County Prosecutor's office opened and Cal Nutt stepped into the hall. Suddenly the reason behind the Sheriff's hang-dog manner became glaringly plain.

It was the Yankee himself who had raked Strayborn's ass over the coals.

If Print hadn't been sure about Cal Nutt before, he was now. The son-of-a-bitch was running this show personally— and had been from the start.

Nutt gave him a scowl that could have drawn blood and stalked off down the hall. Watching the dumpy politician out the door and down the steps, Print had every certainty that the fight had only just been joined. That slimy bastard meant to have him laid out in a box, and no two ways about it.

Bob and the wrangler were so busy thinking about Cal Nutt that their questions were forgotten for the moment. They trooped out of the courthouse in silence, and Print didn't volunteer any information about his talk with the Sheriff until they hit the outskirts of town.

Watching them out of the corner of his eye, he broke the news as if he was discussing yesterday's weather. "Seems like the law misplaced their witness. This fella McDonald got snatched away from his watchdog late last night."

Kelly's face was a study in utter astonishment, and just for an instant he seemed on the verge of saying something. Then he thought better of it and held his peace. Bob didn't say a word, but he looked about as surprised as a loaf of bread.

Print let the silence mount before he spoke again. "Can't rightly say I'm sorry to see McDonald out of the way. Then again, it sure goes against the grain to think of him turnin' up dead somewhere."

They rode along in absolute stillness for perhaps a full minute. Finally Bob slung his jaw out of joint and arched an eyebrow, like a man will when he is suddenly struck by some profound thought. "You know, I'll just bet you that McDonald feller is headed for California. Probably figured it all out for himself and saw the writin' on the wall. Wouldn't surprise me none if we never heard from him again."

Jim Kelly's face was like an onyx stone. "Boy, I got a feelin' in my bones you is dead on the money. Tell you something else, too. That sorry devil must have a good eye for hoss flesh, 'cause last night he done stole one of the best cow ponies in our string."

There was a moment of deafening silence, then all three men broke out in gut-busting laugher. Spurring their horses into a lope, they left Georgetown behind them and headed for home.

That night after supper Print held a meeting on the front porch of the big house with Jim Kelly and the members of his patrol. Pinky Simms had his arm in a sling, but Bob, Lee Wells and the wrangler were playful as bears in a honey barrel. They had rid the country of three more rustlers— four if a man counted last night's little escapade—and their boss was free as a hawk in a summer wind. Along with a bellyful of steak and cream gravy, it was a hard feeling to beat.

After everyone was settled down, Print gave it to them without pulling any punches. "Boys, the cheese is about to get binding. That deal yesterday made Cal Nutt look like a real bonehead, and I've got an idea he's gonna turn the wolves loose. Most likely he'll wait till we've trailed the herds out, then strike when he thinks there's not enough hands left on the place to queer his play."

He waited a couple of seconds to let that sink in thoroughly. "Jim, I've decided to give you four more men for the patrol. That way you can have a bunch out on scout around the clock and it'll leave four guns here in the compound at all times. You're liable to have rough sleddin' till the crew starts driftin' back from Kansas, but I think you boys can handle it."

The men exchanged smiles, and from the looks on their faces he knew his confidence wasn't misplaced. Every one of them just naturally loved a good fight, and whoever was foolish enough to come raiding Sunburst was sure to get a warm reception.

Presently Jim Kelly gave him a searching little side-glance. "When we catches 'em, what does we do with 'em?"

"Same thing you've been doing," Print informed him. "Only different."

Nobody said anything and his gaze slowly swept from face to face. "From now on there's to be no warnin'—none of that *hands up* bullshit. Shoot on sight and make goddamn' sure not one of the bastards gets away. Yesterday showed us which way the wind's blowin', and from here on out we can't afford any mistakes. No witnesses. No prisoners. No nothin'. They just disappear."

"What you're sayin'," Kelly remarked, "is that we should get rid of the evidence and cover our tracks after we does it."

"That's right. There are plenty of places on Sunburst where you can bury 'em so deep they'll never be found.

That way if the law does come nosin' around they won't find nothin'. Not even a sniff."

Bob grinned as though his prospects for a dull summer were quickly taking on a whole new outlook. "Sounds like you think they're gonna be comin' across the creek like smoked bees."

Print's grim scowl was answer enough in itself. "Sport, before first frost you're gonna see enough dead men to last you a lifetime. We've got a war on our hands, and the other side don't play nothin' but dirty pool. That's why I just threw the rules out the window."

Then he paused and looked at each of them in turn. "Watch yourselves at all times. Shoot first and bury your mistakes. When I get back from Kansas I want to see every one of you right here to greet me."

After the men had gone, Print lounged back in the rocker and closed his eyes. What he had told them was the straight of it. They were in a war. Fighting for survival just as surely as he had at Shiloh or a hundred other bloody killing grounds now forgotten. Seemingly nothing had changed from that time to this—neither men nor the motives that impelled them. It remained a savage land—contested over by the ruthless and the strong—and if the meek inherited any part of it, they did so with a headstone planted over their solitary legacy. Six lousy feet with your name carved in crude stone. It hardly seemed enough. Certainly not for him. Or the likes of Cal Nutt. Yet just as sure as the sun rose and shit stunk, one of them would wind up with nothing more to show for his troubles.

A small noise beside him brought his eyes open and he saw his mother standing there. He smiled, straightening in the rocker. "Ma, there's times I suspect you've got more Injun in you than you ever owned up to."

Julia Oliver studied his face for a long while, not returning the smile. "What you told Robert and those men. Is that the way it must be, son?"

"Yes'm, I guess it is. Seems like there's some folks that never heard of the Good Book or the Golden Rule."

"Are you one of them, Prentice?" When he didn't answer she shook her head with profound sadness. "Dead flies cause the ointment to send forth a stinking savor."

"Ma, we're gonna need more'n a few quotes from the scripture before this deal is through." Closing his eyes, he began rocking again. "And don't you worry about them dead flies stinkin' up the place. They'll be buried so deep nobody will ever know the difference."

When he heard a slight scuffling sound he knew she had gone inside. Which suited him just fine. Tonight he wanted to think about killing men. Especially those who threatened Sunburst. Saving their souls—or his own, for that matter—didn't interest him in the slightest.

Only the land mattered. Sunburst. Nothing else.

5

Cal Nutt left the State House in Austin feeling ten feet tall and a yard wide. While the politicos who now governed Texas professed to be straight-arrow reformers, they were no different than past regimes. Only more so. Beneath the guise of their righteous, holier-than-thou attitudes they were merely a new version of an old breed—rogues, charlatans, rascals—all playing for the stakes that had lured men on since ancient times. Power and the strength to rule unopposed.

Williamson County's political boss had come to the Capitol seeking renewed assurances that his murderous little domain would remain inviolate in the days to come. What he had in mind was certain to raise eyebrows across the state, and he wanted a sure-fire guarantee that there would be no interference once he set the plan in motion. Since the gubernatorial election was barely six months away, his timing couldn't have been better. The bargain he proposed was as pragmatic and unadorned as the man himself. He would deliver the vote of Williamson County to the party ticket and in return the State House would keep the Texas Rangers out of his bailiwick.

Curiously, the trading session hadn't gone as smoothly as he envisioned at first. The votes he controlled were direly needed in the forthcoming elections, and there had been much wheedling to strike a deal. But the kingmakers had been highly reluctant to sanction further violence just at this time. Though its figures were suspect, *The Austin States-man* had published an editorial to the effect that more men had been killed across the state in the past year than Texas had lost throughout the entire Civil War. There had even been a barbed reference to the fact that in Williamson County alone no less than twenty men had met death by violent means during this same period. Clearly the newspaper had gotten wind of Cal Nutt's murky schemes and was using him as a pawn in the political struggle that would determine who governed Texas during the next adminis-tration.

More disquieting still, there was a clamor from press and public alike to employ the newly organized Texas Rangers in combating the senseless bloodshed. Already the Rang-ers had swept through Gonzales and DeWitt Counties south-east of San Antonio, killing a whole raft of outlaws and driving what remained into hiding. Even now there was talk in some quarters of increasing the size of the Ranger Batal-lion so that it might speed the job along on a statewide ba-sis. Cal Nutt's overriding concern was that the Rangers be kept as far away as possible from Williamson County. Let them chase desperados down on the Pecos, or in Big Bend country. Anywhere for that matter, so long as they stayed out of his hair over the next six months.

After that it wouldn't make any difference what the Rangers did. Or where. Williamson County would be his to do with as he pleased.

Since Nutt was dealing from a position of strength, dan-gling votes in front of the politicos like a batch of carrots, he ultimately got his way. The Rangers would be kept occupied elsewhere. Whatever happened in Williamson County would be left to the local authorities—at least till election time. Then, if the votes were delivered as promised, the arrangement might be extended indefinitely. That was something only time would tell.

That was also something Cal Nutt didn't give a shit about one way or the other. If he couldn't pull it off within the next six months, then he probably never would. However it was fed into the sausage grinder, it could come out only one way. He was declaring open war on Print Oliver, and before winter came to the San Gabriel one of them would have cashed in.

Ruminating over it now as he turned his buggy back toward Georgetown, the Yankee remained convinced that it was the only way. The Olivers had been a thorn in his side since those first, long-ago days when he had come to Texas. They had thwarted him at every turn, and along with their Secesh neighbors, they represented the only faction in Williamson County still outside his sphere of influence. His campaign to terrorize them off Yegua Creek hadn't worked. They had eluded his cleverly designed scheme to entrap Print Oliver in a murder charge. Whichever way a man sliced it, they had made him eat crow—feathers and all.

But no longer. Not after today.

The Secesh trash would shortly learn that there was more than one way to skin a cat.

Or an Oliver.

CHAPTER NINE

———∙∙∙∙∙———

1

There were times that first week in Wichita when Print almost forgot the troubles awaiting him back on Yegua Creek. Abe Campbell, the Scotch cattle buyer, was in town and for six nights running they had sampled the assorted delights of Kansas' reigning cow capital. Though Campbell's convivial spirits resulted in part from having designs on the Sunburst herds, Print was hardly offended by the mercenary tone of their friendship. He liked the dour little Scotsman, even enjoyed his caustic humor, but that in no way obligated him when it came time to talk turkey.

Three herds were slowly moving northward along the Chisholm Trail, and as they reached Wichita, each would go to the highest bidder. No matter how many wild nights he and Abe Campbell had shared in the red-light district across the river.

Print's boldly ambitious plan for the '74 season had come off without a hitch thus far. Bumpus Moore had trailed out with the Platte herd toward the middle part of April, and Ace Whitehead was only ten days behind with the first batch of steers. Harry Strain and his crew had moved out a week later, and Jay's herd had been headed north the second week in May. Print had stuck with Jay's bunch for a couple of days just to make sure the drive got underway without mishap, then rode on ahead with a pack horse toting his camp gear. South of Ft. Worth he had overtaken Harry Strain and three days later he caught up with Ace Whitehead at Red River Station. From there on out the other ramrods knew he was riding with Whitehead, and had anything gone awry they were instructed to send a courier to fetch him.

But the four herds proceeded northward at an uneventful if somewhat plodding pace and not once was Print summoned to lend a hand. Since no news was good news he stuck with Whitehead clean through the Nations. Yet toward the middle of June he found himself growing dismally bored. Much like a general who had committed his troops on four separate fronts, he was left with nothing to do— and the inactivity slowly began to grate on him. One lazy day gave way to another, then drifted into weeks of a grinding sameness, and by the time they reached the Salt Fork of the Arkansas he had developed a very pronounced itch.

As the crow flies, they were only about seventy miles south of Wichita at that point, roughly a six-day drive to the holding grounds west of town. Print took off like a scalded goose the morning after they had forded the Salt Fork, carrying in a flour sack only enough biscuits and cold beef for a one-night camp. Late the next afternoon he had crossed the toll-bridge over the Arkansas River and ridden into Wichita.

Like most cowtowns, Wichita wasn't much to look at. The railroad had reached the banks of the Arkansas only last spring and around it had sprung up the same old assortment of grungy dives. Main Street and Douglas Avenue, the town's only real streets, were lined with fifteen saloons and gaming parlors, two dance halls, and a single mercantile emporium, the New York Store. The lone hotel was a mammoth three-storey brick structure that looked curiously out of place amidst the sleazy, false-front establishments surrounding it. West of town on the opposite side of the river was Delano, the red-light district. With remarkable foresight, the city council had done its best to separate the shady ladies from the local watering holes, restricting whorehouses of every persuasion to the south bank of the Arkansas.

Though the trailhands were forced to cross the river in search of poontang, they found no scarcity of firewater. The brothel owners nimbly skirted the letter of the law and a man could rinse his tonsils in Delano just as readily as he might in Wichita proper.

Only it was more fun on the southside.

Dixie Lee and Mattie Silks were trying to outdo one another in the swank parlor house trade, and with competition so fierce, fornication had taken on all the overtones of an art form along the banks of the Arkansas. They imported redheads, blondes, brunettes, sloe-eyed Chinese, high yellow octaroons, and perhaps half a dozen who laid claim to being Queen of the Spades. If a man was flush and didn't mind dropping a month's pay to get his tallywhacker pampered in some damned exotic ways he went to the parlor houses.

If he was playing it close to the vest and just looking for a little nookie—plain old wham-bam bang-bang without any pretense of elegance or Frenchified slick tricks—he went farther down the street.

There Rowdy Joe Lowe and the Earp Brothers, Wyatt and James, were running a dead heat to see who could operate the raunchiest two-bit cathouse. Their girls were of the jaded, bottom-of-the-barrel variety, and among the kingdom of whores they were the sorriest looking dogs ever to hit the frontier. Most were so scruffy, in fact, they couldn't even be termed Soiled Doves. Stone cold sober a man either had to be a damn' poor judge of women, or else horny as a Trappist monk, before he could get it stiff. The cowhands who frequented these places were generally one jump away from selling their saddles, and didn't particularly have any choice in the matter. When it came down to the wire, they saved a quarter for supper, four-bits for rot-gut, and two-bits for a short, sweaty minute of dip the wick. Those with weak stomachs brought along their own gunnysacks.

But weak or strong, drunk or sober, it was a rare sort of man who didn't hold his nose when he paid a visit to Rowdy Joe and the Earp boys.

Naturally, Abe Campbell and Print Oliver wouldn't have been caught dead in one of the dicier houses. Not that they had anything against them for those who couldn't afford better. It was just that if a man had a choice between some bloated old cow and a prissy little heifer, he didn't spend a hell of a lot of time debating it one way or the other. They alternated nights between Dixie Lee's and Mattie Silk's, and over the course of the past week the girls had grown to look upon them as the jauntiest sports in the whole town. Instead of suds or popskull, they bought bubbly by the magnum, and unlike most of the customers, they didn't mind sharing their largesse with any girl waiting to turn a trick. They made an odd-looking pair—this tall, dark-skinned Texan and his austere little sidekick—but the ladies couldn't have cared less. They were highrollers of the first order, and when they came through the door the entire house set about catering to their needs with unrestrained gusto.

This particular night, as the two men approached Mattie Silk's place, Print was feeling especially festive. The daring gamble he had taken some three months back had just paid off—with a draft for $63,690.

Ace Whitehead's herd had pulled up on the prairie south of the Arkansas late that afternoon—the first bunch to reach Wichita that season—and after less than an hour's dickering with a saloonful of cattle buyers, Print had sold to Abe Campbell. But he hadn't played any favorites—the Scots-man had paid through the nose and yelled like he was be-ing skinned alive.

What Print had foreseen as far back as last fall had come to pass. The financial panic of '73 had resulted in a shortage of beef in the eastern cities, and demand had driven prices sky high. The cattle buyers had instructions to get the boxcars filled and rolling—whatever the price—and they were fighting tooth and toenail in their eagerness to outbid one another. Already Print had gotten even higher offers for the next two herds—sight unseen. Tonight he meant to let the buyers squirm a little—just for the hell of it. But tomorrow he would strike while the iron was hot. Last summer had shown him the vagaries of the beef market and he had no intention of again getting caught in a squeeze play.

Come morning he would sell to the highest bidder and have done with it. Then, barring any major losses at the gaming tables, he would light a shuck for Sunburst with close to a quarter-million in hard cash.

The only thing that rankled him was the necessity of having the money transferred by draft to his bank in Austin. Even with thirty or so cowhands to guard the chuck wagon, he wasn't rash enough to attempt carting nearly $250,000 in gold across the no-man's-land to the south. Though he still didn't trust Yankee bankers, he had an abiding faith in the road agents and Indians who stood between him and Yegua Creek. One sniff of a haul this size and U.S. Grant himself couldn't have gotten the gold through the Nations.

Bitter as it was to swallow, it seemed he would just have to start trusting Bluebellies. Yet even as he pondered it, he had to admit that for a quarter-million coin of the realm he would have made a deal with Satan himself, and never given it a second thought. Gold had a magic all its own—completely separate from a man's politics or his gods—and with that much hard cash behind him he meant to make Sunburst the godamndest, mind-boggling cow outfit anybody had ever heard tell of.

When he led Abe Campbell through the door of the brothel, Print let out a Rebel yell that shook the house clean to the rafters. They stormed into the parlor to find Mattie Silks and her girls on their feet staring wide-eyed in alarm. Print leaped forward and grabbed the madam's tiny waist in his big paws, then swung her high overhead in a billowing shower of petticoats and thrashing legs.

"Eiiiyow! I'm wild and woolly and full of fleas! Ain't never been curried below the knees!"

Lowering the little madam to face level he gave her a sound smack right on the lips. "Mattie, bolt the doors and lock the windows. I'm buyin' your whole place out for the rest of the night. Girls get ready, 'cause here I come!"

Amidst the squealing cries of her Soiled Doves, Mattie Silks pumped her legs and gave him what for in a throaty rush of words. "Print Oliver, you're drunk as a lord! And rough as a bullwhacker. Now set me down, you big ape. You hear me? This instant!"

Print chuckled deeply and lowered her to the floor. "Aw, Mattie, don't go gettin' bent out of shape. I just struck pay-dirt. I'm filthy rich. Wallerin' in gold. Me and this connivin' little mousefart of a Yankee are gonna knock up ever' girl in your house and drink this place bone dry 'fore daylight."

Mattie Silks was built sort of dainty, with hair the color of cornsilk and a pert oval face that had a way of sticking in a man's mind. But she knew how to handle Texans— drunk or sober, short or tall—and she wasn't about to have her elegant parlor house turned into a three-ring circus. Straightening her gown, she drew herself up about even with his watch chain, and gave him a look that would have withered a young sapling.

"Print, if I'm any judge you've already swilled half the rotgut in Wichita, and you're going to be flat on your kisser before the night's half gone. As for getting my girls in a family way, you're welcome to try if you think you've got the starch to hold out. But only so long as you act like a gentleman. This is an orderly house and I won't have it busted up by anybody. Not even you."

The feisty little madam was closer to the truth than she suspected. The cattleman and his unlikely sidekick had opened the festivities in Pryor's Saloon, then switched to the gaming tables next door at the Keno House, and between them they had downed enough forty-rod to pickle a full-grown ox. Though he could normally soak it up like a healthy sponge even Print had his limit, and he was teetering on the edge right now. Already his knees felt sort of rubbery and unless he concentrated just right he had the pleasant sensation of gazing down upon two Mattie Silks.

Both of whom looked equally delectable.

"Awright, Mattie, don't get your tailfeathers up." Print scooped her up in his arms and gave her a crushing hug. "I just felt like howlin' and I figured the best place to do it was among friends. Why hell, 'fore the night's over I might even get you to show me what you got hidden under all them petticoats."

"Buster, you've got about as much chance of that as a snowball in Hades." Struggling out of his arms, she lifted her chin another notch. "I own the place, I don't work here. Jesus H. Christ and all the tea in China couldn't get you into my bed. You're a fine fellow, Print—salt of the earth—but you're strictly not my type." Then she softened, suddenly recalling his brag about striking it rich. "But these girls love you. Just like a big teddy bear. Don't you, girls?"

Squealing delightedly, the Soiled Doves swarmed over the two men and began dragging them toward cushy sofas along the far wall. Print winked at Mattie good-naturedly and surrendered himself to the girls' playful tugging. One that he had bedded on a previous visit, a flashy redhead with colossal bosoms, backed across the room clutching his hands fiercely. "C'mon, Sugartit. You just sit down here beside Lil and tell me all about it. There's nothin' I admire more than a big, strappin' man that knows how to shake the money tree."

"Watch out, Print!" Campbell howled. "That gal'll pour honey over you and lick you to death." The Scotsman reeled sideways in drunken fits of laughter, crashing onto the sofa in a tangle of arms and legs with the three girls supporting him.

The cattleman was all set with a snappy comeback when he looked up from his own sofa to see a newcomer talking with Mattie Silks. The man bore a remarkable resemblance to the desk clerk at the hotel, but Print decided it was either sheer coincidence or a momentary attack of scrambled vision. The hotel clerk was a real pisswillie if he had ever seen one, much too refined a fellow for the likes of a whore-house.

Then Mattie and the man seemed to float across the room, coming to a halt directly in front of him. The litle madam leaned forward and shook him roughly. "Print, come up and take a deep breath. This man is from the hotel. He's got a message for you."

Print extracted himself from the redhead's embrace and grinned stupidly. "Mister, you sure had me fooled. Never would have figured you for a sportin' man. Just goes to show you."

"Mr. Oliver, you don't seem to understand," the desk clerk said, thrusting a yellow slip of paper under his nose. "This telegraph message came for you. The depot man said it was urgent, so I started tracking you down. When I heard you had come over here I went to Dixie Lee's first, but. . . ."

"Well you've certainly got a nerve!" Mattie Silks' glare was swathed in frost. "Even a dimdot like you ought to know that this is the classiest house in West Wichita."

"No offense, ma'am," the hotel clerk mumbled sheep-ishly. Clearing his throat, he smiled like he expected some-one to boot him in the ass, then made another stab at getting through to Print. "Like I was saying, Mr. Oliver, it came over the wire about an hour ago. Marked urgent. Looks to me like somebody wanted you to get it powerful quick."

The cattleman accepted the telegram with a drunken smirk and slowly opened it. The words fused together in an inky jumble on his first try, but after he blinked his eyes a couple of times it began to look like sure enough writing. Taking it one word at a time, he groped his way through the message.

July 2, 1874
Thrall Station
Texas

Mr. Prentice Oliver
Douglas Avenue House
Wichita, Kansas
URGENT
Request you return home at once. Situation here gone
from bad to worse. Family in great danger but Louisa
and children are well. Your brother.
                    Robert Oliver

The words erupted inside Print's brain like tiny droplets
of fire, searing his head clean of whiskey fumes in the time
it took him to read them. Unfolding from the sofa, he moved
across the parlor with stiff-legged strides. Halfway through
the hall door he paused and looked back. "Abe, old pard,
you take care of them girls for me. I'll catch up with you
next trip." Tipping his hat, he smiled at the little madam.
"Mattie, you're a real gem. Sorry I made such a fuss."

Then he turned and went through the door into the sultry
Kansas night.

2

When Print stepped off the train at Thrall Station five days
later, Bob and Jim Kelly were there to meet him. The first
thing he spotted was that both men were packing a brace
of six-guns. Their faces were grim as death warmed over
and even as they shook hands their eyes moved restlessly
around the station yard. Clearly they felt exposed standing on the platform, and their manner alone alerted him
to the fact that something drastic had taken place in his
absence. But more than words or skittish looks the twin
holsters strapped around their hips brought his hackles
bristling straight up.

In cow country the only men who packed double hard-ware were gunslingers—hired killers. Or men who were being stalked by predators that walked upright and them-selves carried a spare iron.

Since it was plain that Kelly and his brother didn't want to talk in front of the depot, he held his questions for later. They had brought a steel-dust gelding for him to ride, and even before the train chugged out of the station, they were mounted and headed north toward the San Gabriel road.

They rode at a steady clip for perhaps a mile or so be-fore Kelly reined his horse to a walk. The black man had been watching their back trail since they left Thrall and he seemed satisfied they weren't being followed. Bob mean-while had been scouting the road ahead, and he, too, ap-peared to relax. None of this was lost on Print.

The wrangler and his kid brother were working as a team, and it was painfully obvious that they rode with the constant threat of danger—even twenty miles from Sunburst.

Print didn't see any need to hold off longer. "Somebody start talkin'. Whatever it is, I rode a long way to hear it."

Bob glanced at the wrangler and something passed be-tween them. After a moment the younger man spoke up. "Print, you ain't gonna believe this, but the bastards put out a bounty on us."

"Bounty?" The cattleman's head swiveled around, searching both their faces. "What the hell're you talkin' about, sport?"

"Boss, he's givin' it to you straight," Kelly broke in. "They put a price on your heads just like you was wolves. $500 for ever' dead Oliver."

Print was so dumbfounded he couldn't think of anything to say. But a great smoldering anger was starting to kindle deep down in his guts. They rode along awhile in silence before he got hold of himself. "Is the bounty just on Oliver men? None of the hands or any of the womenfolk?"

Bob shrugged, twisting his mouth in a grimace. "So far as we know that's it. The word started circulatin' around town about two weeks after you left. Except for women and kids they just flat made it open season on Olivers."

"You keep sayin' *they*," Print observed. "Does anyone know who *they* are?"

The younger man pursed his lips doubtfully and shook his head. "Not for sure. There's some that says this Grip Crow feller is behind it. But the only thing that's been said outright is that whoever kills an Oliver will wake up some mornin' and find the money on his doorstep."

"And the bounty doesn't go for any of the hands?" Print asked. "Just us."

"That's right," Bob agreed. "Evidently they ain't even interested in Jim."

Print glanced at the black man, then back to his brother. "What makes you single Jim out like that?"

"Hell, they're onto our patrol. Tumbled to it a long time back. More'n likely know that Jim ramrods it, too."

"You're doing a lot of guesswork, aren't you?" Print said skeptically. "Sounds to me like they're just tryin' to throw another scare into us with this business about bounties."

"Boss, he ain't tellin' you all of it," Kelly interjected quickly. "Twice now they've bushwhacked our scoutin' parties. Both times Bob was along, so we sorta figger they was out o' purpose to get him."

"Well, don't go bashful on me," the cattleman demanded. "What happened?"

The wrangler's gaze broke and he looked away. "Nothin' the first time. We jest swapped lead. Second time they got Lee Wells. He was dead 'fore we ever got off a shot."

There was a long moment of silence before Bob added an afterthought. "We got one of them too. Though I reckon it didn't rightly make up for Lee."

"Not by a damn' sight," Print growled hotly. "Why the hell didn't you send for me when you got wind of this bounty crap?"

"Unless we'd sent somebody ridin' after you there wasn't no way till you got to Wichita. Besides, we figured we could handle it ourselves."

Print all of a sudden smelled a rat. "You're hedgin', sport. If you could handle it, why'd you call me back now?"

Bob got a hang-dog expression on his face and he couldn't meet Print's stare. "The night before I wired you they took a shot at the old man."

Print reined the gelding back hard and his dark eyes flashed fire. "Boys, that's gonna take some explainin'. Suppose you just tell me how they got close enough to draw down on Pa?"

Bob started to answer, but Kelly cut him off. "Boss, don't go rawhidin' him. That deal was nobody's fault but mine. Start to finish."

Print just waited, eyes still smoky, and after a few seconds the black man plowed on. "They faked a raid on the ramuda that night and I let 'em sucker us off the home place. While we was out beatin' the bushes one of 'em snuck up and took a shot at your pappy through the winder." Hesitating, he sifted back through the long, confusing night to see if he had left anything out. Then an odd gleam appeared in his eye. "You pappy wasn't shorted when the Lord handed out gumption. He flopped out o' that rockin' chair of his like he'd been hit, then he grabbed up a shotgun and went hunting 'em in the dark. Never got a shot, but I 'spect he got closer'n we did."

"Then he wasn't hit?" Print asked gruffly.

"Not even a scratch," Bob assured him. "The slug took a knob off the rocker a couple of inches from his head. Course, he was madder'n a scalded cat, and Ma spent half the night pickin' splinters out of his neck. But there wasn't nothin' hurt 'cept his feelin's."

With that Print fell silent, taking a little time to digest all he had heard in the last few minutes. Just when they thought he wasn't going to speak again, he looked over at Kelly. "Seems a mite queer they've got your patrols all nosed out."

"Ain't nothin' queer 'bout it," the wrangler snorted. "Some sonovabitch has been spyin' on us. Knowed it since the first time they bushwhacked us."

"Now hold on a minute. Are you talkin' about someone in the compound? One of our own people?"

"Don't rightly know. More'n likely it's one o' them bounty men sittin' out in the brush watchin' us. Might even be one o' the neighbors. Hell, boss, there's 'nough of 'em through there all the time that we ain't got no secrets."

The black man's voice trailed off, and he mulled it over a bit before resuming. "I just got a feelin' in my bones that whatever we gets set to do them owlhoots already knows about it."

Print roweled his horse into a lope and left the thought dangling. They had talked enough. It was time to get home.

Way past time, if he was any judge.

When they pulled up in front of the house along toward sundown Louisa came running out the door. Coming home like this after months on the trail, he was always reminded what a handsome woman she was. Not beautiful, just damn' good-looking. Tall, proud, full of fire and mettle. Through all the years of terror and bloodshed she hadn't cracked, not once. Which took a special kind of woman. Damn' special.

Sometimes he felt guilty about all the whoring around he did up in the cowtowns, yet it never seemed to last very long. It was just a slight twinge of conscience, something every man suffered briefly when he stepped out on his wife. But wives and whores really didn't have anything to do with one another. They were different things entirely. Two distinct and very separate parts of a man's life that had no business even being cast in the same thought. Leastways, that was how he explained it to himself, and how he lived it. So far as he could see, it was nobody's concern but his own.

Bob trailed them into the house and Julia Oliver met them at the door. After pecking him on the cheek, she stepped back and gave him a scrutinizing look. "How did you leave your brothers?"

"Right as rain, Ma," he noted. "Ira's with Ace Whitehead and Jay oughta pull into Wichita some time next week.

From what I've been hearin' they're better off up there than they would be around here."

His mother very calmly ignored that. "What about your cattle? Did coming back here upset everything?"

Her little barb about *his* cattle stung down to the quick, but he didn't let on. Sometimes there was a certain glint in her eyes that made him feel like a runny-nosed little squirt with nothing between his ears but beeswax. It was as though she laid his skull open, seeing everything that went on inside his head, yet finding nothing worth remarking on. Just like she had done when he was a kid. But it didn't change things one way or the other. So long as he was running Sunburst she would just have to pull in her horns and accept it with whatever grace she could muster. Still, it galled him, more than he cared to admit.

"No'm, didn't upset a thing." He grinned, suddenly remembering that there was one good piece of news at least. "I sold all three herds. Left Whitehead there to settle up and bring the hands home."

"Did you get the price you wanted?"

"Matter of fact, Ma, I got better than that. Close to a quarter-million dollars."

Print walked off and left the three of them gaping at one another in open-mouthed astonishment. When he entered the living room Jim Oliver was seated in his now scarred rocker looking fat and sassy as ever. Twisting around at his son's footsteps, his watery eyes twinkled happily.

"See you made it home in one piece. How's tricks in them cowtowns?"

"Never better, Pa. Just like throwin' a bucket of snakes on a hot stove. Understand you had a little excitement around here yourself."

"Weren't nothin' much to speak of. 'Ceptin' the sorry devil ruined my rocker. Sorta gripes me, though, I wasn't able to return the favor by partin' his hair."

Julia Oliver, followed by Louisa and Bob, came into the room just in time to catch this last comment. After a brief staring contest with her husband, Julia sniffed. "Your father is getting flighty in his old age, Prentice. Or maybe Robert didn't tell you how he went chasing off in the dark like someone had invited him to a coon hunt."

Print didn't say anything and his father ignored her completely. Cocking one eyebrow, Jim Oliver gave his eldest son a quizzical look. "What d'ya figure on doin' about them scutters?"

"Pa, I reckon we're gonna have to take 'em down a notch or two. Appears to me the score got a little lopsided while I was gone. Sorta thought I'd get started on it first thing in the mornin'."

Though he had spoken softly and hadn't really said anything outright, everyone in the room recalled his usual method of settling the score. There was a moment of intense silence, then Julia Oliver's biting words sliced across the room. "Let us do evil, that good may come."

The old man grunted and shot her a stinging glance. "Where no law is, there is no transgression. Try puttin' that in your pipe and smokin' it."

Print signed to Louisa and headed toward the kitchen. He was hungry and he just didn't have time to be bothered playing silly games. Somehow it seemed that everytime he returned home it was the cat and mouse all over again. Nothing ever changed. Maybe never would. But it damn' sure got on a man's nerves here and there.

Still, come tomorrow morning it would be his turn to start giving folks the jangles. Only this time he meant to shake them right down to their boot heels.

3

They rode into Georgetown shortly before the noon hour. Print was in the lead, with Bob and Jim Kelly flanked to either side. Pinky Simms brought up the rear. They were spread out in a rough diamond pattern and the significance of their wary little formation wasn't lost on the townspeople. Everyone in Williamson County knew that *somebody* had

put a price on the Olivers, and by now it was common
knowledge that an attempt had recently been made on the
life of the old patriarch himself. Though they gawked, the
citizens of Georgetown weren't in the least surprised and
word went speeding ahead along the street.

Print Oliver was back—looking mad enough to chew
nails—and he had brought his gunhands with him.

While Print didn't care one way or the other what the
townspeople thought, it just happened that they were
dead right about a couple of things. The cattleman had
spread his men out like skirmishers with a definite purpose
in mind. He wanted the word passed around that Sunburst
was ready to fight anytime, anywhere—even in Georgetown. Moreover, he hadn't ridden into town to see the sights
or to refresh himself with a cold beer.

He had come to declare war.

The four men turned off the square and rode straight to
the Bull's Head Saloon. This sent another quake of excited
murmuring through the onlookers, for it was now obvious that Print Oliver meant to flaunt his contempt right in
the enemy's own stronghold.

Over the years Georgetown's most popular watering
holes had become the hangouts of two very distinct and
thoroughly dissimilar factions. Turtle's Exchange, back
over on the opposite side of the square, was a comfortable,
high-class establishment frequented by cattlemen, bankers
and the community's more respectable element. The Bull's
Head, on the other hand, was a common honkytonk, whose
clientele consisted of cowhands, roughnecks and a motley
assortment of characters who evidenced no visible means
of support. Though it was seldom voiced aloud, there was
a tacit agreement among the two factions that Williamson
County's hardcases would confine their brawling and row-
dyism to their own side of town. Which, for all practical
purposes, meant the Bull's Head Saloon.

While it was a matter of some speculation as to *who* had
put out a bounty on the Olivers, it was a pretty safe bet that
the Bull's Head was their enemies' main haunt. For Print

Oliver to walk into the dive with $500 on his head was enough to send a shock wave reverberating clean across town.

The Sunburst men dismounted and trooped into the saloon just like they owned the place. Pinky Simms again brought up the rear, only this time he carried a hammer and a large roll of paper that had been strapped behind his saddle.

When they came through the door Bob and the wrangler fanned out to either side with their backs to the wall. Simms remained standing in the doorway watching the street. Print marched directly to the bar and stopped in front of Bo Thompson, the proprietor. The noon-hour crowd had just begun to collect and every man in the room went deathly still, waiting to see what the cattleman had up his sleeve. Those who might normally have objected to an Oliver's presence in the Bull's Head just kept their mouths shut. With three gunhands backing his play—especially a young scorpion who had already killed at least six men—Print was as safe as a bulldog with a spike collar.

"Bo, if you're not careful they're gonna lock you up as a health menace." Print rubbed his nose and made a sour face. "This place smells so rank it oughta be wearin' fur."

Turning, his eyes casually swept over the hushed customers, sort of like a hungry owl inspecting a nestful of fat mice. "Small wonder considerin' the trade you get. This bunch is riper'n a gassy dog."

Nobody so much as blinked. While the insult was plain enough for anyone with ears, there wasn't a man in the room willing to pick up the challenge. Print Oliver was clearly spoiling for a fight, and he wasn't making any bones about letting the whole town know it. There was something a little frightening about a man who would coolly march into the opposing camp and go out of his way to pick an argument.

Like maybe he was just a bit too anxious. Cocksure. Somehow certain that it would be him who drew first blood.

The Bull's Head regulars didn't flinch under his corrosive stare, but none of them exactly met it head-on either.

Bo Thompson decided he had better turn the damper down before things got out of control. "What can I do for you, Mr. Oliver?"

Print slowly came around and spread his hands across the top of the bar. "Well I'll tell you, Bo. The first thing you can do is wipe that shit-eatin' smile off your face."

The barkeep stiffened and his hand edged automatically toward a bungstarter beneath the counter. "Now look here, mister. You got no call to waltz in here and start bad-mouthin' me in my own place."

"Bo, if you try pullin' that melon thumper on me, I'm gonna kick your ass right up between your shoulders. Don't reckon you'd be the first man that had to take off his shirt to shit."

Thompson's face went white as clabber and his hand froze halfway below the bar. He had seen Print in action before, and near as he recalled it was sort of like getting in a fist fight with a real live gorilla. Better instead to back off and live to fight another day. Right now that seemed a damn' sensible motto.

Print smiled dryly when he saw the other man come un-glued. "Glad to see you're smarter'n you look, Bo. Wasn't any need for you to get your sap up anyway. Fact of the matter is, I came in to ask a favor."

"Yeah?" the barkeep replied skeptically. "What kind of favor?"

"Well you see, Bo, we've been havin' a little trouble out at Sunburst. Nothin' serious, you understand, but here lately it's gettin' a mite irksome. So if you've got no real strong objections I thought we'd post a notice on your wall. Just a friendly reminder to folks about what'll happen to 'em if they cross Yegua Creek. Since that includes some of your regulars I sorta thought you'd want 'em to see it. No sense losin' steady customers needlessly, if you see what I mean."

Bo Thompson saw well enough, and if he had any objections he kept them to himself. "Sure, Mr. Oliver. You just hang it wherever suits you. No problem at all."

"Bo, that's right neighborly of you. Remind me to buy you a drink sometime."

Print wheeled away and headed for the door. Pinky Simms turned and walked toward the wall at the front of the bar, crossing the room like a man who knew exactly what to do and where to do it. After unfurling the poster he tacked it to the wall with a few quick strokes of the hammer, then spun about and retraced his steps to the door. Print had just stepped outside, and as Simms followed hard on his heels, Kelly and Bob backed through the door.

The bat-wings swung shut and the whole room started breathing again. Bo Thompson led the rush toward the front of the saloon and within moments the small crowd was staring goggle-eyed at a concisely worded and brutally frank statement of intent.

PUBLIC NOTICE

All cattle rustlers and horse thieves take heed. Anyone caught driving Sunburst horses or cows will be shot on sight.

Anyone caught on Oliver land without a damn good reason might just get a dose of the same.

Those who ignore this warning will be treated to a sudden demise and a Christian burial.

Bring your own flowers. Burial services on the house.

Print Oliver

The poster was crudely lettered, but there was no mistaking its meaning. Whoever crossed onto Oliver land without one hell of a good excuse wouldn't be coming back. Plenty of men had disappeared out there already, and among those in the Bull's Head this morning, there wasn't one who had an inkling of doubt about the warning. The Olivers would shoot on sight and pray over a man later, which had a certain logic all its own. Persuasive even, unless a fellow didn't particularly care where he got planted.

Ten minutes later Print barged into Ed Strayborn's office without knocking and uncurled an exact duplicate of the first poster across his desk. The old lawdog read it through without stopping, breathing heavier with every line. When he looked up his eyes were round as silver dollars.

"Print, you're plumb loco," he grimly noted. "You put this goddamn thing up and it'll more'n likely get you killed."

"Already put it up, Sheriff. Over in the Bull's Head." When Strayborn started out of his chair Print waved him down. "Don't get yourself riled. We left the place just like we found it. Matter of fact, Bo Thompson was real helpful. Didn't squirm hardly enough to notice when we nailed it up."

"You beat anything I ever seen, Print. You purely do." The lawman reared back in his chair, glowering like a sour-tempered old rooster. "Awright, so you got it posted. Don't expect me to come runnin' when the shootin' starts."

"Never thought you would, Ed. Leastways not till it's over one way or the other."

"Then why'd you come around bothering me?" Strayborn yelled querulously, slapping the poster with his hand. "What am I supposed to do with this thing anyway?"

"Why nothin', Sheriff." Print flashed a quick grin and started rolling the poster. "I just wanted your permission to tack it up on the bulletin board out in the hall."

"Judas Priest! You are daft, aren't you? You haven't got some fool notion that puttin' it up out there is gonna make it legal, do you?"

"Well I can't rightly see how it's illegal. Shootin' rustlers and trespassers has never been against the law before. Not that I recollect anyhow."

When the lawman didn't say anything Print chuckled.

"Hell, Ed, don't get yourself in a dither. Anybody that comes out there ain't comin' back. So forget it. Without witnesses nobody's gonna be about to swear out a warrant, and that lets you off the hook."

Strayborn groaned and a nervous tic started his left eye jumping. "Awright, post the sonovabitch and be damned. Just get the hell out of here and let my head ache in peace."

Print gave him a mock salute and stepped back through the door. Once outside he handed the poster to Simms and jerked his thumb in the direction of the bulletin board. Then he struck off down the hall at a lively clip, still flanked on either side by Bob and Jim Kelly.

"Make it snappy, Pinky," Print called over his shoulder. "We've got to bait some bear traps and get our skinnin' knives honed up."

The black wrangler chortled gleefully as they went out the door and down the courthouse steps.

4

Almost a week had passed, but absolutely nothing had gone according to plan. After publicly challenging the rustlers Print had fully expected them to mount a raid on the compound. They were an arrogant bunch—led by someone double-wolf on sheer gall—and it didn't figure that they would turn the other cheek. Not when the slap in the face had been delivered with such outright contempt.

Though he felt certain they would attack at night, under the cloak of darkness, Print had organized an around-the-clock guard on the compound. They were just cunning enough to try throwing him off by striking in daylight—when the sprawling complex of homes, bunkhouses, barns and corrals was presumably most vulnerable. Only a skeleton crew remained behind during trailing season, and he had to assume that the rustlers would exploit this weakness in one fashion or another. Instead of sending the hands about their range chores he kept them busy around the

compound, mending saddle gear, chopping wood, and re-
pairing leaky roofs. The patrols were still sent out, but
only during daylight hours—and with strict instructions
not to engage any raiding party that had them outnumbered. When darkness fell the women and children were
brought into the big house, and a double guard was posted
throughout the night. Including the cowhands and Jim
Kelly's men, Print had fifteen guns to deploy in his defense
of Sunburst.

Not many—or enough—by any reckoning. But it was the
one reason he had felt absolutely certain the rustlers would
attack.

Yet six grueling days had passed and thus far the gang
had fooled him completely. Kelly's patrols reported in-
creased rustling activity along the outer borders of Sunburst range, which meant the outlaws hadn't turned tail by
any means. More revealing still, neighbors who drifted in
and out of the compound almost daily, brought word that
their own herds hadn't been raided in nearly a fortnight.
Quite obviously—for reasons that as yet remained unclear—
the rustlers were concentrating exclusively on Oliver cattle.
But they hadn't come anywhere near the undermanned and
seemingly defenseless compound.

All of which served to leave Print touchier than a boar
grizzly in rutting season. Somebody—either Cal Nutt or
Grip Crow—was working a few tricks of his own, and he
was more than a little ticked-off by the whole sorry mess.

Seated on the porch, with a rifle near at hand, he was
puzzling over the situation when Jim Kelly came around
the corner of the house. As the wrangler crossed the porch
Print's brow puckered in a small frown. "Don't tell me.
Lemme guess. All's well and not a mouse is stirring."

Kelly dropped into a chair beside him. "Near as I can
tell there ain't nothin' stirrin'. Men included. Boys down
to the bunkhouse is so fed up with sittin' on their back-
sides they've taken to pitchin' pennies."

"Don't blame 'em," Print said disgustedly. "This waitin'
is enough to give anybody a case of the willies."

"Seen Bob?" the black man inquired. "It's gettin' on to noontime and we was supposed to scout up around North Spring 'fore dark."

"Aw, he's probably still home playin' kissy-face with Jenny. Regular couple of lovebirds, them two." Print brought his watch out and checked the time. "Shouldn't Pinky and his boys been back from patrol by now?"

"Yeh, they're overdue, for a fact." Kelly finished rolling a smoke and popped a sulphurhead. "Most likely they're off nosin' some trail that's gonna turn cold 'bout the time they hit the creek."

"I'd damn' sure be surprised if it didn't," Print remarked grumpily. "Seems like this last week it's been nothin' but quiet nights and cold trails."

The wrangler exhaled a small cloud of smoke and glanced at him sideways. "Did you really figure we was gonna sucker 'em into hittin' us here?"

"Hell yes, I did!" Print's gaze darkened and he appeared peeved by the question. "Till Ace gets back with the rest of the hands it's the only chance we've got."

His plan, had it worked, was a good one. Goad the rustlers into attacking the compound—make them fight on the ground of his own choosing. Very likely the outlaws would burn a number of buildings, but the firelight would only make them better targets in the dark. The big house and the main bunkhouse were situated perfectly to protect one another—no matter which direction the raiders struck from, they would be caught in a withering crossfire. Granted, it was a calculated risk—sort of a root hog or die proposition— but until Whitehead returned from Kansas it represented the best odds they were likely to get. With just a smidgin of luck they might easily put the quietus on the gang once and for all.

Kelly puffed on his cigarette for a while, then approached the subject obliquely. "You think there's still a chance of pullin' it off?"

"Maybe. Maybe not," the cattleman admitted grudgingly. "Right now it looks like they're tryin' to bait a trap of their own. More'n likely this stepped up rustling isn't nothin' but a scheme to lure us out in the open. If they could get us to come after 'em in force, then ambush us out in the hills, our goose'd be cooked. You gotta give 'em credit. They're playin' it real smart."

Print chewed it over a moment before tossing in an afterthought. "Whichever way you slice it, though, I still think the wind's in our favor over the long haul."

Snuffing his smoke out between thumb and forefinger, the wrangler flashed a pearly grin. "Now that's the kinda news the boys down at the bunkhouse needs to hear. How you figure we still got the edge?"

"Well, it stands to reason they'll have to do something before Ace and the hands get back. They've always come at us in twos and threes in the past because we had 'em outnumbered so bad. Couldn't afford to attack with the whole gang for fear we'd wipe 'em out in one lick. The shoe's on the other foot now and they know it."

" 'Pears to me it's a Mexican standoff," the black man observed. "They're out there and we're in here. Ain't nothin' but a big fat starin' contest."

"Yeah, but who's gonna blink first?" Print grunted slyly. "If we don't let 'em smoke us out then they'll have to come in sooner or later. This is likely the best chance they'll ever get, and they're not gonna muff it by hangin' fire till our whole crew gets home."

"Maybe they is smarter'n you think," Kelly said.

"What d'ya mean?"

"Maybe they smells the cheese but they ain't willin' to get shot to pieces in the bargain. Could be they're jest gonna bide their time and pot-shoot the Olivers one by one like they meant to do from the start."

Print's brow again wrinkled in a dark frown. "Goddamn' if I don't hate to admit it, but I've been sittin' here thinkin' the same thing myself. Trouble is, we don't know if they're that smart or not. All we can do is sit here and wait."

Kelly was on the verge of answering when the drum of

hooves brought their heads around and they saw a rider coming hell for leather across the compound. Stepping off the porch as he neared, they saw it was Hank Morrison, one of Pinky Simms' scouting party.

Morrison piled from the saddle while his horse was still moving and came running toward them. "Mr. Oliver! We caught 'em redhanded over by Titty Hills. Killed one and got two more hogtied."

Titty Hills were located some four miles to the east, named for their uncanny resemblance to a woman's more pronounced assets. But Print's thoughts just at this moment were of a grimmer nature. "What the hell's wrong with Pinky? I told him to lay low if he was out-numbered."

"Yessir, I reckon you did. But there was only five of 'em and we had an ambush set up so they never knew what hit 'em. Like I said, we sent one up the flume and wounded two more. Them other two just clean got. . . ."

"Never mind," Print barked, looking around at the wrangler. "Jim, get a couple of horses saddled and let's make tracks."

When Kelly took off toward the corral he turned back to the sweat-streaked messenger. "Hank, go find my brother down at his house. Tell him I said to hold the fort while I'm gone. I'll be back by sundown."

Less than an hour later Print and Kelly reined to a halt at the base of Titty Hills. Pinky Simms and two Sunburst riders were squatted across from the rustlers, who were clearly in some agony from their wounds.

Print dismounted, with the black man beside him, as Simms came forward to meet them. "Pinky, I oughta tie a knot in your tail for disobeying orders."

"Aw hell, boss, we wasn't in no danger." Simms jerked his thumb back at the wounded men. "Them poor bastards never had a chance."

"Maybe so, but next time you listen closer." Print's gaze drifted over to the rustlers. "What sorta shape are they in?"

Simms shook his head glumly. "They're dead men, only

they just don't know it yet. One's gutshot and the other took a slug through the lungs. Both of 'em will be stiff as boards 'fore dark."

Print nodded and just stood there staring at the two out-laws. After a while he walked over and took a look at the third rustler, who lay crumpled in the dust where he had fallen when a rifle slug mushroomed through his chest. The broiling afternoon sun seemed to glisten off the dead man's vacant eyes and a swarm of flies had already gath-ered around his open mouth. His bowels had flushed with death and Print turned away from the stench, puzzling again at the risks men took for a few measly dollars. Two hours ago he had been a real live desperado. Now he was just a hunk of meat.

Walking back to Kelly and Simms, he decided how it would be handled. "Pinky, what happened to the cows they were driving?"

Simms pointed toward a brush-choked defile separating Titty Hills from a low hogback to the north. "They skedad-dled in there when the shootin' started."

"Get your boys and go catch up three head." Print's mouth was a thin slit and hardly seemed to move as he spoke. "Drag 'em back down here. Pronto, let's go."

The cattleman's curt manner left no room for questions, even though it seemed like a damn' queer order. Simms and his men mounted and headed for the thorny brush, making loops in their lariats as they rode. Within twenty minutes each of them had returned hauling wild-eyed steers clearly marked with the Sunburst brand.

Print studied the cattle for a moment, then glanced at Kelly. "Kill 'em. Only use your knife. Gunshots might at-tract attention. Then skin 'em and be real careful not to cut the brand."

Without a word Kelly strode forward and cut the throat of each steer in turn. It wasn't necessary to ask questions. He already had a pretty fair idea of what Print meant to do. When the steers had bled out the men got busy skinning them, and before long they had three steaming hides stretched out on the ground.

When they were finished Print nodded toward the dead rustler and the two wounded men. "Wrap 'em up in those hides. Then use whangs to draw the skins around them good and tight."

Simms' eyes went round with disbelief. "Boss, you mean them wounded fellers, too? You got any idea what the sun is gonna do to them hides?"

"Pinky, you told me yourself that those boys were as good as dead. So what the hell difference does it make if they smother to death, or we hang 'em, or they just lay there and bleed out? Dead's dead, and it don't much matter how. Hop to it and quit jawbonin'."

Turning, he found Kelly watching him closely. "Now, Jim, don't go givin' me dirty looks. I don't like this any better than you do."

"Then why're you doin' it?" the wrangler shot back.

"Because, Goddammit, that's the bait that'll suck the rest of the gang into our mousetrap. Once they get a look at these boys the rest of 'em will come lookin' for a fight. And we'll be waitin'."

The gut-shot rustler let out a frightful moan as Simms and his men lifted him from the ground. When they laid him on the bloody hide he suddenly came to his senses and started struggling to get away. They shoved him down and began wrapping him in the skin, taking care to leave the brand mark fully exposed. The outlaw's eyes went white and he started screaming with the mortal terror of a trapped animal. Froth foamed up at his mouth, mixing with blood from the hide, and after a moment his frantic cries for mercy lapsed into the shrill, mindless gibbering of a madman. As the green skin closed over around his neck and the rawhide whangs were snugged down tight, his eyes closed and he sank into the merciful oblivion of unconsciousness.

Print looked away when they started for the second wounded man. Motioning Kelly, he walked toward his horse. "Jim, I want those men hung. Try to get it done be-fore the hides shrink too tight."

"Nothin' to it," Kelly replied. "We'll hang 'em right now 'fore them skins starts bindin'."

"Handle it any way you like, but I don't want 'em found on Sunburst land." Gathering the horses' reins, he started to mount, then paused. "You know that big live oak that stretches out across the road about a mile this side of town?"

"Yeh, I know it. Got a twisty kinda limb over the road that looks like a dog's hind leg."

"That's the one. Hang 'em there. Only wait till after dark so nobody'll see you."

"You mean hang 'em twice?" Kelly frowned. "Here and again down there?"

"Once. Twice. I don't care. Just so they're strung up in that tree outside town. Savvy?"

"Savvy," Kelly said softly, clearly stung by the cattle-man's stringent tone.

"There's good reason, Jim, or I wouldn't ask it. I want everybody in Georgetown to see what happened to these bastards. Once they do, Grip Crow and his outfit won't have any choice but to hit back. Otherwise, they could never show their faces around town again."

"Oh, they'll hit back awright. Don't worry yourself 'bout that." The wrangler slewed a glance over his shoulder as the second rustler began to scream hysterically. "Let's jest hope they don't take any of us alive if your mousetrap don't work."

Print didn't have an answer for that, and as he mounted it occurred to him that the black man hadn't really expected one. After today they would have burned their bridges. Like it or lump it, there would be no turning back.

From here on out, it was no quarter asked, and none given.

Spurring the gelding into a lope, he heard the lungshot outlaw whimpering pitifully, begging Almighty God to grant him a quick death. Perhaps, after a fashion, his prayer had already been answered. Hanging wasn't the fastest way to cash in, but it beat the hell out of a green cowhide.

Thinking about it as he rode away, it came to him that he wasn't especially proud of what he had done here today. It shriveled a man's innards to kill like that—coldly, brutally, no better than an animal slobbering over warm meat. Yet killing was dirty work. Always had been. Always would be.

But that's the kind of world it was. Only the killers survived. Those that didn't have the stomach for it generally ended up begging for mercy.

To a deaf God.

5

Print rode into the compound just at dusk. Though it was perhaps unwise for an Oliver to travel alone these days, he had taken his time on the ride home. After the shooting that morning there was small likelihood he would encounter any rustlers, and he needed some solitude to get his thoughts straightened out. Kelly's remark about what would happen if his trap failed had struck deeper than he let on at the time.

When the attack came—as he was now certain it would—they were sure to be outnumbered. One miscue on his part, some forgotten detail that might shift the advantage to the outlaws, and the Sunburst defenders could be overwhelmed to the man. The women and children were safe enough, so long as they stayed out of the direct line of fire. Not even a scurvy bunch like Crow's outfit would dare to harm a man's family. But it was something to think about all the same.

They damn' sure wouldn't be safe if lead came whistling through the building where they had taken shelter.

Still, the thing that troubled him most was the hands. They would unquestionably give a good account of themselves in the fight to come. They were loyal and they hated rustlers almost as much as he did. Yet this wasn't some isolated little scrape out in the hills, where a few men swapped lead and then called it a day. It would most likely wind up a full-scale battle, and men were sure to be killed. He was asking them to put their lives on the line, with their backs to the wall and no place to run. The more he thought about it, the less he liked it. What disturbed him wasn't that they had gladly agreed to take up his fight, or even that he was put in the position of having to ask. The bothersome part was in knowing that they had unflagging confidence in his ability to bring them through. They were treating it like a schoolboy lark, secure in the belief that he wouldn't lead them into anything they couldn't handle.

While he still had time to call on his neighbors for help, he hadn't even considered that as a possibility. They had their own spreads to protect, not to mention their families, and he wasn't about to become the *widow maker* of Williamson County. Not by a damn' sight!

Besides, the Cattlemen's Association had never been much of an organization anyway. The shoulder-to-shoulder, one-for-all spirit he had envisioned some years back just never seemed to materialize. Everybody was too wrapped up in their own troubles to take more than a passing interest in the plight of their neighbors. Certainly they had helped one another on occasion, but it had been a sometimes thing; a man always had the feeling that the help had been given grudgingly.

Perhaps more significantly—where the Olivers were concerned at any rate—the ranchers along Yegua Creek had grown increasingly envious over the years. To hear old Jim Oliver tell it, downright jealous wouldn't have been far off the mark.

Though most of them had prospered to some extent, they were forever trailing along in the Olivers' shadow. Those who couldn't make a go of it had gladly sold out to Sunburst, and in time the Olivers' holdings in land and cattle had surpassed anything most men would dare imagine. Some blamed the Olivers for their own troubles, calling them range hogs, and it was a feeling subscribed to even by those who remained. Still others thought Sunburst had gone too far in its war on the rustlers. Among themselves they reproached the Olivers for hanging and killing on a mass scale, declaring that it served only to inflame the outlaws further. Not that they were fainthearted or above killing an occasional rustler as a warning, but wholesale slaughter was a bit out of their league. Especially when it was Sunburst cows being stolen.

After all, it wasn't like Sunburst couldn't afford a few hundred head every year. That was just a drop in the bucket for cattle barons like the Olivers.

Reflecting on it as he rode through the countryside that afternoon, Print had found their attitudes grimly ironic. Sunburst had borne the brunt of the outlaw raids, yet instead of being respected for fighting back, the Olivers were condemned as wanton killers. One thought led to another and if it hadn't been so damn' assinine, he might have laughed. If neighbors had been shocked before, they were going to be downright flabbergasted come morning. Once Jim Kelly got through decorating that tree outside town, the busybodies would really have something to talk about.

As he rode into the compound just after sunset, Print had decided the hell with it. A man did the best he could, and there was no sense trying to second-guess the fickle bitch called fate. He was risking everything he had worked for over the years—along with the lives of fifteen damn' good men—in the belief he could whip the living bejesus out of the rustlers when it came down to the crunch. If it didn't work, the pissing and moaning could be left to those who came out of it with a whole skin.

He probably wouldn't be around to comment one way or the other.

After turning the gelding over to one of the hands he tromped into the house, suddenly famished as a wolf on short rations. Tomorrow night, or the night after at the very latest, there was going to be one hell of a fight. In a grisly sort of way he found himself exhilarated by the thought, and for reasons that he neither understood nor questioned, it had done wonders for his appetite.

When he walked into the living room Print came to a dead stop. Jay and Ira were seated around the old man jabbering like a couple of magpies.

"Where the hell did you two come from?" he demanded crossly.

The brothers turned at the sound of his voice and exchanged sly glances. Ira looked the least bit flustered, but Jay appeared his usual smirking self.

"From Kansas, where else?" Jay informed him. "Came in on the noon train. Big brother, I wanna tell you—that sure beats the deuce out of ridin' six hundred miles horseback."

"Is that a fact?" Print growled. "And whose idea was it to hightail it back here?"

"Well, I guess it was mine, really." Jay darted a look at his younger brother. "Ira got all upset when you was called home, so he sent a rider down trail to fetch me. When I heard about that telegram I just naturally figured our place was back here. Any objections?"

"No, not offhand." Though he would have preferred them out of the way just at this time, Print had to admit that two more guns would come in damn' handy. "Might've been a little smarter, though, if you'd waited till we got all this trouble cleared away."

"Print, we won't get in your hair," Ira rattled off. "Honest we w-w-won't. You'll see. We'll pull our s-s-share of the load."

"I know you will, Ira. That wasn't what I was gettin' at." Print's tone softened as he realized that being in on this fight was somehow vastly important to both of them. Every man had to prove himself at some time or another—to his own self, if to no one else. Perhaps this was their time, and he couldn't deny them that. "I just meant it might've been better for some of the family to be out of it. You know, just in case things don't go exactly like we planned."

Jay's mouth twisted in a mocking smile. " 'Pears to me you didn't hang around Wichita waitin' to see how things come out."

"You got me there, bubba. I guess I was sorta like you two. Figured my place was back here."

The boys smiled at one another, sensing that in his own taciturn way Print had just given them a pat on the back. Jay nodded back at the old man, who had quietly drifted off to sleep. "Pa says you ain't had much luck suckerin' the rustlers into a trap. Why don't we just get the hands and go run 'em down?"

Normally Print would have taken offense at being questioned by the likes of Jay. But tonight, for the first time since he could remember, he felt a warm glow of pride in his two brothers. "Bubba, the biggest lesson I learned during the war was that folks who attack head-on generally wind up in the meatgrinder. I reckon we'll just wait 'em out a little longer. Come to think of it, Jim Kelly oughta be puttin' out some bait right about now that I got an idea they'll swallow hook, line and sinker."

Throwing his arms around the boys' shoulders, Print steered them toward the kitchen. "You know something, I'm hungry enough to eat a bear. Why don't we get ourselves some grub and I'll tell you all about it?"

Stepping lightly, so as not to awaken their father, the three brothers marched off toward the mingled aromas of sowbelly and beans and fresh baked cornbread. Jay and Ira were all ears, hanging on Print's every word as they went through the kitchen door. In some curious way it seemed that both of them had grown about a head taller on the train ride back from Kansas.

CHAPTER TEN

───◄◄◄▌ⱱ▐►►►───

1

The three rustlers had been found that morning, just the way Print figured. But the impact on Georgetown wasn't exactly what he had planned. It was worse.

Jeb Kuykendall had stopped by on his way back from town that afternoon, and what he had to say was disturbing, if not outright alarming. The bodies had been discovered shortly after sunup and the Sheriff summoned. Strayborn then carted them into town and a crowd had quickly gathered as they were being unloaded at Fine's Mortuary. The green hides had shrunk so tight that it had taken a knife to free the outlaws from the leathery vise embracing them. According to Jeb, the putrid stench, along with the dead men's bloated features, had been enough to make a buzzard puke. Though he hadn't seen it for himself, he had heard the story all over Georgetown, in at least a half-dozen different versions. One story had it that the rustlers had been shot, then hung, and afterwards wrapped in the hides. Another just reversed the order, having them hung before being shot and mummified. The most widely circu-

lated account, however, made absolutely no mention of
bullet wounds. The victims had been bound inside the hides
and left beneath a broiling sun until they slowly smothered to death. Only then had they been hung. Since this
version was the most inhuman—with just the right touch
of savagery and terror—it was naturally the tale everyone
chose to believe.

But if the townspeople were confused about details and
circumstances, they had no doubt whatsoever as to the per-
petrators of this foul deed. The hides were clearly marked
with the Sunburst brand, and the poster tacked up in the
courthouse hall merely supported what everyone already
knew. The Olivers had murdered the three men in cold
blood, torturing them to death in a fashion that was bar-
baric beyond belief.

There was an immediate outcry for the Sheriff to arrest
the whole family—mad dog killers couldn't be allowed to
run loose in a civilized community. When Strayborn craw-
fished on that score, declaring there was no actual proof
against the Olivers, some folks had gone even farther. The
Texas Rangers should be called in to clean out Yegua Creek
once and for all. Granted cattle rustlers should be punished,
but there was a limit. Sane men just didn't do this kind of
thing. Not even to outlaws. The Olivers were too dangerous to remain at large. They should be locked up. For their
own good and the good of the community as a whole.

Still, as Jeb Kuykendall had laconically pointed out that
afternoon, even if the law worked up the gumption to take
a hand it might well get nothing but leftovers. Word around
town had it that the outlaw gang intended to skin its own
wolf, which in this case meant as many Olivers as they
could catch. Nobody was real sure exactly what the rustlers
had in mind, but everyone in Georgetown knew it wouldn't
be long in coming. The general feeling among the respectable element was that it might be best all the way round if
the Olivers and the owlhoots just killed each other off. Sort
of good riddance to bad rubbish—on both sides of the fence.

Print hadn't been especially concerned about the

townspeople's hostility, though their horrified reaction to the hide incident left him in a bit of a quandary. Why any decent person gave a damn what happened to a grubby cow thief was something that surpassed understanding. What seemed really important was the fact that the rustlers had apparently taken the bait. While the tale related by old Jeb was a mixture of rumor and unfounded speculation, it stood to reason that the gang would attack quite soon. Probably tonight. Delay could only work to their disadvantage. Like a sudden appearance by the Texas Rangers, or the unexpected return of the Sunburst crew from Kansas. Yet, in a matter of speaking, it really didn't matter when the outlaws struck.

Whether it was tonight, or tomorrow night or the night after—Sunburst had to be ready.

Overnight, Print had decided on a switch in tactics. The Olivers and their hands would not fort up in the big house and the main bunkhouse as originally planned. Instead, with the coming of dark, the men would be stationed outside behind trees, wagons and other spots affording cover. They would be positioned to form an inverted V around the open ground directly to the front of the big house. Once the rustlers struck they would be drawn into the wedge-shaped perimeter before the defenders opened fire. Since the Georgetown road and the creek trail were the most likely avenues of attack, it seemed fairly certain that most of the outbuildings would be put to the torch as the raiders moved toward the main part of the compound. They would probably hit fast and hard, planning to sweep through the compound and force the Olivers into the open by firing every building on the place.

What they wouldn't know until too late was that the Olivers and their men were already out in the open. Hidden, waiting with cocked guns, ready to knock them off like ducks in a shooting gallery when they were sucked into the deadly crossfire of the funnel-like defenses.

When Print had brought the hands together that morning to explain the new plan and to assign each man a position, he had also outlined the reasons behind his decision. First, since the raiders expected them to be inside the buildings they would gain an element of surprise that should prove decisive. Next, by already being outside they would have the mobility to adjust their defenses as the fight developed. Lastly, with the fight restricted to the open ground of the compound the gunfire would be drawn away from the women and children in the big house. Though he didn't bother mentioning it, this had been his major consideration in altering the original plan.

While Print would have preferred putting the men through a dry run, he was only too well aware that someone might be spying on them from the surrounding woods. Instead he had sketched out a rough map atop the bunkhouse mess table, then taken the men one at a time to the window in order to point out their assigned positions.

Bob and Jim Kelly were to be stationed on opposite points at the throat of the wedge since these would become critical spots in closing the trap. The rest of the crew, along with Jay and Ira, would be spaced along the legs of the inverted V. For himself he reserved the point at the very top of the funnel. From there he could command a view of the entire compound, and he made it clear that no one was to open fire until they heard his signal. Since he intended to open the fight with a double load of buckshot, there wouldn't be any doubt about when to spring the trap.

The rest of the day had been spent in preparation for the long night ahead. The men carefully cleaned and oiled their weapons, loading rifles and pistols with a solemn intensity that seemed out of place in the normally light-hearted atmosphere of the bunkhouse. Some of those who had fought in the late war, or were accustomed to the smell of gunpowder under other circumstances, wisely took to their bunks for a catnap. But most either swigged coffee in pensive silence, or else took a seat in the poker game that started not long after the noon meal. Though each waited in his own way for the fall of darkness, every man in the room tried to rid his mind of a pervasive and highly disturbing thought. Before morning there was every likelihood that they would have killed a number of men who at this very moment were preparing to kill them. Or vice versa.

Toward sundown a lone rider appeared off the creek trail and held his horse to a walk as he crossed the compound. Print was striding toward the bunkhouse when he spotted the man and recognized him as Fred Smith, a neighbor whose spread lay just west of the Kuykendalls. Smith had had a hard time of it this past year and it was common knowledge among the Yegua Creek cattlemen that he was hanging on by a thumbnail. What with being a small, poorly managed outfit to start with, and the rustlers nearly cleaning him out in the bargain, it seemed that he had just about played out his string. Watching him approach, Print automatically assumed that he had come to ask for another loan. The last time had been less than six months past and while he didn't begrudge lending the money, he felt that it was really nothing more than a polite form of charity. Unless Smith got a license to work miracles, he was only a short jump from being out of the cow business.

"Evenin', Fred," he called as the other man reined in. "What brings you out this time of night?"

"Howdy, Print." Smith made no move to dismount. "Just passin' by. Thought I'd stop in and say hello."

"Glad you did." Print jerked his thumb back toward the big house. "We just finished eatin', but there's plenty left over. Climb down and have some supper."

"Et 'fore I left home. Thanks anyhow, though." The rancher seemed just the least bit on edge, as though being there somehow made him nervous.

Print couldn't help but notice the man's unease and it struck him as being slightly out of character. Smith was a shiftless, easy-going sort of fellow who rarely let anything nettle him. He had grown fairly stout from too many years of swilling rotgut and piling his plate high enough for a plowhorse; his main preoccupation in life seemed to be in fathering a passel of lard-bellied, snot-nosed kids who were the spitting image of their ne'er-do-well sire. So far as Print knew, the man had never worried about anything in his life. Still, the Oliver compound wasn't the safest place on earth right at that moment, and it seemed reasonable that even a jughead like Smith could get a case of the willies trying to be neighborly.

"Well, light and have a cup of java then," Print said. "Always got a pot simmerin' on the back of the stove."

"Naw, can't spare the time tonight." Smith tossed his head back toward the Georgetown road. "Got to be in Rockdale bright and early tomorrow mornin'. Feller over there went busted and I'm hopin' to pick up some cows dirt cheap. Saved most of that money you lent me just waitin' on a chance like this."

"Well I'm mighty glad to hear that, Fred. I'd be real proud to see you get back on your feet. Hope it works out the way you want."

While the two men talked the last faint glow of dusk had departed the land and an inky blackness fell over the compound. As Smith gathered his reins to leave, the bunkhouse door suddenly opened and the hands trooped outside. The spill of light through the door glinted off the rifles they carried and it took only a glance to see that they were armed to the teeth. Smith watched in silence as they gathered in a small bunch before the building, waiting till the last man had shut the door before he spoke.

"Guess I'd best be makin' tracks, Print. Thanks for the invite. Maybe I'll take you up on it when I come back through tomorrow."

"Do that, Fred. You're welcome any time."

Smith reined his horse about and Print dismissed him from his mind even as he turned back to the bunkhouse and the waiting crew. The night had begun and with it their vigil was about to start. The first step was to spot the men in their positions and make sure each understood there was to be no noise, no smoking, and above all, no moving around.

Then the waiting would begin. Perhaps an hour, perhaps

all night, that was anybody's guess. But of one thing he was sure. The raiders would come, and when they did, Sunburst would be ready.

Late that night, as the stars sparkled brilliantly against the blackened velvet overhead, Print eased his game leg into a new position and let his eyes drift across the compound. In the pitch darkness it was impossible to see more than ten yards in any direction, and only the dim glow of the starlight allowed him to make out the roof tops of distant buildings. As near as he could reckon it was getting on toward midnight, which meant that he had been waiting for close to five hours. With nothing to show for it but a damned stiff leg and a growing exasperation.

Seated behind an elm tree about halfway between the main house and the bunkhouse, he peered around the trunk and strained to catch any movement or sound out of the ordinary. Cradled over his arm was a double-barreled ten-gauge greener and his Winchester lay on the ground within easy reach. Tonight he was even packing an extra six-gun and the pockets of his coat were stuffed with rifle shells. He was loaded for bear and primed to fight, but it was beginning to look like there weren't any varmints out and about on this particular night. Maybe they weren't coming after all, not tonight anyway. Or maybe they were just holding back till everyone on Sunburst got tired of waiting and had been lulled into a dreamy state of carelessness.

Though he had had all lights extinguished some two hours back, he really didn't figure it had fooled anyone watching from across the creek. Had he been raiding this compound he would have done exactly what they were probably doing. Delayed long enough for the defenders to get numbed with waiting and start counting stars out of sheer boredom.

Just as he shifted his leg for the tenth time in the last hour something about the night changed, and for a moment he couldn't put a name to it. Then it dawned on him that instead of hearing some noise that didn't belong, he was miss-

ing a night noise which had been there only moments
before. Abruptly it came to him.

The frogs along the creek bank had stopped croaking.
Something big enough to scare a barrelful of frogs—probably a large body of horsemen—had just crossed the creek.

Suddenly gunfire erupted from the woods along the east
side of the compound. Rising to his feet, he glanced around
the tree and saw the orange wink from the muzzle flashes
of perhaps ten guns. Yet even as he watched he knew there
was something fishy about this deal. The slugs were passing overhead, or thudding haphazardly into buildings
around the compound. Whoever was doing the firing didn't
have the least idea of where his men were hidden.

But they damn' sure wanted to know! The bastards were
trying to draw fire so the Sunburst hands would expose their
positions.

"Sunburst, hold your fire!" His voice thundered across
the compound like the roar of an angry bull. *"Don't give
away your positions."*

Then he heard it. The steady rumble of hooves as at least
a dozen horses rounded the bend in the creek and galloped
headlong toward the big house. Somehow the sons-of-bitches
had known his men were waiting outside the buildings!
The gunfire from the woods had been merely a diversion. A
calculated and brashly cunning attempt to get the defenders to reveal themselves with return fire. Once that was accomplished the mounted raiders would charge them from
the rear, the gunmen on foot would close in on the flank, and
it would be all over. Except for burying the dead—if there
was anybody left alive to handle a shovel.

But he might just still have a surprise in store for the
dirty bastards. The riders were committed now and it didn't
figure they would turn back. They were headed straight
into the funnel he had planned all along, and if his men
would wait only a few seconds more the jaws of the trap
could be closed with a deadly crossfire. A great calmness
settled over him, as it always had on the killing grounds of
times past, and he slowly raised the shotgun to his shoulder.

Then the hoofbeats were almost upon him and a rider loomed up out of the darkness, not twenty feet directly in front of the tree. Print triggered both barrels almost simultaneously and in the blinding roar of light saw the rider snatched from his saddle as if a giant gust of wind had bowled him over. Suddenly the V-shaped wedge came alive with the muzzle flashes of sixteen rifles and a hail of lead buzzed back and forth across the open ground in the center. Print grabbed his Winchester and looked back to see a swirling hell of horses and riders desperately attempting to break free of the hornets' nest that had them encircled. Though some of them returned the fire, there was never any thought of trying to fight back. They wanted only to escape, to be gone from this deadly little island ringed by blinking death. But whichever way they turned there seemed to be another rifle, then another, and still another spitting flame and lead with relentless ferocity.

Print brought his own Winchester into action, triggering shots as fast as he could work the lever. Over his sights he saw riders flung from their saddles, horses screaming in terror as they toppled to the ground; all about him there was a pall of gunsmoke mixed with the fetid stench of men and animals caught in the final struggle with death. Then, as quickly as it began, it ended. Only three horses remained standing, and the compound was littered with the bodies of the dead and the dying.

Within the space of a heartbeat he remembered the woods. *"Sunburst! The woods! Start firing on the woods."*

Before the words were out of his mouth the night again erupted with blinding flashes and a maelstrom of lead raked the woods to the east. But the volley of rifle fire was met with complete and utter silence.

The last of the raiders had retreated without so much as a parting shot.

Walking forward Print dropped his empty rifle and drew both six-guns. Some of the sons-of-bitches might still be alive, and tonight they were taking no prisoners. Whoever had fallen would never rise—they had come for the last time to the land of the Olivers. Then he chuckled silently to himself, recalling the last line of the poster nailed to the Bull's Head wall. *Bring your own flowers. Burial services on the house.*

God damn their souls to hell. Now they knew what he was talking about. The brag had worked. The trap had been sprung. They had been sucked into the meat-grinder and spit out like so much bone and gristle. Never again would the backshooting, bushwhacking cocksuckers set foot on Sunburst.

Instead, they would be buried there!

Suddenly Print froze in his tracks as Jim Kelly's rumbling voice boomed from somewhere out of the dark.

"Boss! Come quick. They done got Jay."

2

Though it was a warm summer night, Jim Oliver had taken a chill when he saw Jay carried through the door. A roaring blaze had been kindled in the fireplace and the air in the living room was stifling, yet no one seemed to notice. Dr. Clement Doak, assisted by Julia and Louisa, had been working over Jay on the kitchen table for more than an hour, and it was this grim struggle for life that claimed their every thought.

The only woman in the room was Elmira, Jay's wife. Hunched forward in her chair, she stared sightlessly into the fire, almost as if the flames somehow dulled the shock of having seen her blood-splattered husband laid out on the kitchen table like a side of beef. She had broken down completely when they first brought him in, sobbing and wringing her hands helplessly as he was carted through the living room. Julia Oliver had gently shut the kitchen door in her face and with Louisa's help had gone to work trying to staunch the flow of blood. Ira had led Elmira back to a chair before the fire and there she had remained throughout the long, agonizing hours of the night.

While Print had sent a rider to fetch the doctor only moments after the battle ended, he had scant hope that Jay would pull through. The slug had passed completely through his chest and exited to leave a gaping hole between his shoulder blades. Print had seen wounds like that during the war, and to the best of his recollection men rarely if ever survived such a mortal blow.

Waiting now with the rest of the family, he tried not to think about it. Off in the back of the house he could still hear children whimpering and crying, even though the gunfight had ended hours ago. Emma and Jenny had done their best to calm them, but some of the youngsters remained too frightened for sleep. The crashing volley of gunfire, mixed with the screams of dying men and wounded animals, wasn't something a child could easily put out of mind. Thinking about it, Print knew exactly how they felt.

It wasn't something he was likely to forget either.

After seeing Jay into the house, Print had gone back outside and called for lanterns. The eerie, flickering lights had illuminated a scene of carnage and death as grisly as anything he had witnessed during the war. Three Sunburst hands and eleven outlaws had been killed in the murderous exchange of gunfire—which from beginning to end had lasted less than thirty seconds. Two other hands had been hit, though not seriously, and Pinky Simms had taken them into the bunkhouse to bind up their wounds. Among the fallen rustlers there were also eight dead horses, and of the three animals still standing when the fight ended, one was wounded so badly it had to be put out of its misery.

Walking through the welter of bodies, gazing upon the grotesque contortions that had stiffened them in the moment of death, Print could only reflect that it was a hollow victory indeed. Three good men, and very likely a brother, were the price Old Scratch had demanded in return. Drained, empty of even the slightest comfort at the triumph he had wrought, he could only stare and mutely curse the one who remained alive.

The slimy bastard who had sent hired killers to do his dirty work.

Print's instinctive thought had been to load the bodies on a wagon and dump them in front of Cal Nutt's office in Georgetown. But reason shortly replaced blind rage. The Yankee probably knew by now that the raid had failed, and there was little to be gained by depositing eleven dead men on his doorstep. Moreover, after the hide incident of yesterday, such an act would only serve to inflame the townspeople to even greater howls of moral outrage. While he would have liked nothing better than to fling the dead outlaws one by one at Cal Nutt's feet, it would have been an uncalled-for recklessness that Sunburst could ill afford just at the moment.

Just the story alone—once it became common knowledge in Georgetown—would doubtless bring lawmen of every description swarming over Oliver land.

Though it went against the grain, he reluctantly ordered the hands to begin burying the dead. But not together, he had hastily added—the rustlers in a mass grave somewhere back in the hills and the Sunburst men in separate graves on a small knoll overlooking Yegua Creek. It was a herculean task, considering that there were also nine horses to be disposed of, but the crew had tackled it straightaway without a murmur of protest. After the bloodiest night of their lives they weren't about to sleep anyhow; in a way, they welcomed the chance to keep busy at something. Even the gory business of planting stiffs beneath ground.

Besides, there wasn't a man among them who wanted the women and children to see the outcome of this night's handiwork. Some things a fellow could be proud of, and in a casual sort of way, might even brag about. But the terrible jumble of stinking, bullet-shredded corpses spread before them at that moment was hardly the kind of thing a man wanted to be remembered for. Just living with it himself—waking in a cold sweat from the nightmares that were sure to come—that alone would be enough. Perhaps more than enough.

Thinking about it now, Print calculated that the hands were probably close to being finished with their ghoulish chore. Through the window he could see the dusky glow of false dawn, and somehow it reminded him that later he must go up and say words over the Sunburst dead. It was the least he could do. That and send some sort of compensation to their next of kin. Which raised another disturbing question in his mind. How could money alone serve as repayment for a man's life? Especially when he went under not for some grand, earth-shattering cause, but merely as a thirty-a-month hand fighting to protect another man's cows. One lived and got rich, while the other went to meet his maker with nothing but the clothes on his back. There was an injustice about it—perhaps even a certain shabbiness—that chaffed on his soul.

Like many things about tonight, it was something that would bear reflection.

But before anything else he must first await the verdict on Jay. Once, years back, it had been him laid out on that kitchen table, and in a very real sense, he found himself wishing it was the same again tonight. Him instead of Jay.

Though he hadn't brought the boys back from Kansas, he should have sent them away when they returned unannounced. Or assigned them to guard the women and children—anything to have kept them out of the fight. Neither Jay nor Ira had the stomach for killing, and God in His eternal bumbling had a way of winnowing out those who least deserved to die.

The funereal atmosphere of the living room along with his own nagging thoughts was suddenly more than he could take. He signaled Bob and headed for the front porch. Outside they spent a few moments rolling and lighting smokes, then lapsed into a silence almost as profound as that back in the house.

After awhile Bob glanced over at the sun burning its way up out of the earth's bowels. "Wonder if Jay'll ever get to see another sunrise?"

Print watched the splinters of light spilling over the

distant hills as if seeing them for the first time. "Christ Jesus, I hope so, sport." Then he paused, dragging deeply on the cigarette. "Much as I hate to say it, though, I reckon we'd better get set for the worst."

"You don't think he'll make it then." Bob's reply wasn't so much a question as a statement.

Print shuddered deep down in his guts, remembering what he had seen on the kitchen table. "Did you see the hole in his back?"

"Yeah. It ain't something a feller's likely to forget." Bob swallowed around a hard lump in his throat. "Looked like you could put your fist through it with room to spare."

"The old man's takin' it hard, and the women are gonna need us even worse. Whatever grievin' we've got to do, we best get it done with before they start."

"Print, you ain't foolin' nobody. You and me grieve the same way. By going after the sorry sonovabitch that did it."

The cattleman stared out over the compound, seeing again in his mind's eye the roar and flash of that bloody half-minute. "That's the way of it, awright. Last night didn't finish it, not by a damn' sight. Just added to the list of them that's owed."

Bob's eyes slewed around quizzically. "You talkin' about the gang? Hell, we broke their back. That only leaves Cal Nutt."

"Maybe," Print said deliberately, frowning as his mind again drifted back to the fight. "Don't it strike you as just the least bit queer that those turdknockers knew we weren't holed up inside the buildings?"

"Now that you mention it, I remember thinkin' that, the minute they opened up on us from the woods. But it don't hardly make sense one way or the other. Not unless they had somebody spyin' on us when you put the boys in position last night."

"No, that won't cut it. First off, it was so dark anybody nosin' around would had to've gotten in mighty close for a look-see. If they were plannin' to attack, they wouldn't have risked us catchin' their scout. On top of that, they only knew we was out there. They didn't know *where*. The way they started sprayin' lead all over the place proves that."

"That's right! They was tryin' to draw our fire so we'd give away our hidin' places." Bob's gaze narrowed and he studied his brother's face intently. "Goddamn. What you're sayin' is that some shit-heel told'em we was layin' for them outside, but he didn't know enough to tell 'em where we was spotted."

"That's the way she looks to me," Print acknowledged. "Somebody sashayed in here, saw what was happenin', then scooted back to give 'em the lowdown."

"Well, hell, if that's the case it could only be. . . ."

"Fred Smith." Print finished it for him. "The only ones that came by yesterday were him and Jeb Kuykendall. And Jeb didn't see nothin' that would've tipped anybody off."

"Yeah, but Goddamn. Fred ain't got the spine of a piss-ant. Where would he get the nerve to pull a stunt like that?"

"Hard tellin'. But he was nervous as a whore in church all the time we was talkin'. I recollect thinkin' at the time that he was mighty skittish about somethin'. And you boys had no sooner come out of the bunkhouse totin' rifles than he took off like a ruptured duck."

"Which means he hotfooted it down the road and told 'em we was gettin' set to snooker 'em in a trap."

"More'n likely. Leastways that's how I got it figured."

Before they could explore it further, Jim Kelly came across the yard and mounted the porch steps. Print had ridden with the black man long enough to sense he was fairly bursting with some juicy bit of information. "Jim, you look like a pup that just flushed his first covey."

"Better'n that, boss." The wrangler's mouth parted in a pearly grin. " 'Pears we done clobbered the he-wolf his-self. While we was buryin' them nightriders I went through their pockets. Found this on one of 'em."

Kelly held out a faded envelope that was crusted with dirt and sweat. Print took it and Bob moved around to look over his shoulder. What they saw was the near illegible scrawl of someone thoroughly unversed in penmanship.

MR. GRIFFIN CROW
GENRAL DELIVRY
ROUND ROCK TEXAS

When they looked up the black man had a gloating smile plastered across his face. "Boss, I ain't much of a hand at readin' but it looks like Mr. Grip Crow done bit the dust. The letter inside is from his mammy back in Georgia. Sounds like a real nice lady to've whelped a sorry devil like him."

"Wonder who got him?" Bob mused aloud. "I'd give my left nut to know it was me."

"Boy, I hate to disappoint you, but it 'pears like your stones ain't in no danger." Kelly's gaze shifted from the youngster and he gave Print a sly glance. "Mr. Crow took a double load of buckshot straight up the gizzard. Cleaned him out like a gutted hog."

Print's dark eyes brightened and his mouth set in a grim line. "One down and two to go."

"Two?" Kelly echoed with a surprised frown.

"Cal Nutt and Fred Smith." The cattleman shot Bob a quick look. "Nutt is up for grabs but hands off Fred. That's one Judas I aim to finish off personal."

"Boss, what the hell's Smith got to do with. . . ."

Kelly never got to finish the question. Clement Doak stepped through the door just at that moment and cleared his throat softly. The pudgy little doctor looked bone-weary and his somber features told the tale. "Print. Bob. I think your folks need you inside. Jay just passed away."

Without a word the two brothers moved across the porch and through the doorway. The physician shook his head sadly, then filled his lungs with a draught of fresh morning air and followed them inside. After a moment the black man went down the steps and trudged off toward the bunkhouse.

Somehow, though the sun was a red ball of fire cresting

the eastern hilltops, the day had suddenly turned bleak and
dismal.

Bitterly so.

3

After the doctor had finished with Jay's body, Julia and
Louisa dressed him in his Sunday suit. The brothers then
carried him to his old room and laid him out gently on the
bed. Jim Oliver still hadn't stirred from his rocker by the
fire, almost as if some essential part of his being refused to
admit that his second son was gone. But the old woman,
trailed by the girls, showed up only moments later with candles and her Bible. Elmira was disconsolate with grief, but
her shuddering sobs had slowly given way to a pale, be-
numbed state of shock. Emma and Jenny supported her as
they waited at the foot of the bed, and Louisa came to
stand beside Print. Julia placed candles on tables at either
side of the bed, then lighted them and stepped back. Her
eyes closed and a gradual serenity spread over her features,
as though by sheer force of will she had summoned some
inner strength to see her through the moment. Within the
space of a few heartbeats she drew a deep, quaking breath,
sank to her knees, and opened the Bible. The others knelt
to the floor and sorrowfully bowed their heads.

Her voice strong and unwavering, Julia Oliver began
to read. "The Lord is my shepherd; I shall not want. He
maketh me to lie down in green pastures: He leadeth me
beside the still waters. He restoreth my. . . ."

Print didn't hear the rest. Reading over the dead had
always seemed to him a pagan ritual that did little to con-
sole the living and nothing at all to comfort the dead. When
a man cashed in his chips there was little to be gained by
heaping pieties on him like lard over fresh cured sau-
sages. When the spark departed he was alone, left to the
uncertain mercies of whatever God he had worshiped in
life. Prayer and a barrelful of scripture readings weren't

likely to help him at that point. If there was a hereafter, his fate had been decided long before he went up the flume— by someone who was stone cold deaf to the mumbled entreaties of those left behind.

Wherever the dead went—whether to everlasting paradise or eternal damnation—the ancient rites performed over their remains would do little to ease their journey. But there was always the remote possibility that in some way as yet unrevealed to the living, the dearly departed might just get a chance to sneak a look back over his shoulder. If Jay got that chance, Print didn't want him to see a bunch of slobbering, teary-eyed Bible-thumpers spouting empty psalms. He wanted the boy to know that something far more practical was being done to consecrate his passing. Like an eye for an eye—a life for a life—another ancient and equally pagan rite known as retribution.

That was the kind of memorial a dead man could take real comfort from—wherever the hereafter led.

And at the same time, it gave the living a damn' sight more gratification than mouthing stilted mumbo-jumbo from the Good Book.

Print eased to his feet just as his mother finished the psalm reading and without so much as a deep breath started on the Lord's Prayer. Louisa glanced around uneasily but he motioned for her to stay put and stepped into the hall. When he reached the living room the old man was still staring vacantly into the fire and he decided not to disturb him. After buckling on his gunbelt, he took a shotgun from the gun rack, loaded it, and started out.

Bob caught him just as he was going through the door. "Hold on, brother. You wasn't thinkin' of leavin' me behind, was you? I got a stake in this deal too, you know."

Print's look stopped him cold. "Sport, I reckon this time you'll have to stay home. Like I said, it's personal. I'm takin' Kelly to watch my back, but otherwise I'm playin' a lone hand."

"Well that don't hardly seem fair," Bob said indignantly. "Jay was just as much my brother as he was yours."

"That's right, he was. But Jay's dead and there are only three of us left. If anything happens to me somebody's gotta take over the family. That sorta makes you *it*."

The light reference to the childhood game of tag didn't lessen the impact of Print's words. He had called the shot exactly as it lay. Ira couldn't anymore assume responsibility for Sunburst and the family than he could sprout wings and fly. Should anything befall the eldest brother, the mantle of leadership would then rest squarely on Bob's shoulders. They both knew it, and there was no need to belabor the point with a lot of fancy talk.

Bob nodded soberly, then smiled. "Good huntin'. I'll look after things till you get back."

Impulsively, Print clasped the youngster in an affectionate bear hug, then stepped back feeling somewhat easier about what lay ahead. But as he turned to leave Julia and Louisa appeared in the doorway.

"Prentice, have you no sense of decency?" The old woman's astringent words hit him like a slap in the face. "Your brother is not yet in his grave and you're off to start the killing again."

"Ma, a man does what he has to," Print said quietly. "Jay and me were never real close, but he was my brother. Fred Smith got him killed and I aim to square the account. I reckon I owe Jay that much."

Julia Oliver's eyes bristled with wrath. "No, Prentice, it was you who got your brother killed. Forever grasping for more land, more cattle, more money. Had we lived simply and humbly as God intended, none of this would have happened."

Louisa gasped, shrinking back from the old woman. "Mother Oliver, that's wicked and vile. How can you say such horrid things about your own son? Everything Print's ever done has been for the family. Just the family."

"Lou, let it drop." Print's sharp tone brought her up short, and she fled back into the house with a muffled cry. For a moment he was tempted to go after her, then thought better of it and turned instead to face his mother. "I'm sorry you feel like that, Ma. But in a way you're about half right. I only built this place partly for the family. Mostly it was for myself. Just to show everybody what a big hombre Print Oliver really was. Maybe that's why I figure it's me that has to square things for Jay."

"Vengeance is mine; I will repay, saith the Lord." Her gaze bored through him like shafts of fire. "Another killing won't help Jay now. It will only damn your soul more than it already is."

"Then I guess I'll just have to run the risk of hell's fire and brimstone. 'Less He moves damn' fast, I'm gonna save the Good Lord a lot of time and bother with a couple of fellas."

Spinning on his heel, Print went down the steps and stalked off in the direction of the corral.

But Julia Oliver wasn't finished yet. Her strident voice rang out across the compound. "God is not mocked! For whatsoever a man soweth, that shall he also reap. Turn back, son. Turn back before it is too late."

Print didn't even look back. Jim Kelly had the horses saddled and waiting, and he wasn't about to call it quits now. It was like a man holding aces full in a table stakes game. Even if he was raised he had to play out the hand. There were times a fellow just couldn't turn back.

Not and live with himself after it was over.

Some twenty minutes later Print and the black man drew up before a bend in the Georgetown road. This was as good a spot to wait as any, and unless he missed his guess Fred Smith would be along shortly.

Last night the rancher had said he had business in Rockdale, and perhaps he did. That remained to be seen. But Smith was the kind of fellow who never bet a hunch. Chances were better than ever that he had actually ridden to Rockdale and was now on his way home with a cast-iron alibi. More than likely he intended to stop off at Sunburst and stand around with his mouth open trying to look shocked when he heard about the raid. Then he could trot on home with nobody the wiser that he was the sorry son-of-a-bitch who had sold out his neighbors.

Thinking about it, Print was reminded that he had missed a golden opportunity to put the damper on his mother. If ever she had loathed a man it was the one who had betrayed the Good Lord for thirty pieces of silver. Whatever hate she had in her bones, it was reserved for weasels who slunk through life double-crossing their own kind. Had she known he meant to hunt down Yegua Creek's own personal Judas, she might have been far less touchy about the whole thing.

Then again, perhaps she would have thrown it right back in his face. After all, Judas had strung himself up in a tree. Which was a pretty fair testament to the fact that the Lord had His own ways of dishing out vengeance.

Still, it seemed damn' unlikely that Fred Smith would ever stretch his own neck. No matter what kind of hocus-pocus the Good Lord hit him with. Some people were just naturally so sorry that they had no more shame or conscience than a hungry lizard.

Suddenly the cattleman's ruminations came to an abrupt halt as Fred Smith rode around the bend. Though there was a fleeting instant of shock etched across Smith's face, he sucked up his nerve and kept right on coming. Clearly he meant to brazen his way through, never for a moment suspecting that anyone could tie him to last night's raid.

"Mornin', Fred," Print called out. "How's things over in Rockdale?"

"Fine, Print. Looks like I might just get me some cows." Smith was smiling but his eyes flicked nervously over the shotgun.

"You know, I was thinkin' about that last night after you left. The fella that went busted, I mean." Print sounded as casual as if they were passing the time of day. "What d'ya say his name was?"

"Why, I don't recollect sayin', now that you mention it." Smith's reply seemed a bit rushed and beads of sweat began forming on his pudgy cheeks. "Not likely you'd know him. Just one of them two-cow outfits nobody ever heard of."

"I expect you're right, Fred." Print hawked and spit, watching the other man out of the corner of his eye. "Guess you heard about the ruckus out at our place last night?"

"Shore did. It's terrible, Print. Just terrible. Don't know what this country's comin' to."

"Been thinkin' the same thing myself. Where d'ya hear about it?"

"Why, back in Georgetown. Stopped off on my way through. Whole town's talkin' about it. Doc said it was the bloodiest mess he ever seen."

Print eyed him speculatively for a moment. "You must've done some pretty fancy ridin'. That's a long piece over to Rockdale. 'Specially on a hot mornin'."

Smith smiled weakly. "Well, you know me, Print. Never was one to let the grass grow under my feet. Always believed in pushin' right along."

"Yeah? Then how come your horse isn't lathered up?" Print's voice had suddenly taken on a raw edge. "I've got an idea you're lyin' through your teeth, Fred."

"Say now, that's. . . ." Smith gulped audibly and a wary look came into his eyes. "Print, what the devil's eatin' you anyway?"

"Suppose you heard they killed Jay. You remember him don't you? My brother, Jay."

"Well, of course, I do. Knowed Jay all his life. Can't tell you how sorry I was. . . ."

"No, go on, Fred. Tell me how sorry you were. Hundred dollars. Two hundred. Or maybe you just took the same old thirty pieces of silver."

Smith's face went pale as a ghost. "Print, you don't think I had anything to do with that? God as my witness I never. . . ."

"God's busy this mornin', Fred. He ain't gonna be a bit of help to you. Now suppose you just tell me who paid you off to come in there and report what we were plannin'."

"Nobody. Jesus Christ, man, I wouldn't do a thing like that. You're my neighbors. You loaned me money."

Print swung the shotgun around on line with Smith's belly and earred back both hammers. "You got about three seconds to start talkin'. Otherwise my finger's gonna twitch and you'll get splattered to hell and gone. Once more—who paid you?"

The rancher seemed hypnotized by the cavernous holes of the scattergun and the words spewed out of him like hailstones. "Wait, Print. Don't do anything hasty. I'll tell you. 'Fore God, I will. It was a feller named Grip Crow. That's his name, honest. Grip Crow. He's the one that bosses them rustlers."

"How much did he pay you?"

"Nothin'. Not a red cent."

"Nothin'? You mean you just did it for free?"

"You don't understand, Print. They broke me. Stole all my cows. Run off my livestock. Got me in hock to the bank up to my eyeballs."

"Fred, you're not makin' sense and that gets on my nerves." Print wiggled the end of the shotgun. "Who's they?"

"Why, Cal Nutt. That's what I'm tryin' to tell you." Smith was sweating freely now and kept licking his lips. "He bought up my mortgage at the bank and threatened to foreclose if I didn't spy for him."

"How long ago was this?"

"Last fall. After they'd done rustled all my cows."

"Well I guess that explains a lot of things. Sure made it easy for 'em, didn't it? Just pull your spigot and you'd start squirtin' information like a beer keg."

"Print, honest to God, I never meant for it to go this far. They said they was just gonna scare you. If I'd knowed what. . . ."

"Fred, I reckon we've talked enough." Print's eyes went cold as chilled stone. "But I'd like for you to know that if it weren't for Jay I wouldn't feel obliged to kill you."

"Jesus Christ, don't! Gimme a chance. I'll make it up to you. Listen. . . ."

"I said the talkin' is done with. The only chance you've got is strapped around your hip. Use it. If you beat me you ride out a free man."

Smith glanced at Kelly who was idly slouched in his saddle at the side of the road. One of them was sure to get him, but he didn't have a hell of a lot of choice. With a gun in his hand he at least had a chance. Without it he was buzzard bait for sure.

The lard-faced rancher clawed at the Colt holstered on his hip. His sweaty thumb slipped off the hammer but it cost him only a fraction of time. The gun cleared leather and there came the metallic whirr as he earred it back to full cock.

It was the last thing Fred Smith ever heard.

Print waited till he had the pistol leveled to fire, then jerked both triggers on the shotgun. The top of Smith's skull simply disappeared in an explosive scarlet spray, raining bones, brains, and scraps of pinkish matter clean across the road. The rancher collapsed like a doll that had lost its stuffing and toppled off his horse.

Reining about, Print kneed the gelding into a trot and signed to the black man. "Let's go home, Jim. We've had a long night."

Back in the road, under a scorching noonday sun, Fred Smith and the flies started to get acquainted. The buzzing swarm gathered without haste, slowly inspecting the remains. Though it looked promising there was no need to hurry. They had all day. Perhaps even longer.

4

Chairs had been brought from the church for Julia and Jim Oliver, but the rest of the family stood around the open grave. Kelly and three hands slowly lowered Jay's rough-hewn wood coffin into the ground, then pulled the ropes free and stepped back. The men removed their hats as the preacher took his place at the head of the grave. Stooping, he gathered a handful of earth, then opened his Bible and began the burial service in a heavy, somber voice. As he read, he let the moist dirt sift through his fingers onto the coffin below. It made a gentle pitter-pat sound as it splattered on the wood, like lightly falling rain on a shake roof.

Looking on, Print tried to erase from his mind the sallow, washed-out face of the man lying in that coffin. He wanted to remember Jay as he had been—pungent, irreverent, cleverly taunting—instead of the cold, lifeless stranger they had placed in the box that morning. Somehow, lifting him from the bed and nailing the coffin shut had been the hardest part. There was that last glimpse of the ashen face and as each nail was hammered down it struck a note of grim finality unlike anything Print had ever known. Though he had killed many men, ruthlessly and with never a trace of remorse, he was unprepared for the dry, hollow ache that came with burying one of his own.

The deep well of sorrow that eddied brackishly in his guts sickened him worse than any pain or hurt he had ever borne. There was something crippling about it, as if a part of him had withered and died with Jay's passing. While in life they had forever been at odds with one another, he now felt diminished in some strange way by his brother's death. A gnawing, oppressive sense of loss with which he was unable to cope came over him, and the tears that might better have stained his face instead festered corrosively within his soul.

After loading the coffin in a wagon that morning they had brought Jay to the Lawrence Chapel, a small country church about halfway to Georgetown. There he had been baptized as a boy, and though he wasn't what most folks would call a practicing Christian, there he had worshiped the one God. Julia Oliver had insisted that there also would he be buried.

Emma and Jenny had stayed back to care for the children, and Print had left seven of the crew behind to look after things. Just in case whatever was left of the rustlers got any bright ideas. The older hands, like Jim Kelly and Pinky Simms, he had brought along. After their many years at Sunburst they seemed like part of the family, and it was only fitting that they be there to see Jay off.

Gathered around the grave now, the hands off to one side, the two boys standing behind their mother and father, Louisa supporting Elmira with a strong arm, it made a sorry spectacle. The low, choking sobs, their tear-streaked faces, the preacher blathering away in his consoling, graveside voice, it was a sight a man wouldn't soon forget. One which brought bile rushing to Print's gorge and left him determined that never again would it be repeated.

Olivers would die, well enough. From sickness and old age. Perhaps even disease and cattle stampedes. But so long as he lived, never again would one of his own be cut down by gunfire. There was a way, an out he should have taken months ago, back in the spring. Standing here at Jay's graveside had forced him to the realization at last, crystallized his idle thinking into the firm, resolute decision to act.

Before it was too late.

The preacher finally wound down but it was some moments until Print came to his senses and saw everyone staring at him. Nodding his thanks to the minister, he motioned for the boys to bring their parents along, then moved over to give Louisa a hand with Elmira. Kelly and his boys fell in behind, and as they started out of the little cemetery Print could hear the sexton begin to shovel dirt into the grave.

No longer did the earth sound like gentle drops of rain falling lightly from the sky. It sounded exactly like what it was. Clods of dirt being dumped on a dead man who had been mourned, prayed over, and left to the tender mercies of fat litle worms awaiting the feast.

Rounding the corner of the church, Print froze in his tracks. Ed Strayborn and two deputies were waiting beside the buggy. Without turning, he rattled off instructions over his shoulder.

"Ira, take the women and Pa back behind the church. Kelly, you and your boys fan out and follow my lead. No trouble unless I start it."

Glancing sideways at Bob, he smiled tightly. "C'mon, sport. Let's go see what the big, bad lawdog's got on his mind."

The brothers walked forward, watching the peace officers for any sudden moves, and the hands spread out about ten yards to their rear. As they drew nearer, Print noted that Strayborn's face was taut with strain, and the two deputies were strung tight as cat gut. Clearly, something had happened to raise the stakes, otherwise the Sheriff would never have brought along extra guns. When only a few paces separated them Print came to a halt.

"Ed, if this is official, you picked a damn' poor time. We just finished buryin' my brother."

"I'm sorry it had to be this way, Print." Strayborn took a swipe at his mustache and cleared his throat. "We was headed out to the ranch when we seen the wagon and buggy and I figured we might as well get our business settled here as there."

Print's mouth clenched so tight it looked like he had a broken jaw. "What business is that?"

The lawman met his gaze levelly. "I've got a warrant for Bob's arrest. Charged with the murder of Lawson Kiley."

"Shit!" Bob snarled. "Kiley drew first and everybody knows it. 'Sides that, it was more'n a year ago."

Print nodded agreement. "He's right, Ed. That was self-defense, plain and simple. Gonna be damn' hard to make it stick after all this time."

"Well, first off," Strayborn said, "there ain't no statute of limitations on murder. You oughta know that since we're still holdin' a warrant on you for the hangin' of them alleged rustlers. Next thing is, we got a witness who says Bob started the fight and shot Kiley before he had a chance to draw. That sorta rules out self-defense."

Bob snorted contemptuously. "Witness? Who the hell you kiddin', Sheriff? There must've been ten men saw Kiley go for his gun."

"Can't rightly say," Strayborn observed. "All I know

is, Luke Grady says you gunned him down in cold blood and he's swore to it."

"Wait a minute," Print demanded. "Are you talkin' about that no-account rummy that runs the pool hall?"

"That's the one. Says his conscience finally got the better of him and he felt duty-bound to come forward."

"Is that a fact?" Print fired back. "And I suppose it never occurred to you that somebody made it worth his while to get religion. Somebody like Cal Nutt, maybe?"

The lawman flinched slightly, but he didn't back off. "That's something for the court to decide. I just serve the papers."

"Goddamn' if you don't!" Print flared. "Now I guess you're gonna tell me Bob'll get a square deal from that bunch of brown-nosin' jellyguts back in town. Shit, they'd have him out o' court and hung before you could turn around."

"That ain't my bailiwick, Print." Strayborn squared his shoulders and took a hitch at his belt. "The law says he's gotta be arrested and that's what I come to do."

"In a pig's ass!" Print growled, dropping his hand to his side. "Your kinda law is a little too ripe for me. If you want Bob you're gonna have to try takin' him."

The Sheriff's gaze went past Print to Kelly and the three hands. After a moment he looked over at Bob, who was tensed like a coiled spring, ready to draw at the first hostile move. Finally his eyes came back to Print. "I was hopin' you wouldn't get your hackles up. Guess it didn't figure, though."

Print just waited, saying nothing. They stared at one another for a while, then Strayborn shook his head ruefully. "I reckon you know I could have the Rangers in here no later'n tomorrow. After that slaughterhouse you rigged up the other night the newspapers have been roastin' Governor Coke over the coals somethin' fierce. Likely he's just itchin' for an excuse to send the Rangers in here and let 'em settle your hash once and for all."

"Fish or cut bait, Ed. I haven't got all day to stand around jawbonin'."

"Print, lemme give you some good advice. Times have changed. You can't be your own law no more. Like killin' Fred Smith. You're just lucky there weren't no witnesses on that one. Now maybe you figure the deck's stacked against you, that ain't for me to say. But like it or not, you're gonna have to submit to the law as other folks see it. Otherwise they'll get the Rangers in here and wipe you out like a nest of rattlers."

The Sheriff turned and walked toward his horse, trailed closely by two very relieved looking deputies. When he was mounted, Strayborn twisted around in his saddle for a last word. "I'll wait till mornin'. If Bob ain't in my office by then, I'm sendin' for the Rangers."

Print didn't acknowledge the threat one way or another. Without a word, he spun about and headed toward the church.

When they arrived back at the compound early that afternoon Julia immediately put the old man to bed. The last two days, culminating in Jay's funeral, had been more than he could take. Plenty of rest and absolutely no excitement was what Julia prescribed, and he grumpily allowed her to bed him down. Though it wasn't mentioned openly, it was apparent to everyone that Jim Oliver's once-great vitality had been dangerously sapped. The constant strain under which they had lived throughout the summer had taken its toll, more than any of them cared to admit.

After the house had settled down, Print called his mother and the boys into the living room. Facing them, he laid it out fast and without frills. "We're finished in Williamson County. Cal Nutt owns the sheriff, the courts, everything he needs to put the law on his side. Any time that's not enough, he can even get his scalawag friends down in Austin to sic the Rangers on us. I should've seen it a long time ago, but I guess I just couldn't admit he had me whipped. What happened this mornin' finally woke me up."

"Well a dog don't lay down just one way," Bob said, slewing a quick glance at his mother. "What I'm sayin' is, maybe without Mr. Nutt around we'd be fresh out of problems."

The old woman raked him with a baleful frown. "Don't mince words, Robert. You're talking about another killing so just come right out and say it."

Print silenced them with a curt reminder. "That wouldn't solve nothin' anyway. The Unionists control this county and it's time we admitted it. They hate our guts and God Himself couldn't change that. If we got rid of Cal Nutt somebody else would just take his place. The plain fact is, they mean to get us sooner or later, and it don't matter much who's callin' the shots."

Julia Oliver stared at her son for a long moment before she spoke. "Your mind is made up, isn't it, Prentice? You mean to take the family north."

"Yes'm, I guess that's what I'm gettin' around to sayin'." Print deliberated an instant, choosing his next words carefully. "I'm gonna have to send Bob up there anyhow. Otherwise the Rangers will get him sure. One way or another, I expect they'd get me and Ira too if we hang around here long enough. I've thought it out backwards and forwards, and I don't rightly see we've got any choice."

When his mother didn't respond immediately, he tried a lighter vein. "It's not like we was trekkin' off into the wilderness. That 'Exodus' stuff went out of style a long time ago. We've already got an operation started up there, and inside of a year we'll have a spread that'll make this place look like a cabbage patch."

The old woman's eyes drifted around the room, lingering wistfully on the hand-hewn beams, the pegged floors, the great stone fireplace before which she had reared four sons. "Your daddy built this house with his own hands nearly thirty years ago. The day he finished, he said, 'Julia, it ain't a palace, but we'll make it into one.' I never told him, but that's what it always was to me." After a moment her dark eyes came to rest on Print. "Dreams die hard, but I suppose it's never too late to start over. When do we leave, son?"

"Bob leaves tonight. After spring roundup the rest of us will head north with all the cows we can drive and enough wagons to haul our goods. Between now and then I'll figure out some way to keep the law off our backs."

They talked a while longer about the Platte country and the new life they would build there, then Julia went off to the kitchen to start supper. Once the brothers were alone, Bob shot Print a sly look and grinned like a tomcat.

"Maybe you got Ma fooled, but you ain't pulled no wool over this child's eyes. You're going after that Yankee tonight, ain't you?"

Print's reaction was gruff and to the point. "Where I'm going is no concern of yours. You're headed for the Platte and I don't want no back-talk. Savvy?"

Bob shrugged, grimacing with just the right touch of boyish resignation. "You're the boss. Dammit."

"Just don't you forget it either." Print punched him playfully on the chin, then threw his arm around the youngster's shoulders. "C'mon, let's go see how the old man's doing. More'n likely he needs some cheerin' up right about now."

Matching one another stride for stride they marched off toward the back of the house. Not until they were out of the room did Ira ease out of his chair and head for home. Sometimes he got the feeling there was a nigger in the woodpile back along the line. Like about nine months before he was born.

Leastways that was how it seemed any time he got to puzzling over his brothers. They were just so goddanged ornery. Not like him at all.

Somehow it just didn't seem natural. Or fair. Sort of like being the runt of the litter.

5

Print rode into Georgetown just as the courthouse clock struck ten. Though he had come to kill a man, he was feeling loose and very cool. He had killed so many in the past few days that one more hardly seemed to matter. Even if his name was Cal Nutt.

The cattleman's impassive manner was due in no small part to the fact that Bob was on his way to the Platte. After supper Bob had made his farewells to the family and the hands, then Print had walked him down to the corrals. The hardest part for the youngster had been in leaving Jenny behind. She had cried something terrible, hanging on to him till he went through the door. But it could have been worse. One hell of a sight worse.

The Rangers were sure to come pounding on the door, and if ever they took him into custody the youngsters' goodbye kiss would have been of the forever variety. Not just a matter of a few months. Jenny had known that as well as Bob, and they had reconciled themselves to the wisdom of a brief separation. Come summer they would be together again, with the killing and the threat of a murder charge behind them. Then it would all seem like some spooky apparition out of a distant nightmare, and they could begin building a life for themselves on the high plains.

Where the land was free and wild, and the law was what a man made it. Unfettered by the grubby structures of little men and their little ways.

The two brothers had parted at the corrals with the quick handshake of strong men who find words difficult at such times. They had shared much over the years—a kind of bond not formed by blood ties alone—and neither needed to be reminded of it with mere words. They knew, and the knowing in itself was enough.

Bob had headed north, with a pack horse in tow, where before morning he would pick up the Chisholm Trail. Then it was on to Kansas and from there northwest to the Platte and the valley of the Loup. Print had watched him off with a feeling of immense relief, content now that no matter what happened tonight, the Olivers would have a strong hand to guide them in the days ahead.

Yet while Print was feeling loose and limber, Jim Kelly was fit to be tied. For the first time in years Print wasn't taking the black man along to cover his back. Depending on how things went tonight the repercussions could be damn' serious. Maybe Cal Nutt's sudden demise could be rigged to look like self-defense and maybe it couldn't. That was something the law would decide in its own fashion. But whichever way it went, Print meant to see that the wrangler wasn't involved in any way, shape or form.

The rest of the crew would be returning from Kansas any day now, and Sunburst would then be safe from threat. With Ace Whitehead and Jim Kelly to look after the outfit, he could rest easy that his plan for a spring exodus to the high plains would come off without a hitch.

Regardless of what might happen to him tonight.

Thinking about it as he entered the outskirts of town, Print remained convinced that what he proposed to do was the only way. So long as Cal Nutt lived, Sunburst and the Oliver family were in constant danger. While the gun battle two nights past had destroyed one gang, another could always be formed. The Yankee had money and connections, not to mention a stranglehold on the law, and it wouldn't be difficult for him to assemble another pack of cutthroats to do his dirty work.

But if he were dead—there was another kettle of fish entirely. Once Cal Nutt cashed in, the political machine of Williamson County would come apart at the seams. There would be an immediate struggle, with some damn' fierce infighting, to determine who emerged as the new kingfish. Animosities and old grudges would likely nudge the bloodletting along even farther, and it was entirely possible that the county would be kept in a turmoil clean into election time. Though the ultimate winner would be a dyed-in-the-wool Unionist, and therefore hostile to the Olivers, it was a matter of no great consequence. While the jackals were scrambling for power, Sunburst would have ample time to get the hell out of Texas.

Then, too, there was the matter of Jay. On that, Print wasn't fooling anybody, least of all himself. No one killed an Oliver and walked away clean. Perhaps Cal Nutt hadn't pulled the trigger, but he had engineered the raid, which amounted to the same thing. All other things aside, it was sufficient reason to kill him. So far as Print was concerned, the Yankee had signed his own death warrant.

The first place he looked was Nutt's office. But the windows were dark and the place was quite obviously deserted. That left the hotel and Tuttle's Exchange. He decided to try the saloon. Nutt generally held court there each evening with his political cronies, and it wasn't likely he had returned to the hotel at such an early hour.

Print dismounted in front of the saloon and draped the reins over the hitch rack. Loosening his gun in the holster, he crossed the boardwalk in two swift strides and peered through the large, lightly tinted window that was Tuttle's pride and glory. His luck was running strong.

Cal Nutt stood at the bar talking with three of his underlings.

Print turned toward the door, but even as he moved, steps sounded on the boardwalk behind him and a gun was rammed into his back. His first thought was that Sheriff Ed Strayborn had him cold, and not a damn' thing he could do about it. When a hand jerked his pistol from its holster and tossed it into the street he began cursing himself for a witless fool.

"Now, brother, you hold real still. I'd hate to have to shoot you in the leg just to make you stay put."

The voice was unmistakeable. *Bob!* He started to turn and the gun barrel jarred his spine. "Print, I ain't funnin'. I just dealt you out o' this party."

"Goddammit, get that iron out of my back." The gun didn't move and neither did he. Bob was just ornery enough to put a slug through his leg. "Where the hell did you come from anyway? You're supposed to be on the trail north."

Bob chuckled softly. "Well I'll have to admit I had to do some pretty fancy ridin' to circle around and catch up with you before you got to our friend in there. I take it Mr. Nutt is inside. I mean, you weren't just lookin' for a drink, were you?"

"Sport, you listen to me and listen good. You're playin'
the fool. If Strayborn catches you in town you're a dead
goose. Now you get your ass on a horse and make dust out
of here. Let me worry about Nutt."

"Sorry, brother. No dice. You kill Nutt and they'll
have you strung up to the nearest tree. But if I do it they're
gonna have to come all the way to the Platte to get me.
Which don't seem too likely. You begin to get the drift?"

Print got it all right, but he didn't like it. Crouching, he
spun about, swinging a looping right as he came around.
Cold steel thudded upside his head and great splinters of
fiery light exploded before his eyes. Without a sound he
went limp and crumpled to the boardwalk.

Bob glanced quickly up and down the street, then holstered his gun and stepped over Print's inert form. When
he came through the door of the saloon the hubbub lingered
on for a few seconds until men around the room started rec-
ognizing him. Gradually the talk died out and within moments Tuttle's Exchange had gone still as a tomb.

Cal Nutt looked around and his face blanched, but he
didn't move a hair. His three underlings prudently backed
away from the bar, clearing a path between him and young
Oliver.

Bob smiled like a short-fanged wolf. "Evenin', Mr. Nutt.
How's the rustlin' business these days?"

Nutt took a sip of his drink and set the glass down very
carefully. "Oliver, if I were you I'd get out of here before
the law shows up."

"Couldn't do that, Mr. Nutt," Bob chortled. "Then I'd
miss hearin' you tell these fellers how you sent that scum
out to our place and got my brother killed."

"That's a. . . ." Nutt suddenly thought better of what
he was about to say. "I had nothing to do with that, and
you'll pay hell proving different."

"Why, I've got all the proof I need. Feller named Smith
spilled his guts about you. Turns out you're not just a damn'
Yankee, Mr. Nutt, you're a goddamn liar to boot. Not to
mention cattle rustlin', murder, and a few odds and ends."

Nutt wouldn't look at him and after a couple of moments Bob decided the game had gone far enough. He enjoyed toying with the slimy bastard but time was growing short, and come daylight he had to be long gone.

"Guess it's time to get down to brass tacks. I came here to kill you, so let's get the music started."

That brought Nutt's head around, and for the first time he appeared shaken. "I'm not armed. Wouldn't be stupid enough to fight you even if I was."

"Mister, a sonovabitch like you has to go heeled." Bob shrugged indifferently. " 'Course, it's up to you whether you use it. I'm gonna kill you either way."

Glancing around, Bob caught the eye of the bartender, who was frozen in place like a statue. "Barkeep, you do exactly what I tell you. When I give the word you toss a bottle up just as high as you can pitch." Looking back at Nutt, he grinned. "Yankee, you got your chance while that bottle is in the air. When it hits the floor you're a dead man."

Nodding to the bartender, who had hastily grabbed up a quart bottle, he growled, "Now!"

The barkeep flung the bottle toward the ceiling, then dove headlong behind the counter. Cal Nutt didn't wait around to see what would happen. His hand darted beneath his coat and jerked a silver-plated revolver from its shoulder holster. Wheeling away from the bar, he brought the gun to bear, trying desperately to stop his hand from shaking.

Suddenly a Colt appeared in Bob Oliver's hand and spat a sheet of flame a yard long. Twice more it roared in rapid succession. Three bright dots appeared on the Yankee's shirtfront as he was slammed up against the bar. Then his knees buckled and he fell face down in the sawdust.

There was a moment of dead silence before the bottle crashed to the floor.

Smiling, Bob let his eyes drift over the stunned faces for a couple of seconds, then backed through the door.

Print was just coming to his feet as the youngster brushed past him. Lurching about, he steadied himself against the wall and tried to sort out the jumble of words the boy flung back.

"Get a move on, brother. There's work to do. We'll be waitin' for you on the Platte."

Then Bob was gone around the corner of the building, and in a moment came the sound of hoofbeats thundering down the alley.

Print didn't even bother to take a look in Tuttle's. Cramming his hat on his head, he retrieved his gun and crawled aboard the gelding. Then he reined the horse around and headed him toward Sunburst.

That damn' fool kid was right. There was work to be done. But it sure as shit wouldn't go begging.

Not now.

Epilogue

---◦◦◦---

Print brought the gelding to a halt on a small knoll about a mile ahead of the caravan. Less than an hour's march to the north lay the Red River. Tonight they would camp on the prairie south of the station house and come morning begin the crossing. Turning in the saddle, he squinted against the harsh glare of the sun and let his eyes rove back over the trail.

The vanguard was comprised of ten lumbering freight wagons, the biggest he had been able to buy. Those carrying the women and children had been rigged similar to the covered wagons used by sodbusters. The rest were simply loaded to the gunnels with a lifetime's accumulation of furniture, bedding, personal effects and assorted equipment. Junk, gewgaws and play pretties, Print had labeled it when the loading began. But the women had been adamant, presenting a solid front, and before their peppery caterwauling he had finally backed off. Everything that wasn't nailed down had somehow been crammed into the wagons, and Print could only hope that the rivers were running dry this year. Should one of those cumbersome vehicles ever hit deep water it would sink like a rock attached to a lead weight.

Yet, in a way perhaps more profound than the women realized, Print had known exactly how they felt. When the last tarp was lashed down over the last wagon it was as though a finish had been written to Sunburst. There he had played as a child, romping through the wooded hills, learning the ways of wild things in their secret haunts. There also had he grown to manhood, gone off to war, married, fathered his children. While perhaps unimportant except to himself and those of his breed, it was on Sunburst that he had also participated in the great Texan experiment. The birth of the cattle industry.

Throughout the years following the war he had solved the riddle of taming longhorns, and afterwards been among those who blazed trails across a vast, uncharted wilderness to establish a market for their beef. Along with men of lean, leathery grit, who possessed the boldness to match their vision, he had brought an era of plenty to a land stricken by the holocaust of war. Texas had risen from the ashes of defeat to again become a proud, sovereign giant—and in no small degree, it had ridden every step of the way atop the backs of the most ungainly, cantankerous eyesore God ever invented. The Longhorn.

Still, these were things that couldn't be packed in a barrel or lashed down in a wagon. They were of the mind and heart, perhaps even of the soul, and no matter what a man left behind this was the stuff that went with him wherever he might roam. Locked inside him, somehow private and warmly cherished, it was the part that could never be lost.

It was his past—the agony of defeat, the dizzying, skull-popping thrill of hewing an empire from the wilderness—in some curious way, the stuff of hopes and dreams for what lay ahead.

But if Print put Sunburst behind him, he left it much as Jim Oliver had found it thirty years before. The old man had never risen from his bed after Jay's funeral. Even when they told him stories of the Platte and the mighty spread they would build together on the high plains, he had listened with only passing interest. It was as if he had lost the will to struggle longer, or perhaps he simply made up his mind that Sunburst was where he wanted to die. They never knew, for Jim Oliver never said. The spark withered, flickering ever dimmer with each passing day, and shortly after Christmas he quietly passed away in his sleep.

When they buried him beside Jay out behind the Lawrence Chapel, Julia had observed that the only reason he stuck around that long was to see the kids gathered about the Christmas tree. It had always been his favorite time of the year, and stubborn old bogger that he was, he had just plain fought off Old Scratch till he could see the mistletoe and holly once more. Though the house was filled with sorrow for a time, the mourning of Jim Oliver had been as he would have wanted it. Brief and without any wailing or gnashing of teeth. He had lived a long, full life, and unlike lesser men, he had picked his own time and place to call it quits.

Besides, had he hung around till after the New Year, the old man would have been the first to say it—there was just too damn' much work before them for anyone to sit around sniffling and snuffling over a fellow who had gone out riding St. Nick's coattails.

When winter broke the crew had gone into the brush after the longhorns. Over the next two months they had worked from dawn till dusk, seven days a week—grabbing meals when they could, falling into their bunks only when they were too exhausted to stay in the saddle a moment longer. Toward the end of May they had gathered three herds of roughly twenty-five hundred head each, mostly cows, yearlings, young heifers, and a handsome assortment of bulls. Though at least another three thousand head remained scattered throughout the hills, Print had declared the roundup finished.

They had gathered all the cows they could possibly drive north, and more than enough to stock the lush grasses awaiting them in the valley of the Loup. The rest they would leave behind, to roam the hills of Sunburst free and wild—the way it had been when the first Oliver crossed Yegua Creek.

The end of roundup had also brought news from the Platte, in the form of a terse but electrifying letter from Bob. Bumpus Moore and the hands were fat and sassy. The cows had come through a high plains winter like woolly buffalo. The spring graze was growing an inch a day, and as far as the eye could see it belonged to the Olivers. Bob had closed with the joshing reminder that he sort of missed Jenny and wished to hell Print would get the lead out. Time was a-wastin'.

While Print still had a bone to pick about the clout he had taken that night in Georgetown, he couldn't have agreed more with the youngster just at that moment. Time was vital. They had to have the herds bedded down on the high plains—the new Sunburst—no later than the middle of August. With even a smattering of luck they would make it, and by first snow they would have a herd of better than ten thousand butterballs ready to face the winter.

There was nothing holding them back—the dead had been buried, their worldly possessions were stowed aboard the wagons, the last gather had been made—and Print ordered the drive to commence with sunup the next morning.

After the wagons pulled out and the Sunburst compound was deserted of any living thing, Print had hung back for a final moment. The place seemed to abound with ghosts, memories mainly of the good times—yet hardly lacking in thoughts of the killing and death and terror that had dwelled there alongside the rest. Before him arose Cal Nutt, Grip Crow, and the score of rustlers who had gone under attempting to break the Olivers. Again he saw Ed Strayborn nervously licking his cookieduster as he explained to a company of Rangers that the young gunslinger they sought had vamoosed to parts unknown.

Then as if the last ghost was the one who would endure after all else had faded, his mind's eye caught a glimpse of

Jim Oliver striding across the compound toward the corral. Just as he had in the old days when he was a robust, yoke-necked bear of a man.

Perhaps one day another family would settle this land, flush the longhorns from the thickets, make it live again with laughter and happiness the way it once had. But while Jim Oliver walked it alone, a grizzled sentinel of what once had been, he would never see the Sunburst he had wrought with his own two hands desecrated by strangers.

Gathering firebrands, Print had gone from building to building, saving the big house for last, and put them to the torch. Only when the compound was wreathed in smoke and three decades of labor were engulfed in a holocaust of flame did he mount the gelding and ride north.

Soon the flames would die, the ashes would be borne away by the wind, and the vibrant hill country wilderness would flourish again. Then the old man could wander across Sunburst in peace—seeing it forever as he had the first time so many years ago.

Watching the wagons trundle onward, with the herds strung out ten miles behind them over the plains, Print came at last to a reckoning with himself. What he had done was neither more nor less than what other men had done—what men had always done. One man fought another man for the land, red or white made little difference, then waited for the next man to come take it from him. It was the scheme of things—the way nature, or God, or whatever force that shaped men's lives meant it to be. Men lived and fought and died only to be replaced by other men who did likewise, and when they were all gone nothing had changed.

Man's days were few and full of sorrow, but the earth endured forever.

Feathering the gelding with his spurs, he came off the knoll and rode toward the caravan. When he came abreast of the lead wagon he reined about and kneed the bay alongside. Doughbelly Ketchum was driving, an honor befitting his position as boss cook over all Sunburst cooks. Beside him sat Louisa and next to her rode the dowager herself, Julia Oliver.

Over the creak and grinding screech of the wagon wheels, Print called, "River's just over the rise. We'll camp there tonight."

His mother exchanged glances with Louisa, then looked back. "Does that mean we'll finally get to see the Nations you men raise so much fuss about?"

"That's right," Print hollered, "wild Indians and all. Say, tell me something. Now that we're almost there, how's it feel to be leavin' Texas?"

The old woman's eyes went misty for a moment then brightened and she smiled softly. "Son, it's just like the Good Book always said. We're going to the Promised Land."

Print flashed a wide grin, for once fully in accord with the scriptures. "That's as good a name as any, Ma."

Chuckling to himself, he waved with his hat, slapped the gelding across the rump, and took off at a lope headed north. Maybe it wasn't the Jordan River they would cross come morning but it would do nicely. Damn' nicely indeed.

Across it lay the rest of their lives. Sunburst. The Olivers' tomorrows, all juicy crisp and shiny bright.

The Promised Land.